CW01023824

# THE BODIES

*Also by Sam Lloyd*

The Memory Wood
The Rising Tide
The People Watcher

# THE BODIES

### Sam Lloyd

bantam

TRANSWORLD PUBLISHERS
Penguin Random House, One Embassy Gardens,
8 Viaduct Gardens, London SW11 7BW
www.penguin.co.uk

Transworld is part of the Penguin Random House group of companies
whose addresses can be found at global.penguinrandomhouse.com

Penguin
Random House
UK

First published in Great Britain in 2025 by Bantam
an imprint of Transworld Publishers

A CIP catalogue record for this book
is available from the British Library.

ISBNs
9781787636248 (cased)
9781787636255 (tpb)

Text design by Couper Street Type Co.

Typeset in 13/16pt Dante MT Std by Jouve (UK), Milton Keynes
Printed and bound in Great Britain by Clays Ltd, Elcograf S.p.A.

The authorized representative in the EEA is Penguin Random House Ireland,
Morrison Chambers, 32 Nassau Street, Dublin D02 YH68.

Penguin Random House is committed to a sustainable future
for our business, our readers and our planet. This book is made
from Forest Stewardship Council® certified paper.

Dedicated to Jim Stuart.
Not just one of the good guys,
but one of the best.

As he bumps his car along the track through Jack-O'-Lantern Woods, peering out of the windscreen at the night, he still can't quite believe this is happening. Can't quite believe what he's about to do.

What *they're* about to do.

His headlights paint the trees in shades of emerald and bone. So far, they haven't seen another vehicle. This late, they're unlikely to meet one. The overnight carp fishermen often set up camp around Critchfork Lake, a few miles east, but they don't use this track to reach it. Not until dawn will the first dog walkers arrive. By then, there'll be nothing to see.

On his left, beyond a pile of sawn logs and branches, he notices a clearing. Stones pop and crunch as he turns the wheel. 'Here's a good spot,' he murmurs, wiping the sweat from his forehead. The temperature outside has barely dropped since sunset, but the humidity hasn't stopped climbing. 'No chance of being disturbed.'

Fronds of giant bracken fold beneath the bonnet, their stems crushed by the tyres. He kills the engine, then the headlights. Moments later the cabin lights fade up, turning the windows into black mirrors. When he sees his passenger, he hardly dares breathe – as if she's a creation so fragile and finespun that the merest movement of air will dissolve her into smoke-like threads.

But breathe he does. Her perfume is a hot and languid flower in his throat. Beneath it he detects her real scent – teenage musk and sharp fresh sweat. On her breath, something vaguely like blood.

Did she eat steak before she came out? He's heard that red meat, like oysters or avocados, can boost female arousal. His eyes slide over her, taking in her watermelon-pink minidress, her tanned legs. She's done something to her eyelashes, he thinks. And to her lips. Her cheekbones shimmer. Her blonde hair has a liquid sheen.

And it's all for him.

His fingers twitch. He feels like he's sitting in a Heston Blumenthal restaurant, staring at a concoction so artfully assembled it's almost too perfect to eat.

She's been quiet so far, but now she releases her seatbelt. The leather upholstery squeals against her bare thighs as she turns to face him. 'It's so *hot*. Can you put the windows down?'

He thumbs two buttons on his door rest. Warm night air feathers in, carrying sounds of the forest. Close by, something shrieks in the darkness.

She glances past him, through his side window. Then she grins, flashing white teeth. It feels like an invitation – and suddenly he can't wait any longer. He needs to touch her, taste her, mess up that Michelin-starred perfection and hear her breathing quicken.

She's still grinning when he kisses her, when his tongue pushes into her mouth. And then he's popping his own seatbelt, hissing with satisfaction as his hands start to map her curves.

For a while, he loses himself to sensation – until he feels pressure against his sternum and realizes it's her hand, pushing him away. Confused, he pulls back. And when he sees her smeared lipstick, her flushed cheeks, his heart thumps with excitement.

'Easy, Romeo,' she laughs, wiping her mouth. 'I don't know what you're used to. But with me you don't get everything all at once.'

He smiles, lunges forward, snatches another kiss. 'Is that right?'

'Play nice,' she tells him. 'Be a good boy. And eventually you'll get rewarded.'

'How nice?' he asks. And realizes that once again she's looking past his shoulder at the night.

She frowns. 'You hear that?'

He cocks his head, turns to the open window and scans the darkness. 'Nope.' Firstly because he can't, and secondly because he doesn't care. Rearranging himself in his seat, he slides his hand up her thigh.

She squirms away. 'Seriously, I think I heard something.'

'We're in the woods, at night,' he tells her. 'Of course you're going to hear something.'

'Still, maybe we should find a different spot. Somewhere closer to town.'

'Are you fucking kidding me?'

His frustration slips out and he knows, instantly, that he's screwed up. Her expression changes. He sees the thought as clearly as if she'd voiced it: a calculation of just how far she is from help, should it come to that. His gaze travels down her legs to her footwear: strappy pink heels, not exactly tuned for running.

He hears the snap of a twig, but it's only a night creature nosing around in the undergrowth. The unease he sees in her eyes is no longer focused on anything outside the car.

He reaches out, touches that liquid hair. Feels, beneath it, the warm skin of her scalp, the smooth curve of her skull. 'What if I don't want that?' he asks.

She blinks. 'Don't want what?'

'To be a good boy.'

# ONE

Joseph Carver wakes in darkness, to a hand shaking his shoulder.

As always, the first moments of consciousness belong to the *before* and not the *now*. As always, he bites down on the name forming on his lips before he spills it. Joseph feels his heart plummet into depthless chasms before adjusting for its boomerang return.

That all this occurs in the space of heartbeats, far quicker than it once did, amazes him, appals him – love and loss and sheer brute willpower pulling in different directions until the ragged strata of his waking mind grow taut.

Finally, he takes a breath.

*'Joe.'*

He frowns, concentrates.

Cool air on his face from the fan. Erin's hand, still shaking him. He smells her perfume, her night breath. 'Mm,' he says. 'Uh-huh.'

*'There's someone downstairs.'*

A gap in the curtains admits a lick of moonlight, revealing the bedroom's vague contours. His first question: 'Where's Max?'

'He's staying at a friend's tonight,' she hisses. 'Remember? And his car isn't here.'

Hearing that, Joseph drags himself upright. He'd closed those curtains tight before coming to bed. Erin must have parted them, peered down at the driveway, checked.

'But he's not insured,' he says. Nor will his son's Honda even qualify for insurance until it passes its MOT. Still, that's hardly a thought for right now. Joseph reaches out to the fan, switches it off, waits for its blades to fall silent.

He hears something, then, or thinks he does, even if he can't describe it. Maybe he just senses it. A wrongness about the house. A feeling that something chaotic has crept in while he's been sleeping. Something ruinous and wicked.

His chest tightens. Instantly, he's wide awake. Because he knows that overcoming the threat, however it manifests, is *his* task; and because the role of protector is one for which he's uniquely unsuited – a role he's failed before, with spectacularly painful results.

In a blink he's spun back five years. To the *before* and not the *now*. To a different bedroom; a different night; a different wife. To a nightmare that had begun much the same way. Back then, he'd believed that home was a safe place, unassailable. He doesn't believe that now.

A clinking from somewhere deep inside the house, a creaking. A shushing, as if of wind. Hard to explain why those sounds seem so insidious, but they do.

'Where's your phone?' Erin whispers.

'Downstairs, I think. Yours?'

'Charging, in the kitchen.'

'Shit.'

Joseph swings his legs out of bed. He places his feet on the carpet, carefully so they don't thud. Adrenalin lightens his stomach, shortens his breath. Naked except for his underwear, he pads to his wardrobe. Opening the door, he reaches in. Erin doesn't know what he keeps in here, behind the shirts and the suits, the ties and winter scarves, the bereavement box still too traumatic to open. A man haunted by past failures is wise to plan ahead.

Just last winter a doorstep seller – some coin-eyed addict who flashed a homemade ID – wedged his foot inside the front door until Joseph handed over twenty pounds for three squeegees and a pack of J cloths. Erin wasn't home, but Max and Tilly were in the living room, watching TV. If the guy had tried to force his way inside, Joseph couldn't have stopped him. His adversary had been stronger, fitter, far more aggressive. Joseph, by contrast, had never fought anyone in his life; he wasn't even sure he knew how.

Failing his family once had been devastating enough. To have failed a second time would have been worse than inexcusable – an utter dereliction of his duty – and he'd just come perilously close.

Immediately afterwards, he started investigating home defence options. His research led him to a YouTube channel dedicated to the subject. The host – a ripped and balding American around Joseph's age – exploded a lot of myths and talked a lot of sense.

No point buying a full-sized baseball bat if you didn't have room to swing it. No point buying a machete if you couldn't imagine cutting flesh. Calling the police was always a priority, particularly if you couldn't escape. But planning for a confrontation was vital.

Americans, of course, could arm themselves pretty much how they pleased. Even when using deadly force, they faced little danger of prosecution. Here, the law seemed to favour the intruder. Keeping any kind of weapon for self-defence classed a homeowner's actions as premeditated. The only legal products, Joseph discovered, were rape alarms and criminal identifier aerosols that dyed an assailant's skin.

The YouTube host's advice for his British viewers was characteristically blunt – *Better to be tried by twelve than carried by six.* The axiom lent itself readily to adaptation for Joseph's purposes: *Better to face jail than bury another loved one.*

Packages started arriving at the house soon after. Joseph didn't stop buying until every room was stocked with something he could use in an emergency. Whether a screwdriver tucked beneath a sofa cushion, or a ball hammer hidden inside the cloakroom cabinet, each new purchase helped him feel marginally more prepared, marginally more capable of shouldering the awesome weight of responsibility for the safety of those he loves.

Here in the bedroom, hidden in his wardrobe, he keeps his two most lethal purchases, bought after a week of nightmares where he repeatedly watched his wife, his son and his stepdaughter being cut down around him: a five-shot pistol crossbow and a midnight-black tactical tomahawk with a carbon steel axeblade and spike; stored beside them, a set of police-issue cuffs and a torch that produces a 4,000-lumen beam designed to blind and disorientate any attacker.

Now, though, when it matters, Joseph realizes that the confidence his preparations gave him was false and fleeting – because he isn't a buffed and combat-ready YouTube host. He's a guy who'll get a screwdriver torn from his fingers and buried in his head; a guy who can't recall how to assemble his crossbow or load arrows into the speedloader – and certainly won't manage those feats in the dark.

Joseph touches the tomahawk's polymer handle. When he wraps his fingers around the grip, he feels instantly sick. He retrieves the weapon regardless, along with the torch. Then he moves to the bedroom door.

Downstairs, he hears the yawn of a hinge; a thud. He no longer merely feels sick; there's a very real risk he might pass out.

'What're you doing?' Erin whispers, from the bed.

'Getting my phone.' Joseph remembers, now, where he left it before following Erin to bed: on the arm of the sofa, stacked between the TV remote and his paperback. 'Stay here. If something bad happens, lean out of the window, start screaming. Then barricade this door until help arrives.'

'What about Tilly?'

*Christ*, he thinks. *It's not even a good plan.*

'I won't let anyone get up here with you.'

Silence, for a moment. Then: 'Joe?'

'What?'

'Is that a fucking *axe*?'

Erin's incredulity sends his heart-rate skyrocketing. Because if his own wife doesn't believe in him, how the hell can he? Joseph closes the door on her and takes four quick steps along the hall to Tilly's room. He ducks his head inside, hears his stepdaughter's breathing, knows from its rhythm that she's asleep.

At the top of the stairs he pauses in a narrow triangle of moonlight. He wants to grab the bannisters, steady himself, but in one hand he holds the torch, still unlit, and in the other he grips the tomahawk.

*The ridiculous tomahawk*, he thinks. *A weapon more suited to an SAS operative than a middle-aged guy with two kids.*

He clenches his teeth and descends, sinking into purest black.

The ground floor is an alien place, bereft of oxygen or light. Joseph feels like he's arrived at the bottom of an ocean trench.

The pressure down here is enormous. His ears pop; his jaw aches. He hears movement in the kitchen, the scrape of something across the floor. There's no tell-tale glow around the doorframe. Whoever's inside is operating in perfect darkness.

The tragedy of five years ago had struck in the depths of winter, not late summer, but it had arrived just as unexpectedly – a few minutes of insanity stealing his late wife's life and robbing Max of his mother.

In his head, he hears his last conversation with Claire, terrifyingly similar to the one he just had with Erin:

'Joe, wake up. I heard noises. I think someone's downstairs.'

'Just the heating, probably.'

He'd gone back to sleep, hadn't even heard her leave their room to investigate. He'd woken next to her scream; followed, moments later, by a terrible low-pitched moan. Even then he'd lain there in confusion for a handful of seconds before leaping up.

The burglar Claire had disturbed clubbed her three times with a metal bar before fleeing. Only one of those blows had proved fatal. A handful of seconds might have made all the difference.

Claire's antennae for danger – always more finely tuned than his – had been surpassed only by her instinct to protect their son. He should have trusted her, should have known she'd wouldn't ignore a suspicious noise.

He should have gone in her place.

Sweat rolls cold from Joseph's armpits. It makes him shiver despite the night's heat. He thinks about shouting a warning, scaring off whoever's there. Odds-on they'll flee, but what if they don't? He'll have alerted them to his presence, squandering the advantage of surprise.

His first plan is a superior one: retrieve his phone, get back upstairs, call the police, guard the landing.

Joseph swims forward through the gloom. He remembers leaving the living-room door ajar. It might be dark, down here in the hall, but he knows this house, can navigate it without fear of striking furniture or other obstacles – until his toe catches one of Erin's ballet flats and sends it spinning across the wooden floor to the wall, where it ricochets off a bookcase.

The sound is an artillery strike. An orchestra's percussion section. But what Joseph hears from the kitchen, moments later, is even worse – the unmistakeable scrape-slide of a knife being drawn from its block.

And then silence.

He thinks of the YouTube guy, of how he talked so confidently about situations exactly like this. Of how he's probably never come close to facing one. Certainly not two.

Hearing commotion in the hall, Joseph's intruder could have fled but hasn't, has instead chosen to draw a knife.

Erin is upstairs. Tilly, too. Joseph can think of few people less qualified to protect them than himself. He wants to creep back upstairs to his wife and stepdaughter and wait for help. But help isn't coming, not yet. Even if he grabs his phone and manages to call the police, they'll take time to arrive – if they show up at all. A confrontation, now, feels inevitable. Perhaps he should try to seize the initiative.

He can't control his breathing. His body feels as insubstantial as air. Joseph kicks open the kitchen door, advances over the threshold.

He raises the torch in his fist and thumbs the power switch, throwing out a cone of light so brilliant he's almost blinded but not quite, because he does see the knife that flashes through the air towards him, and when he jerks backwards even as his momentum carries him forward, it's not enough to avoid the blade, which slices him clean across the abdomen – and then he's skidding on his heels, crashing on to his tailbone with a jolt that rattles his teeth.

The torch flies from his hand. It clatters across the floor, throwing carnival shadows around the kitchen. When it comes to a rest, Joseph is pinioned by its light. Four thousand lumens is three times brighter than a car's full beam.

It fills his head, washes away colour, reduces his world to monochrome.

He squints, peers down at himself, can't figure out why there's no blood. And then, across his abdomen bleached white by the torchlight, a black line appears, finer than a papercut. It opens like a mouth, as if to speak, but instead of words it gushes black ink. Illusion or not, Joseph can't help thinking that this really is the truth of what's inside him.

And then the pain hits.

# TWO

Pain that makes him clench his teeth and groan. That makes him puff his cheeks and blow. Pain that makes him forget, just for a moment, that he isn't alone in here. That this isn't over.

The tomahawk lies near Joseph's right hand. It's a stark silhouette more suited to an apocalyptic movie scene than a suburban kitchen. He scissors his legs, tries to get them under him. His heels scribe wet, black skid marks across the floor. With each contraction of his abdominals, his torso spills more ink. He snatches at the tomahawk, grateful that he's blocking the door, that his family is still behind him. From somewhere beyond that halo of white light he hears movement. He raises his free hand in front of his face, anticipating another knife slash. Instead he hears a voice, a name. It scoops up his brain and whirls it around and around, because only one person in the world has ever called him that: 'Dad?'

It's phrased as a question, framed in shock and disbelief. Joseph groans. Despite the pain of his injury, he pushes himself to his feet. Recovering his breath, he reaches out to the wall.

'Don't,' Max hisses, but Joseph's fingers have already touched the switch. Overhead, the LED spots banish the shadows so abruptly that the room seems to flip, nearly throwing Joseph off balance. Colour floods in. Black ink morphs into bright blood. And there's a lot. Smeared wet across his torso – across the floor, his legs and his feet. But what Joseph sees before him frightens him even more. He feels like he's stepped into an alternate reality to confront a time-shifted version of himself. They've always looked similar, he and Max. Right now, though, except for their age difference and the weapons they're both clutching, they appear almost identical. Max is in his underwear, too. And he's similarly streaked with blood.

Joseph stares, aghast. Did he swing the tomahawk without thinking, eviscerating his son in the dark? If so, that's a scenario so shocking even the YouTube guy didn't foresee it.

He drops his weapon on the worktop. Across the kitchen, Max keeps his blade high, as if he's thinking about slashing his father again. There's a cornered-animal look to him, a white-faced terror Joseph hasn't seen since the night, five years ago, that delineates the *now* from the *before*. His eyes are wild, unfocused – as if captured, still, by whatever trauma they just encountered.

Max blinks, flinches. The knife slips from his fingers, clatters to the floor. Suddenly he looks present in a way he hadn't moments earlier. When he speaks, his words come out in a rush. 'Oh Jesus, Dad, Jesus, I'm sorry, I wasn't thinking, I just freaked. I never heard you come down. I thought . . . My head's all over the place. I thought someone was . . .' His gaze drops to his father's abdomen. 'Ah *shit*. I can't— We've got to stop that bleeding.'

'Are you hurt?' Joseph asks, stumbling forward. He seizes his son's shoulders, searches in vain for visible injuries.

When he cups Max's head, tilting it to examine his neck, the boy pulls away.

'I'm fine, Dad. Seriously. You're the one who's cut. Let me get the first-aid kit. We need to—'

'Joe?'

Erin's voice, from the landing. It's almost too much to process. Joseph had asked her to stay in the bedroom. Clearly, she hadn't trusted him enough to do that. Looking around the blood-spattered kitchen, he can hardly blame her.

'It's OK,' he shouts. 'It's just Max.'

'*Max?*'

Now, he hears footsteps on the stairs. His eyes meet his son's. Frantically, the teenager shakes his head. Joseph backtracks across the floor. 'Don't come down here, Erin,' he says, closing the door and bracing it.

But Erin has already reached the hallway. He hears her bare feet slap towards the kitchen.

'What's going on?' she demands.

'I just need to talk to him. Please, go back to bed.'

'Joe, it's three *a.m.*'

'I know. I'm sorry. We'll be done soon.'

He hears her approach the door, senses her on the other side. The doorknob turns in his hand. He grips it tightly. 'Erin, seriously. Go back to bed. I need to talk to Max. Father and son, alone.'

Even through the closed door he knows that he's wounded her, that this will only exacerbate the problems their marriage has been facing.

The pressure on the doorknob ceases. Silence, now, from the other side. Joseph senses his wife's thoughts – all the responses running through her head. Finally, she retreats, back along the hall and up the stairs.

Only when their bedroom door thumps shut does Joseph allow himself to breathe again. He re-examines the kitchen:

bloody footprints across the floor leading from the bloody mural where he fell; a red handprint on the nearest worktop; a red glimmer on the light switch.

There's blood on Max's side of the kitchen, too – on the taps, and the floor beneath the sink. It looks darker than Joseph's, rustier. More like paint flecks than fresh blood. Through the arch to the utility he sees rust marks on the washing machine door, hanging open. Beneath it lies a pile of Max's clothes and a pair of bloodstained trainers. On the work surface above the machine stands a box of washing powder beside a bottle of whisky, uncapped, and an empty snifter.

Joseph limps to the kitchen roll spin stand. He tears off a long sheet and presses it to his stomach. He's still bleeding freely, but the wound isn't deep, just messy.

'Dad, for God's sake, I know this stuff. You've got to let me take a look.'

Joseph waves him away. From a drawer he grabs a box of clingfilm and wraps plastic around his torso, fixing the kitchen roll in place. 'We'll clean up this mess,' he says. 'Then we'll sit at the table and you'll tell me exactly what's going on. You won't spin me a tale, lie by omission, any of that stuff. You'll tell me the truth, all of it, and then we'll figure this out.'

He watches Max's eyes closely, looking for the tell-tale glance – up and to the right – that in childhood indicated dishonesty. Because as fiercely as Joseph loves him, he knows he hasn't managed to fully heal his son from the trauma of five years ago. That even now there are things that remain unsaid. Often, these days, the boy seems more comfortable around his stepmother and stepsister than his own father.

Now, though, instead of deceit, Joseph sees something infinitely worse – an expression on Max's face utterly alien. It makes him fear that the truth of what's happened will be more devastating than he can bear, that the last safety line tethering him to his son has been severed, and that from here there's no way back.

The thought is so crushing it drives the air from Joseph's lungs. He clenches his fists and vows that whatever this is, he won't fail Max tonight like he's failed him before. He'll protect him no matter what.

No matter what.

# THREE

They work side by side in strained silence. For Joseph, despite his dread at what he might soon discover, it's an opportunity to breathe, order his thoughts, process what just happened.

Max stands at the sink with a dish scrubber, scouring dried blood from his nails. Joseph uses more kitchen roll to soak up his own spilled blood. He mops the floor with detergent. Then he adds a few squirts of bleach to fresh water and mops the whole thing again. He returns the whisky bottle to the cupboard and puts away the snifter. In the utility, he wipes down the washing-machine door.

While Max cleans the kitchen taps, Joseph examines the pile of discarded clothes beneath the machine: his son's shorts, grey T-shirt and white socks. The shorts and socks are spotted with rust stains. The grey T-shirt is more heavily soiled, the blood on it still wet. Briefly, Joseph considers loading the clothes into the drum and running a boil cycle. Instead, he double-bags them in bin liners, along with the ruined trainers.

When he turns back towards the arch, he finds Max staring at him from the kitchen. Again, he sees something deeply troubling in his son's expression. It lifts the hairs on his arms, wicks the moisture from his mouth.

'Let's sit,' Joseph says.

'I'd rather stand.'

'Sit.'

For a handful of breaths, Max doesn't move. Then, without breaking eye contact, he goes to the breakfast table by the bifold doors and pulls out a seat.

'Drink?' Joseph asks. The tension between them is palpable. He needs to find some way of slackening it.

Max shakes his head. He rests his forearms on the table edge, inspects his fingernails. Then he hides his hands in his lap. 'I can't talk to you.'

'Why not?'

'This . . .' Max licks his lips. 'You were never meant to see it.'

Joseph opens the fridge. He grabs a Coke Zero, pops the tab and takes a long swallow. Then he sits opposite. 'Whose blood is that?'

Again, Max shakes his head.

'What happened tonight?'

'It's best you don't know.'

'Was it a fight?'

'Dad,' he begins. Then he grimaces, closes his mouth.

Abruptly, Joseph realizes what's been frightening him about his son's expression. It's as if he's seeing two people struggling for supremacy inside the same face. One is the boy he loves; the other is a traumatized stranger. The battle twists back and forth. Moments ago, his son resurfaced. Now, the stranger has reappeared, watching with wary eyes.

Joseph wants to reach out, take Max's hands, create a physical connection if not an emotional one. Deeper instinct tells him the time isn't right. Better to proceed cautiously, and wait for his son's return.

Max – or Not-Max – lifts his gaze to the worktop, blinks. 'Is that an axe?'

'A tomahawk.'

'Jesus, Dad.'

'Erin woke me. Said she could hear someone poking around downstairs. We thought you were stay—'

'What were you going to do?'

'Get my phone, call the police. The tomahawk was just a deterrent. But it was a stupid—'

'I've never seen it before.'

'I keep it hidden.'

'Where?'

'Back of the wardrobe,' Joseph says, and wishes, instantly, that he hadn't. 'Look, that's not important. What—'

'Does Erin know?'

'Max, listen to me. You're down here in pitch darkness, in the middle of the night, covered in someone else's blood. I don't want to talk about the tomahawk. I don't want to talk about anything other than whose blood it is, what's happened, and whether you're both OK.'

His son – or perhaps it's still the stranger – shakes his head. 'I can't talk about it.'

'You don't have a choice. I'm not—'

'Dad,' he says softly. 'What you need to do is go back upstairs, pretend this never happened. That means you tell no one about what you saw, not even Erin. *Especially* Erin. It's the only way this ends well.'

Max must know that no responsible parent in the world would agree to what he's asking. The idea that Joseph could climb into bed and go back to sleep is absurd. Joseph glances at the wall clock, sees it's well past three. He has the sense of time running down, running out – the window for fixing this shrinking by the minute.

He leans forward, searching Max's face. 'Why did you grab a knife?' he asks. 'That might have been Erin walking in on you. It might have been Tilly, getting a glass of water. Swinging out like you did – you could've slashed her throat.'

Max's face creases in pain as he considers that. 'I don't know what to tell you. I just wasn't thinking straight. First thing I heard was whatever you kicked over in the hall. And when the door burst open, and that torch beam shone in my face, I . . . I guess it took me back to . . .'

Max's words peter out, but he doesn't have to finish the sentence. Clearly Joseph's not the only one, these days, to see danger in what should be the safest of places.

'What happened tonight?'

The boy shakes his head.

'Max, you've got to tell me.'

'I can't.'

Joseph's heart thumps. He knows he can't walk away from this, which means his only option is escalation – raising the stakes and hoping it works.

He stands, grimacing as the wound across his abdomen reopens. Crossing the kitchen, he opens the door. The rest of the house is still dark, but there's enough light to see the hall. He steps over Erin's ballet flat, pauses at the base of the stairs. No way of knowing if his wife has gone back to sleep unless he goes up there, but at least she hasn't come down again.

He retrieves his phone from the living room and returns to the kitchen. He doesn't like what he's about to do. If he were a better parent – wiser and more emotionally literate – maybe he'd devise a better plan. But this is all he has.

He sits opposite Max, places the phone on the table between them, tries to control his breathing. 'Here's the deal. And there really isn't another. You tell me, right now, exactly what's happened tonight. No lies, no evasions. The truth. If you do that, this conversation – everything we talk about – remains strictly between you and me. And I mean for ever. No one else will ever know, not even Erin. I give you my word on that. From there, if it's bad, we figure a way out. Together.'

Joseph pauses, forces a calmness into his voice he doesn't feel. 'But if you won't talk to me, Max – if you insist on silence – then I'll phone the police right now and tell them what I know. Because that blood came from someone's son, or someone's daughter.'

Max blinks. 'You wouldn't do that.'

'I would. And I will. I'll give you to the count of five. Then I'm picking up that phone and calling.'

'If you think this is—'

'One,' Joseph says.

'I've already told you I'm—'

'Two.'

Max drops his gaze to the phone.

Joseph wonders if he'll try to snatch it, thinks he probably won't. 'Three,' he says.

'Please, Dad, you're—'

'Four.'

A nerve twitches in Max's cheek. 'There's no—'

'Five,' Joseph says.

He picks up the phone and dials 999, and as his finger descends on the call button, Max says, 'I hit someone.'

# FOUR

Joseph puts down the phone.

'You hit someone?' he asks. 'In a fight?'

Max rubs his hands together, as if he's washing them beneath a tap. There's no damage to his knuckles, no scuffing of the skin. His fists can't be responsible for the spilled blood.

Joseph touches his abdomen. He recalls the knife blade flashing in the dark. And suddenly he's very frightened indeed.

The face opposite seems to cycle through different identities: Max the child; Max the teenager; a person who's barely Max at all. 'Not a fight,' says one of them.

Joseph runs his tongue around his mouth, tries to work up some moisture. 'What, then?'

Max holds his father's gaze a while longer. Then he hangs his head. When he speaks next, his voice cracks with emotion. 'Once I say, everything changes. And I'm not ready. Because afterwards we can never go back.'

Joseph reaches across the table, takes Max's hands, squeezes them. 'Between you and me,' he says, 'nothing changes. Nothing ever changes. I'm your dad. That's for ever. Whatever this is, let me help you.'

Max lifts his chin. He looks past Joseph to the wall clock as if he, too, has started to sense time running inexorably down. Again, his head drops.

'I was driving,' the boy whispers – because eighteen years old or not, to Joseph he's still very much a boy. 'Next thing I know, someone's in the road. There was . . .' He shudders. 'There was nothing I could do.'

In the ensuing silence, the refrigerator's soft buzzing is the only sound. Joseph cannot breathe, cannot speak. He gets up from the table, shakes his head – as if by dislodging his son's words he can cancel their meaning. 'Nothing you could do to avoid them?'

When Max lifts his gaze to his father, his eyes are wet with tears. 'Nothing I could do to save them.'

The overhead LEDs brighten. The refrigerator's buzzing increases in pitch. It's as if a power surge has just hit the house, but Joseph suspects it's a dump of adrenalin sharpening his senses. 'You're saying you . . . that they're *dead*?'

Max wipes his eyes, nods.

'No. That can't be. Maybe that's what it looked like. You knocked them unconscious, or—'

'Dad,' he says. 'I'm telling you.'

Joseph crosses the kitchen, comes back, sits down again. He can't make sense of what he's hearing. Its sheer enormity. 'You called the police?' he asks, knowing the futility of the question, knowing that Max wouldn't be here, in this kitchen, if he had.

'I was going too fast. Uninsured, in a car that isn't road legal. That probably means prison time. It definitely means a record.'

Joseph puffs his cheeks, blows air. And can't help voicing what he's thinking, brutal though it is. 'You're meant to be starting medical school in a month.'

'I know.'

'They'll run an enhanced DBS check before you start.'

'Yeah. And if anything comes up, out of the door you go. No second chances.'

Joseph rocks back in his seat. Max's childhood passion for medicine grew exponentially after his mother's death. In recent years he's volunteered in hospitals and surgeries, attended conferences. He's grilled countless doctors and specialists, has thrown himself into his studies with a commitment bordering on obsessional, all in the hope of ensuring other families avoid the same devastating loss.

How could he possibly have caused the very thing he's been working so hard to prevent? How could the universe have permitted such brutal irony?

'What was your plan?'

'I came back here to clean myself up, think it over.'

Joseph recalls the bottle of whisky, the empty snifter. He closes his eyes, recalling his earlier promise: *This conversation – everything we talk about – remains strictly between me and you. And I mean for ever. No one else will ever know, not even Erin. I give you my word on that. From there, if it's bad, we figure a way out. Together.*

When he opens his eyes, he sees Max watching him. That same cornered-animal expression. 'Jesus,' he says. 'Jesus.'

He goes around the table, puts his arms around his son, squeezes him so tightly it becomes something more than an embrace. He smells the boy's hair, his sweat. 'As if we needed this,' he whispers. 'As if we needed it.'

'I'm sorry, Dad. I'm so sorry.'

'Did anyone else see?'

'No.'

'You're absolutely sure?'

'Hundred per cent.'

Joseph takes a breath, sighs it out. He's still holding Max

far too tightly, but his son seems immune to the discomfort. At last, he forces himself to disentangle. When he stands, he feels fresh blood seep from his abdomen and winces.

'Dad, we really should take a look at that. It may need stitches or glue.'

'It's fine. The person you hit. Did you recognize them?'

Max shakes his head. And Joseph wonders if he just spotted the first flicker of dishonesty in his son's eyes.

'A stranger?' he presses.

'I guess.'

'You guess?'

The boy grimaces, as if he just swallowed a mouthful of bile. 'It was pretty bad. It could have been Tilly and I doubt I'd have recognized her.'

Joseph puts out a hand to the worktop. That Max would choose his stepsister for the comparison is more than a little chilling, particularly as they're so close. 'It was a woman?'

'A guy.'

'Where did this happen?'

'One of the roads that cuts through Jack-O'-Lantern Woods.'

'What were you doing out there?'

'Taking a short-cut.'

'To?'

'A friend's.'

Again, that tell-tale flicker. Dishonesty, or something else?

'Which friend?' Joseph asks. He's played taxi service often enough to know where most of Max's friends live. He doesn't recall ever taking that route.

'Just a girl.'

'Someone I know?'

'Dad – it was just a girl.'

'Was she expecting you?'

'Why does that—'

'It matters. Everything matters. Was this girl expecting you?'

'Yeah.'

'And you didn't turn up.'

'No.'

'So who was it?'

'Dad, I . . .'

'Max, for God's sake. If someone died in those woods tonight, and someone else knows you were driving through them, and then you never turned up to see them afterwards – it matters.'

The boy goes still. His eyes flare, as if he's just grasped the danger his father has highlighted.

'So tell me, Max. What's her name?'

'Drew,' his son replies.

'*Drew?* As in Tilly's best friend?'

'We've been keeping it quiet.'

'Have you spoken to her since?'

'No.'

'Does Tilly know? About you and Drew, I mean.'

Again, Max shakes his head. 'We've been figuring out how to tell her.'

'OK,' Joseph says. 'OK.' He drums his fingers. 'So, right now, where's the . . .' he begins, and finds he can't bring himself to say *body*. He pauses, unsticks his brain, tries again. 'This guy you hit. Where is he?'

Max's jaw bulges. Then he says, 'In the boot of my car.'

# FIVE

Joseph groans, feels like he's just taken a cricket bat to the gut. Because this keeps getting worse.

Watching his father's reaction, Max says, 'I thought about calling the police, explaining. Then I remembered about the insurance and MOT. I couldn't just leave the guy in the road. So I . . . I dragged him out of sight. After that, I drove home to figure out what to do.'

'Wait,' Joseph says. 'You've been back here once already? Why didn't you wake me? *Talk* to me?'

The boy meets his eyes. It's a while before he speaks. Eventually, he says, 'Because you've already been through so much. Because, on top of everything else, you really didn't deserve this.'

'Max,' Joseph says, and doesn't know how to continue.

'I grabbed a spade from the shed, some other gear. And then I went back. I know how it sounds, how it makes me look, but I didn't know what else to do. If I go to the police, say anything, then the one thing I could do to make up for this, even slightly – med school, the foundation programme, trauma and orthopaedics – will be toast. Plus, I knew what seeing me go to jail might do to you.'

Tears are running freely from his eyes again. 'I was

going to bury him in the woods. Then I realized it's the first place the police might look. They might get sniffer dogs out there. Cadaver dogs. So I wrapped him in that tarpaulin we sometimes take camping and loaded him into the boot. On the way home I realized that . . . I guess I needed more time to think it through.' He runs his hands through his hair. 'I don't know, Dad. Maybe I deserve everything that's coming.'

'Don't say that. Where's the car, now?'

'Berrylands Road.'

*Close to here but not too close,* Joseph thinks. *A quiet road with few streetlights. The kind of place I might park a car containing a dead body while figuring out what to do.*

'Is there much damage?' he asks. 'To the car, I mean.'

Max shakes his head. 'The guy saw me, fell backwards just before it happened. The car . . . it kind of went over him rather than through him.' He pauses. Then he says, 'Did you mean what you said earlier? That you'd keep this between you and me? No matter what?'

Joseph fills his lungs. He knows Max's question is the right one. At present, it's the only question that matters. He studies his son, seeing the boy he was and the man he might one day become. He sees the tiny white scar on his lip from nursery, when another child swung a tennis racquet without looking behind him. He sees the sprig of hair that insists on standing proud however often it's wetted, the downy facial hair beginning to track across each cheek. He sees the features inherited from Claire: the oval jaw, the high forehead, the aquiline nose. In contemplating them Joseph braces himself against all the pain bound up with her memory.

'You're my son,' he says simply, because to add anything more would bring tears, hard sobs. And because, really, there's nothing more to add.

Max nods, his own throat bobbing.

'I'll grab us some clothes,' Joseph tells him. 'And then we'll get the car.'

Five minutes later, they're fully dressed. Before they leave the house, Joseph collects up everything they used to clean the kitchen: the blood-soaked and bagged-up sheets of kitchen roll; the mop he used for the floor; Max's bloodied clothing; the washing-up bowl and the dish scrubber.

'Where's your phone?' he asks.

Max produces it. Joseph turns it off, hands it back, checks his watch. It'll be dark for a while yet. Leading his son through the back door, they creep down the path beside the house, carrying the binbags between them.

The Carvers live in a cul-de-sac of identical four-bedroom homes, each with a double driveway and front lawn sloping down to a shared turning circle. The boundaries of each property are marked not by walls or fences but borders of low shrubs. Next door, a monkey puzzle tree grows in the Robinsons' front garden. Other than that, there's little cover from prying eyes.

Joseph steps on to the pavement, into the orange glow of the cul-de-sac's three streetlamps. Immediately, his neck prickles, as if unseen eyes are watching him. Except for Ralph Erikson's place, the neighbouring houses are all dark. There, the curtains are undrawn, the ground-floor lights all on. Joseph doesn't see the widower inside, but that doesn't mean the man isn't watching from somewhere upstairs.

His prickle of awareness doesn't leave him until the circle of houses is out of sight. At the end of the street, he turns left on to Hiltingbury Lane, then right on to Berrylands Road. They pass the driveways of three homes hidden by giant leylandii before they come to the car, a twenty-year-old sky-blue Honda Jazz.

Officially, the vehicle still isn't Max's. Until she died last Christmas, it belonged to Joseph's mother. It's been sitting on the Carvers' driveway since probate, waiting for replacement parts.

*And now there's a dead man in the boot,* Joseph thinks. *Wrapped in the tarpaulin we take on family camping trips.*

The horror of it, mixed with the everyday mundanity, feels unreal.

After checking the street for activity, he moves to the rear of the car and puts down his load. 'You'd better unlock it.'

Max squeezes the key fob and the vehicle's hazards flash. Joseph glances at his son, tries to read his face in the shadows of the street. A wild hope takes him that this is all some monstrous hoax; a hideous gotcha filmed for TikTok. Max will open the boot and balloons will burst out, rising into the night. The boy's friends will emerge from hiding, filming Joseph on their smartphones and collapsing into hysterics. Erin will appear. Tilly, too.

But Max has never been one for cruel jokes. And now, silent, he swings up the boot lid.

It's too dark to see inside. Dialling his torch to the lowest setting, Joseph turns it on. He sees a green polythene-wrapped bundle, bent in the middle and secured with three yellow bungees.

His torch beam trembles. Joseph extinguishes it. Then he reaches into the boot and gently squeezes the tarp.

If he harboured any doubts, he doesn't now. There's no mistaking the contours of a human body. To think that not long ago this was a living, breathing individual sickens his soul, suffocates him with sadness.

During the walk from home, perhaps to protect himself, he'd been thinking about this purely in terms of a corpse he intended to hide. But of course it's not that at all. This is a man just like him – maybe a little younger, maybe a little older, but with hopes and fears just as real, with real family and friends expecting to see him again soon. He has a bank account, a list of favourite foods, a particular way he takes his tea or coffee, a favourite book. He probably has a private space, filled with objects meaningful to him.

'Get in the car,' Joseph says. He closes the boot, loads what they brought from the house on to the back seat and goes around to the driver's side. Once he's behind the wheel, he says, as calmly as he can manage, 'We're not going to bury him.'

Max twists around. 'What?'

'We can't change what's happened. But the choices we make from here have consequences. There are his loved one to consider, for a start. If we try to cover this up, they're the people we'll be torturing, because they'll never find out the truth. There'll just be this terrible hole in their lives. This awful abyss.'

'What're you saying?' the boy asks. 'I should hand myself in?'

Angry, Joseph shakes his head. 'You think I want your life ruined over a single, tragic mistake? Because it *would* be ruined, you're right about that. A criminal record would slam shut the very door you've spent all these years in education trying to open. How many lives does the average trauma surgeon save in a career? Hundreds? Thousands? You think I'd get in the way of that?

'But *this* . . . To pretend it never happened. To leave another family without answers. We have no right to do this. I can't live with the thought of people suffering for the rest of their lives because we decided to cover this up. And I doubt you can, either.'

Joseph wraps his fingers around the steering wheel. He tightens his grip until the plastic squeals. 'So here's what we're going to do. And I want you to listen carefully, and take in all in, because I know you won't like it, even though it really is the best solution.'

He licks his lips and tries to swallow, but his throat is so dry he nearly retches. 'After we dump what we brought from the house, we're going to drive back to the spot where this happened and put things back exactly as they were. Then you're going to walk home, get rid of the tarpaulin along the way. I'll wait a while. Then I'll call the police, say I fell asleep at the wheel, that I—'

Max rears away. 'Dad, no. You can't—'

'I told you to *listen*,' Joseph hisses. 'Because this makes sense. Think about it. I haven't been drinking. I've got a perfect driving record. And at least I'm insured. We can cope with the consequences, however they play out. It won't be disastrous.'

'You're going to let Erin think you *killed* someone?' Max shouts. 'Tilly, too? Have you even considered what that might do to them?'

Joseph's heart aches. Because he hadn't, not yet, and because it still doesn't change his mind. His loves his wife, regardless of their difficulties, but he loves his son more. 'This kind of secret,' he says. 'It would eat away at you. Until there's nothing left.'

'And you being in prison wouldn't? Fucking hell, you're delusional, Dad.'

'Max, you don't underst—'

'No, *you* don't understand.'

'Put your seatbelt on.'

'I'm not putting my—'

'Max—'

'*You don't have all the facts!*'

Joseph freezes, his hands still clutching the wheel. Because that voice didn't sound like his son's. He twists around – convinced, suddenly, that the words came from behind him, possibly from inside the tarpaulin.

His horror is a noose drawing tight around his windpipe,

choking off his breath. It's too dark to see anything back there, to see if that bungee-wrapped package has sat up straight.

Abruptly, Joseph's reason floods back. The voice might not have sounded familiar, but he knows that it belonged to Max. He thinks of how he'd felt in the kitchen, his sense that he was talking to a stranger. 'I told you earlier not to hide anything. So if I don't have all the facts, what am I missing?'

Max breathes slowly, through his nostrils. Then, in a tone far different from any Joseph has heard before, he says, 'You're not going to like it, Dad, and I wish more than anything I didn't have to tell you. But when I stopped the car, the guy was still alive.'

# SIX

Headlights appear at the end of the street. Joseph tries to formulate a question, but his brain seems to have seized again. He feels his eyebrows fluttering, worries he's about to pass out. The headlights grow brighter. He hears the whine of a battery motor, the clink and clatter of glass. Three parked cars from theirs, a milk float pulls into the kerb. The driver jumps out, grabs a carry crate and disappears up a nearby driveway.

'You remember the deer?' Max asks.

Joseph's stomach yawns away from him. Because he knows, immediately, what his son is talking about.

The milkman reappears. He transfers his empty bottles to the float and starts to refill his crate.

They'd hit the deer last summer, driving home. A fawn had sprung from the undergrowth and bolted across the road. Joseph managed to avoid it, but he couldn't avoid the mother, who followed an instant later. The impact took her in the flank and sent her pirouetting past his window.

Joseph stopped the car, got out. The doe was a mess of broken legs, wild eyes and frothing blood. He stared at her for a while. Then he fetched a torque wrench from his car and did the only humane thing possible. His first strike didn't kill her, just distressed her further, turning her chest into forge bellows. His second attempt cratered her skull and ended her life. When he turned around he found two sets of eyes watching him: the fawn's and his son's.

'Max,' he croaks, now.

'I . . . It was obvious he wouldn't make it. He wouldn't even have lasted long enough for an ambulance. And he was in so much pain. I thought it was for the best. That deer you hit, in our old car. Remember how you said it was kinder to . . . to . . .'

He twitches, seems to veer from that thought.

The milkman finishes loading his crate and walks up the street towards them. Max seizes Joseph's shoulder and pulls him level with the dashboard. Moments later, footsteps pass the passenger door.

'I know what you're thinking,' Max whispers. 'But I'm not a killer, Dad. I'm not. It was a kindness, what I did. Just like you and that deer.'

Joseph closes his eyes despite the darkness. He can't believe what he's hearing. Doesn't know how to react. Max understands the difference between an injured deer and an injured human being, of course he does. He understands you don't treat them the same way, apply the same brutal logic.

*Claire*, he thinks, finally invoking the name that appears on his lips each time he wakes. As always, it brings pain so exquisite his body contorts to withstand it.

Joseph clenches his teeth, bites down on his guilt. *Claire*, he pleads, eviscerating himself. *What do I do? This isn't our boy, this isn't. When did I stop paying attention?*

A personality change as stark as this should have been obvious for a while, should have been observable in a thousand different ways, but Joseph appears to have been blind to it – because for far too long his eyes have been firmly closed.

For two years after Claire's death, he'd lived in a state of purgatory, of permanent torture, his guilt too enormous to address, his only focus Max. Then he'd met Erin. Within months she'd become the centre of his world. He'd abandoned his guilt entirely, immersing himself in the elixir of new love, but in the process he'd also abandoned his son. Max, cast adrift, had withdrawn from the world around him.

Then had come marriage, and a new family home. Trying to make it all work, Joseph had spent more time establishing a relationship with Tilly than he had on Max.

He'd hoped, as everything settled down, he'd feel less torn. But that hadn't really happened. Thank God Erin had spotted Max's isolation. With love and patience she'd rejuvenated him. Tilly, too, had played her part. That had been Joseph's wake-up call.

This last year, determined to rebuild, he's poured all his focus into his son. But in doing so he's distanced himself from Erin, with predictable consequences for their relationship.

He's been a weathervane blown by guilt, each pivot causing further heartache. Worst of all, his efforts with Max might have come too late to make a difference.

His late wife doesn't answer his call, as he'd known she wouldn't. Perhaps that, in itself, is her message: this is his responsibility to fix. But before he can even think about trying to put his son back together, he has an even more pressing crisis to tackle. Because Max's latest revelation means the calculus has fundamentally changed. And Joseph's earlier options have all but disappeared.

He hears the milkman return to the float. The whine of a motor. He sees a brief wash of headlights and wonders if the vehicle is equipped with a dashcam – and if it'll record the car's registration plate.

Max releases his shoulder. They sit up straight in their seats. Joseph can't seem to breathe without shuddering. 'Keys,' he says.

Max passes them over. 'Where're we going?'

'Just don't say anything for a while. OK?' Joseph tells him. 'Please, just let me think.'

He pulls out of Berrylands Road and heads east. All the while, Max's words replay in his head: *He was in so much pain. I thought it was for the best.*

No one in their right mind believes that. No one.

Up ahead, he sees the twenty-four-hour BP garage and instinctively checks the Honda's fuel gauge. When he looks up, he realizes two things simultaneously: he's drifted across the road's white centreline and a police patrol car has rolled off the BP forecourt, signalling to turn right towards him.

Joseph corrects with a flick of the wheel. The Honda rocks back into its lane. As he passes the patrol car he gets a close-up view of its occupants and makes fleeting eye contact with the driver – a sharp-faced male a decade or so younger than himself. The officer in the passenger seat is older and fleshier, focused on opening a sandwich box.

Joseph glances in his rear-view mirror, willing the other vehicle to follow its indicated route. Instead it turns left, falling in step behind them.

He locks his arms, grips the steering wheel with trembling hands and tries to prevent the car from weaving.

'Dad,' Max mutters.

'I know.'

Behind them the headlights grow closer, a pair of hunting eyes. Joseph checks his speed. He hasn't seen a sign, can't remember if this is a thirty zone or a forty. Or possibly even a twenty. Too slow and it'll look suspicious. Too fast and he'll get pulled for speeding.

The road swings left and right. The white eyes in the rear-view mirror swell as if with hunger. Then, shocking even in their silence, a rack of flashing blue ones joins them.

Teeth clenched, Joseph lifts his foot from the accelerator.

He steers towards the kerb, gently touches the brakes. Behind him, accompanied by a howl of rubber, the lights swing away into darkness.

For a moment, Joseph can't work out what's happening. Then the realization hits him that the white eyes were intent on different prey. He groans, swears, wipes sweat from his forehead.

In the passenger seat, Max exhales explosively. Then he leans forward in his seat. 'Are we going where I think we're going?'

A few minutes later they arrive in Saddle Bank, where winding residential roads serve widely spaced bungalows. This is where Joseph's mother had lived for the last fifteen years of her life. Her home has been up for sale since probate. So far, thanks to a tanking housing market, there's been little interest.

The clicker for her electric garage door is on the key fob. Joseph pulls on to the driveway, activates the door and rolls into the garage. Once he's turned off the engine he presses the clicker again, sealing them in darkness.

Bringing the dead man to his mother's feels worse than obscene, but Joseph can think of nowhere else. He sits in silence for a while, recalling the near-miss with police. 'We'll leave the car here,' he says, retrieving his torch. 'Just until I've figured out what to do. First, though, I've got to see what we're dealing with.'

Opening his door, he edges along the Honda. He rests his hand on the boot lid, gathering his courage. Then he swings it open, dials up the torch's brightness and clicks it on.

White light with the brilliance of burning magnesium fills the boot. In its incandescence, there's nowhere for the horror to hide. The green tarpaulin glitters, each ridge and hollow thrown into a sharp relief of light and shadow. Earlier, Joseph had relied on touch to confirm what lay beneath. Now, it's obvious from the shape alone.

Max climbs out of the car. 'Dad, you don't need to—'

'Quiet,' Joseph snaps, more harshly than he'd intended – because it won't take much to dissuade him from this task, and he knows he can't avoid it. From his pocket he takes a second torch and hands it to his son. 'Last time I was here, I left a roll of duct tape on the workbench. See if you can find it. There should be a few old blankets kicking around, too.'

With Max occupied, and with his own torch gripped between his teeth, Joseph unclips the bungees securing the tarpaulin and rolls back the first layer. With his knife, he slices through the remaining material. Doing this in semi-darkness, the colours of his surroundings corrupted by white LED light, makes the job even more ghastly.

Finally, he eases aside the tarp's severed edges – and confirms that five years after Claire's death, the wheels of his life have once again jumped the rails and plunged into the realms of nightmare.

# SEVEN

What he exposes is no longer a face. It's a reddish, blackish crust from which rise the recognizable contours of a human skull. There are teeth, splintered into points. A ruined eye.

The damage is so severe, so shocking and grotesque, that all Joseph can do is stare. His mouth floods with saliva. Before he can react, a fat bead of it rolls down the shaft of the torch still gripped between his teeth. It extends from the bezel and into that crusted mass. For a moment, he's connected to the dead man by a single, glistening filament – until, with a splash, it breaks.

Joseph flinches. And when the light pans back and forth it gives the illusion of movement – a tongue moving inside a black mouth – as if his saliva has brought about a revival of sorts, a reanimation.

Instead of a stranger's voice, though, Joseph hears his son's: *He was in so much pain. I thought it was for the best.*

Beneath the cloying richness of blood and butchered flesh he smells a woody cologne similar to one he used to wear. It throws him into fresh turmoil, reinforces his awareness that he can't think of this as a corpse, however gruesome its presentation. This is a human being, recently passed, who demands not just respect but reverence.

Joseph has made promises to Max, to Max's late mother, and he'll die before seeing the boy go to prison. But the consequences of those choices don't weigh lightly.

'I'm sorry,' he whispers. 'You didn't deserve this. I can't make it right, but I hope you're at peace. He . . . I know how it sounds, but he's a good kid, I swear. He's just lost. That's my fault, not his. I've got to find a way to bring him back.'

Briefly, Joseph closes his eyes. Ahead is another task as vital as it is distasteful. Slicing through more of the tarp, he exposes the rest of the body.

The dead man is wearing navy shorts, deck shoes and a short-sleeved linen shirt saturated with blood. His skin looks grey rather than summer dark, perhaps due to whichever processes of death have already begun. On his forearm is a raised mole the size of a ten pence piece. Hairs have sprouted from it like the spines of a cactus.

An Omega Seamaster hangs from his left wrist. Encircling the pinkie finger of his right hand is a gold signet ring, set with a green stone. Joseph stares at it, emotions roiling inside him. It's a while before he can tear his eyes away.

Overall, the dead man looks in good shape. The pair of them might be similar in age. It's hard to tell.

Joseph presses his hand to the left front pocket of the shorts. Through the material he feels nothing but cold thigh muscle. He slides his hand into the pocket regardless, but it's as empty as he suspected.

Checking the right front pocket is more difficult. The dead man lies in the foetal position, partially on his side. Joseph has to reach his arms around the torso, bringing his face to within a few inches of that gruesome reddish-black mask. This close, it's clear that decomposition has already started. The odour of meat bloat mixed with cologne curdles his stomach, makes him want to retch.

The right front pocket is empty, too. Joseph slides his

fingers into the two back pockets and finds nothing there either.

Max returns with the duct tape and two oil-stained blankets. 'What're you doing?' he asks. 'I had him all sealed up.'

'Looking for a phone.'

'Dad, come on. You think I've been driving him around this whole time without even checking if a phone was pinging away in his pocket?'

'Did you find one?'

'No.'

'That's weird.'

'Is it?'

Joseph maintains eye contact. 'You don't think?'

'Maybe.'

'There's no wallet, either.'

The boy shrugs.

'You didn't find anything – personal possessions, whatever – near where you hit him?'

'No.'

Joseph frowns, continues to study his son. 'And you checked?'

'Dad, there was nothing.'

'You're positive?'

'Yes. Why do you want his wallet?'

'So I can figure out who he is – and who might be looking for him. He's going to be missed by someone, I guarantee it. He's wearing a watch that could pay your first year's tuition fees.'

'There wasn't a phone,' Max says. 'Nor a wallet.'

Joseph doesn't push it further. He takes the duct tape and reseals the tarp's severed edges. Rolling the top flap back into position, he re-ties the bungees and throws the blankets over the top. Then he shuts the boot and locks the car.

Against the far wall leans his mother's shopping bike and

an ancient Dawes racer. Indicating them with his torch, he says, 'Let's go.'

They peddle home through sleeping streets. Joseph uses the silence to focus on what comes next. He's on a timer, now. The dead man can't stay in his mother's garage long – twenty-four hours, maybe; forty-eight at best. He has an incredibly short window in which to figure out a cover story, analyse its holes and ensure they're all plugged. Most pressing is what he'll tell Erin. Doubtless she'll want to know why he kept her out of the kitchen tonight – and, at some point, the whereabouts of Max's car.

He's spent his entire adult life being honest. Now, he'll have to become a liar – and a competent one, at that. If he fails, Max will go to prison, and Joseph will have broken the most sacrosanct vow he'd made to his late wife: to protect their son from further harm.

As they arrive home, he checks the neighbouring houses. Ralph Erikson's windows are now dark like all the others. After shutting the bikes in the shed, he unlocks the back door and leads Max inside. 'Straight up to bed,' he says. 'Get some sleep. We'll talk more in the morning.'

Max looks for a moment like he'll reply. Like he wants to get something off his chest. Instead, nodding, he disappears upstairs.

Joseph goes into the living room. In the mirror over the fireplace, he examines his reflection. His eyes look different. Like they're missing something important.

*If I hadn't given Max the car, he couldn't have driven out there to visit Drew tonight. And if I hadn't married Erin, Max wouldn't have met Tilly or Drew. He'd have had no reason to be in those woods.*

There are fresh stains on his T-shirt, he sees. Probably from when he leaned in close to search the dead man's pockets. Stripping it off, he bags it in a Sainsbury's carrier and hides it at the back of a kitchen cupboard. Then he retrieves his ridiculous tomahawk from the worktop. Foolish to have left it in plain view. If he's to help Max survive this, he'll have to think faster and clearer.

One thing he wants to understand is what the dead man was doing in Jack-O'-Lantern Woods. If he was walking out there so late, surely he'd have been carrying a phone. Joseph didn't find any car keys in his pockets, but that doesn't mean there weren't any. He can't rely on Max's claim that no belongings remain at the scene – the stakes are simply too high.

If he's learned anything from books and TV, it's that guilty parties shouldn't revisit crime scenes. And yet that's exactly what he feels he must do.

Upstairs, he pauses outside his bedroom. Beyond the landing window the sky is beginning to lighten. From Erin's breathing, it sounds like she's gone back to sleep. He wonders if she's faking – and then he flinches from that thought. He's just hidden a body inside his late mother's house – and already he's projecting his dishonesty on to his wife.

Joseph hears movement behind him. Turning, he sees Tilly emerge from her bedroom. His stepdaughter is barefoot, in a white cotton nightdress featuring a yellow Pokémon. She might be the same age as Max but she's several years younger in looks. Her dark hair, recently styled by Drew, is messy from sleep.

Tilly pauses when she notices him, rubs her eyes. 'Joe?'

'Hi, sweetheart.'

'Is that an axe?'

He looks down at the tomahawk. 'Your mum thought she heard an intruder. But coast is clear.'

'Lucky for the intruder,' Tilly mutters, padding past him to the bathroom.

Joseph goes into his bedroom, closes the door. He returns

the tomahawk to its hiding place. In the ensuite, he switches on the light. In the mirror over the sink he sees, once again, that look of something missing in his eyes. When he breathes, he smells the dead man's clotted blood. He grips the basin, thinks for a moment that he'll vomit. From the family bathroom, he hears the toilet flush.

Closing the ensuite door, Joseph strips off the rest of his clothes. He unwinds the clingfilm from around his torso and flushes the blood-soaked sheets of kitchen roll down the toilet. He showers carefully. Afterwards, he cuts a wide length of Elastoplast and secures it across his abdomen. Then he rummages through the medicine cabinet for the bottle of Sauvage, still in its packaging, that Erin bought him last Christmas. Peeling off the cellophane, he tears open the box and douses himself. It's a good smell, different to what he smelled on the dead man. He sprays it on his fingers and dabs the skin beneath his nose. Once he's cleaned his teeth, he creeps into the bedroom, dons fresh underwear and lies down beside Erin.

She sighs and mutters something in sleep. For the first time in months, Joseph feels the urge to spoon up to her, press his face into her hair, but even after his shower he doesn't feel clean enough. His hands have touched death tonight. He doesn't want to transfer that to his wife.

And physical intimacy now, when it's been absent for so long, might make Erin question what's changed. So Joseph remains on his back, eyes open and gritty.

*Claire, if you're watching, if you're seeing all this, please tell me what to do. Tell me how to protect our son. Show me what he needs.*

He listens to the darkness, heart thumping. Claire doesn't respond, but suddenly the answer is clear. Climbing out of bed, he tiptoes along the hall and slips inside his son's room.

Max is lying on his bed, eyes closed, still fully dressed.

Carefully, Joseph lies down beside him. He listens to his son's breathing for a while. Finally, he hugs him close. 'I love you,' he whispers. 'I'll always love you. I might not have been here for you in the past. But I'm here for you now, no matter what.'

Max's breathing changes, just slightly.

Exhaustion falls over Joseph like a cloak.

# EIGHT

He wakes as he always does, into the *before* and not the *now*; into a world unblemished by shame or regret. It survives for the space of a breath before folding. Joseph's heart collapses through the bed, through both floors of the house, through millions of tons of earth, through crust and mantle and right into molten rock. There, abandoned by gravity, it ignites and burns – until he clenches his fists and his heart rockets upwards, trailing smoke and ashes, back towards duty and a crisis almost too awful to comprehend.

He gasps, opens his eyes, tightens his arms around empty space. And realizes he's in Max's bed, all alone.

Bright sunlight is pouring through the window. Joseph checks the bedside clock, sees it's past nine. He springs off the mattress, hurries to his room and pulls on jeans and a shirt. During the night, the smell of the dead man has returned, hovering at the periphery of his senses. In the ensuite, he spritzes himself with cologne until the stench has gone.

Downstairs, Tilly is eating a bowl of muesli at the break-fast bar. Behind her, the kitchen's bifold doors are open to the garden. Outside, it's a perfect August morning. Blue sky, bright sunshine. The air is fragrant with lavender and geranium.

By the nearest worktop, Erin is fussing over the espresso machine. 'The dead finally rise,' she says, her blue eyes appraising him.

Joseph cringes, wondering for a stupid second if she knows something. But it was only a throwaway comment, more for her daughter's ears than his, there to paper over what might otherwise have been a silence. The coolness of her gaze tells the real story.

He knows he hurt her again last night. Recently, the distance between them has felt like an ocean, as if they're two life rafts pulled apart by opposing currents. His fault, not hers. Like so many other things.

This morning, Erin looks full of summer vigour: denim cut-offs, yellow gypsy top, blonde hair piled up. Her skin is smooth and clear – the product, he suspects, of a clean diet and an even cleaner conscience.

Tilly, hearing her mother's words, raises an eyebrow. 'He was roaming the house with a war axe last night, like some kind of Viking. Or did I dream that?'

'No dream,' Erin replies. 'Just me, mistaking Max for a burglar. I heard someone downstairs and sent our Viking, here, to investigate. Where did you get that thing?' she asks Joseph. 'I'm really not sure I want it in the house.'

'I—'

'Hey, Thor,' Tilly says. 'Does it come back like a boomerang if you throw it?'

'Thor carries a hammer, not an axe,' Erin tells her, handing Joseph a cup of coffee. She lifts her nose and inhales. 'Is that the one I bought you last Christmas?'

For a moment, Joseph doesn't know what she's talking about. Then, recalling his cologne, he mumbles an acknowledgement.

Erin examines him with interest. 'Congratulations, you finally took it out of the box. You want some toast?'

'Thanks, but I'm not hungry.'

She tilts her head. 'Was everything OK last night? You slept in Max's room.'

'All good. Have you seen him?'

'I think Sally offered him extra hours this weekend. He must have left first thing. Oh – weird one. Have you seen the washing-up bowl? Or the dish scrubber?'

Joseph shrugs.

'So why has he run off with them?'

'Because . . . teenager?' Tilly suggests, as if she isn't one herself.

'I'll pick up replacements while I'm in town,' Joseph says.

Erin pastes on a grin, again for her daughter's benefit over his. 'I think we've got enough teenagers. You're going into Crompton?'

'I need a new shirt,' he tells her, because it's the first explanation that enters his head.

'New scent, new clothes. Did someone order me a Joe Carver Mark Two as an early birthday present? Don't forget we're hosting the neighbours tonight. You're on bar-becue duty.'

Joseph grimaces, because the party had completely slipped his mind, and because this endless charade in front of Tilly is exhausting. Glancing out of the window, thinking of his mother's airless garage and the dead man wrapped in plastic, he asks, 'What's the forecast today?'

'Hot,' Erin says. 'And I mean Death Valley hot. You might want some lotion if you're going out – I don't want you burning, and frightening away all our guests. You can collect my meat order from Samsons while you're on the high street. Save me a trip.'

'Can I get a lift into town with you, Axe Man?' Tilly asks.

Right now, company is the last thing Joseph needs, but he

knows he has to act normally – and normally he'd agree to his stepdaughter's request without complaint.

Before they leave the house, he returns to his bedroom and closes the door. From the back of his wardrobe he retrieves the bereavement box he keeps there and places it on the bed. Holding his breath, he removes the lid.

When Joseph sees the first few items – Claire's passport, a pair of her sunglasses, a battered copy of *Perfume*, her favourite novel – emotions crash over him like breaking waves. He delves into the box regardless. His fingers press past old concert tickets, anniversary cards, a silk scarf. At the bottom he finds Claire's iPhone, still in its sequinned case, which he slips into his pocket before returning the box to the cupboard.

He pauses there, closes his eyes. Is he doing the right thing? Last night, had the steady drip-feed of revelations affected his thinking? At first, he'd thought he was dealing with a tragic accident. Only as he was preparing to drive to Jack-O'-Lantern Woods and take responsibility had he learned that the dead man survived the initial impact, and that Max had intervened to cut short his suffering.

Would he have acted differently if he'd known that from the start? It's not too late to change his mind about how he handles this.

Downstairs, still reeling from his encounter with the touchstones of his previous life, Joseph grabs his keys and calls to his stepdaughter that he's leaving.

Crompton isn't huge. A single high street intersected by two roads into which more shops and restaurants have spilled. There's a roundabout at one end, a cenotaph at the other.

'You can drop me at the Grind House,' Tilly says. From her pocket she retrieves Max's phone. 'Guess which med-school-student-in-waiting forgot this when he left for work? Step-sis rides to the rescue as usual.'

'You should have said. I could have saved you the trip.'

Tilly grins, shakes her head. 'Leverage, dear Joseph. This way Max owes me a favour. Got to keep him sweet.'

'For what?'

'Free carrot cake, for a start.'

'You're your mother's daughter.'

'*Naturellement.*'

Joseph pulls up outside the coffee shop. Tilly unclips her seatbelt, hesitating with one hand on the door. 'Joe?'

He glances over.

'What you told Mum – is everything really OK? Last night I thought I heard . . . I don't know. Were you and Max up late talking? Wasn't he meant to be staying at a friend's?'

Joseph reaches for the aircon, thinks better of it. 'Just university chat. Everything's fine.'

'You're going to miss him. Aren't you?'

'Everyone leaves home eventually,' he says, because no words exist to describe his turmoil at Max's upcoming departure. Now, even more so.

'Well – you've still got me and Mum. We're not going anywhere.'

'You'll be off some day, no doubt.'

'Uh-uh. I'm staying right here. Got to look after Mum. *And* my current favourite stepdad.'

'Noted, regarding the current.'

Tilly grins. 'And for as long as you continue to behave.' She leans over to kiss his cheek, then swings open the door. 'Black,' she says, glancing over her shoulder. 'The shirt, I mean. If in doubt, choose black.'

Joseph thanks her, waves her off. He parks in the multi-storey above the Sainsbury's and takes the stairs back to ground level. On his way he passes two CCTV cameras and forces himself not to look. He doesn't see any cameras outside the vape shop on the high street, where he pays cash for a 120 GB data-only SIM card. In the Costa Coffee opposite, he orders an Americano and carries it to an empty table. Then he takes out Claire's iPhone. His thumb slides over the case, feeling the empty spaces where some of the sequins have come loose.

*You like how I've ABBA'd it up, Joe?*

*I'm sure Benny and Björn would be proud.*

When he pops the phone from its case, a scrap of notepaper falls into his lap. With shaking fingers he unfolds it. There, in his late wife's handwriting, he sees a list:

Max school shoes
Washing machine guy
Max dentist appt
Joe passport photo
Clothes for Friday
Make hair appt
Toby birthday present
Call Jane

Suddenly, it feels as if all the air's been sucked out of the coffee shop. He's looking at a simple to-do list, hurriedly scrawled and long since forgotten. And yet it radiates the aura of a sacred artifact, his own Rosetta Stone.

Typical that Claire had prioritized the tasks benefitting him or Max. Incredible that he doesn't even remember Toby or Jane. Their names trigger no memories whatsoever, belonging firmly to the *before* and not the *now*.

Joseph refolds the slip of paper and tucks it into his wallet. Using the tool that came in the package, he swaps Claire's old SIM card with the one he just bought. Then he connects her phone to a brick charger in his pocket and switches it on. The Apple logo appears, replaced a few seconds later by Claire's old screensaver.

It's a snapshot from six years ago, taken by a waiter in a Tuscan restaurant – Claire and Joseph and Max, surrounded by fairy lights and raising their glasses to the night. Claire is resplendent. Max is guffawing. Joseph – his face unmarked by the fathomless loss to afflict him a year later – is barely recognizable.

The image blurs. Air rushes back into the shop. He clutches the table, breathes deep, rocks back and forth until he's fully returned to the present. Then he goes online and searches *crompton missing person*. When nothing comes up, he tries again at a county level, but the most recent news story is from a week ago, about a young woman from neighbouring Shipley reported missing four days prior.

Joseph sweeps the coffee shop with his gaze. Then he types *how long corpse start decomposing*.

The answer, he discovers, is between twenty-four and seventy-two hours. During the first stage, autolysis, a build-up of carbon dioxide leads to increased acidity in the tissues, causing cell membranes to rupture.

The second stage is bloat. Enzymes leaked during autolysis begin to produce gas. The corpse increases in size, sometimes dramatically. Bacteria, reproducing exponentially, cause skin discolouration. An unpleasant odour attracts insects and carrion feeders.

The third stage, he learns, is active decay. Fluids begin to leak from orifices. Organs and muscle start to liquefy.

Joseph stops reading, waits for his nausea to pass. Then he adds *hot weather* to his search query and confirms that when the ambient temperature is higher, a corpse produces gas at a much faster rate, creating more openings in the skin for flies to lay their eggs.

He stands up so abruptly that a couple at the next table reel away from him. Stumbling out of the Costa, Joseph leans against a lamppost and recovers his breath. He needs to dispose of the dead man urgently, and think about what to do with the Honda once it's done.

Fortunate, at least, that he hasn't yet transferred ownership from his mother. He has her death certificate and a copy of her will naming him as executor, which means he can sell the car without ever registering as its owner. Whether that will prevent police from linking it to him or Max, should either of them fall under suspicion, he doesn't know. It might depend on whether an ANPR camera snapped the Honda last night – and whether the patrol car that followed him from the BP garage was equipped with one. Because if police *start* with the Honda, rather than with Max, its connection to Joseph will doubtless be unearthed.

The only men's tailoring business in Crompton is Grayson's, a dark and Dickensian establishment with crown glass bay windows and uneven floors. Inside, Joseph parts with three times more than he'd usually spend and walks out with a Stenströms shirt in black linen. In a homewares shop five doors down he buys a washing-up bowl, a mop and a dish scrubber. Then he visits Samsons.

Erin's meat order is far larger than he'd expected. The butcher takes a while to box it all up. Joseph stands in the sweltering heat, his nose filling with the smell of raw meat. While he waits, he stares through the glass-sided display at the neat rows of steaks, short ribs, topside joints, briskets, gammon hams and pale slabs of pork belly the colour of the dead man's flesh.

From the back he hears what sounds like bones being cut by a band saw. At the end of the counter he sees another butcher feeding a smoked bacon through an aluminium slicer. As he's paying Erin's bill, a wasp flies into the wall-mounted zapper and is fried with a crackle that makes him jump.

Joseph carries his purchases to the car, his stomach flopping. Halfway up the steps of the multistorey, he feels the wound across his abdomen split open again, as if the butcher just ran the slicer over his skin. Grimacing with pain, he pauses in the stairwell to check his clothes. Fortunately, the Elastoplast seems to have stopped any blood from leaking through.

After dropping off the meat, he retraces his steps to the high street. He'll have to buy something in Sainsbury's to validate his parking, but first he wants to check on Max.

As he recalls his son's words from last night – *It was a kindness, what I did* – an image comes to him of the dead man's ruined face. Batting it away, he hurries across the street.

# NINE

The Grind House is more akin to an upmarket opium den than a coffee shop: Moroccan rugs, mosaic-inlaid tables, low sofas crowded with kilim cushions. Candle flames bob and smoke inside iron lanterns set with tiny stained-glass windows. Over the hiss and splutter of the espresso machine, an Arctic Monkeys track is playing.

Tilly and Drew are sitting in semi-darkness, at a table furthest from the window. Unlike most days, Drew's only make-up this morning is a scarlet slash of lipstick. Her turquoise hair, feathered to baby blue at the tips, spills through the back of a white baseball cap. She looks about as uncomfortable as Joseph has ever seen her – cheeks flushed, eyes downcast, her focus on the phone case decorated with turquoise rhinestones beside her coffee cup. Max, wearing a black T-shirt beneath a hessian barista's apron, is standing over the table, looking just as awkward. Clearly, they hadn't been expecting Tilly – and now, partly thanks to Joseph, they've been caught.

Tilly's gaze moves between her stepbrother and her best friend, her expression difficult to read. Perhaps she's starting to figure out what's going on between them.

As Joseph manoeuvres around the other tables, Max

glances up and spots him. Something passes between them that Joseph can't define but worries him even so.

'Hi, Dad,' the boy says, looking relieved at the distraction. 'You want a coffee? Staff discount?'

'Thanks, no. I just grabbed a Costa.'

'Oof. Don't let Sally hear you say that.'

From somewhere Drew finds a smile. 'Hey, Mr Carver,' she says, her nose twitching. 'I am *loving* the new *parfum.*' But when she picks up her coffee cup a moment later, the rim rattles against her teeth.

Max glances at her, then back at his father, eyebrows raised. For a moment, Joseph has the craziest thought that his son is jealous – and that it's a dangerous kind of jealousy. But Tilly is watching him strangely, too.

*Can they read my thoughts?* he asks himself. *Can they tell that last night I drove a dead man to Saddle Bank, in the boot of my late mother's car? Do they know that I've been researching how quickly a corpse decomposes? How it bloats up and starts to leak fluids?*

Abruptly, he realizes they're probably just wondering why he's here. 'I was in Samsons,' he says. 'Picking up the meat order. Thought I'd come by and remind you about the party later.'

Max nods. 'Barbecue, right? We'll be there.'

'Wouldn't miss it,' Drew says.

'Great, you're very welcome,' he tells her, although he doesn't really mean it. He's always had a lot of time for his stepdaughter's best friend – a decent girl saddled with an unreliable father and abandoned by an even more unreliable mother – but right now he wants the fewest possible visitors to the house.

'Drew's bringing her dad tonight,' Tilly says.

'Even better,' Joseph lies.

He makes his excuses and leaves. Back inside his car, the

raw meat smell of the Samsons order is so heavy it makes him retch. He drives home with the windows down and the aircon on full blast. When he carries his shopping into the house, he finds Erin in the kitchen, cutting into slices what at first he thinks is a human heart – until reality rushes back and he sees it's simply a beetroot.

'Good,' she says, sucking beetroot juice from her thumb. With the point of her knife she indicates the sofa near the bifold doors. 'You. Sit.'

'I'll just put the meat—'

'Uh-uh.' She jabs with the blade. 'Sit. Talk.'

Joseph leaves his purchases on the side and eases himself on to the sofa.

Erin, still holding her knife, perches on the coffee table opposite.

'Something's up,' she says. 'You're being weird.' With her free hand she squeezes his knee. 'Weirder than usual, I mean.'

He flinches at her touch – as much from surprise as guilt. These last few months, physical contact between them has been rare. Her sudden effort to address it has him spooked. 'I am?'

'What happened last night? Your chat with Max. What did he say?'

Joseph shrugs. 'He . . . got some things off his chest.'

'Like what?'

*Here it is, then,* he thinks. *The moment of departure. The point where my deception truly begins.* Joseph breathes deep, and starts with something that may not be a lie at all. 'Max is seeing Drew.'

Erin blinks. Her mouth drops open. 'Max and *Drew*? Wow. Of all the things you might have hit me with, Joe Carver, I wasn't expecting that.'

'Me neither. I don't know how Tilly will react. Apparently, they haven't told her.'

'Ouch.'

'What?'

'I'm just not sure that'll play well.'

'Why not?'

'Because Max has always worshipped her, for a start. And because Tilly's had him around her little finger for as long as we've been together. I don't think she'll appreciate her best friend intruding. It might feel a little claustrophobic. Still, at least it won't last long, this thing with Drew.'

'What makes you say that?'

'He's a good-looking boy – and next month he's going to be hundreds of miles away in St Andrews, surrounded by smart and single young women.'

'You don't think Drew's smart?'

'I think she's whip-smart. Ambitious, too. Even with all those hours at the salon, she's still finding time for that college course. A few years from now she'll be opening her own place, no doubt.

'But Drew's still a homebody at heart. She'll likely never leave Crompton. Whereas Max just wants to spread his wings. Which means I guarantee this is just a bit of summer fun until they go their separate ways.'

'Can we avoid telling Tilly, then? I don't like keeping secrets, but I promised Max I wouldn't say anything – and I don't want to mess up these last few weeks before he goes.'

'I won't blab. But if Tilly asks me a direct question, I won't lie.'

'That's fair.'

Erin slaps his leg and stands. 'OK, Carver, you're released. There's heaps to do and we're running out of time.'

Joseph sighs out his breath. He climbs to his feet, trying to mask his discomfort, and crosses the kitchen to the door.

'Oh, I almost forgot,' Erin adds, behind him. 'What happened to Max's car?'

Joseph turns, meets her gaze. And discovers that his wife is studying him far more closely than he'd expected. His scalp shrinks on his skull. Has she been deceiving him all along? Pretending to hoover up his bullshit while saving the tougher questions until he's off-guard? Was her earlier physicality a ploy? Does she *know* something?

He blinks, as if waking from a daydream – and castigates himself for his lack of trust. Bad enough that he's concealing the truth. Projecting his guilt on to Erin helps no one.

'Joe?'

He hasn't prepared for this, needs to shut down her curiosity fast. Only one explanation feels remotely plausible. 'I drove it over to the bungalow last night, locked it in the garage. Less temptation for Max that way. At least until we get it road legal.'

He replays his words, trying to decipher Erin's look. For better or worse he's committed himself, now, to a version of last night's events.

'You drove over to Saddle Bank at three o'clock this morning?'

'I took Max. Harder to escape a lecture when you're trapped inside a moving vehicle.'

She nods, as if something just clicked inside her head. 'And then you cycled home, the pair of you.'

'How'd you know that?'

'I took the gazebo out of the shed earlier and saw the bikes.' Erin searches his face. 'Joe, is everything really OK?'

'Of course.'

'You'd tell me if it wasn't?'

'Everything's fine.'

Joseph's heart is a stone in his chest as he says that. Because his wife looks like she believes him – and because lying to her was far easier than he'd imagined. She comes over. After a moment's hesitation, she loops her arms around his neck, breathes him in. 'I *do* love that scent on you. Did you get a new shirt?'

'Uh-huh.'

'Do I get a sneak peek?'

Again, he baulks at her closeness. Because this simply isn't how things have been. 'There's loads to do, remember?'

'It's only a barbecue and drinks.'

Joseph disentangles himself, can't bring himself to look at her. As he leaves the room, he feels Erin's gaze like two scorch marks on his neck.

# TEN

Upstairs, Joseph undresses and peels off the blood-encrusted Elastoplast. He showers, redresses his wound and puts on his new shirt. Then he douses himself in cologne until he can no longer smell the ghost stench of the dead man.

With the ensuite door locked, he sits on the toilet and goes back online. This time he doesn't check news sites; in hindsight, the police won't be searching for an adult male missing for less than twenty-four hours. Nor will any journalist be reporting the disappearance. If he's lucky, a missing person report might not even have been made. His focus, right now, should be appropriate disposal of the body.

The internet, as usual, offers a wealth of advice from people with no clue. Joseph dismisses almost all of it. He's not going to build a funeral pyre, pour an acid bath, feed body parts to wild pigs or hire a wood chipper and spray a nearby forest with gore. His only real option is burial – and for that he needs a suitable location.

Jack-O'-Lantern Woods is a non-starter for obvious reasons. His late mother still retains her allotment in Saddle Bank, but that feels like another short-cut to disaster.

Crompton is reasonably close to the South Downs. It might be his best bet. After another ten minutes of internet surfing he settles on Black Down in West Sussex, an hour's drive from home. He'll go tonight, once the barbecue's over and Erin's asleep.

Downstairs, making himself useful, he reels out extension cables, plugs in speakers and lights, buffs drinking glasses, makes ice cubes and stocks the overflow fridge with beer and wine.

While he's setting up outside, Erin prepares four different salads and the same number of desserts. Mid-afternoon she disappears into town and returns a few hours later with styled hair, a new outfit and freshly lacquered nails.

The first guests arrive around five. All are cul-de-sac neighbours: the Robinsons, the Taylors and Ralph Erikson, the insomniac widower whose house was lit up last night.

The Robinsons live next door. Gemma Robinson, a keen runner, is close to Erin's age. This afternoon she's swapped her Lycra and running shoes for a floral summer dress and strappy leather sandals.

'You *do* scrub up well, Joe Carver,' Gemma remarks. She breathes deep as she embraces him, clearly another fan of his new cologne.

Joseph mumbles his thanks. Then he shakes Greg Robinson's hand and welcomes the other arrivals. With every physical interaction he imagines himself transferring a trace of the dead man's essence to his guests' skin. Quickly the thought grows too much, and he retreats to the safety of his shed on the pretext of fetching charcoal. When he turns to shut the door, Erin is standing on the threshold, so close that he lurches backwards, nearly colliding with the lawnmower.

'Whoah, there, Jumpy,' she laughs. 'Here, I got you a present in town. Now's probably a good time to give it to you.'

She hands him a black box, long and narrow. It looks, to Joseph, like a miniature coffin. For a moment, he's too disquieted to open it – worried, irrationally, that it'll contain a tiny replica of the dead man, complete with a tiny caved-in face.

Clenching his teeth, he prises off the lid. Inside is a seven-inch Victorinox meat cleaver with a polished maple-wood handle. Carefully, he removes it from the box. The blade gleams when he angles it.

'I know you've always wanted one,' Erin says. 'It'll go through ribs, beef bones, you name it.'

Joseph looks past her to his neighbours drinking and chatting on the lawn. He imagines a journalist interviewing one of them a few weeks from now:

*When did you start to suspect Joseph Carver?*

*When I saw him prowling around his garden party with a meat cleaver, that's fucking when.*

He hears himself tell Erin he loves his present and feels himself cringe-grin his thanks.

'I got you this, too.'

Her second gift, wrapped in tissue paper, is a brown leather apron. Branded across the front are the words: WORLD'S OKAYIST COOK.

'I'll be honest,' she says. 'I mainly bought it to cover up whichever gross old T-shirt you'd chosen to throw on. And then, against all expectations, you suddenly discover an interest in fashion. It's a shame to cover up your new shirt, but at least this way you won't ruin it.'

Erin touches his shoulder, then flicks it, as if removing lint. 'Joe?'

He braces for another question about last night. 'Yes?'

'I'd really like to get back to the way we were.'

Joseph lifts his gaze to his wife's face – and is surprised by the fragility he sees in her expression. Fine lines have appeared around her eyes, almost as if she's in pain. 'The way we were?'

'You must know what I'm talking about. Sometimes it feels

like we're two strangers living in the same house. I know it's partly my fault. I've been spending far too much time at work. But being married to you – it's been lonely at times, particularly these last six months. I mean, we don't even . . .'

She sighs. 'Are you happy, Joe? With me and with Tilly? Do you still want this?'

Joseph stares at her, dismayed. In the space of a few breaths, another crisis has blindsided him. He has a sense, suddenly, of something incredibly delicate balancing between them – a crystal vase teetering on a high shelf.

'It's not your fault,' he says. 'And yes, I still I want this, of course I do. I always will.'

Has it taken the horror of his current situation to show him that? Perhaps it's only natural to crave most intensely what's most in danger of being lost. Last night, in the kitchen, he'd feared that the last safety line tethering him to his son had been severed. Now, it seems the rope he'd known was fraying is down to its very last thread.

But just as he can't share with Erin the events of last night, nor can he share the depthless chasms of guilt into which his heart plunges each morning when he wakes; the increasing reserves of energy he expends daily to separate the *before* from the *now;* the crippling shame he still feels for his abandonment of Max in the early stages of his new relationship.

To love someone completely, perhaps one needs to be complete. He loves Erin, but only with what's left of the man he was five years ago. Increasingly, that feels like not much of a man at all.

Although he's tried to hide it, this year has been one of the most difficult he's faced. Max's departure date has felt like an enormous black hole, creeping inexorably closer. Focusing all his attention on his son, he's deliberately turned his back on his wife. He need look no further than Erin's face for evidence of the pain that's caused.

Her lungs fill. 'Are you sure there's nothing else you want to tell me, Joe? Nothing else at all?'

'Only that I'm sorry. And that I'll try harder.' He returns the meat cleaver to its box. 'Thanks for this. It was a very romantic gift.'

'Maybe you could butcher something for me. Reconnect with your inner caveman.'

'I'll work on that.'

Back outside, and with the barbecue coals lit, Joseph rejoins his guests. More people are arriving, now: the Cheungs, who live next to Ralph Erikson, others from further up the street.

Someone hands him a beer, which he drinks far too quickly and vows is his last. He might wish to take the edge off his anxiety, but he needs to keep a clear head.

Soon, he finds himself among a group gathered around Owain Dart, the cul-de-sac's newest resident. Owain is finishing a rambling anecdote that grows more grotesque each time Joseph hears it.

The gist is that after burying his dead guinea pig in his garden, Owain had been presented with it a few weeks later, courtesy of his grave-dirt-spattered miniature schnauzer. In this retelling, Owain has nearly coaxed the carcass from his dog's jaws when the Schnauzer bites down hard and showers Owain in rotten guinea pig.

Everyone in the circle cries out in pantomime horror, including Gemma Robinson, who catches Joseph's gaze and grins.

He looks past her, tunes out, sweeps the garden for Erin. He spots her near the gazebo, clutching a white-bearded man by the shoulder and doubling up at something he just said. The old man laughs too, delighted by her response. Erin excuses herself with a squeeze of his forearm. Then she moves on, effortlessly joining another group.

Joseph watches, newly captivated by his wife. She's a fairy presence among their guests, sprinkling magic dust. Her gift is in forging instant connections, in making each person she greets the centre of her world. She listens, *really* listens. And she touches constantly – a nudge here, a press there, a squeeze or a tap or a gentle stroke. She communicates with her eyes and her fingers, with her body posture and her laugh. The combination is bewitching, intoxicating. In her wake she leaves people smiling, then flinching as if waking from a dream – and discovering that the reality to which they've returned isn't nearly so pleasurable as the Erinland they'd briefly inhabited.

Joseph should have been celebrating, every day, the miracle of her love for him. Instead, he's made her miserable. However desperate his current situation, he sees now that it's not just Max he has to fix.

'And how's life treating *you*, Joe?'

His name is a hook, yanking back his attention to the group. Quickly, he replays Ralph Erikson's question. 'Pretty good,' he says. Then, because everyone's still watching him: 'Pretty tired, I guess. But you know what's it like, living with teenagers.'

Obviously, Ralph doesn't know that, because his late wife couldn't have children and Ralph never remarried, facts known by everyone in the circle. Embarrassed by his gaffe, Joseph swigs from his beer glass before remembering it's empty, proving that he's a moron as well as a shit.

'Not sleeping?'

He shrugs, forces a grin. 'Erin hauled me out of bed last night to confront a burglar. An *imaginary* burglar,' he adds hastily, when everyone reacts. 'I think she's been watching too many true crime shows on Netflix.'

'Ouch – my ears are burning,' Erin laughs, appearing at his side. When she slides her arm around his waist, Joseph tries not to stiffen. 'You haven't just revealed my dirty secret?'

'Oh, God, you're not alone,' Gemma Robinson tells her. 'You start watching and suddenly an entire evening's disappeared. The American ones are the worst because they're so extreme – and so *addictive*. But I always feel mucky afterwards.'

'What time did she haul you out of bed, Joe?' Ralph asks.

'Must have been around three,' Erin says, before Joseph can move the conversation on. 'I'm so cruel.' Gently, she squeezes his ribs.

'And the burglar turned out to be Max, right?' Ralph says.

Joseph flinches at that. He studies his neighbour more closely.

Ralph Erikson, in his late sixties, is always eccentrically dressed. Even on this late-summer afternoon, he's wearing a thick alpaca-wool poncho, brightly coloured, as if the blood flowing through his veins is cellar-cool.

'Wow, Ralph,' Erin says. 'Where did you learn your detective skills? I don't believe for one minute that you're as mucky as me and Gemma, debauching yourself on true crime.'

'I don't believe for one minute that *anyone's* as mucky as Gemma,' Greg Robinson says of his wife, and takes an elbow jab to the midriff. He spits beer, sniggers.

'No detective skills required,' Ralph says, addressing Erin. 'My doorbell camera is motion-activated. It records whenever it's triggered – and sends an alert to let me know. I can view the live footage on my phone.'

'Sheesh. Well, I'm sorry if Max's homecoming woke you,' Erin replies – as if it's *their* fault Ralph Erikson aimed a camera at their house that buzzes him every time someone farts.

'Oh, I wasn't asleep. I hardly seem to sleep at all, these days. Seems like you couldn't either, Joe, after your scare – judging by your early morning bike ride.'

Joseph opens his mouth, closes it.

'A bike ride at three a.m.?' Gemma asks. She looks at Erin and tips her a wink. 'Now *that's* suspicious.'

Ralph smiles, clearly enjoying the attention. 'More like four a.m. by the time he and Max returned.'

Gemma sips from her wine glass, giggles. 'Wowsers – I predict a Channel Five four-parter in all our futures.'

Joseph's fingers twitch. Right now, he'd quite like to throttle Ralph Erikson. 'I never realized you watched us so closely,' he says.

Erin flashes him a look. Then she touches Ralph's arm and rubs it appreciatively. 'I don't know about anyone else, but I feel a lot safer knowing that you're looking out for us.'

'You don't feel safe with me?' Joseph asks, regretting the question even as he voices it. Again, his mouth seems to be working faster than his brain. But Erin, albeit accidently, has just pressed her fingers into his deepest wound.

Greg Robinson grins. Then he shakes his empty beer bottle. 'Going to hunt out another of these.'

'And I've got to pee,' Gemma adds.

Joseph watches them go. Then he returns his attention to Ralph. If the widower saw them return home on bikes last night, presumably he also saw them leave on foot. Did that anomaly escape his attention? Or did he leave out that part deliberately, to see what Joseph would say? Had he noticed what they'd been carrying or had the darkness saved them?

'You know, I've been meaning to get one of those doorbell cams for a while,' he tells the widower. 'Maybe if you have time, over the next few days, I could drop by for a quick tutorial.'

'I'd be delighted,' Ralph says. 'We're lucky this is such a safe area – there's been one burglary on this street in the thirty years I've lived here – but I do enjoy my doorbell cam. With the sensitivity dialled up, it captures all sorts of wildlife I might never see.'

Her hand still around his waist, Erin squeezes Joseph again: *Well done, Carver,* her touch seems to say. *For a while that was kind of awkward, but now your tram wheels are firmly back in their tracks.*

Joseph looks around the garden. Tilly and Drew are in the gazebo, helping themselves to drinks. Max is standing near the kitchen's bifold doors, watching them.

'Time to start burning the meat,' Erin says.

Sweat, cold and oily, flows down Joseph's back.

# ELEVEN

Joseph hasn't eaten all day. And now, dressed in his ridiculous apron, advertising himself as the WORLD'S OKAYIST COOK, he won't be able to eat all night.

On the barbecue, hissing and sputtering, lie rows of pink sausages, red burgers and kebabs. There are prawn skewers, tuna fillets and racks of glazed ribs, even a couple of tomahawk steaks that Joseph will sear and Erin will finish in the oven.

Usually, the competing aromas of beef and pork and fish would have him salivating. Now, they roil his stomach. The fizz and whistle of burning fat sound to him like squeals of pain – as if, rather than barbecuing dead meat, he's torturing live animals on his grill. As he cooks, he tries to avoid thoughts of the dead man. And when someone hands him another beer, it takes all his willpower to refuse it.

'Dad?'

Joseph nearly drops his tongs, turns.

Max is looking at him in disbelief. 'What the hell? You're *barbecuing*?' He checks no one's in earshot before adding, 'Have you completely forgotten about last night?'

'Of course not,' Joseph hisses. And suddenly his emotions

ignite. 'You think I want to be standing here, wearing this stupid fucking apron, cooking cheeseburgers for Gemma fucking Robinson and all the rest of them?'

Max takes a step back. A few people glance over.

'Look,' Joseph says, through clenched teeth. 'I have a plan, but I can't just disappear from a party I'm meant to be hosting. How do you think that would look?'

Max raises his hands. 'OK, understood. I'm sorry.' He lowers his voice. 'So what are we going to do?'

'What *you're* going to do is stay here, ideally with people who can vouch for you later if needed. I don't want you involved in what comes next. Once the party's over, I'll take care of it.'

'Dad, you're not doing this alone. I'm—'

'That's not up for debate, Max. Did you know Ralph Erikson recorded us leaving the house at three a.m.? And coming back an hour later on bikes? That he's been *telling* everyone? I've got to figure out how to get rid of his doorbell camera and its footage. Until I do, I don't want it capturing us again, especially not at any weird times of day or night. So – put on a smile and act like you're enjoying yourself.'

Max sighs. Then he indicates Joseph's abdomen. 'How is it today? Are you keeping it clean?'

'It's fine.'

'You want me to take over here for a while? Give you a break?'

Joseph shakes his head. 'If you want to help, you can carry this tray of kebabs over to the gazebo.'

Max looks at him as if he's thinking about saying more. Instead, he takes the tray and turns his back.

Drew's dad arrives around eight, wearing white socks and sliders and a Manchester United shirt from when Vodafone were still the sponsors. Enoch Cullen is stubbled and shaven-headed, his ears so cluttered with piercings they look to Joseph like hybrid musical instruments. He heads straight to the gazebo, emerging with two cans of Strongbow. He pops the tab on one, chugging down the contents in a couple of swallows. Then he opens the second and takes a long sip. Shuffling over to the barbecue, he punches Joseph's arm with a fist that's all sharp knuckles, the blow hard enough to bruise.

'Joey-boy,' he mutters, and belches cider fumes. 'Ain't seen you in a while.'

'How are you, Enoch? Keeping busy?'

'Ain't no work, is there? 'Less you want peanuts. 'Less you're happy taking shit from some jumped-up toddler just out of nursery. Knocked the last one out sparko. Then everyone got excited.'

The sun sets. The sky darkens. Overhead, a spray of stars glitters. In Joseph Carver's back garden, wine corks pop, prosecco fizzes into glasses, jaws and tongues and teeth masticate barbecued flesh. Erin switches on strings of globe lights. Someone cranks up the music.

Joseph checks his watch constantly. Eleven p.m. comes and goes and the party's still in full swing. At midnight, a few of the older guests start leaving, Ralph Erikson among them. By one a.m., a core of twenty drinkers remains. When Erin drags Greg Robinson into the kitchen to arrange a tray of sambuca shots, Joseph groans – and not just because he's left with Gemma Robinson, whose dress straps keep sliding off her shoulders and who can't seem to stand upright without snatching at him for balance.

The more Gemma drinks, the more flirtatious she grows. She tells Joseph he understands her, that Greg, her husband, doesn't realize she's a woman. She fingers the buttons on his new shirt and repeatedly tells him how good he looks.

Gemma glances towards the house, where Greg, his face flushed with alcohol, is emerging from the bifold doors with the sambuca tray. For a moment it looks like he'll stumble, until Erin, following behind, puts a stabilizing hand on his shoulder.

'I met him at university,' Gemma says. 'Freshers Week. Can you believe that? We were both off our faces and he wheeled me across campus in a shopping trolley. That was my criteria for a future husband: can push me on wheels while pissed.'

'Might be handy when you're both eighty.'

Gemma snorts with laughter. She touches Joseph's collar, smooths it. 'How did you and Erin meet?'

'A bereavement group,' he replies.

'Oh God, of course. I remember Greg telling me. You were married before, both of you.' She hiccups. 'Your first wife, she—'

'Yes,' Joseph says.

'And Erin's husband. I heard he—'

'Took his own life over a gambling debt.'

'S'really sad,' Gemma continues, leaning into him again. 'Horrible. But it's good you found each other.' She puffs out her lips, blowing alcohol breath all over him. 'You know, there's an upside to meeting later in life. Trouble with marrying young, if you ask me, is that your other half hasn't stopped growing into the person they're going to be.'

She waves a hand in the direction of the gazebo, where Greg Robinson is trying to extinguish a flaming sambuca that's spilled down his shirt. 'And what I never quite realized when I married Greg was that one day he'd grow into, well . . . that.'

Joseph nods, disentangles himself, casts his gaze over his guests. Across the garden, Max has joined Tilly and Drew. As Joseph studies his son's interaction with his stepdaughter and her best friend, he realizes that Drew has noticed his interest. Quickly, he looks away – but over the next ten minutes they make eye contact again and again. Joseph can't figure out if he keeps glancing over because he knows she's looking at him or if it's the other way round.

Just like at the coffee shop, he wonders if she can somehow read his thoughts – and knows what he plans to do once everyone else is asleep. Whatever the explanation, her scrutiny is deeply uncomfortable. Once or twice he catches Max frowning at him, and can't decide if the boy feels threatened or if he's simply anxious for his father to fulfil tonight's task.

By two a.m., the core of twenty revellers has dropped to eight. Half an hour later, the Robinsons are the last guests to stagger home. Erin's eyes are heavy. Tilly's too. Joseph helps them both upstairs. When he returns to the kitchen, Max is waiting. The boy's eyes are red-rimmed, from alcohol or tiredness or both.

'Go to bed,' Joseph says. 'You look exhausted.'

'I need to know what's happening.'

'No. You don't.'

'But I can't just—'

'We already had this conversation. I don't want you any more involved. What I *do* want is for you to go to bed and let me deal with the rest. Afterwards, we can talk all you like, but right now you're holding me up – and I don't have much of a window to get this done.'

Max's shoulders slump, but at the kitchen door he hesitates, turns back. 'Dad?'

'Yes?'

'Do you think I'm a monster?'

The question stops Joseph dead.

*It was a kindness, what I did.*

'No, of course not,' he says. 'I love you. More than any-thing else in this life.'

'Loving someone and thinking they're a monster aren't mutually exclusive. At least, they don't have to be.'

'I don't think you're a monster. I do think you suffered a massively traumatic event at a really vulnerable age. And I think we're still feeling the effects of that – the echoes of it – all these years later.'

'I know I've said it before, but I'd give everything to go back in time, to have handled everything differently.'

'It probably sounds horrible,' the boy says, 'and I don't mean it to be, at all, but I'm glad Mum's not here to see this.'

There's crushed glass, suddenly, in Joseph's throat. In his eyes, too. He folds his son into a hug, hoping to hide his tears. 'Don't say that,' he croaks. 'Don't say it. I love you. We'll get through this. Don't say it.'

'I miss her so *much*, Dad,' Max moans. 'I didn't think it could still be this painful but it is. I miss her, I miss you. I miss *us* – the way we used to be. But mainly I just miss Mum.' He trembles once, like a tree struck by an axe, and then he's shaking, sobbing.

Joseph tightens his grip. He tells Max it's OK, even though he knows it isn't. And he wonders – if this is how life now feels to his son – whether it might explain Max's actions in Jack-O'-Lantern Woods. Because if life is pain, one might be forgiven for thinking that those who cut it short aren't demons, after all, but angels.

'And now I'm losing you, too,' the boy whispers.

'No, you're not. Of course you're not.'

'Yes, I am. After what happened to Mum, I swore to myself I'd look after you, and now I've dragged you into a nightmare.'

'It's not your job to look after me, Max,' Joseph says.

'It's my job to look after you. I might not have done it very well in the past, but I'm going to do it now.' He kisses his son's ear, then turns him by the shoulders and ushers him into the hall. 'Go,' he urges. 'Straight up. We'll talk more tomorrow.'

Thankfully, Max complies without further protest.

Joseph watches him climb the stairs. Then he gets to work.

# TWELVE

Outside, he grabs his bike from the shed and lowers it over the brick wall that divides their property from the Calthorpes, who live behind them. He isn't going to let Ralph Erikson or anyone else on the cul-de-sac know that he's embarking on another three-a.m. bike ride. At the party, the Calthorpes were drinking heavily. Doubtless, by now, they'll be comatose. Their lean-to carport offers easy and inconspicuous access to the neighbouring street.

Ten minutes later, Joseph arrives at his mother's. He leaves his bike in the hall and edges through darkness to the kitchen. In here, it feels safe enough to use his torch. He switches it on, angling its beam around the room. He sees empty worktops, a stack of post, the Honda's spare key hanging from its hook. When he grips the handle of the garage's connecting door, he thinks he hears movement on the other side: the scrape of a foot, perhaps; or maybe the drag of an axe head across the concrete floor.

Joseph freezes, heart thudding in his chest. He knows his fear is irrational, but he can't rid himself of the notion that the dead man has somehow escaped the car boot and is waiting for him in the darkness, his face a bloodied crater.

It takes all Joseph's willpower to push the door open and aim his torch beam inside.

Workbench. Old paint tins. Blue Honda.

And, even from here on the threshold, an unmistakeable odour. It isn't strong but it's there, and it's the worst thing Joseph's ever experienced – the smell of Dead Guy Rotting In Hot Weather.

He pauses in the doorway, staring at the car. Something about it feels wrong. He doesn't want to get closer until he figures out what. For a minute or more he stands there, his torch beam aimed at the bonnet.

This is the first time he's seen the front of the vehicle since he found out about the dead man. On Berrylands Road, where Max had parked after returning from Jack-O'-Lantern Woods, they'd approached from the rear. After driving it here last night, Joseph had gone around to the boot so he could search the dead man's pockets. Immediately afterwards, he'd left via the same garage door through which he'd entered.

Now, Joseph passes his torch over the car's headlights, its bumper, its grille. He recalls Max's words while they'd been sitting in the front seats: *I know what you're thinking. But I'm not a killer, Dad. I'm not. It was a kindness, what I did. Just like you and that deer.*

The doe Joseph clubbed to death had weighed maybe a hundred kilos. He'd been doing just under forty when he hit it. The impact had shattered his driver's side headlight and ripped off his wing mirror. The damage had cost him over a thousand in parts alone.

The Honda, by contrast, looks largely intact. Admittedly, the grille has a few dinks and the bumper looks scratched, but Joseph isn't sure those marks weren't there before. Of course, he doesn't know how fast the car had been travelling, but Max already admitted that the dead man was still alive when he pulled over, so it couldn't have been *that* fast. And there aren't many places inside Jack-O'-Lantern Woods where you can really floor it.

Standing there in semi-darkness, he's struck by a possibility almost too dark to contemplate: what if Max was lying? What if the collision was a fabrication? What if events unfolded some other way?

Shaking himself free of that thought, he steps inside the garage and edges along the car to the driver's door, breathing through his mouth. A fat bluebottle buzzes past his head. It performs long and lazy loops, its shadow distorted grotesquely by the torchlight.

Joseph climbs into the driver's seat and presses the button for the motorized garage door. While it's lifting, he clips Claire's iPhone into the holder fixed to the dash. He selects the Maps app and loads his destination. Then, starting the car, he reverses on to the drive, reactivates the garage door and pulls on to the road.

He won't entertain such traitorous thoughts about his son. Max might be troubled but he's not psychotic. Plenty of animals killed by cars never even scratch the paintwork. That must be true of humans, too.

*It was a kindness, what I did.*

Joseph drives with the windows down and the cold air vents on full – and still can't eliminate the stink of the dead man. It coats his tongue, clings to his throat. He feels like he's *tasting* the putrefaction. Even though he left the bluebottle pulling barrel rolls around the garage, he still hears its buzzing in his head. He imagines opening the boot and releasing a black cloud of flies – and then he's not just tasting putrefaction but stomach acid.

Even worse than all that is his creeping sense that he's left this too late – that he simply doesn't have enough time to complete tonight's task. It's already quarter to three. He has an hour's drive ahead of him. The sun will rise at six, but he'll need to have finished the job long before then – not just for fear of being seen, but because he needs to be back in Crompton before the rest of the family wakes. That gives him, at best, ninety minutes at Black Down to dig a grave and fill it in.

*Not long enough*, he tells himself. *Not even close.*

The journey, at least, is uneventful. He sees few other vehicles – and mercifully no police. Soon, he's climbing a gently winding road towards Black Down's summit, his headlights illuminating the heath. He spots a dusty, unpaved track and turns on to it. Half a mile later he pulls over.

When he gets out of the car, the wind singing through heather and gorse is the only sound. It's cooler up here, fresher. Joseph holds his breath and opens the boot. Thankfully, the cloud of bluebottles doesn't materialize. He grabs his spade and walks one hundred paces into the scrub. There, he picks out a gorse bush larger than the rest, with a trunk so twisted he'll remember it. Then he switches off his torch.

The stars, as they reveal themselves, are of a purity unsurpassed. *Look at us!* they appear to demand of him. *Will you desecrate our beauty by digging an illegal grave while we watch? By tipping a dead man into a hole and covering him up?*

A moment later, Joseph realizes he'll do no such thing. At least, not tonight. Because with his first downstroke, his spade rebounds off the sun-hardened earth as if from concrete or even steel.

Ten minutes into his task, with sweat pouring down his face and his shirt clinging wet to his back – knowing it's fruitless but persevering anyway – he's excavated a hole barely deep enough to conceal a human head. He needs a pickaxe as well as a spade; an entire evening instead of an hour. After thirty minutes of sweating and swearing, he encounters a gorse root that stops his progress dead.

Joseph tosses down his spade. Then, unable to contain himself, he throws back his head and yells at the night. Around him, ground-nesting birds explode from the heath, cawing and flapping. Nearby, something four-legged screeches and bolts.

He sees himself as if from above, an awful silhouette inside a rising cloud of carrion feeders. Suddenly, the earth beneath his feet doesn't feel solid or still. It feels like it's seething, countless millions of worms and grubs convulsing with excitement at the prospect of the meal he'd intended to feed them.

Joseph's stomach clenches. He falls to his knees and vomits up a torrent of stinking bile water. It pours into the hole he just excavated and sinks into the soil. He imagines the worms and grubs writhing more furiously, delirious in their unexpected bath. And then he's heaving again – and again. After a while he starts to think the contractions will never end, that once his stomach is empty he'll vomit up a liver, a pair of kidneys, a lung or even a heart, and that what will follow afterwards will be even worse, blackness without form: derelictions, resentments and betrayals.

Exhausted, purged at last, he rolls on to his back. Above him the vast dome of stars turns kaleidoscopic. For the first time since Claire's death, he hopes she isn't watching him from up there, that she cannot see what he's become.

*That* thought is so terrible it forces him to his feet. He fetches his spade and fills in the vomit trench. Then he picks his way back across the stony ground to the car.

During the drive home, he finds himself addressing the dead man directly, and wonders if this is how madness starts. 'Listen,' he says. 'I need to know the truth. Because it doesn't make sense to me that you were walking in those woods, late at night, without a wallet or a phone. Nor that you'd be there without a car. So what was really going on? What isn't Max telling me? What aren't *you* telling me?'

Fortunately – for his sanity, at least – the dead man refuses to answer. Joseph parks inside his mother's garage and cycles home. It's five thirty a.m. Above him, the indigo sky has erased all but the most persistent stars. He tosses his bike over the Calthorpes' back wall and scrambles after it.

Inside the house, he checks on Max. The boy is asleep, one arm slung across his face. Erin is snoring, too. Joseph showers and spritzes himself with cologne. Then he sets his alarm and crawls into bed beside his wife. She murmurs something incoherent, snuggles up to him.

Lying there, he thinks about the coming day. The dead man has now been ripening inside the Honda for thirty hours, give or take. It feels like the situation couldn't grow any more critical. But Joseph fears it will.

And five hours later, it does.

# THIRTEEN

Sunday mornings during the football season, Max is out of the front door by eight. In summer, he rises late – although not, it seems, today. Just before nine a.m., after a paltry three hours' sleep, Joseph checks the boy's room and finds it empty. Downstairs, he discovers Erin in the kitchen. Despite her heavy drinking at the party, she looks like she spent the previous evening alternating between meditation and yoga. Joseph, by contrast, sank one beer and feels like his head might explode.

'He left hours ago,' she replies, when he asks after Max.

'Did he say where he was going?'

'No. Maybe he was off to see you-know-who. He was out of the door before I could ask. You want some coffee? I'll be honest, Carver – you look like you need a saline drip.'

'I'll get it,' he says. Rinsing out the portafilter, he pushes it into the electric grinder's jaws.

'Was it a bad dream?'

'Dream?'

'When my alarm went off, you were thrashing about, muttering some very strange stuff indeed.'

'Like what?'

Erin's features pull into a leer. '*Feed it, feed the machine,*' she says, in a witch's voice. '*More meat, fingers and legs, got to feed the machine.* You could have been auditioning for a horror film. If it were anyone else it'd be creepy. Actually,' she adds, 'I'm being too generous. It *was* creepy.'

Instantly, Joseph recalls his dream. He'd been in Samsons, the butcher's on Crompton's high street, feeding the dead man's body parts into a grinder. But however many limbs he pushed through it, there were always more. Soon, he was knee-deep in red mince. Then, thigh-deep.

He shudders. 'Is that all?'

'That's not enough?' She looks at him strangely, grabs her purse. 'Right, I'm heading out – got to pick up some print work for the next fundraiser. Don't forget I'm in the London office tomorrow. I'm updating the board on our high-value donor push. I'll be leaving this afternoon.'

Joseph had forgotten, but the news is a relief. Tonight he needs to drive out to Black Down and succeed where last night he failed. Now, he won't have to lie to Erin about his whereabouts. 'What time's your train?'

'After lunch.'

'When are you back?'

'Some time tomorrow evening. I'll make sure I'm not late.' She touches his arm, wrinkles her nose. 'I know – it isn't ideal. But once this fundraiser's wrapped up, things will settle down – at least, until the next one. I meant what I said last night. I'd really like things to get back to the way they were.'

'Me too.'

'Tilly took the bus into town so you've got the place to yourself for a while. Garden looks like a war zone if you're feeling up to it, but I'll tackle it when I'm back if you're not.'

Once she's gone, Joseph brews coffee and loads the toaster with bread. He still isn't hungry, but he hasn't eaten since Friday night and he's starting to feel faint. He manages one slice before the ghost scent of the dead man wrecks his appetite again.

Upstairs, he showers and brushes his teeth. Then he douses himself in cologne and dresses in clean clothes. On the landing he pauses outside Max's bedroom. He doesn't want to do this, but he can't see any alternative.

Gingerly, he pushes open the door. The room is characteristically tidy: the bed made, the floor clear. On the desk stands a collection of football trophies, along with a human heart of dense foam, which opens to reveal a detailed interior. Claire had bought the heart, along with the foam brain beside it, when Max first took an interest in biology. Tacked to the wall above the desk is a human anatomy poster, one side illustrating the skeletal structure, the other side illustrating the musculature. Peering from the skull's red half is a single bulging eye. It looks, to Joseph, uncannily like the dead man's stare from Friday night.

Grimacing, he opens Max's desk drawer. 'Sorry, buddy,' he mutters. 'But you've given me no choice.' Inside the drawer he finds ID cards, loose change, pens, bookmarks, a couple of ancient fidget spinners, a birthday card from six years ago with a handwritten message from Claire, an orienteering compass, an old GPS watch, a pocket knife Joseph once bought him for camping trips, spare boot studs, a brick charger, old phone leads, old batteries.

The birthday card slows Joseph down but doesn't stop him. When he finds nothing of interest in the drawer, he turns his attention to Max's bookcase. He slides his hand along the narrow gap above each row. Then he opens the boy's wardrobe and searches the two wicker baskets on the bottom shelf. He finds clothes, shin pads, odds and ends; everything he might expect.

The space beneath Max's bed houses several nine-litre storage boxes. Joseph pulls them out one by one, prising off their lids and searching through them. He unearths certificates, old school exercise books, Lego instruction manuals, chemistry sets, comics – and toys that haven't seen daylight in years.

Right at the back, near the wall, he discovers something that makes him feel ugly for invading his son's privacy, because he has one just like it – equally priceless – in his own room.

Max might not call this a bereavement box but that's exactly what it is: a shoebox filled with memories of Claire. There are letters, cards, photographs; even a pair of old football socks into which she'd stitched Max's name label.

While Joseph has kept one of his late wife's scarves, Max has kept her favourite woollen cardigan. Wrapped inside it is the Cabbage Patch Kids doll from her childhood, along with her wooden recorder. There's a gift aid card for a local charity shop with Claire's signature, and a mug Max once chose for her birthday with the legend, MAMA BEAR.

Joseph repacks the box as carefully as he can and puts it back where he found it. Then he replaces the storage boxes in their original positions.

Feeling dirty, but doing it anyway, he searches Max's bedside table and checks down the back. He's about to leave the room when his gaze falls on his son's wooden footstool, a christening present from Claire's parents. The front is inscribed with Max's name and date of birth. Inside the seat is a secret compartment accessed on the underside by a sliding panel.

Joseph turns it upside down – and hears something flop

around inside it. He slides open the panel, revealing a dark interior. Then, holding the stool above the bed, he flips it back over. On to the duvet falls a black leather wallet.

*Oh, Jesus Christ,* Joseph thinks. *Oh, you foolish, foolish boy.*

Because he knows whose wallet this must be. He's working out what to do next when, downstairs, the doorbell rings.

# FOURTEEN

Standing in Max's room, staring at the wallet on his son's bed, Joseph hears the doorbell chime a second time. So many thoughts erupt inside his head that he finds himself paralysed. He doesn't want to touch the wallet and yet he must. He doesn't want to answer the door and yet he has to know who's calling. Worst of all is the discovery that his son has not only killed a man but has lied to Joseph about key details – details which could see them both jailed.

Wrenching himself around, he steps into the hall and leans over the bannisters. Through the privacy glass in the front door he sees a pair of dark shapes.

*Police*, a part of him insists.

*Paranoia*, insists another.

Joseph dips back inside Max's room and scoops the wallet off the bed. The leather feels warm, alive. Grimacing, he slides it into his back pocket. As he hurries down the stairs, he recalls the coin-eyed doorstep seller from last winter, who'd forced one foot into the hall and wouldn't leave without payment.

A lot has changed since then. Joseph has filled the house with weapons he dare not use, and a nightmare far worse than any he'd envisaged has crept up on him unawares.

When he swings open the front door, he finds Tilly and Drew on the step, in novelty sunglasses and summer dresses. The sight is such a relief that he blows out his breath like a punctured football.

'It was a flight of stairs, Joe, not the Matterhorn,' Tilly says, as she comes inside. 'Maybe it's time to invest in a gym membership. Work on that cardio.'

Joseph flashes a sickly smile. Closing the door, he follows the girls into the kitchen. The wallet sliding against his buttock feels like a just-cooked steak. 'I thought you went into town.'

'Only for suntan lotion. Today's all about lazing in the back garden like a couple of hungover hogs.'

'You're suffering?'

'Not overly.' Tilly dumps a carton of coconut water on the worktop, goes to the bifold doors and opens them. Her sunglasses are shaped like pineapples, with yellow lenses and green plastic crowns. Lowering them to the tip of her nose, she says, 'I'm going to root out our sun loungers from the shed. Do we have blueberries?'

'Some.'

'Ginger?'

'Possibly.'

'Kale?'

'I think your mum has a bag in the crisper drawer.'

'OK if Drew makes us a couple of hangover smoothies?'

'They're your tastebuds.'

'Shuh-*weet*,' Tilly says, and disappears outside.

Drew's sunglasses, with wide pink lenses, are shaped like a pair of flamingos. Joseph can't see her eyes but he knows she's watching him. He recalls the way her coffee cup had rattled against her teeth yesterday morning in the Grind House. And her close observation of him last night. She looks as uncomfortable now as she'd looked then. And trying hard not to show it.

'We need a magic bullet,' she says. 'Do you have one?'

'A magic what?'

Drew takes off her sunglasses. Today, he sees, she's back to full make-up. Her eyes only meet his own for a moment. 'Sounds like a vibrator, I know. But it's actually a smoothie maker.'

Joseph indicates the corner cupboard by the toaster. 'I don't know if it's the same brand, but look in there.'

Drew checks the cupboard and lifts a large grey appliance on to the worktop. Then she goes to the fridge and digs out the blueberries, kale and fresh ginger. 'Bananas?'

Joseph points, Drew nods. She looks through the bifold doors, to where Tilly is crossing the lawn with two sun loungers. As she slides past him to the smoothie maker, she leans forward and says, deep into his ear, 'I know what you did for Max, and I think it's really brave.'

The calm that follows is like the ocean just after a depth charge has exploded. Despite the enormous energy wave racing upwards, the surface looks tranquil, flat.

Drew reaches the end of the worktop and turns to face him.

Joseph can't breathe. That pressure wave races closer. Then, from the bifold doors, his stepdaughter says, 'You think what's really brave?'

Finally, the ocean turns white. Moments later, a mountain of water climbs heavenward. Hundreds of tons of spray.

Straightening, Joseph watches Tilly step into the kitchen. Her gaze moves from Drew to him and back, her expression amused-quizzical. 'Drewster?'

Drew grins, but she's no poker player. She grabs a banana and begins to peel it, turning to Joseph for help.

'We were talking about kale,' he says. 'I was explaining how I avoid most forms of roughage in my diet.'

'Avoiding roughage is brave?'

'It is if you're his colon,' Drew replies, finally recovering her composure.

Tilly wrinkles her nose like she's still not quite in on the joke. 'Right now, I'm a little too hungover to think about colons.'

If Joseph's jaw clenches any harder his teeth will shatter. Avoiding Tilly's gaze, he makes his excuses. In the downstairs cloakroom, he locks the door and yanks the pull cord light. From the kitchen he hears the smoothie maker begin to blitz.

In the mirror over the basin, Joseph stares at his reflection. He can't think about Drew's comment, not yet. Nor its awful implications. Instead, he fishes the wallet from his back pocket, cringing once again at its flesh-like feel. On the bottom edge is a logo he vaguely recognizes – a plump six-pointed star inside a white circle.

He doesn't want to examine the contents, doesn't want proof, irrefutable, that Max has lied to him. What troubles him even more is the prospect of learning the dead man's identity – and details of the life his son has destroyed.

Joseph flips open the wallet. Inside he sees six credit card slots, two slip pockets and a full-width pocket for banknotes. Embossed into the leather on the right-hand fold is MONTBLANC.

*That's* why he'd recognized the logo. On his fortieth birthday, Claire had given him a Montblanc fountain pen. Its cap had featured the same plump white star.

The wallet's frontmost card looks like a driver's licence. Joseph eases it half an inch from its slot. He's not ready to look at the face of Max's victim, but he does want to learn his name, which he discovers is Angus Oliver Roth.

Out in the hall, he hears the snick of a key, the rattle of the door latch. If Tilly's already home, and Erin just left for the print shop, it must be Max. Joseph slides the wallet back into his pocket. He grips the wash basin, takes five long breaths. Then he unlocks the cloakroom door.

The hallway is deserted, as is the kitchen. Through the bifold doors he sees Tilly and Drew carrying their smoothies across the garden. As they set up their loungers, Drew throws Tilly furtive looks. She seems spooked, as if she knows she just messed up and is wondering if she got away with it.

Joseph returns to the hall and creeps up the stairs. He pauses outside his son's room, gathers himself. The door is closed but not fully. He gives it a gentle push.

Max is hunched over on his chair, muttering to himself in an urgent, animated tone. His words are indistinct but the emotion in them is clear. He sounds wretched, distraught. When he notices Joseph, he lurches off his seat, so violently that he nearly collides with his desk. Tear tracks glisten on his cheeks.

'Dad,' he says, dragging his shirtsleeve across his face. 'You scared the hell out of me.'

Joseph stares at his son, trying to reconcile himself with what he's seeing. 'What,' he says, 'the fuck,' he continues, 'is going on?'

Max flinches as if he's just been struck. 'What're you talking about?'

'What am I talking about? How about you start by telling me where you've been this morning, and what you've been doing? I woke up and you'd disappeared.'

'I went out.'

'No shit. Where?'

'To the hospital.'

Joseph baulks. 'The *hospital*?'

'Mealtime support,' Max says. He raises his hands as if in surrender. 'My old volunteering role. I called them yesterday, arranged it. I just . . . I just wanted to do something positive, you know? Start paying back.'

'And you thought now was a good time for that?'

The boy opens his mouth, blinks hard. 'I didn't think it wasn't.'

'Maybe you weren't thinking at all. Why didn't you tell me?'

'I don't know. I . . .' He shrugs, swallows. 'I don't know.'

'Honestly, you're really starting to worry me, here, Max. I'm beginning to doubt your judgement.'

'Dad,' the boy says. He looks frightened, confused even – and, somehow, small. 'Other than doing a volunteer shift at the hospital, and forgetting to mention it, what exactly do you think I've done wrong?'

Joseph opens and closes his mouth. Half of him wants to put his arms around his son. The other half wants to shake some sense into him. 'Have you spoken to anyone? About what we're trying to deal with?'

'Of course not.'

'Really? You didn't tell Drew? You didn't tell her what happened in Jack-O'-Lantern Woods? That I'm helping you to *bury* this guy?'

The boy licks his lips. 'No, I—'

'Max, you fucking schoolboy!' Joseph hisses, slapping the doorframe in frustration. 'She just *told* me.' He shakes his head in disbelief. 'Apparently, she thinks – and these are her exact words, by the way, which is just fantastic – "it's really brave". I mean, is there— Do you *want* us to go to prison?'

Max's holds his father's gaze a moment longer. Then he goes to the bed and slumps down on it. 'She shouldn't have said that.'

'Maybe, just maybe, you shouldn't have told her.'

'I'm sorry. It won't happen again. I promise you.'

'You do realize that both our futures might now depend on whether Drew knows how to keep her mouth shut?'

Max runs his hands through his hair. 'She won't say anything.'

'Well, I'm delighted you're so confident. She's certainly made an excellent start.'

'Dad, please. Not the sarcasm. Not right now.'

Joseph is so surprised – so shocked and outraged by his son's response – that he laughs. 'My God,' he says. 'What is going on here? What is happening inside that brain of yours?'

'Look, I said I'm sorry. It was a dumb thing to do, but Drew won't say anything, I guarantee it. Our focus should be on where we go from here. I realize this must have spooked you, but I'm not flaking out. You can trust me – and my judgement. I'm not going to let you down.'

'I hope you're not just saying what you think I'm hoping to hear.'

'I swear to you, Dad.' He massages his neck, grimaces. 'You haven't told me about last night. Is it done?'

'Yes, it's done.'

Max frowns, holding his father's gaze. 'So where is he now?'

'It's best you don't know.'

'And my clothes? My trainers?'

'Burned,' Joseph says. 'Gone.'

'What about the car?'

'Back at your grandmother's place.'

'What do we do with it? There might be traces of the guy's blood. His DNA.'

'I'll deal with that on Monday, when everything reopens. Best thing you can do, in the meantime, is stay here, keep out of trouble and resist the temptation to blab about this to anyone else.'

He searches Max's face for any sign of dissent. Then he says, 'I need to ask you something. And I want a one hundred per cent honest answer.'

'Sure.'

'Do you really have no idea who this guy is?'

When Max begins to respond, Joseph holds up his hand. 'Don't just say the first thing that comes into your head. We're in trouble, here, you and me. We've a lot of work to do to dig ourselves out of it. This may get much worse before it gets better, and if we can't even be honest with each other, we've no hope. So think about your answer first. I only want the truth.'

'Dad,' Max says, his gaze wandering to the wall. 'I have absolutely no idea who that guy was.'

Joseph's heart breaks, then – because he knows without doubt that his son is lying. Even worse is the realization that if Max can lie to him about something so fundamental, perhaps the good-hearted boy he knew before Claire's death somehow died alongside her.

He shudders, expelling that thought as forcefully as the bile he vomited up last night.

*There's a way back,* he thinks. *There has to be.*

'And you found nothing where he fell?' he asks. 'No car keys, no wallet, no phone?'

'I already told you. More than once. None of that stuff, I swear.'

'Look at me, Max.'

As Joseph stares into his son's eyes he feels, for the second time since Friday night, like he's looking at a stranger. Briefly, he considers confronting Max with the wallet. But admitting that he searched the boy's room will obliterate trust rather than reinforce it, and he's not ready to do that just yet.

'OK,' he says finally. 'Let's leave it there. But remember what I said: stay at home, keep a low profile, and for God's sake steer clear of Tilly and Drew. You think you can do that?'

'Absolutely.'

'Is there anything else you want to tell me? Anything at all you think I should know?'

Max shakes his head. No longer a stranger. More like a scared and exhausted child.

Joseph goes to the bed, puts his hand on his son's shoulder, squeezes. 'I know how difficult things have been. I mean, since—'

'Please, Dad. You don't have to say it.'

'You know I love you.'

'And you know I love you too.'

Joseph nods, turns away, closes the door behind him. As he heads back downstairs, he hears a single hard sob from Max's room. Then silence.

# FIFTEEN

Sunday morning at ten thirty a.m., Gabriel Roth drives past his brother's place on Hocombe Hill without slowing but not without looking.

The houses along this stretch – mansions, most of them – hide behind a thick screen of trees, their canopied driveways allowing only the most fleeting of views. The architecture is eclectic: Modernist, Arts and Crafts, Gothic revival, Art Deco.

As Gabriel passes Thornecroft, the mock Tudor place his brother built after tearing down what preceded it, he sees many of its first-floor windows hanging open. Parked outside are three vehicles, including a white van that might belong to a maintenance company.

Someone is definitely home.

Further up the hill, Gabriel finds a parking spot on a grass verge shaded by elm trees. Reclining his seat, he pairs the hire car's entertainment system to his phone and opens Spotify. The music he selects is 'Plum Blossom in Three Movements' by Huan Yi, a musician from the fourth century Eastern Jin Dynasty. This version is played not on a flute, as is traditional, but a seven-stringed guqin.

Gabriel breathes in through his nose and out through his mouth. He closes his eyes and visualizes: pink plum blossom falling on to the surface of a slow-flowing river. He imagines floating downstream among the petals, the water cool and cleansing against his skin.

When he steps out of the car five minutes later, the world feels no better than before. He sees no beauty in the lines of the Mercedes, in the overhanging elms touched by summer sun. Walking up Thornecroft's drive, he wonders if his appreciation for those things is lost for good. He crunches across the gravel, climbs the five steps of the front porch and presses the bell. As he waits, he studies the parked vehicles.

Stencilled on the side of the van is SNOW WHITE CLEANING AND GARDENING SERVICES. A white Tesla is parked beside it. A grey rain cover protects his brother's wood-framed Morgan Plus 8.

An iron bolt draws back. One leaf of the huge entrance doors swings open. In the half-arch, peering out, stands Teri Platini. She's small and sad-eyed; a thirty-year-old woman with all the confidence squeezed out of her.

As Gabriel watches, Teri's heels lift from the floor then reconnect. She reminds him of a prey animal trying to make itself larger – and quickly abandoning the attempt.

Was she always like this? Really, it makes little difference; because however his brother's women start out, this – invariably, inevitably – is how they end up.

Teri is barefoot, in pink jersey shorts and a ribbed vest. Her nails and make-up are flawless. She'll have learned that lesson early – and the importance of not forgetting it.

'Gabe,' Teri says. When she smiles, she lowers her gaze and shifts her weight to one leg.

He glances at her jutted hip, inclines his head. The silence between them builds. Finally, Teri pulls the door wide.

'Sorry, I'm sorry. I'm forgetting my manners as usual. You want to come in?'

'Thank you.'

He follows her along a marble-laid hall and into an orangery the size of a small church. Despite the summer sun blazing through the windows, the aircon is cool enough to raise goosebumps on Teri's bare skin.

She indicates one of two bamboo sofas and sits opposite. As she draws her legs beneath her she flinches, eyes widening, and begins to stand.

Gabriel waves her back down. 'Please,' he says. 'I don't need refreshments. We can ignore all that. I just want to talk.' He looks through the orangery's windows at the expanse of perfectly manicured lawn rising towards an ancient oak, then back at Teri's perfectly manicured nails.

It confuses him, all this wealth – at least, the ostentatious display of it. Gabriel is identical to his twin in many respects, but he's uninterested in material possessions. Everything he owns fits into a single duffel bag.

'You know today's date?' he asks.

Teri nods.

'You know the date three days ago?'

She blinks five times in quick succession. 'H . . . Happy birthday,' she stammers. 'I'm sorry, Gabe. I didn't – w . . . *we* didn't – send a card.'

Hearing her panic, seeing it in her face, Gabriel feels even wearier. This time, it seems, his brother's really gone to town. Teri reminds him of a Jenga tower in the final stages of a game. The merest touch or sharp exhalation and the entire edifice will come crashing down. 'I didn't need a birthday card,' he tells her. 'And besides, I was travelling – you wouldn't have known where to send it.' He looks around the orangery. There's no fireplace in here, no mantelpiece. 'Did Angus receive mine?'

'It's in the living room,' Teri says. 'Pride of place.'

'Tell me, because I'm intrigued, and because I know how hard it must be to find a gift for a man who appears to have everything – and against all logic seems to crave even more. What did you choose?'

She opens her mouth, closes it, opens it again. 'It's kind of private,' she says. 'Sort of . . . embarrassing.'

Gabriel remains silent. With people like Teri, it's often his preferred strategy.

'I had a . . . I organized . . . well . . . I think they're called boudoir shoots.' Teri glances at her lap. 'It's not porn. Nothing like that. Glamour photography is sometimes what they call it. Except . . . maybe it was a bit more than that. I had one of the images blown up and framed for him. To go above our bed.'

Gabriel considers this for a while – and how his brother might have reacted. 'You let another man see you naked? Take intimate photographs of you?'

Blanching, Teri shakes her head. 'It was an all-female team. I would never . . .' She takes a breath. 'I would *never*.'

Gabriel suspects that Teri's gift would have symbolized, to his brother, the final surrender of her dignity; would have demonstrated that the game was effectively over, because nothing remained worth playing for – because, to Angus, the only thing less interesting than a slave is a willing slave. 'Well, it was certainly thoughtful,' he says. 'Did he take you to dinner afterwards?'

'Thursday night?'

'Thursday night.'

'Thursday night, I think he was . . .' Again, Teri's eyelids stutter. This time, a single tear spills down her cheek. 'I think he was with one of the others.'

From his pocket, Gabriel retrieves a handkerchief and offers it. 'I'm sorry. That must have been tough. I'm guessing things have been difficult for a while. Has Angus stopped paying you as much attention? Stopped trying to make you happy?'

Teri dabs at her eyes, careful to avoid her mascara. Finally, she nods.

'Who was the girl?'

'Someone new, I think. Someone younger than me. A lot younger.'

'Where's my brother now?'

'I'm guessing he's still with her.'

'You haven't seen him since Thursday?'

'No.'

'Have you heard from him?'

'Not yet.'

Plum blossom falling on to slow-flowing water. Cotton-white clouds passing over Mount Huangshan. Gabriel breathes long and slow. 'Have you tried to contact him?'

Teri shivers. Again, she shakes her head.

From outside comes the buzz of a leaf blower. A muscular-looking guy in overalls appears around the side of the building. As he passes the orangery, he glances through the windows at Teri. When he spots Gabriel on the opposite sofa, he quickly averts his eyes.

'I don't know if you've heard this story,' Gabriel tells her. 'Maybe you have, but I think it's worth repeating. One year, when we were a lot younger, Angus was in Pana-jachel, Guatemala, on our birthday. He was out of money, had nothing of value to trade. He found a fisherman with a mobile phone on Lake Atitlan, but the man wasn't willing to hand it over. Angus beat him bloody and used the phone to get in touch.'

Gabriel grimaces. 'I can never decide if that's a story about savagery or love, but that's not really why I'm sharing it. The point is, every year since our lives took separate paths, Angus has always made contact on our birthday.'

He pauses, lets that sink in. 'Most people understand that the bond between twins is something special. But when those twins grew up in care, as we did, that connection eclipses everything. You know what Angus said to me Thursday night?'

'No.'

'He said nothing, Teri, because he never called.' Gabriel searches her expression. 'What do you make of that?'

'I'm sorry, Gabe, I—'

'Please. You don't need to keep apologizing. I'm not holding you accountable. I *see* you, Teri. I see what Angus has done to you. I know you're not capable of hurting anyone, but I do want to know my brother's whereabouts.'

'Gabe, I don't *know.*'

'And I understand that, I do, but you likely know something, even if you haven't realized it. Something that might point me in the right direction.'

When Teri starts to respond, Gabriel holds up a hand. 'Listen,' he says. 'I know you're frightened. And I can understand why. But Angus is missing and I intend to find him – because my brother is all I have. And if he's come to harm . . .'

Gabriel's hand grips the sofa arm, crushing the bamboo. For a while, he cannot continue. He blows out his breath, tries to slow his heart. He knows through brutal experience what can happen when his blood is up. Gradually, the pulse in his ears surrenders to the whine of the leaf-blower. At last, it's safe to continue. 'You said you thought he was with someone Thursday night. Someone a lot younger. What made you say that?'

Teri scratches her cheek hard enough to leave track marks. 'I sneaked a look at his phone. While he was in the shower.'

'You saw messages between them?'

'Uh-huh.'

'This was on . . . Messenger? WhatsApp?

'WhatsApp.'

'You saw a photo?'

'Yes.'

'Can you describe her?'

'I can't . . . I mean, it was only a tiny picture. She . . . Well, she was pretty, obviously. Blonde hair. Eyes, I couldn't say.'

'You saw her contact details?'

'I didn't have time.'

'You must have seen her name.'

'It . . .'

Gabriel waits.

'Barbie Girl.'

'Barbie Girl?'

'I think it was an alias.'

'Teri,' Gabriel says. 'I think you're probably right about that.' He watches her frantic breathing for a while. Then he folds his hands in his lap. 'You know what we're going to do now? We're going to rewind. Much earlier than the arrival of this new young thing who's caused you all this misery. We're going to talk about everything that's been happening in Angus's life – and yours – these past six months, every little detail. You're going to tell me about his work, how he's been spending his free time and where he's been meeting these other women. Are you with me, Teri?'

She nods her head so furiously that in any other circumstances it might be amusing. But Gabriel senses that something serious has befallen his twin, and if that's true there'll be no room for laughter in this world. Only pain.

Teri talks. Gabriel listens. After an hour, they break for

coffee. While Teri, in the kitchen, presses buttons on a chrome-plated monstrosity that looks like it should run on aviation fuel, Gabriel checks the front of the house and sees that the Snow White Cleaning and Gardening van has gone.

Now, it's just the two of them, in this enormous private space. Returning to the kitchen, watching Teri froth milk in an aluminium jug, he observes how girlishly she's started to behave. It manifests in her body language, her diction, even the pitch of her voice. He's astute enough to know it's deliberate. Clearly, Teri thinks she's most likely to illicit his sympathy by putting all her vulnerabilities on display, exaggerating them with a little play-acting.

Aware of her ploy, the resulting performance strikes him as coquettish rather than innocent; mildly perverse. Instead of eliciting empathy, it does the opposite.

He starts to question his earlier assumptions, his earlier reassurances: *You don't need to apologize. I'm not holding you accountable. I see you, Teri. I see what Angus has done to you. I know you're not capable of hurting anyone.*

Maybe he was wrong about that. Maybe she's a far better actor than he first thought. Maybe her bad acting is in itself an act. A cunning double bluff.

The atmosphere in the kitchen changes; the tension between them climbs several notches. When she turns towards him and knocks over one of the cups, spilling coffee across the quartz worktop, she blushes deeply and apologizes.

'It's fine,' he tells her. 'Just an accident. Now clear it up and start again.'

Back inside the orangery, holding a cup of perfectly brewed Yirgacheffe, he probes Teri further about Angus. She can hardly meet his gaze any more, answering his questions with her eyes locked on her bare knees.

As Gabriel listens, he finds himself imagining the secrets concealed beneath her high-cut jersey shorts and ribbed vest. It creates in him an enmity that she should provoke him so deliberately, that she should attempt to distract him from his task.

'Where's Angus's laptop?' he asks.

'In his study.'

'His mobile phone?'

'I haven't seen it.'

'Any other devices?'

'There's his iPad. But he doesn't use it much.'

'I'll be taking the laptop. The iPad, too.'

'I don't know the passwords,' she says. 'Or how to unlock them.'

'I do. If something's there, I'll find it.'

She swallows. 'What now?'

'I think we're done.'

'Should we . . . will you call the police?'

'The police? Do you think we should?'

'I . . . Maybe.'

'So why didn't you? You've had three days.'

The fear in her eyes is instant. 'I told you. I assumed he was with that girl.'

'So what's changed? Why worry now, if you didn't worry before?'

Teri opens and closes her mouth several times before she manages to get out any words. 'Because I didn't know that *story* you told – about how he always calls you on your birthday, how this time he didn't. That changes things, doesn't it? And I didn't *know*.'

Gabriel breathes. In through his nose. Out through his mouth.

He thinks of Huan Yi; of plum blossom falling on slow-moving water; of cotton-white clouds above Mount

Huangshan. He imagines the warmth of Teri's skin; the feel of the firm flesh beneath.

Uncrossing his legs, he stands.

Teri struggles up too, hopping away from him as if he's contagious. She shifts her weight to one leg again and Gabriel decides it's high time he left his brother's house.

'Teri,' he says. 'Do you know where Angus is?'

Wild-eyed, she shakes her head. 'If I did, I'd say. I *promise* you, Gabe.'

He nods, fists clenched. 'Thank you for making the time.' His voice sounds strange – as if it's coming from far away. Sweat breaks out across his forehead. It pricks from his arm-pits and runs down his sides.

Teri turns on her toes. Gabriel follows her through the house to the entrance hall, breathing like a boxer after twelve hard rounds.

She reaches for the iron deadbolt. Her painted nails flash like red teardrops.

His gaze drops to her calves. It climbs to the backs of her thighs disappearing into those high-cut jersey shorts. It settles on her bare shoulder.

He can smell her, now; a scent that calls out to him.

The right-side door swings wide. Gabriel sees the gravel driveway, the grey rain cover protecting Angus's Morgan.

His face contorted, he closes his hand on Teri's shoul-der. She gasps, twists around. And then he's dragging her aside – urgently, not savagely – and striding out into summer sunshine. He pants for breath, doesn't look back. Gravel crunches like broken bones beneath his feet. Behind him, the door to Thornecroft slams shut. He keeps moving, keeps walking, one foot in front of the other.

He needs to find Angus. But first he has to get away from Teri Platini.

Gabriel hears the crunch of gravel no longer. When he

looks down, he sees he's standing motionless. Another few steps and he'll have crossed Thornecroft's boundary. From there it's only a few hundred yards to his car.

He's so close.

From the canopy of one of the elm trees comes a crow's harsh call. Like a weathervane, Gabriel pivots. He stares at his brother's house, at the place Angus built to hoard and protect his treasures.

Gabriel finds he's walking again. He climbs Thornecroft's porch steps and rings the bell. A minute passes before the door reopens. Teri blinks at him from the hall.

They stare at each other for long seconds. When Gabriel speaks, his voice is low. 'I love my brother,' he says, 'but I'm not blind to his flaws. We might be twins but we're not the same.'

She raises herself on to her toes again, her face waxy with fear.

'Angus likes to dominate,' Gabriel says. 'He also likes to humiliate. And the women he selects – women like you, Teri – are so infatuated they let it happen. Then, once he's broken them down completely and they've lost their self-respect, he moves on to someone new.'

A pulse beats in her throat. 'Gabe,' she begins.

'You'll struggle to put him behind you, Teri. I know because I've seen it happen. After you leave this house, you'll go into mourning for what you lost. It's going to be lonely. Difficult.'

His gaze travels over her small frame, her perfect hair and nails. He wonders if she knows that desire is a natural consequence of grief, a repudiation of it.

'I'd like to see that picture,' he says. 'The one you framed for your bedroom. Will you show me?'

Her expression is of glazed horror. 'Angus wouldn't . . . I'm sorry, Gabe, but that's private. It wouldn't be right.'

'Angus has moved on,' Gabriel says. 'He no longer has any interest in you – nor in what you might choose to share with me. I'd like to see it.'

Teri's lungs fill. Gabriel's lungs fill, too. When she shakes her head and starts to close the door, he puts out a hand and stops it.

# SIXTEEN

An hour later, Erin returns from town. In the downstairs office, she packs an overnight bag with work files and printouts. Then she throws in a few clothes. 'I bought a couple of ready meals for this evening. Or there's food in the freezer if you feel like cooking. Try not to get up to any mischief while I'm gone.'

'I'm sure it'll be a quiet one.'

He drops her at the train station in Crompton. On the way home, he detours through Jack-O'-Lantern Woods, taking the main road north to south. He passes no police vehicles, spots no evidence of anything amiss.

Pulling into a rest spot, Joseph climbs out of the car, retrieves the wallet from his pocket and flips it open. This time, he fully removes the driving licence from its slot. When he sees the photo he leans against the doorframe – because, despite the cranial injuries he observed on Friday night, and the washed-out colours of the licence, this is, indisputably, an image of Max's victim.

The dead man's face bears all the hallmarks of a high-testosterone individual: hollow cheeks, square jaw, strong chin. His eyes are set wide apart, his stare unsettlingly intense.

According to the licence, Angus Roth is thirty-eight years old. His home address is on Hocombe Hill, a few miles from Jack-O'-Lantern Woods.

Joseph checks the banknote pocket and counts ten fresh twenties. In the left-hand slip pocket he finds a couple of petrol receipts. In the right-hand pocket he finds a heart-shaped pink Post-it. Written on it in pencil are the words, *If you dare.* Below them, a mobile number.

Joseph removes the remaining cards and cycles through them: an Amex Platinum card, a British Airways Executive Club card, two First Direct debit cards.

He returns the cards to their slots and gets back in the car. Then he programmes his satnav with the postcode from the licence.

The journey from Jack-O'-Lantern Woods takes ten minutes. Hocombe Hill is one of Crompton's most affluent roads, lined with huge properties screened by mature trees. Joseph passes Thornecroft, Angus Roth's place, too fast to get a proper look. At the top of the hill, he turns around and drives back. This time, slowing to a crawl as he reaches Thornecroft's entrance, he sees a grand mock Tudor residence designed to radiate power. The place must be worth a couple of million.

Joseph's stomach somersaults. Teeth clenched and temples throbbing, he puts his foot down and gets out of there. None of this is good. None of it.

Back at home, he grabs a bottle of Evian from the fridge and drinks till his thirst is slaked. In the garden, Tilly and Drew are still draped across their sun loungers. Watching them from the bifold doors, Joseph wonders how much Drew knows.

Has Max told her everything? Or an edited version? Surely he didn't make the same claim he made to his father: that he'd done the dead man a kindness by staving in his skull.

Joseph recalls Erin's assessment of his son's relationship: *This is just a bit of summer fun until they go their separate ways.*

If she's right, what happens after the break-up? Drew might stay quiet for now, but what might she do once they split? Admittedly, that's not a concern for the next twenty-four hours, nor perhaps even the next few weeks. But it's still another tsunami rushing towards him.

So intensely is Joseph focused on these thoughts that it's a while before he notices that Drew has turned her face towards the bifold doors. Her sunglasses obscure the focus of her gaze, but then she raises them – and he realizes she's been watching him all along. Worse, he sees that Tilly, her expression faintly mystified, has noticed their wordless exchange. Conscious of just how creepy he must look, he abandons the kitchen for the hall.

Briefly, Joseph considers doing what he failed to do earlier – confronting his son about the wallet. Because if Max lied about that, it's possible he lied about the dead man's phone. If he hasn't turned it off, it'll lead anyone searching for it straight here.

Despite the danger, Joseph isn't ready to look into his son's eyes and listen to another lie. Instead, he goes upstairs and locks himself inside the ensuite. Taking out Claire's iPhone, he opens the browser.

He's always assumed that a grave should be six feet deep, but he finds no modern-day justification for that online. The practice seems to have sprung up during the plague years of the sixteen hundreds; back then, the deeper the victims were buried the better, and six feet was likely the maximum depth a man could dig while comfortably shovelling soil over the lip.

These days, most cemetery graves run to a depth of four feet, allowing three feet to the top of the coffin. Joseph isn't burying a coffin – he's burying a man wrapped in a tarp – but four feet still seems a good target. At that depth there's little chance of scavengers uncovering the remains, or a storm washing away the topsoil.

He's about to unlock the door when he remembers Max's mention of cadaver dogs. Back online he goes, where he discovers a number of facts to make him nauseous, among them that American cadaver dogs are often trained on rotting human placentas. Finally, he lands on a site that claims they can detect human remains even under fifteen feet of soil. There's zero chance of him digging down that far, so he may as well accept that if a dog is deployed he's fucked.

Joseph checks his watch, sees that it's gone three. If he sets off from his mother's bungalow in four hours' time, he'll arrive at Black Down near sunset. That'll give him a while to pick out a grave site before the sky grows fully dark. After brushing his teeth a second time, he daubs more Sauvage on his upper lip.

At six thirty, he leaves a note in the kitchen, saying that he's off to see a friend, will be back late, and that the fridge is stocked with ready meals for anyone who gets hungry. Then he fetches a bike from the shed and walks it through the side gate. Ten minutes later, he arrives at his mother's bungalow in Saddle Bank.

The stench hits him the moment he steps inside the garage, immeasurably worse than last night. Decomposition seems to be progressing far quicker than his online research had suggested. Joseph breathes through his mouth, but the tainted air still fills his lungs. While he hunts around for his father's old pickaxe, three huge bluebottles perform aeronautic displays. He flails wildly whenever they come close – and when one of them lands on his arm he cries out in disgust.

He discovers the pickaxe in a pile of rusting garden tools. Holding his breath, he opens the Honda's boot. Three more flies loop out of it. Dry-heaving, Joseph tosses the pickaxe inside and slams shut the lid.

Back in the bungalow, he fills the bathroom basin with cold water and submerges his face until his breath runs out. Then, returning to the garage, he climbs into the car and uses the remote to raise the garage door. For the second time in twenty-four hours, he reverses on to the driveway and drives the dead man to Black Down.

# SEVENTEEN

When he arrives, the sun is a red fire on the horizon. By the time he's picked out a grave site, the sky is purpling. He breaks ground shortly after.

The pickaxe helps. Joseph works in shifts of twenty minutes' swinging or shovelling soil, followed by five minutes' deep breathing. After the first hour, he's drunk half the water he's brought along. Ten minutes into the second hour, he's finished the bottle.

The stars come out. The temperature begins to drop. Joseph opens the Honda's boot so the stench of decomposition can dissipate.

'You have any kids?' he asks, as he continues to dig. 'I hope not. I don't mean that unkindly. But the fewer people you've left behind, the fewer people we'll hurt. Being dead is pretty shit, I'll grant you, but I guarantee you one thing – being left behind is *really* shit.'

Joseph pauses, wipes sweat from his forehead. He's down to a depth of three feet. Not deep enough to fool a cadaver dog – but another foot or so should be good enough to deter scavengers.

'Were you a religious man?' he asks. 'Claire and I – we never really took Max to church. And after what happened . . .

Well, I could never reconcile myself to a God who allowed that. Erin's the same way.'

From the car boot, the dead man doesn't comment. In all likelihood, he probably doesn't give much of a toss.

'I know I said it before,' Joseph continues, 'but Max is a good kid. He's just . . .'

*Lost?*

*Is that what you were about to say? Because we're all fucking lost, aren't we? Some of us more than others. But we don't all go around doing kindnesses for strangers by shattering their skulls after driving over them.*

Joseph runs his tongue around his teeth and spits. He climbs out of the hole, throws down his spade and inspects his work. 'OK, I think that's about as good as I can make it. I'm sorry you won't get a gravestone. Or even a coffin, come to think of it.'

He gazes around him at the moon-touched heath, at the dome of stars above and the ragged sails of travelling night clouds. 'But you do get all this. From what I've seen of cemeteries, I'd say you're better off.'

Returning to the car, he stares at the tarp-wrapped bundle. 'I'll be as gentle as I can. But I'm on my own, here – so things might get a little bumpy.'

*Are you losing your mind, Joseph? Apologizing to a corpse? Why not go the whole hog – sprinkle the path between here and that hole you just dug with rose petals. You think any of this matters?*

'Yes,' he says. 'I know it matters.'

Joseph holds his breath and slides his hands around the tarp. Then, tightening his grip, grimacing in revulsion at what he's doing – knowing that he needs to do it now, all in one go, because he might not find the courage for a second attempt – he hauls the dead man over the lip of the boot. He tries to lower him slowly, but gravity and inertia defeat him. The dead man slips from his fingers and thumps to the ground, emitting a moan like a kicked bagpipe.

Appalled, Joseph leaps backwards. It takes him a full minute to recover. The cadaver still has airways, he realizes – and by now they're probably filled with decomposition gases.

'Sorry,' he says. 'Hardly dignified. But that's the worst part over, I think.'

Gripping the dead man's ankles through the tarp, he drags him across the stony ground towards the trench. A minute later, he's pulled him inside it. Joseph sits on the lip of the grave, panting for breath. Sweat rolls down his cheeks, his armpits and his back. He's dirty, dusty, itchy as hell. His muscles burn. His feet ache.

'You want me to say a few words?' he asks.

The dead man doesn't answer. This time, not even a moan.

Joseph nods, claps soil from his hands, pulls himself to his feet. 'Then let me say this. If you have a God, I hope you're reunited with Him. If you don't, I hope you've found peace. If you're looking down on this' – he pauses, shaken by the very thought – 'then I know I don't deserve your forgiveness, so I won't even ask. I hope things look better from up there than they do down here. I'll spend the rest of my life atoning for what's happened. I'll make sure Max does the same.'

Picking up his spade, he peers into the grave, clears his throat. 'Here lies Angus Roth. I hope he rests in peace.'

Joseph begins to shovel in soil. He doesn't stop until the job is finished. Afterwards, there's a huge pile of leftover dirt. He spends a good hour distributing it as far and as wide as he can. If someone walks through here tomorrow, they'll doubtless spot the disturbance. But a week from now, a month – hopefully by then the ground will have recovered. Enough of the summer remains for weeds to grow, for heather and gorse to spread.

Tossing the spade and pickaxe into the car, Joseph climbs

behind the wheel. His body feels heavy, his arms leaden. Starting the engine, he checks the dashboard clock: two eleven a.m.

He drives back to Saddle Bank faster than he drove to Black Down. Partly because he's no longer as worried about being stopped; partly because he wants to escape this place and for ever erase it from his memory. Along the way he spots a couple of industrial bins outside a retail park and dumps the bag of bloodied clothing, the mop, the dish scrubber and washing-up bowl.

Shortly after three, he pulls on to his mother's driveway and hits the switch for the electric garage door. As it starts to winch open, light spills out.

He frowns, trying to remember if he flicked off the fluorescent strip before he left, but as the door raises higher, it reveals something in the middle of the garage that wasn't there before. The winder motor continues to churn. The door continues to raise.

Joseph realizes he's looking at a hooded human figure, sitting cross-legged on the garage floor.

His hands tighten on the wheel. As he watches, the figure begins to lift back the hood.

Joseph presses himself into his seat, fearful beyond all rationality that he's about to come face to face with a presence that defies everything he's come to believe about the world; something older than the stars; something that has stalked humanity across millennia.

But what he sees is worse. He sees his son.

Joseph shivers, knows this is going to be bad. The headlights are shining right into the garage, so he knows Max can't see him; and yet the boy stares directly ahead.

His first thought – from the depths of his lizard brain – is to throw the car into reverse and put as much distance between himself and what's happening here as he can.

Shame envelops him an instant later. Because this is his son; because this is the flawed and wonderful human he created with Claire thirteen years before she passed; because this is the best thing he has ever done, perhaps the only good thing.

Joseph kills the engine, then the headlights. He opens the car door and climbs out. Tentatively, he steps closer. 'Max?'

No lights shine from the homes either side of this one, nor from those across the street. He wonders how many eyes are watching this exchange behind darkened windows. Just one suspicious resident could be enough to sink them.

Max's shoulders lift and fall. Perhaps it's a trick of the light, but the boy's cheeks glisten as if wet. Joseph closes the remaining distance and steps into the garage. He hits the door release and waits for the clanking, grinding motor to seal the pair of them inside.

The silence that follows is terrible.

He crouches in front of Max. This close, the tear tracks on his son's cheeks are far more obvious. 'Hey,' he says.

Slowly, the boy emerges from whichever horrors he's just been contemplating. 'I didn't . . .' he manages to croak, before his voice fails him. He shudders for breath, rocks forward. 'I don't know how . . . Why are you even here?' A high-pitched keening issues from his throat – the most awful sound Joseph has ever heard.

'Max, what is it? What's happened? *Talk* to me.'

Only now does Joseph see something he hadn't noticed before, or perhaps had managed to block out: his son's hands are gloved in blood. In one of them is the pocket knife Joseph spotted yesterday in the boy's desk drawer.

It feels, in that moment, as if every molecule of oxygen has been sucked away, as if he isn't in his mother's garage at all but an outpost on the moon where the airlock has just failed. He hears the beat of his heart as a pressure inside his head. When he stands, the gravity seems all wrong.

Max tries to struggle up too, but his bloodied hands slip on the concrete and he crashes back down. 'Wait, please. Don't go in there, Dad. I don't want you to see.'

Ignoring his son's plea, stumbling past him to the bungalow's connecting door, Joseph has to correct course several times.

Inside his mother's kitchen, it really does feel like he's swimming inside a vacuum. His boots make no sound on the linoleum. The rasp of his breath echoes as if an astronaut's helmet encloses his head.

The kitchen looks identical to the last time he was here. In the living room, where he goes next, a table lamp throws out a homely glow entirely at odds with what it illuminates.

His mother's armchair has been pushed to the nearest wall, along with her glass coffee table. Spread across the carpet is a heavy-duty plastic sheet. Upon it, eyes fixed on the ceiling, lies Drew.

# EIGHTEEN

Joseph swims closer, hampered by the lack of gravity. When he calls Drew's name, he barely hears his own voice.

She's dressed differently than she was at the house, her floaty summer dress switched for a tartan miniskirt and a high-necked white halter cut to the midriff.

In his head, he hears his son's words from earlier this afternoon: *Drew won't say anything, I guarantee it.*

Joseph moans, sinks to his knees.

Drew looks like she died from a single stab wound to the neck. Blood has sheeted down her throat, soaking her halter top. It covers her hands, too, all the way up to her elbows, as if she tried in vain to stem the bleeding before she died.

A few days ago, save for their occasional banter, Drew Cullen had rarely featured in Joseph's thoughts. Now, in death, he appreciates just how unutterably precious she was, and what the world has lost.

Even worse is the knowledge that he could have prevented this – that the responsibility for her death rests with him. He cups his hands over his mouth, forces himself to look at what his choices have brought about. So intense is his grief that it's a while before he realizes Max has sunk to his knees beside him.

When the boy draws breath, the air sounds like it's rushing through dusty catacombs. When he speaks, his voice is so bereft that Joseph hardly recognizes it. 'However I try to explain this, I lose you.'

'Try,' Joseph croaks.

Max claws bloodied fingers through his hair. 'I was wrong,' he says. 'Drew would have talked. She got scared, Dad. She was saying she had to tell someone. If she'd gone to the police, she'd have ended up implicating you. We'd have both gone to prison. And you'd have lost Erin – Tilly, too. Our whole family broken apart.'

Joseph hears the words but he can't really comprehend them. The full impact of his actions, and his role in this tragedy, breaks over him. 'What have I done?' he whispers. 'I could have stopped this Friday night and I didn't, but I never for one moment thought you'd . . . Oh my God, you've taken Drew's *life*, Max. Her *life*.'

He wants to scream those words. Wants to grip his son's head, pull it close and yell them so forcedly that they detonate like landmines inside the boy's brain. He feels Max's hand on his shoulder, wants to shrug it off, wants to beat him with his fists, wants to crush him in a hug.

He gags, gasps for air. Right now, his entire reality feels under threat, as if a single false move could rent it with holes through which nameless horrors could pour.

The warmth from Max's fingers spreads across his back. 'It's not your fault,' his son says, beginning to sob. 'Please, Dad. Don't blame yourself. This isn't on you. I don't know how else I can—'

'I should have gone to the police. Taken responsibility. I should have told them I hit that guy driving home.'

'No. I never would have let you. And without me, you'd never have got them to believe you. Please don't say this is your fault, because it isn't.'

Joseph begins to weep, too. Once he's started, he can't stop. He cries for the dead man. He cries for Tilly, for Erin, for Max. He cries for Claire, dead these last five years, who would have prevented this tragedy had she lived, because she'd have given Max the love and guidance the boy so desperately needs.

But mostly he cries for Drew.

He feels Max's hand slide up and down his spine, and it seems to him that they've swapped roles, son trying to comfort father.

'Her parents . . .' Joseph begins. 'Enoch and Paula. My God, what have we *done* to them? We've killed them, too. This isn't just one death, it's three.'

'Enoch's an alcoholic, doesn't care about anyone except himself. Paula cares more about cocaine than she does about her daughter.'

'Oh, Max,' he mutters. 'What are you saying? What difference does that make?'

'It doesn't make any difference. That's not what I mean.'

'Then don't say it. Because it's entirely fucking irrelevant.'

Max licks his lips. He's silent for a while. Joseph rocks back and forth, his gaze on the precious, tragic human lying in front of him.

There's no blood on the carpet or any of the walls. Which means Max must have rolled out the plastic before Drew arrived, killing her when she walked in here and stepped on to it.

Joseph can't think about that for long. It's simply too horrific.

Time passes. How much, he doesn't know. Because time, like everything else, has temporarily lost its meaning. He breathes, he weeps. He paddles through chaos and loss, trying to stay afloat.

Beside him, Max says, 'You left a note at home, saying you

were going to see a friend. I had no idea you were coming here. It was only when I checked the garage that I realized you must have collected the car. When that door opened, I thought it was the police, here to arrest me.' He shakes his head. 'What were you even doing, driving around in that?'

When Max receives no answer, he takes his father's wrist and lifts it. Joseph stares at his own fingers. He sees the dirt caked under his nails. The dust and grime on his shirtsleeve.

'You buried him tonight,' the boy says, his voice flat. 'Didn't you? Not last night, like you made out.'

'There wasn't enough time last night. The ground was too hard. I left it too late.'

The room feels like it's beginning to pulse in time with Joseph's heart. He breathes deep, tries to focus. 'I know what I told you wasn't true. And I know what I said this morning – about the need for us to be honest with each other.'

'Doesn't matter. You were trying to protect me, I get it. This,' Max says, turning to his father with haunted eyes. 'I guess, in a way, this is like protection, too.'

Joseph coughs, chokes. Realizing he's about to be sick, he staggers to his feet and lurches towards the hall. In the bathroom, he heaves into the toilet bowl until his stomach is purged. There's not much to bring up – a little toast from breakfast, that's it – but the contractions continue regardless.

What is he going to do? There's no way back, and no conceivable path forward. Drew is dead, and there's no way back because Drew is dead.

How did his attempt to keep his boy out of jail turn into this? How did one death – which he'd believed was an accident, a tragic one-off – turn into two?

He can't cover this up. He won't wrap Drew in plastic and drive her out to Black Down.

Is he going to hand in his son? Could he actually bring

himself to do that? If he does, he'll be condemning Max to a fate far worse than the one he'd previously feared. But what other option does he have?

Could he give himself up instead? He'd be trading his life for the life of his boy. And while he might think that a viable exchange, could he do it in the knowledge that this might happen again? And that next time he'd be in jail, powerless to prevent it?

*Like you prevented this?*

He flushes the toilet, clambers up. At the sink, he rinses his mouth and confronts his reflection in the mirror. 'Are you going to lie to Erin?' he asks. 'To Tilly? Are you really going to let them think you did this?'

'Dad?'

Joseph flinches. When he glances behind him, he sees Max standing in the doorway.

'Who were you talking to?' the boy asks.

'No one.'

'You mentioned Erin. Tilly, too.'

'I'm just . . .' He wipes his mouth on his sleeve. 'I'm just trying to process this. Just trying to get my head around it.'

'Does Erin know something?'

When Joseph hears his son's tone, the blood drains from his head. 'Erin doesn't know a damned thing. She's in the dark about this – *totally.*'

Max raises his hands. 'Oh Jesus, I didn't mean anything by it. I know this is horrific. I can't even begin to . . .' His face creases. 'Are you OK? I heard you throwing up.'

'I'll survive,' Joseph says, grimacing at his choice of words.

'What happens now?'

'What do you mean?'

'What're you going to do? Now you know about Drew. About all this.'

'Max, I just can't believe what you've done to her.'

'Dad, I don't know how to . . . From the start, I just wanted to protect you. I never—'

'By taking her *life*?' he asked, dumbfounded. 'Have you any idea how batshit crazy that sounds?'

'That's not what I meant. I meant I was going to deal with this myself, so you wouldn't have to be involved.'

'Of course I'm involved!' Joseph shouts. 'You thought you'd keep this one secret, is that what you're saying? Because when Drew was reported missing, there was no danger that I'd put two and two together? I'd just think it was a fucking coincidence?'

Abruptly, as if he's a marionette whose strings have been severed, Max sags against the doorframe, all the strength going out of him.

Joseph stares at his son. At the wreckage Max has become. And then, because he's a father, and because he'll never stop loving his boy, no matter what Max does, no matter how much devastation he wreaks, he limps across the bathroom and gathers him in an embrace.

He thinks of Drew's parents, Enoch and Paula. Drew's wider family. He thinks of Tilly, his stepdaughter. All those lives about to be changed. He thinks of the poor dead girl lying in the living room – of all the joys and losses and fierce and furious moments of life that were rightfully hers and are now for ever lost. He thinks of how different the world will be because of this. How the ripples of what happened here will spread. How they'll echo in the smallest of ways and the largest. How he'll only ever grasp a tiny fraction of the impact. And how Max might not even grasp that.

Except . . . except his boy isn't a monster; he's not.

He's just lost.

'Dad? What are we going to do?'

'Nothing,' Joseph says finally. 'Not tonight. This is just . . . it's too big, Max.'

'I know.'

'So – we're going to go home, sleep. Or at least we're going to lie down and get some rest. But before that, I need you to think for me. Because the very *worst* outcome would be for someone else to discover what's happened here before we figure out what comes next. Did Drew have her phone with her? Could someone track her here because of it?'

Max shakes his head. 'She promised to leave it at home.'

'And you're absolutely sure she did?'

'She didn't have it with her. I checked.'

'Did anyone else know she was meeting you?'

'No one else even knows we were seeing each other. Only me and you. And Drew, obviously.'

*And Erin.*

*Thanks to your loose mouth.*

'Have you texted her at all since you've been seeing her? Contacted her on social media? Commented on her Instagrams? Any of that stuff?'

'Not even once. Tilly would have picked up on it, which is why I never did.'

Joseph files away Max's answers for later, when he has the headspace to think. 'I want you to get out of here,' he says. 'Right now. Straight out the front door.'

'We're not leaving together?'

'We're not. And I don't want you going home directly, either, to get tagged by Ralph Erikson's camera. Go to the Calthorpes, sneak into their back garden and over the wall to ours. Understand?'

'Sure.' Max licks his lips. 'Do we wrap her up first? Put her in the—'

'No,' Joseph tells him, louder than he intended. 'We don't touch her. Not a hair.'

'You're just going to leave her out in the open like this?'

'We don't touch a hair.'

'OK,' Max says.

A minute later, he's gone.

Joseph returns to the living room. He stands in the doorway for a while, looking at Drew. Two nights ago, staring at the dead man folded into the Honda's boot, he'd felt a bone-deep duty to treat him not just with respect but with reverence.

But what Joseph feels now is on a scale incomparable. This is someone he knew in life. He can close his eyes and see Drew's smile and hear her laugh.

He goes to the kitchen and roots around under the sink, finding matches, a saucer, a stub of candle. Back in the living room, he kneels on the floor and lights the candle, securing it to the saucer with a drip of wax. Then he turns off his mother's lamp.

He doesn't know what he's doing. He's never believed in a God, in a guiding spirit, in a heaven or a hell or an afterlife. But nor did he ever believe that his son could kill another human being. Certainly not two.

If a shred of Drew's spirit remains in this room, he'll wait here a while until it departs. He owes her that – and a lot more besides.

He doesn't speak, because no words exist for what he wants to say. When the candle dies an hour later, plunging the room into darkness, Joseph senses he's required here no longer. Climbing to his feet, he walks through his mother's house, feeling his way by touch. Beneath him, all around him, the earth turns towards dawn.

# NINETEEN

When the doorbell goes, Monday morning, Teri Platini is in the orangery, FaceTiming with Brittany Moore. Teri has turned off her camera, but at least she can see her friend.

'You think that's him, babe?' Brittany asks.

'I don't know. It could be the brother again.'

'This is messed up. Don't you dare open that door.'

'It's not my house.'

'Of course it's your house. You've been living there long enough.'

'Cohabiting,' Teri says. She climbs off the sofa, wincing, and limps from the orangery to the hall.

'Cohabiting?' Brittany asks, screwing up her face. 'What the hell is *that* shit?'

'It means it's Angus's house, not mine. Legally, I have no right to stay.'

From the entrance hall, Teri steps into Thornecroft's formal dining room and peeks through the mullioned windows. On the driveway, parked next to Angus's tarp-covered Morgan, she sees a police car. 'It's not him,' she whispers. 'I've got to go.'

'So who the f—'

Teri cuts the call dead. Then she steps out of the dining

room and into the downstairs cloakroom. In front of the mirror she examines her face. Her make-up conceals some of the damage, but there's no escaping the swollen eye or split lip.

The doorbell rings a second time. Quickly, Teri zips her hoodie, hiding the bruising around her throat. From her pocket she removes sunglasses and slips them on. Then she goes to the front door and opens it.

Two police officers, male and female, are standing on the driveway below the covered porch.

'Morning,' the female officer says. Her eyes sweep over Teri, then past her into the house. 'PC Hopkins – and this is PC Kenner. Hope we didn't disturb you. Looking for Angus Roth. Is he home?'

'Not at the moment,' Teri says, standing a little straighter. 'Sorry, can I help? I'm his girl . . . his partner.'

'Mr Roth owns a blue Lexus RC F?'

She nods.

The woman checks her notebook and reads out the registration.

'That's the one.'

'We had a call. You know Jack-O'-Lantern Woods, west of Crompton? Car's partially blocking one of the Forestry Commission access roads.'

'Sorry,' Teri says.

'They didn't report it Friday, thinking the owner would move it over the weekend. But now it's Monday, and they need it shifted. If Mr Roth isn't home, can I take a contact number for him?'

'I can move the car, no problem,' Teri says. 'I'm so sorry it's in the way.'

The police officer's eyes travel over her once again. 'You know where it's parked?'

'Uh-huh,' Teri says. 'Angus likes to run. Often, he'll leave it there and run all the way home.'

She lies partly because she's frightened of what Angus might do to her if she doesn't – and partly because she's afraid of the police officer. The woman seems to have her shit together in a uniquely frightening way. Teri feels like she's being inspected and assessed. She bites her lip, forgetting it's swollen – and flinches.

'OK, good,' the officer says. 'I'll just take Mr Roth's number for the record, since we're here.'

Blushing, Teri recites it.

'And what's your name?'

'Teri. Teri Platini.'

'You live here, Teri?'

'Yes.'

'Your mouth looks a bit sore,' the woman says. 'And that's a nasty scratch on your neck.'

Teri's hand flies up. Earlier, doing her make-up, she hadn't noticed a scratch, but now she feels it beneath her fingers, and the tiny bobbles of crusted blood along its length. 'Sorry,' she says, and winces. It must be the millionth time she's apologized. 'Basketball injury.'

'Ouch. Where do you play?'

'I don't, really. Just practice.'

The officer nods. 'Is everything OK at home, Teri, if you don't mind me asking? Anything you want to talk to us about?'

'Everything's fine.'

PC Hopkins glances at her colleague. Then she digs a card from a pocket and hands it over. 'My details. You can get in touch any time. About anything you like. In the meantime, I'd be grateful if you could move that car as a priority, so we can stop getting calls about it.'

Teri takes the card, feeling her cheeks grow hot again. She thanks the officers and quickly closes the door.

# TWENTY

Joseph's first task, Monday morning, is to call his boss at the architectural firm in Shipley and tell her he'll be working from home. Then he cancels all his meetings for the day.

Immediately afterwards he goes into Max's room. The boy is lying beneath his duvet, his breathing slow and rhythmic. Asleep, he looks far younger than his eighteen years. Seeing him like this, it's difficult to imagine him capable of a bad thought, let alone a bad deed.

Clutched in Max's hand is a purple scrunchie that once belonged to Claire. It wasn't in the bereavement box Joseph found yesterday. Somewhere, the boy must have a second stash of his mother's things.

Five years since her passing, it's obvious how intensely he still misses her. Does that change anything, Joseph wonders? Even slightly? Is Max's ongoing heartache in some ways a spark of hope? Does the humanity it represents offer proof, however slight, that not *everything* is lost?

Tentatively, he touches his son's shoulder – needing, suddenly, to feel the life flowing through him, the swell of his lungs as he breathes.

Joseph remains that way for some time, connected to Max

physically if not by other means. Inevitably, his thoughts return to Drew, lying dead in his mother's living room, and the unconscionable theft of her life.

Could he ever contemplate these lungs falling still? This heart failing to beat? To lose a wife, he's learned, is to experience agony so devastating it cleaves a person in two. But to lose a son, or a daughter: how could anyone possibly survive that?

Downstairs, the house is silent. Joseph makes coffee and carries it to the breakfast bar. There he sits and drinks. He doesn't have long to decide his course. He's conscious that these quiet minutes of contemplation might also be his last moments of liberty.

The options he considered last night are the only ones left on the table: either he hands in his son or himself. Each prospect is uniquely terrifying.

He can't break his promise to Claire – that he'll protect Max from harm and ensure he reaches his potential, because that vow is sacrosanct. But if he does persuade everyone that he committed these acts he'll be in prison, unable to monitor Max's behaviour, unable to mentor him, unable to intervene should something like this threaten to happen again.

Compounding his indecision is his inability, even now, to accept that his son is capable of such barbarity.

Joseph looks around the kitchen. This house, in truth, has never felt like the home he once built with Claire – perhaps because back then home had been a place of safety, inviolable – but he'd hoped, for Max's sake, that he'd created something close. Now, examining his surroundings more critically, he realizes that virtually nothing from his old kitchen has made it into this one.

The stools at the breakfast bar are new, as is the sofa near the bifold doors, the coffee table in front of it, the table and chairs beneath the pendant lights. There's different crockery in the cupboards, different cutlery in the drawers. Different art hangs on the walls, and different vases and pots crowd the sills. Even the smaller, everyday items are different: the coasters, the placemats, the chopping boards, the kettle, the toaster, the loaded fruit bowl.

Wandering through the house, Joseph sees that it's the same in the living room, the dining room and the hall: everything is new – a celebration of the now; a denial of the past. The framed photographs on the mantelpiece and side tables, and the collection of monochrome images that marches up the stairs, are all of him and Erin, him and Max, Erin and Tilly, Max and Tilly – or all four of them together.

Why are there no pictures of Claire? Did he put them away because looking at them was too hard? He doesn't even know where they are.

Overwhelmed by an urge to escape, he grabs his keys and locks the front door behind him. Across the street he sees Ralph Erikson's house – and the doorbell cam pointed this way.

Joseph climbs into his car and drives without a destination in mind. Twenty minutes later he finds himself on Hocombe Hill for the second time in twenty-four hours. When he rolls past Thornecroft, Angus Roth's mock Tudor mansion, he sees a police patrol car in the driveway. Two police officers are talking to a scared-looking woman on the covered porch.

*They're coming for you. They know something's happened.*

With the aircon on full-blast, Joseph accelerates away. He knows where he's going, now. Ten minutes later, he pulls up a short distance from Crompton's police station.

# TWENTY-ONE

It's a two-storey building clad in grey concrete, designed by someone whose intention appears to have been the suffocation of all hope from those compelled to enter.

Staring at it, Joseph knows the last sand in his timer is running out. The police are already at Angus Roth's house. Pretty soon, Enoch Cullen will report his daughter missing. Meanwhile, Max's mental health seems like it's falling apart.

His phone buzzes against his leg. When he checks the screen, he sees a message from Erin:

Afternoon meeting cancelled. Catching an early train.
Can you please grab something for dinner?

Joseph sends a reply. Then he switches off the ignition and closes his eyes. Erin will be back in a few hours. Tilly is already home. He has a duty to protect them from not just physical harm, but the fallout from what's already happened. He has a duty to ensure that Drew's death is the last – and that no more families suffer. But he also has a duty to Claire. And, of course, to Max. Which one of those ranks highest? Truthfully, painfully, he can't answer.

*It was a kindness, what I did.*

Joseph's jaw claps shut so hard he catches his cheek in his teeth. He tastes blood, makes a decision. And then the passenger door opens and Max slides in next to him.

'Dad,' the boy says.

He looks ill, desperately so, his eyes red and rheumy and his skin grey, as if life is draining from him by the second and he's only a few hours from death. Turning his attention to the police station, Max hunches forward in his seat. 'Miserable-looking place, don't you think?'

Joseph stares through the windscreen, his heart knocking against his ribs. A woman walks past, pushing a pram. An older man passes in the opposite direction, carrying shopping. Twenty yards away, a courier van bumps two wheels on to the pavement and the driver hops out.

This is how a hostage must feel, looking at the street from inside a bank, an embassy, or some other everyday place where horror has descended without warning. Suddenly, a single sheet of glass separates normality from nightmare. On one side life continues. On the other life is paused, suspended.

Max says, 'I woke up and you weren't there.'

'I needed to get out of the house for a while.'

'To Hocombe Hill?'

'Among other places.' Joseph purses his lips. 'How did you know that? How did you find me?'

'I was tracking you on the Life360 app. I figured you might end up in Crompton so that's where I headed. I wasn't expecting you to come here. Why did you?'

'I don't know.'

Max's shoulder twitches. He rubs at it, tries to hold himself still. 'You know what I think? I think you were about to walk in there and confess to something you haven't done. And that scares the shit out of me, Dad, because I'd have had to go in there straight after you and tell them you were lying.'

Max pauses, turns his head. Softly, he adds, 'Unless I've got that wrong. And you came here to tell them about me.'

Joseph avoids his son's gaze. This no longer feels like a hostage situation. The car has become an ocean submersible, miles below the surface, subjected to pressures beyond its tolerance. Any moment, cracks will filigree the windscreen. A millisecond later, the car will squish flat, liquidizing them both. Perhaps that will be a mercy.

*A kindness.*

'Is that what you were about to do?' the boy asks. 'I deserve to know, don't you think?'

Joseph watches as a man a few years younger than himself passes the car, arm in arm with a woman a few years younger than Claire would have been had she lived. His teeth squeal in his mouth. 'Of course not,' he whispers.

'Is that what you want to do?'

'It couldn't be further from what I want.'

'What *do* you want, Dad?'

'Max,' Joseph says, his voice cracking. 'I want you to survive this. I want . . .' He pauses long enough to wrest back control of his emotions. 'I want to make sure this isn't the end for you. I want to keep my promises to your mum. I want you to have a good life.'

He closes his mouth, inspects the windscreen for cracks, wonders if the car is about to implode.

Max turns in his seat until he's facing his father directly. 'Even if that means hiding the truth about Drew?'

Here it is, then. The decision that will damn him.

'Even if it means that.'

Now that he's said it, Joseph knows there's no going back. He searches his son's face, appealing to the boy he loves. 'But Max, this has to stop. It must.'

'It will. It already has.'

'No matter what happens from this point, however bad things get, you never, ever do anything like this again.'

'I won't,' Max says, and it's almost a wail of anguish.

'Promise me.'

'Dad, I swear it.'

'How did Drew die? Tell me what happened.'

Max seems to shrivel in his seat – as if it's not just life that's leaving him but actual, physical matter. 'You don't need to hear that.'

'But I should hear it. Because I'm part of it. And because I'll have to live with that girl's death, and the consequences for all those who loved her, as much as you will.'

'Dad,' he says. 'There's so much I'd like to say to you that I can't. So much I'd like to go back and change. There's no good option in front of me any more. No safe route through. I can't—'

He chokes, seems to dry-heave. 'I don't even know how to protect you. As for what happens tomorrow, next week, next month . . . It's all so . . . I don't want to talk about Drew. I'm not *going* to talk about her. Certainly not to you. I wanted to shield you from this. If Erin hadn't sent you downstairs, Friday night, maybe you wouldn't be looking at me the way you're looking at me now – like I'm some kind of sick freak. This is an awful situation, I realize that – beyond awful. I'll spend the rest of my life making up for it. And that still won't be enough.'

Joseph is silent for a while. He doesn't like the way Max's voice changed, just then, when he mentioned Erin. As if the boy has somehow decided this is her fault, just because she asked Joseph to investigate what she thought might be a burglar.

His eyes drift towards the police station. He wonders if they've set up an incident room in there, or whether that kind of thing happens at the regional headquarters. Reaching out, he squeezes Max's shoulder. 'I don't think you're a sick freak,' he says. 'I'd never think that. I do think you might need help with some of this stuff, but we can figure that out together. We can.'

Max puts his hands on the dash, braces himself. 'I can't even . . . I do love you, Dad,' he says, and Joseph is surprised by the depth of emotion in his son's voice. 'You give yourself such a hard time – especially about Mum. I wish you wouldn't.'

Joseph's throat is so tight it's hard to speak. 'I love you, too,' he says. 'Always will.'

'The other night . . . I lied. I said I was glad Mum wasn't around to see this. But I wish, more than anything, she was here.'

'I know you do.'

'Fucking hell,' the boy moans. 'It feels like only yesterday since she died. It never gets easier.'

Joseph closes his eyes, a brief respite. 'Let's walk back to the high street, grab an early lunch. Then we can pick out some flowers and go and see her.'

# TWENTY-TWO

From the passenger seat of Brittany Moore's Audi TT, Teri Platini stares at her best friend's hands and wonders if she should have taken an Uber instead of asking for a lift.

Brittany's nails are so outlandishly long that she can't curl her fingers around the steering wheel. Instead, she exerts pressure with her palms, fingers splayed. Sharp turns require a move like a mime artist impersonating a window cleaner. Teri wonders how her friend buttoned her blouse this morning, or applied her false lashes.

'I know, hon, believe,' Brittany says, as if reading Teri's thoughts. 'Try flossing with these claws – or wiping your butt. Still, since I grew 'em out, there's a whole bunch of bedroom stuff Leon just doesn't ask for any more.'

'I guess that's a win,' Teri replies. Her own nails, perfectly manicured, are the Angus Roth regulation length. Angus, of course, never asks for anything in the bedroom. He knows what he likes – and takes it when he pleases.

Overhead, the tree canopy blocks out the early afternoon sun. Brittany hunches forward and wrinkles her spray-tanned nose. 'Did we not come this way already, babe?'

Teri glances at her Google Maps app, shakes her head. 'We've checked everywhere west of the lake. But this bit's new.'

The car hits a rut. The steering wheel spins like a roulette wheel beneath Brittany's hands. 'Freakin' *nature*!' she shrieks. 'Why can't they properly *pave* this shit?'

Ahead, a narrow dirt track peels off to the left. Teri checks it as they pass. Just where it kinks out of sight into the trees, she sees a glint of blue paintwork. 'Stop!'

Brittany hisses, hits the brakes. The car shudders to a halt. 'Tell me I didn't kill one of them grey stripey things.'

'Sorry, it's OK. You didn't. Can you back up?'

Brittany curls her fingers around the gearstick, trying to select reverse – and Teri suddenly understands why Leon's stopped asking for certain favours in the bedroom. Finally, the car lurches backwards. A couple of metres later, the turn-off reappears. Brittany shifts into first and palm-spins the wheel. The Audi noses around and bumps along the track. When they reach the bend, Angus's Lexus RC F reveals itself. Even though it's parked with two wheels in a clearing, Teri can see why the Forestry Commission have had a hard time passing.

'OK, you can drop me here,' she says.

Brittany squints through the window at the trees. 'Are you sure? I've got to say – this place has kind of a horror movie vibe. I mean, Jack-O'-Lantern Woods? Tell me which lunatic dreamed up *that* creepy shit.'

'I'll be fine.'

'You meet any freaks, you scratch their eyes out. Hear me, babe?'

Teri nods. A minute later, she's alone.

Inside her hoodie are the spare keys from Angus's desk. The Lexus's doors will open automatically if the keys are nearby – and then she won't know if they'd been locked. Knowledge is power and power is security – and security is something Teri has started to value very highly indeed. Pulling out the keys, she drops them beside a bracken patch.

She knows what Brittany means about these woods. They're giving her the heebie-jeebies, too. On either side of the track, the trees grow so close that it's hard to see more than twenty feet. Fifty killers in Ghostface masks could be hiding within spitting distance. Worse – and this thought turns Teri's insides to water – they might even hide the Roth twins.

Steadily, she closes on the Lexus. Four days, now, since she's seen or heard from Angus. Four days since she presented him with that excruciating boudoir image. And four days since she sneaked a look at his phone and saw his exchange with Barbie Girl.

Teri reaches the car and peers through the glass. The front seats are empty, as are the two rear ones. Glancing around, she sees no one watching from the undergrowth.

The driver's door is unlocked. Teri swings it open and ducks in her head. The interior is clean and uncluttered – no scrunched-up petrol receipts and festering gym gear like her Tesla. She checks the door pocket, the centre console. All she discovers is a locking nut in a grip-seal bag. There's nothing of interest under the front seats or behind them. Stuck to the passenger seat headrest is a long blonde hair. Teri finds another in the floor well.

*Barbie Girl*, she thinks. She'd told Gabriel Roth that the thumbnail WhatsApp photo was too small to reveal detail, but in truth she'd expanded it and stared at her rival for a full minute. And contrary to her claim that she hadn't seen the girl's mobile number, she'd committed it to memory. What Teri doesn't yet understand – and still hasn't worked through – is whether Barbie Girl represents an opportunity. Despite her treatment by Angus, she's grown used to her lifestyle at Thornecroft. She doesn't intend to give it up.

Retrieving the keys from where she left them, Teri climbs

inside the Lexus and starts the engine. Then, putting on her sunglasses, she reverses on to the main track.

No way Angus drove into these woods and abandoned his car willingly. Something bad has happened. Or perhaps something good. Just like Gabriel, she needs to establish the truth. Fortunately, she has the Lexus, and he does not. And she knows what Barbie Girl looks like, and how to make contact.

On the way back to Thornecroft, Teri places her palms flat on the wheel and examines her nails, comparing them to Brittany's four-inch claws: *Since I grew 'em out, there's a whole bunch of bedroom stuff Leon just doesn't ask for.*

If an image from a boudoir shoot hangs above Brittany's bed, undoubtedly it'll be of Leon, chained and gagged. For the first time in what feels like months, Teri permits herself a smile.

# TWENTY-THREE

They eat at Meghan's, a place on Crompton's high street that
serves a Mediterranean-inspired menu. Max orders a steak.
Joseph orders a falafel and cauliflower shakshouka, his first
full meal in days, and demolishes it in under a minute. Calling back the waiter, he requests hummus and flatbread,
halloumi fries and a pot of scotch bonnet mayo.

It feels worse than crass to be filling his stomach while
Drew lies dead in his mother's living room, but once he's
started eating, he can't stop. Only when he's paying the
bill does he realize he avoided anything on the menu containing meat.

A few doors down at Hannah's Flowers, they pick out
some blooms. Greenacre cemetery is a twenty-minute drive
from Crompton. Claire's grave lies near the summit of a
grass rise.

There's no need for words. Joseph hands Max the flowers,
and together they approach. As always, he can't look at
Claire's headstone directly. He knows the shape because
he chose it from the brochure, and he knows the words
inscribed on it because he wrote them himself, but he hasn't
laid eyes on the finished piece. Nor will he.

Strangely, although he can't look, he can touch, perhaps

because he knows the headstone extends into the earth, forming a conduit of sorts between him and his late wife.

The granite is cool beneath his fingers. Beside him, Max kneels and arranges the blooms. Then he stands beside his father and bows his head. For a minute or more they're both silent.

Finally, the boy says, 'You and Erin. Things have been difficult recently. Haven't they?'

Joseph frowns, dropping his hand from Claire's headstone.

'When you first met her,' Max continues, 'it was like she brought you back to life. But now, this last year . . . Do you still love her, Dad?'

'Of course I do.'

'Are you sure? Because you don't act like you do.'

'I love her as much as I always did.'

For two years following Claire's death, Joseph had existed in a permanent state of torture. Healing Max from the trauma of losing his mother had been his only concern. Not that he'd ever been much good at it.

And then he'd met Erin.

After such a crippling bereavement, after so long without emotional or physical intimacy – it *had* felt like a rebirth. Their love was all the more fierce because of its genesis in grief, and the losses they'd both suffered.

But in Joseph's full-tilt run towards what had seemed at the time like salvation, he'd horribly neglected Max, leaving the boy to flounder. He'd hoped things would improve after the marriage, with everyone living in the same house, but by then the distance between them had seemed insurmountable.

This last year, with university fast approaching, he's done what he can to repair the damage. It's all been too little too late – and by holding Erin at arm's length throughout, he's also caused terrible damage to that relationship.

Max puts his hand on his father's shoulder. 'I'm not trying

to make you feel bad. It's just . . . if things keep going the way they are, you're going to lose her. The only reason I'm telling you is because I don't want you to end up alone.'

Joseph lifts his head, less fearful of what Max *is* telling him than what he isn't. 'Why would I be alone? I've got you.'

'I just want you to think about the future and how that looks. Because if Erin is part of it, you need to commit to her, Dad. If she isn't, you really need to decide now while you still can, while there's still time to start afresh.'

He pauses, then adds, 'Maybe, when I go to university, you and her could go away for a while, take a long holiday somewhere. Escape all this and give yourselves a chance to figure everything out.'

'Listen,' Joseph says, after a moment to collect his thoughts. 'I appreciate the advice, Max. I appreciate that you're thinking about this stuff – about me and Erin, and about the future – but let's put it into perspective. You just killed two fucking people, OK? Which means there's quite a lot to deal with right now. I think we should focus on that. And worry about the marriage guidance stuff later.'

Max recoils, shoving his hands into his pockets. He stares at his father, his cheeks filling with blood. 'OK,' he mutters.

'Is it? I mean, stupid question, but are you handling this? Do you need to talk?'

'I'm fine.'

Joseph isn't convinced, but this doesn't feel like the right moment to push it. He shouldn't have let emotion overcome him, or have spoken to his son so harshly. Squeezing Claire's headstone in goodbye, he puts an arm around Max and leads him back to the car.

'Dad?'

'Uh-huh?'

'We need to decide what we're doing about Drew.'

'I'm working on that.'

'We can't leave her where she is.'

'I know.'

'Something else I've been thinking about,' he says. He takes a deep breath. 'I think I should defer. Go to St Andrews next year. It won't make much difference, not really. And if I'm at home I can make sure that—'

'No. There's no reason for you to be here.'

'But, Dad—'

'I said no. You've worked too hard. And it wouldn't achieve anything, anyway. Better for us to carry on exactly as planned.'

Traffic is light on the way home. When Joseph pulls into the driveway he sees, parked in front of him, a white Mercedes he doesn't recognize.

Max frowns. 'Whose is that?'

'I'm not sure.'

'Is Erin back from London already?'

'Maybe,' Joseph says, remembering the text he received outside the police station.

'Did she say anything about having visitors today?'

He shakes his head. Conscious of how it might look if they remain in the car too long, he opens his door and climbs out. As he walks past the Mercedes, he peers inside. On the centre console and the interior glass are stickers barring occupants from smoking. It might be an Uber, dropping Erin home – but if so, where's the driver? Could it be a police pool car?

Joseph goes to the front door and slides his key into the lock. In the hall, Erin's travel case stands near the stairs beside her discarded heels. 'Hello?'

'In here.'

He opens the living-room door. On the sofa, one foot tucked beneath her, sits his wife. In the armchair opposite sits the dead man.

# TWENTY-FOUR

The room tilts. Joseph freezes in the doorway. If this is a hallucination, it isn't dissipating. The dead man watches him, fingers steepled in his lap. Somehow, his terrible facial injuries have healed. No blood, no broken bone, no shattered teeth.

Joseph blinks, tries to unstick his muscles. Slowly, he turns his gaze towards Erin. Despite her relaxed pose, he sees a noticeable tension in her expression, a tightening of the muscles around her mouth.

'Joe,' she says, uncurling her foot from beneath her. 'I'd like you to meet someone.'

Joseph turns to Max, behind him, and flicks his head towards the stairs. 'Give us a few minutes,' he says, and closes the door before the boy catches sight of their guest.

The dead man stands, extends his hand. There's no grave dirt beneath his nails. No indication that he clawed his way out of the pit Joseph dug last night. There's no stink of putrefaction rolling off him. His palm, when Joseph shakes it, is cool but not cold.

'Joe, this is Gabriel Roth. Gabriel, this is my husband, Joe,' Erin says. 'Gabriel's here about his brother.'

Joseph's ears pop, then roar with equalizing pressure.

He sways on his feet, tries to anchor himself. Not a hallucination, then. Nor some kind of demonic reanimation. But that still doesn't explain Gabriel Roth's presence in his living room. Joseph retrieves his hand, tries to focus.

They have to be twins. There's no other explanation. Standing this close to a duplicate of someone he so recently buried is too hideous to bear. He goes to the sofa, sits beside his wife, runs his tongue around his mouth and tries to work up some moisture. 'Your brother?'

Gabriel's eyes are unsettlingly intense. 'Angus Roth,' he says, enunciating the name as if it's a deity. 'I take it you've met?'

Joseph tries to slow his breathing. He wonders if anyone's noticed the rapid rise and fall of his chest. 'I don't believe so. At least, not that I recall.'

'Gabriel's concerned about his brother's wellbeing,' Erin explains. 'Apparently, nobody's heard from Angus since Thursday. And he hasn't returned any of my team's calls.'

Joseph tries to digest that last comment, but it sticks in his throat like a fishbone. He turns to his wife, confused. 'You know him?'

'Remember that regional fundraiser I took you to last Christmas, at Huntington Manor? Angus was one of the guests. Afterwards, he made a significant donation. We've kept the conversation going since, hoping to develop the partnership.'

'I've been going through Angus's contacts,' Gabriel says. 'Which is where I found your wife's details.'

It's starting to feel like the steel blades of a food processor are spinning inside Joseph's head, pulping his brain to soup. He remembers the fundraiser – a black-tie event Erin had arranged for affluent donors and prospects. She'd rented tuxes for Joseph and Max, had given Tilly and Drew money for new outfits. Joseph doesn't remember meeting the dead man that night, but Erin had introduced him to lots of people.

That all six of them were at the same event surely can't be a coincidence. Which means Joseph needs to re-evaluate everything, including Max's claim that the chain of tragedies since Friday began with a random car accident. He thinks of the damage to the Honda, or lack of it, along with his son's explanation that the killing blow was a kindness intended to end suffering.

He replays, too, what his wife has just revealed. Erin's donor recruitment campaigns, targeting specific high-net-worth individuals, stand little chance of resistance. It's why she's so sought after in the industry. Had Angus Roth lived, no doubt his wallet would shortly have grown much lighter.

With a lurch, Joseph remembers that the man's physical wallet is still in his back pocket – and that Gabriel Roth is within touching distance of learning what happened to his twin. His head pounds as if he's being strangled, as if the blood has nowhere to go. He wants to loosen his collar, gasp for breath.

Across the room Gabriel watches him, unblinking. Finally, he turns his attention to Erin. 'When was the last time you saw each other?'

'We caught up for coffee last week. He said he'd be in touch again soon.'

'You've had no contact since? No emails, texts?'

'I left him a voicemail. So did my PA, I think. But we didn't hear back.'

'How close would you say you've grown to him?'

'Getting closer. Obviously, the charity's keen to encourage his philanthropy. I really hope he's OK. If there's anything I or my team can do to help, we'll be ready and willing the moment you ask.'

When Erin falls silent, Gabriel doesn't acknowledge her

offer. 'Do you know anyone else locally I should be talking to? Anyone who might have fallen through the cracks?'

'Not really. As I said, it's a relatively new partnership.'

'Did he ever mention if he was seeing someone?'

'I think he lives with his partner.'

'I meant someone new. Someone a lot younger.'

Erin frowns, shakes her head.

Gabriel returns his gaze to Joseph. Then, standing, he says, 'Thank you for making the time.'

Erin stands, too. Barefoot, she's a good eight inches shorter than their guest. Joseph is conscious of how vulnerable she looks. He wants to climb off the sofa and put himself between them, but he's worried that Angus Roth's wallet will fall from his pocket and that Gabriel will recognize it. There's something badly off about the man. Something malignant lurking close to the surface.

He glances around the room, mentally locating his various home defence weapons: the screwdriver tucked beneath his sofa cushion; the Stanley knife taped behind one of the radiators; the pewter candlestick bases at either end of the mantelpiece. His other weapons are too far away to be of use.

Gabriel digs into his pocket and removes an identical Montblanc wallet. From it he withdraws a card and hands it to Erin. 'My number,' he says. 'Should Angus get in touch.'

For a moment he looks like he's going to say more. But then something catches his eye. He crosses the room to a cabinet on which stands a collection of framed photographs. He picks one up and examines it: a shot of Erin at the Huntingdon Manor fundraiser, her arms around Tilly and Drew. Tilly's hair is longer, pre-dating her recent pixie cut. Drew's is blonde instead of blue.

'Your daughters?' Gabriel asks.

Erin smiles. 'One is.'

He taps the glass with a nail. 'Got to be this one. You can see the resemblance, clear as day.' He replaces the frame and picks up another. 'Your son?'

Erin's smile grows a fraction tighter. She throws Joseph a subtle eyebrow.

Gabriel glances up. 'He has more of his father's look, wouldn't you say?'

'Probably because I'm his stepmother.'

'That would explain it.'

The man has grown very still. Joseph slides his hand behind him, into the gap between the sofa back and the seat cushion. His fingers brush the screwdriver's resin handle, then curl around it. He doesn't know what's happening here but he knows it isn't good. Even Erin has started to look nervous – and that's not something he sees often, if at all.

After what feels like a minute, but is probably no more than a handful of seconds, Gabriel replaces the photo frame. 'You have a beautiful family,' he tells Erin.

'Thank you.'

'Families are precious.'

'They are.'

'And vulnerable.'

'Vulnerable?'

'More vulnerable than you might think. But we do what we can to keep them safe.'

Erin's smile has reached its tolerance. She folds her arms, unfolds them. Then she moves to the door and opens it, revealing Max.

The boy lurches upright, realizes he's been caught. When he sees their guest, his facial muscles slacken.

'And here he is,' Gabriel says.

Max steps backwards, nearly collides with the bannisters. His brain seems to be performing the same paroxysms as Joseph's a few minutes ago.

'I'll show you out,' Erin says. As she leads Gabriel to the front door, the boy's hands tighten into fists.

Worried that his son is about to do something that will sink them both, Joseph jumps up. Only as he steps into the hall does he realize he's still clutching the screwdriver.

Erin opens the front door. Gabriel walks to his car without looking back.

Once the Mercedes has reversed off the drive, Erin turns towards her stepson, eyes flashing. 'That was inappropriate. Why on earth were you eavesdropping?'

'Because I . . . Who was that?'

'The brother of a work contact.'

'What was he doing here?'

'He's concerned about his brother. Why?'

Max's eyes flare. And in that moment a memory comes to Joseph from last summer, of the fawn that had watched from the undergrowth as he'd killed its mother. The fawn couldn't have comprehended the death sentence Joseph had just served it too, but it had understood well enough that something seismic had happened.

Right now, his son looks similarly stricken.

'Max,' Erin says, her voice softening. 'Is everything OK?'

When she steps towards him, he steps back. When he reaches the stairs, he charges up them to his room.

Erin watches his departure. Then, indicating the kitchen with a flick of her head, she leads Joseph along the hall and shuts the door. At the table near the bifold doors, she makes him sit. 'This feels like déjà vu.'

'What does?

'Putting you in the chair. Demanding you talk.'

'What do you want to know?'

'Joe, come on. I'm not stupid. Things have been weird in this house for days. I know you know what I mean. I thought, maybe, that I'd been imagining it, that when I got back from London everything would be back to normal – or as normal as it's been – but it's all just as strange as it was. We don't keep secrets. At least, we never did. Has something happened, between you and Max? Is he in some kind of trouble?'

'Like what?'

'I was hoping you might tell me. I still don't understand why you felt the need to drive him over to your mother's place in the middle of the night. Nor why you slept in his bed afterwards. Now he's creeping around, listening at doors. He looks scared as hell.'

'He's about to start university, with all the stresses and insecurities that brings. I think we can forgive him a few road bumps in the lead-up.'

Erin takes both his hands, squeezes. 'What about you and me? Are we OK? Even vaguely? Because it certainly doesn't feel like it. We haven't really talked since the barbecue. If there's something you want to say, I'd rather you just took the plunge and came out with it.'

'Like what?'

Erin leans closer, searches his eyes. 'I don't know. But you're jumpy as hell. Worse than Max, even. You've started talking in your sleep, thrashing about.'

'Honestly, Erin, there's nothing.'

She holds his gaze, squeezes his hands harder. And Joseph recalls his conversation with Max at Claire's graveside:

*Do you still love her, Dad?*

*Of course I do.*

*Are you sure? Because you don't act like you do.*

*I love her as much as I always did.*

*I'm not trying to make you feel bad. It's just . . . if things keep going the way they are, you're going to lose her. The only reason I'm telling you is because I don't want you to end up alone.*

At the time, he'd angrily shrugged Max off. The boy's

analysis had been clinical – sharp enough to cut. Now, though, Joseph sees that his anger had blinded him to something important: not merely the truth of his son's words, but the love, empathy and understanding wrapped up in them. They were, indisputably, the thoughts not of a monster but of the boy he raised with Claire. Is there a clue in that? A source of hope?

He forces himself to study Erin's face, seeing the laughter lines and worry lines that have begun to appear around her eyes and mouth, the subtle signs of aging.

One of the intimacies of love rarely described is the slow reveal of a partner's mortality, evidenced in degradations of flesh. Taking that journey together, Joseph knows, is a painful privilege – but it's filled with as much beauty as pain. Because the essence of a person never diminishes until it leaves, even if mind and body do. Time and experience leave scars that tell stories as poignant as those left by childbirth.

The pain of Claire's passing nearly broke him; but he'd accompany her on that journey again, a thousand times, and die another thousand at the end.

And now, here, he has the same painful privilege. His love for Erin is different to his love for Claire – maybe it's only possible to love one person a certain way – but this love is just as real, just as strong. In some ways, tempered by the loss in which it was forged, it's even stronger.

The realization forces him to confront another truth: just as he has to protect his son from the situation unfolding around them, he has to protect his wife. What's almost too unbearable to contemplate is the knowledge that he might not manage to do both.

He watches the delicate movement of Erin's throat as she swallows. The gentle pulse of blood in her neck. If she stares into his eyes much longer, she'll doubtless read the truth in them. Fortunately, his wife's instinct for when to press and when to relent seems as reliable as ever. Releasing his hands, she stands. 'That guy creeped me out.'

'Me too.'

'The way he was looking at those photographs, staring at Tilly and Drew.'

'And Max,' Joseph says. 'What's his brother like?'

'Kind of intense. But nothing like that. Did you pick something up for dinner?'

'Ah, shit. Sorry.'

'When Tilly gets home, how about I phone in an order to Mr Wu's? I've a hankering for some chicken chow mein and crispy chilli beef.'

'Deal,' Joseph says, although he can't think of anything worse. Since his huge lunch at Meghan's, he's started to feel nauseous again – and his intensified awareness of what's at stake has hardly reawakened his appetite.

Erin slaps his shoulder, smiles. 'I've got one bit of good news. The estate agent called while you were out. We finally got a viewing on your mother's place.'

Joseph blinks. 'When?'

Erin looks at her watch. 'Actually,' she says, 'right about now.'

# TWENTY-FIVE

Thirty seconds later, Joseph is in the car. He reverses off the driveway so fast that when the car bounces into the street, the front bumper sparks against the tarmac. Hauling the wheel around, he finds first gear. He floors the accelerator, smoking his tyres. On the passenger seat, his phone lights up. Over the car's speakers he hears its ringer. The dashboard screen shows Erin's name.

Joseph reaches the end of the street, hits the brakes, checks for traffic, sees none. He guns the engine again, screeching on to Hiltingbury Lane and changing up through the gears.

The phone goes dark. A moment later, it relights – Max this time. Joseph jabs at the dashboard screen, trying to turn it off. He must hit the wrong button because immediately his son's voice issues through the speakers.

'Dad, what's happening? I overheard some of it but not everything. That guy was his *brother*? Why was he at our house?'

Ahead, a learner driver is pootling along at half the speed limit. Joseph overtakes, swerving back into his lane just in time to avoid a lorry coming the other way. Its air horn blasts. Joseph swears. He grips the wheel with one hand, wipes sweat from his forehead with the other.

'Dad? Talk to me. Why'd you run out like that?'

'Get off the phone, Max.'

'Tell me what's going on.'

He grinds his teeth, realizes how hard he's breathing. 'The bungalow,' he says. 'I just heard there's a viewing.'

'When?'

'Like, right now.'

'But Drew—'

'I know.'

Max groans. 'I *told* you we had to move her! We should have done it last night. What's going to happen when they—'

Joseph punches the screen, disconnects the call. He has to clear his head of distractions, focus on what's important. That means getting to Saddle Bank as fast as he possibly can.

He shrieks to a halt behind two cars stationary at a set of lights, fingers drumming the wheel.

Since Friday night, he's tried to anticipate every possible gotcha, every tiny mistake that would see him lose his boy. And now, three days later, it looks like his downfall might come thanks to a goddamned fucking estate agent.

The lights change. The cars ahead of him begin to move. When Joseph reaches the junction, he rips the wheel left, taking the A road towards Saddle Bank. He accelerates hard towards the tail of traffic in front of him. Veering into the opposite lane again, he overtakes three vehicles in a row.

He's doing twice the speed limit, now. If he hits something, he's dead. If a tyre blows out, he's dead, too. There was a time, not too distant, when he might have welcomed the oblivion, but he won't abandon his boy, regardless of what his boy has done.

Hunchedforwardinhisseat, Josephgripsthewheelwithtwo hands, ready to react should a vehicle pull out in front of him.

His phone lights up again. At this speed, he daren't even

look. Spotting the turning for his mother's road, he stands on the brakes. Taking the corner, he almost loses the rear.

Ahead, the road curves in a long crescent, revealing itself bit by bit. Any moment he expects to spot a line of police cars, an ambulance, maybe even a few news crews.

Finally, he sees his mother's bungalow. Parked on her driveway is a silver Skoda he doesn't recognize. Joseph skids to a stop, clambers out of his car and sprints past the Skoda to the front entrance. He plunges his key into the lock, bursts into the hall and slams the door behind him. There he pauses, hands braced against his thighs, sweat dripping from his nose, heartbeat thumping in his ears.

The house is quiet. Mortuary still.

Before Joseph can even catch his breath, a shadow falls over him. He straightens, hears the clatter of the door knocker behind him and side-steps into the living room.

His mother's armchair remains by the wall where he last saw it, along with her glass coffee table. Spread across the carpet is the same heavy-duty plastic sheet. Drew, lying upon it, is wearing the same tartan miniskirt, the same high-necked halter cut to the midriff. Overnight, the pool of blood has dried, its surface dull.

Joseph sinks to his knees. Grabbing the plastic sheet's leading edge, he lifts it up. Behind him he hears the machine-gun rattle of the knocker, harder now.

He folds the sheet over Drew and tucks it tight around her body. Outside, he hears another vehicle pull up. From the sound of it, right behind the Skoda. A car door opens.

'I'm sorry,' Joseph says, and doesn't know if he's talking to Drew, to Max or to Erin. Gripping the bottom of the folded sheet, he heaves upwards and rolls Drew on to her front, encasing her in more plastic. He hears a groan of expelled breath and leaps backwards, half expecting her to start clawing herself free. Then he remembers the dead man's identical protest last night.

Footsteps, outside. Someone passes the front window. Joseph glances through the net curtains a fraction too late to see. Multiple voices, now, outside the front door.

He rolls Drew over a second time, a third. Gathering the plastic below her feet, he crimps it like a Christmas cracker and drags her across the room.

Behind him, from the hall, a key snicks into the lock. As he pulls Drew into the kitchen, the front door squeals open. With one hand he opens the garage's connecting door.

There's the Honda, parked just where he left it. Joseph tows Drew across the concrete. He knocks over a rake, sends a glass demijohn rolling, finally gets Drew into position behind the car. Dropping the bunched plastic, he searches his pockets for the keys. Did he even bring them? He can't remember.

Voices in the front hall. Keys in Joseph's right hand. He unlocks the boot, yanks up the lid.

Pulling the dead man from the car was straightforward. Lifting Drew into it won't be nearly as easy. Dead bodies are dead weight, difficult to manoeuvre – but the adrenalin in Joseph's bloodstream thinks otherwise.

Wrapping his arms around Drew's plastic-wrapped torso, squeezing her into a bear hug, he powers out of his crouch. A muscle screams in his shoulder. Beneath his right buttock, something pops.

Drew tumbles into the boot. Joseph collapses to the floor. The pain comes instantly – maybe a torn hamstring. He drags himself up regardless, putting all his weight on his left leg. He slams the boot, locks it, limps around the car, trips over the rake, goes down on one knee, hears it crack against the concrete.

Sparks erupt behind his eyes. He staggers up a second

time, so crippled by agony he can hardly believe he's still moving. Crashing across the garage, right leg dragging behind him, his momentum carries him into the kitchen, where he falls against the worktop. He braces his arms, pivots on his good leg and smiles through his teeth at his audience.

# TWENTY-SIX

Three people are standing in the living room: a woman in her twenties and an older couple. The younger woman is wearing a trouser suit and big hoop earrings. Joseph remembers her name is Miah. She's holding an iPad, a set of house keys and a few sheets of stapled paper. The couple, in their seventies, are dressed in golfing attire.

Nobody speaks. Everyone looks uncomfortable.

Joseph's hamstring hurts only marginally less than his kneecap. If he opens his mouth to say something, he can't guarantee he won't scream. If he clenches his teeth any harder, he'll likely spray the kitchen with enamel.

Miah stares, wrinkles her nose. 'Hi,' she says. 'It's Mr Carver, isn't it?'

A bead of sweat rolls down Joseph's nose and drips off the tip. He wheezes for breath, tries to stop his body from contorting in agony.

'I think my colleague spoke to your wife about a viewing? This is Roger and Mary Boyd. They're looking to downsize.'

'Hello,' Joseph hisses.

The Boyds recoil a little.

'I'm sorry,' Miah tells the couple. 'I thought we'd be alone.

Still, it's a good opportunity to ask the vendor any questions you may have.'

Mary Boyd is standing on the very patch of carpet where Drew was lying not a minute ago. Briefly, she glances at her husband. Then she says, 'Have you ever had any problems with Japanese knotweed?'

Joseph doesn't know how he ends up outside. Nor can he recall any of the nonsense he spouted inside the bungalow. He limps down the drive, conscious of the unseen eyes that might be watching behind lace curtains across the street. Only once he's back in his own car with the door closed does he allow himself a shriek of pain. He sounds like a camp kettle reaching its boil.

He cannot believe what just happened, nor how narrowly he averted disaster. The knowledge that right now the estate agent is showing a couple around the very property where Drew's body is hidden is almost too appalling to contemplate.

Did he even lock the boot? No prospective buyer with a shred of sanity would expect to look inside a vendor's car, but during his time in the property market, Joseph's met plenty of oddballs – although perhaps none odd enough to use their mother's garage as a makeshift mortuary.

Cringing, he starts the car and tentatively touches the accelerator pedal. The lance of pain is bad but not incapacitating. Maybe he hasn't torn his hamstring, after all. Maybe it's just a muscle sprain.

Putting the car in gear, Joseph pulls away from the kerb. He doesn't want to sit outside the bungalow, but he can't leave until he's made sure his visitors have gone. If the unthinkable happens and his secret is revealed, he wants to know about it even if he's powerless to intervene.

A few doors down, he turns around and pulls up behind

a parked van. If he leans across the passenger seat he can monitor the bungalow, the Skoda and the estate agent's car behind it.

Ten minutes later, Mary Boyd emerges and starts nosing about in the shrubbery. She doesn't look like she just discovered a dead girl wrapped in plastic. Her husband appears on the front step, followed by the estate agent. The three have a short conversation. Then they get into their cars and drive off. Joseph waits a while longer before twisting his keys in the ignition.

His brain is so fried by the close call that he doesn't notice the white Mercedes parked across the street.

# TWENTY-SEVEN

Late afternoon, Teri Platini arrives back at Thornecroft. She makes an early dinner of salad and hard-boiled eggs, opens a bottle of Chablis and pours herself a small glass. Rarely does she drink alcohol during the day, but she hopes the wine will take the edge off her nerves.

She eats in Thornecroft's formal dining room, taking Angus's seat at the head of the table. From there she looks through the window at his Lexus. Four days, now, since he disappeared. Far too early to assume he isn't coming back, but long enough for it to be a possibility. She needs to plan, covertly, for the latter, while avoiding any repercussions should he reappear.

Amazing, really, that she's even worked up the courage to think like this. Ironically, Gabriel Roth's toxic little speech, Sunday morning, was the catalyst.

*Angus likes to dominate. He also likes to humiliate. And the women he selects – women like you, Teri – they're so infatuated they let it happen. Then, once he's broken them down completely and they've lost their self-respect, he moves on to someone new.*

Hard to admit, but Gabriel had been right. She *had* offered Angus everything; she *had* lost her self-respect. Over the last six months she's allowed him to dominate her completely. She'd even accepted his infidelity.

Fortunately, whatever dark magic he'd weaved to imprison her at Thornecroft is weakening with each passing hour. Four days ago, she'd been living like a medieval concubine, the willing inmate of a luxury open prison. Why had she ever tolerated it?

*You'll struggle to put him behind you, Teri. I know because I've seen it happen. After you leave this house, you'll go into mourning for what you lost.*

That's where Gabriel's analysis had failed. Because she's already putting Angus behind her; and should his disappearance endure, she doesn't intend to leave this house at all.

Remaining at Thornecroft won't be easy. It'll take courage, imagination – and calculated risk. Strangely, though, in the twenty-four hours since Gabriel's visit, her hunger for reparation has grown even stronger than her fear.

Her gaze still on the Lexus, Teri thinks about the hairs she found inside: one on the passenger seat headrest and another in the footwell.

Do they help her cause or hinder it? Assuming, for a moment, that something fatal *has* befallen Angus, is it better for her that his disappearance remains unexplained? Or are indications of foul play beneficial?

Teri places the police officer's card from yesterday beside her plate. PC Hopkins had urged her to call anytime. Clearly, she'd suspected domestic abuse. With Angus still missing, does Hopkins remain an ally, or is she now a potential threat?

Finishing her lunch, Teri climbs the stairs to the master bedroom, her body aching with the effort. The huge photo canvas she gave Angus is leaning against one wall. Staring at it, she feels revolted and ashamed.

In her walk-in wardrobe, she rifles through her drawers until she finds the lingerie set she wore for the shoot. Picking up the canvas, she limps back down the stairs.

Outside, she smashes the frame's wooden batons. Then she bunches up the canvas and throws it on to Angus's brick-built barbecue, along with the lingerie set. Squirting everything with lighter fluid, she tosses a lit match on top.

Teri stands there and watches it all burn. The taller the flames reach, the better she feels. Pulling out her phone, she calls Brittany Moore.

'Hey, hon,' her best friend says. 'What's up?'

'Are you still in touch with that solicitor friend of yours?'

'The dodgy one?'

Teri grimaces, but the chances of anyone monitoring this conversation are low. 'The one you told me about.'

'I'm happy to hook you up, babe, but if you're thinking about dating him, I've got to say he's kind of gross.'

'I'm not after a date.'

'So what do you – ohhhhhhhh,' Brittany purrs, with obvious relish. 'Gotcha. Yeah, he's great. Totally reliable. What you might call an ethics-free zone. For the right price, he'll do whatever you ask – although it's a pretty hefty price.'

'I'd like a conversation.'

'Leave it with me, hon. You planning some kind of alpha-bitch power move?'

'I just want some advice.'

'Yeah, right,' Brittany says, chortling. 'OK, I'll stop digging. Any word from the Antichrist?'

'Not yet.'

'Halle-fucking-lujah. OK, gotta go. I'm in the nail bar, getting my scratchers polished, but I'll message lawyer guy and pass on your details. You just promise me one thing. You take that arsehole for every penny you can get.'

Teri hangs up. Leaving her bonfire to burn, she goes back inside the house. Her smile lasts until she returns to the dining room. Through the windows she sees Gabriel Roth's Mercedes bounce across the drive and stop in a shower of gravel.

# TWENTY-EIGHT

Joseph drives home cautiously, hoping to balance the karma of his white-knuckle race to the bungalow. Erin, phone in hand, confronts him the moment he comes through the door.

'Joe, seriously,' she says. 'What the hell is going on? We're in the middle of a conversation, then you grab your keys and hare off like a lunatic. And now you're limping.' She steps closer. 'Jesus, you're *bleeding*. Did you crash the car? Are you hurt?'

He glances down at himself. His trousers are torn at the knee, the fabric stiff with drying blood. 'I'm fine,' he says. 'I just tripped.'

'Tripped where? Where did you go?'

'I had a . . . a work thing I forgot about. A document I was meant to send. And then you mentioned the bungalow and I realized I left my laptop there.'

'What was your laptop doing at the bungalow?'

'I took it there yesterday. I thought I'd do an audit of the furniture. Put some of it on eBay, declutter the place a bit.'

He's about to say more when Erin's mobile rings. She

checks the number, accepts the call. 'Hi, Miah. Thanks for calling back. Yes . . . How did it go?' She listens for a while, then says, 'Look, bit of a weird one, but can I just check: did my husband turn up during the viewing?'

Erin stares at Joseph as she listens to the answer. Then she thanks Miah and ends the call.

'You phoned the estate agent?' he asks.

'You weren't picking up. I wanted to know where you'd gone.'

'I'm sorry. I should have . . . I know I haven't . . . I know I've . . .' Joseph begins, and realizes, suddenly, that he's gasping for breath. He's trying to figure out what's wrong when the strength drains from his limbs. His head nods forward, and even as he jerks it back upright his knees sag and he staggers towards the newel post at the base of the stairs. Somehow he prevents himself from falling, but the hall is yawning all over the place.

Erin rushes close, sliding an arm around his waist. Then she yells for Tilly. 'Joe? What is it? What's wrong?'

Tilly thunders down the stairs. When she sees what's happening, she takes half Joseph's weight. Together, they lead him into the living room and lower him on to the sofa. 'Get him some water,' Erin tells her daughter.

'No, get me a beer.'

'Joe, bad idea. Tilly, do as I say.'

'It's just my knee. I must have banged it worse than I thought.'

Erin fetches a footstool and positions it under his heel. Then she grips the tattered edges of his trousers. 'They're ruined, anyway,' she says, ripping a larger hole. 'So let's just – oh, *Jesus*.'

When Joseph sees the damage, he groans. His knee looks like something Max might meet in the woods and decide worthy of his mercy – a swollen mess of blood and tattered skin. Still, he knows the injury wasn't the reason he collapsed. The stress of the last three days, and the last half an hour in particular, appears to have momentarily doused his lights.

Tilly returns with a glass of beer. 'Here you go, Axe Man.'

Joseph cringes when he hears that, a reference to the ridiculous tomahawk he'd hoped they'd both forgotten. He drinks down the beer in two long gulps and hands back the empty glass. 'I'm going to take a shower,' he says. 'Then I'll patch this up.'

'You can't—'

'Yes, I can. I'll clean the knee, put a dressing on it. I just need you to help me up. Where's Max?'

'He went out looking for you.'

'Bloody hell.'

Once Tilly and Erin have hauled him off the sofa, Joseph limps up the stairs to his bedroom. Locking himself in the ensuite, he turns on the shower and strips off his clothes. Then he removes the first-aid kit from the medicine cabinet and puts the Montblanc wallet in its place. Beneath water as hot as he can bear, he scrubs himself clean, watching the water run red, then pink, then clear. Afterwards, he dresses his wounded knee, steps into fresh clothes and douses himself in cologne.

He feels marginally better than he did – less like he's actively dying and more like he's on life support – but it's only a temporary reprieve. He knows he hasn't fooled Erin. She'll be watching him ten times more closely from now on. When he opens the bedroom door, Max pushes him back inside the room so forcefully that he collapses on to the bed. His knee and his hamstring scream in tandem.

The boy is pale-faced, shaky with adrenalin. 'Dad, what the *fuck*?' he hisses. 'You tell me there's a viewing, that people are at the bungalow, and when I ask you about it you cut me off?'

'I couldn't—'

'And then, after leaving me hanging for over half an hour, you come home and take a shower, without even bothering to *contact* me?'

Abruptly, he realizes how hellish the last sixty minutes must have been for Max. 'I'm sorry,' he says. 'You're right. You're completely right. I was so—'

'What happened? Did they see her?'

Joseph cringes, holds a finger to his lips. He struggles up, checks the hallway and closes the bedroom door. 'No. I got there just in time.'

'Where's Drew now?'

'Keep your voice down.'

'Where is she, though?'

'*In the Honda,*' he mouths.

Max stares at him, wild-eyed. His fists clench and unclench. 'Dad,' he says. Then his shoulders slump. He sits on the edge of the bed and puts his head in his hands. 'This is exactly what I worried might happen. You get involved in something and the next minute you've taken over. You can't keep shutting me out. You're going to make a mistake, get us both caught. I wanted to protect you from this, not drag you deeper into it. We've got to get Drew out of there.'

'I know,' Joseph says. 'We will.' He sits back down beside his son, stares at the carpet. 'Have *you* told *me* everything?'

'Of course.'

'You've missed nothing out?'

'No.'

'In the woods, Friday night, you never found anything? Anything that would have identified that guy?'

'No, I already told you. Multiple times. I swear to God.'

Joseph nods, squeezes Max's shoulder. Then he gets off the bed, limps into the ensuite and returns with the Montblanc wallet. 'I wonder what God would make of this.'

Max stiffens when he sees it, inhaling sharply through his nose. Watching his son's reaction, Joseph decides to go all-in. 'Last night I checked the car, went over every inch. It looks the same as it always did. No dents. Not even a scratch.'

'I told you. He—'

'Yeah, I know. It was dark, he fell, you drove over him – and then his wallet bounced all the way from Jack-O'-Lantern Woods to here, where it landed inside your footstool.'

'Dad, you don't have to—'

'Did you know he knew Erin?'

'Absolutely not.'

'I'm meant to believe that's just a coincidence?'

'It was just some random guy, out walking in the woods.'

'Max—'

'It's the truth.'

Joseph indicates the wallet. 'Like this was the truth? For God's sake, I can't be clearer. If you aren't honest with me – and I mean total honesty – there's only one outcome. You just gave me a kicking for shutting you out, and rightly so, but it's about time you took your own advice. Otherwise, as you say, both our lives are over.'

Max sucks in a breath, puffs out his cheeks.

And then Erin calls up the stairs, asking for any requests from Mr Wu's.

'Think about it,' Joseph says, opening the bedroom door. 'Let's talk after dinner.'

The food order arrives within forty minutes. In the kitchen, Joseph pulls lids off plastic containers and empties prawn crackers into a bowl.

As usual, Erin's ordered far too many dishes. 'I thought Drew might drop in,' she explains, removing the foil from a bottle of Sancerre. 'You know how she has a sixth sense for barbecue spare ribs.'

Joseph grabs a pale ale from the fridge and makes a mess of pouring it. Slurping foam, he goes to the dining table and sits. Already, the rich smells of plum sauce and fermented black beans are beginning to turn his stomach. Erin joins him at the table. Tilly traipses in, placing her phone beside her plate. Max sits opposite.

The meal is a feast of eyes: Max watches Joseph; Joseph watches Tilly; Tilly watches her phone screen; Erin watches everyone. The dearth of conversation accentuates the sounds of eating: the beetle-back crunch of crispy seaweed, the wet mastication of noodles and rice; the pulverizing of chicken and pork. They bite, they chew, they drink, they swallow. They suck meat from bones, smack their lips, probe their teeth with their tongues. For Joseph, it's almost too much – a horrifying aural affirmation of their squishy organic states. He wants to cover his ears and drown it out. He grabs his beer glass, nearly swipes it off the table. Takes a long gulp.

Erin looks at him sidelong. She's about to speak when Tilly's phone rings. 'Oi, Missy,' she tells her daughter. 'You know the rules when we're eating.'

But the device is already at Tilly's ear. 'Oh, hi,' she says. 'I was going to text you, but then I realized I didn't have your number.' She listens for a while, her eyes meeting those around the table. 'No . . . No, she isn't . . . You haven't? . . . Wait, since when?'

A longer pause, now. Joseph feels Max's gaze and forces himself not to meet it. An awful pressure is building in his chest. There's no doubt in his mind who's calling. The fall-out from Drew's disappearance was always going to arrive sooner than Angus Roth's. Surprising, really, that Enoch Cullen waited this long before reaching out.

Worst of all is the knowledge that he's witnessing, in real time, the opening beats of another man's tragedy. One that he could have prevented.

Joseph knows what it's like to lose a wife. He can't begin to imagine the horror of losing a child. At last, the true cost of protecting Max is becoming clear: not simply how much of his own humanity he's prepared to sacrifice, but how much inhumanity he's prepared to inflict on others. Because if he does with Drew's remains what he did with Angus Roth's, he'll heap even greater torment on Enoch – the unendurable pain of not knowing, the imposition of a life spent searching for answers that will never come.

'Uh-huh,' Tilly says. 'No . . . yeah . . . I don't . . . Just some guy she was meeting. I don't even know that . . . No, I'm sorry, it was all pretty secretive . . . Yeah, exactly. Not at all.'

Finally, Joseph looks across the table at his son. Max has put down his fork and is leaning forward in his chair, watching his stepsister closely. His breathing, although silent, is laboured.

Tilly catches her lower lip between her teeth, releases it. 'Just . . . yeah, anything . . . Of course. I'll do it now.' She listens again, then frowns. 'And what did they say? . . . *How long?* . . . OK . . . Yes . . . Guaranteed.'

She ends the call and opens an app, typing with palpable urgency.

'That didn't sound great,' Erin says. 'Everything OK?'

Tilly shakes her head. 'That was Enoch. I *knew* something was up. He says Drew never came home last night.'

'Has he heard from her?'

'No.'

'Have you?'

'I've been messaging her all day with no answer. She hasn't even viewed what I sent.'

Erin looks at Joseph, then back at her daughter. 'Has anyone else heard from her?'

'That's what Enoch wanted me to find out.'

'Did you say something about a guy she was meeting?'

'A new one, yeah,' Tilly says. 'Not that I could tell you much about him – because Drew's been so weirdly tight-lipped about the whole thing.' She flicks a look at Joseph, then returns her attention to her phone. 'She said it was someone a lot older. Someone she thought would freak me out completely, hence all the secrecy. I told her it didn't matter but she still wouldn't open up.'

'Who was the last person to see her?'

'Right now, I guess that's Enoch. Drew was here most of yesterday. Then she went home to get changed before meeting this new guy. Enoch says he saw her before she left.'

Joseph is still reeling from the look Tilly just threw him. Surely she doesn't suspect a tryst between her stepfather and her best friend – that he's somehow responsible for Drew's disappearance?

He recalls his visit to the Grind House, Saturday morning, and how Drew had greeted him when he approached their table: *Hey, Mr Carver, I am* loving *the new* parfum.

At the time, catching Max's expression, he'd had the craziest notion his son was jealous. But Tilly had looked at him strangely, too. Had that innocent coffee shop encounter planted a seed of suspicion in his stepdaughter's head? How terminally ironic if a throwaway comment from Max's victim ends up implicating Joseph.

He needs to head this off quickly, before Tilly's seed can germinate. Trouble is, the Grind House conversation isn't the only problematic one. Yesterday lunchtime, making smoothies in the kitchen, Drew had leaned into him and dropped another grenade: *I know what you did for Max, and I think it's really brave.*

Tilly, arriving from the garden and catching the tail end of Drew's disclosure, had asked her *what* was really brave. If she hadn't accepted the explanation, where might her mind have gone?

His problems don't stop there. Earlier, attempting to justify his madcap dash to intercept the estate agent, he'd told Erin he'd visited the bungalow yesterday. And now Tilly, albeit unknowingly, has turned that excuse into a reason for further suspicion by claiming Drew's secret liaison was with a far older man.

Abruptly, he realizes that he hasn't spoken a word since Tilly's phone rang a minute ago, and that his silence might incriminate him further. 'Where's Enoch now?' he asks.

'At home.'

'Is anyone with him?'

'I don't think so. Let's face it – he's not the type of guy to have a dependable support network. He was slurring a bit.'

'I presume he's called the police?'

'They told him Drew's not vulnerable or at risk, so he needs to hang tight a while.'

'Useless,' Erin says. 'One of us should drive over there, make sure he's OK – and that he's letting all the right people know.' She glances at her watch, then at Joseph. 'Maybe the two of us should do it.'

Joseph nods, even though Enoch's is the last place he wants to be, because to do otherwise would look strange. To Tilly, he says, 'What happens when you call Drew's phone?'

'It was ringing earlier. Now, it goes straight to voicemail. I'm guessing it ran out of charge.'

Joseph prays that the phone isn't hidden in Max's room,

and that the boy was telling the truth about Drew leaving it at home last night. 'Don't you have one of those tracking apps?' he asks. 'Where you can keep tabs on each other's location?'

'Not really Drewster's thing.'

Erin turns to her stepson. 'You're pretty quiet. Any thoughts?'

Max pauses with a forkful of chicken fried rice halfway to his mouth. He glances at his father, then back at Erin. 'Thoughts on what?'

She blinks, fractionally tilts her head. 'Have you not been listening? On Drew's whereabouts. And what might have happened.'

A coldness spreads across Joseph's shoulders as he considers what Erin might be thinking. He's been sitting here, fearful that she's been putting together the puzzle pieces and steadily assembling his picture, but maybe she hasn't been doing that at all.

Saturday morning, she'd pressed him about his three-a.m. conversation with Max. To throw her off the scent, he'd told her about the boy's covert relationship with Drew. Now, that deflection might be about to bite him hard. Erin had agreed to keep quiet about what she'd learned, but Joseph knows her promise won't hold in an emergency. Worse, he hasn't even given Max a heads-up that his secret has been shared.

'Why should *he* know anything?' Tilly asks, looking up from her phone. Her gaze moves from her mum to the fork still suspended halfway to Max's mouth. The tension in the room skyrockets, suddenly too obvious to miss. 'Mum?'

'Max?' Erin asks.

Carefully, Max puts down his fork. 'I have no idea where Drew is.'

Tilly is frowning, now. Again, she looks around the table

before her gaze returns to her mother. 'I don't even know why you'd ask him.'

Joseph watches his son, utterly impotent. He wants to communicate a message, but anything he says will likely implicate them both. In the early hours of Saturday, he'd assured Max that everything they talked about would remain between them, for ever. He'd vowed that he wouldn't even tell Erin – especially not Erin. Across the table, Max looks like he's trying to work out how much of that promise his father has broken, and the consequences of being caught in a lie.

'What's going on?' Tilly asks. 'Seriously, you're all scaring me. I'm sure Drew's fine. She's probably just holed up with this new guy somewhere, and they've lost all sense of time.'

Erin reaches out, touches her stepson's wrist. When she speaks, her voice is melodic, mesmerizing. 'Max, look around you,' she says. 'Look around this table. I know I'm not your mum, and I know Tilly's not your sister, but we *are* your family. And in a family, even a blended family like ours, especially like ours, there aren't any secrets. This house is your sanctuary, a place where you can be honest – about anything. Whatever happens out there doesn't affect what happens here. Whatever we talk about within these four walls stays between them. There are no recriminations, only love. I'm sure your dad's told you that – I know Tilly would, too, if we asked her – but it's important you hear it from me.'

When Erin's in the zone like this, she's difficult to resist. Even Joseph finds himself being hypnotized, and he's not the subject of her attention.

Max stares at his stepmother, unable to look away. 'I don't know what you're talking about,' he mutters, but there's no conviction in his words.

Erin squeezes his wrist harder. 'Your dad told me every-thing, Max. I've known for two days. I haven't said a word to anyone outside this family, but I need to hear it from you, and then we can discuss the implications.'

Joseph, unable to catch his son's eye, is reduced to slowly shaking his head and hoping that Max will notice. The boy looks like he's about to confess everything – the killing not just of Angus Roth but also of Drew; and even Joseph's part in the cover-up.

'*Please* tell me what you're talking about,' Tilly begs.

'I think we need to hear it from Max.'

Joseph feels like his head has been packed with explosives and his wife has just lit the fuse.

'OK,' Max says finally. His gaze moves around the table, from Joseph to Erin and, finally, to Tilly. 'OK, I'll tell you.'

# TWENTY-NINE

Gabriel Roth pulls up outside Thornecroft's front entrance, grabs two suitcases from the boot, climbs the porch steps and rings the bell. When no one answers, he holds his thumb against the button. Instinct tells him Teri Platini is inside.

A minute later, he's proved right. The door opens an inch; then, falteringly, it swings wide. Teri stares at him with large, dumb cow eyes.

He pushes past her into the entrance hall and drops the suitcases beside the stairs. 'You've got five minutes.'

Teri blinks. 'Sorry?'

'You don't live here any more. Take those cases, pack your things and get out.'

'You can't just—'

He swipes at her, a clubbing open hand that strikes her cheekbone and knocks her sideways. She crashes into a console table, splintering its legs. The huge vase perched on top hits the floor and shatters. Daggers of sharp porcelain slide across the marble.

Gabriel shakes the sting from his fingers. He retrieves his wallet and pulls out a wad of cash.

'Here,' he says, bending over her. 'For a hotel.' Teri kicks her legs and tries to scoot away from him, blood pouring from her mouth. He presses the money into her hand and closes her fingers around it. 'Four and a half minutes.'

He still hasn't heard from Angus. These last few days, the universe has seemed increasingly bleak – as if the scales of a cosmic balance have tilted, upsetting the equilibrium. Everything is starting to feel wrong: the sky; the air in his lungs; the beat of his heart in his chest; even the skin on his knuckles and his scalp.

A few hours ago, at Erin Carver's house, he'd seen Joseph Carver's expression as he walked into the living room. The man should never play poker, because he'd reacted to Gabriel as if to a doppelganger, the horror etched deep into his face.

Minutes after leaving, a car Gabriel had spotted on the Carvers' drive overtook him on the road towards Crompton, driving recklessly fast. He'd followed it to an address in Saddle Bank, where he'd watched Joseph Carver race inside as if pursued by a pack of hungry wolves. Whatever Carver had done in there, he'd clearly wanted to finish it before an estate agent arrived to show the place.

His nose twitches. From somewhere he smells smoke. Going to the orangery, he sees something burning outside. Throwing open the doors, he crosses the lawn to his brother's barbecue. On the grill he discovers what's left of the boudoir image Teri had given Angus for his birthday. The remains of a lingerie set is smoking in the ashes.

It's certainly a statement.

Gabriel returns to the house. In the hall, Teri and the two suitcases have disappeared. He hears her moving about upstairs, checks his watch. Ninety seconds left. He flexes and unflexes his fingers.

Teri comes down the stairs, dragging the two suitcases behind her. One side of her face is swelling. The blood from her mouth has spilled down her sweatshirt.

'You didn't give me enough time!' she gasps. 'I've got an entire wardrobe of clothes up there that I—'

'Buy new clothes.'

The look she throws him is pure murder. She leaves the suitcases by the front door and limps to the dining room, where she snatches a business card off the table.

Gabriel's eyes glide over her. He has no difficulty visualizing what lies beneath Teri's hoodie and leggings, but it no longer interests him. During his last visit, he'd forced her to show him Angus's birthday present. He'd wanted to see it because he wanted her, and before he left he'd intended to have her.

But the fake sensuality he'd seen in that image had turned his lust into revulsion. No wonder his brother had gone elsewhere.

Sixty seconds.

Teri comes out of the dining room. On all fours by the smashed console table, she searches through the wreckage for her car keys. Then she drags her suitcases to the front entrance.

'Thirty seconds,' Gabriel says.

Teri fumbles with the latch. But when she tries to pull open one of the huge half-arched doors, her luggage gets in the way.

'Ten seconds.'

She sobs, a sound of distilled humiliation and rage. Finally, she manages to haul the door wide, but the gap isn't wide enough for both suitcases. Panicking, she tugs in vain at the carry handles.

Gabriel takes three steps and kicks Teri hard in the backside. She shoots forward, hands tearing loose of her luggage. Pitching off the porch's top step, she hits the gravel and slides across it face-first.

He picks up the first suitcase and bounces it off Teri's

head. The second suitcase lands on her back, driving the breath from her lungs.

Gabriel closes the door.

As he contemplates the wrecked console table and the shards of broken porcelain, his urge for violence recedes. Back in the kitchen, he searches Angus's cupboards for a broom.

# THIRTY

To his stepsister, Max says, 'I've been seeing Drew.'

Joseph, who just moments ago was fearing an even more damning revelation, sinks into himself like a punctured inflatable mattress.

Across the table, Tilly recoils, then laughs in astonishment. 'What? No, you haven't. Since when?'

'A few weeks. We were going to tell you.'

She looks at him stonily. 'Bullshit. I don't even know why you'd say that.'

'Because it's true.'

'No, Max, it's bollocks. Drew's seeing an older guy, not a younger one. And *certainly* not you.'

'I'm not saying she hasn't been seeing someone else too. In fact, I think she may well have been.' The boy glances at his father. Then his gaze returns to his stepsister, his expression pleading. 'I know we should have told you, Tilly. We just didn't know how. We didn't want you to feel you were somehow being edged out.'

Max pauses. Then he adds, 'Whatever you might be thinking, this doesn't change anything else, anything at all. It certainly doesn't change anything between us. I swear to you.'

Holding his breath, Joseph studies Tilly's reaction. She sits there a while, blank-faced, and he wonders if she's recalling – and reframing – all her recent interactions with her stepbrother and her best friend. Finally, reaching across the table, she squeezes Max's hand. 'You should have told me,' she says. 'I wouldn't have felt edged out, far from it. But I get why you didn't. Maybe Drew went out last night to split up with this older guy.'

Erin's hand is still encircling Max's wrist. Now, though, she removes it. 'When was the last time you saw Drew?'

'In the garden, yesterday afternoon,' the boy says.

'And last night?'

'Last night?'

'Max, if Drew's disappeared, and the police find out you've been seeing her, they'll want to know your whereabouts last night.'

'He was here, Mum. With me. We heated some microwave meals and watched *Oppenheimer*, just the two of us.' When Erin looks at Joseph for confirmation, Tilly adds: 'No point asking him, he left us to it, but it's the truth, I swear. If something's happened to Drew, Max has nothing to do with it.'

Erin turns to Joseph. 'You went out last night, too?'

'Mum, seriously, stop. I don't understand why you're being so suspicious.'

'I'm just trying to get my head around this. Joe?'

'I went to the bungalow,' he says. 'Like I told you. With you in London, it felt like a good opportunity.'

He feels Tilly's eyes on him and doesn't want to meet them. The note he'd written last night, before leaving to bury the dead man, had explained that he was visiting a friend. But if he repeats that lie in front of Erin, she'll want to know which friend, and to that he has no answer.

Silence, now, around the table. Joseph tries to work out

what everyone's thinking. Through Erin, Max has learned that his father broke his promise to keep the relationship with Drew secret. Tilly now knows about the relationship, too. From the strange look Tilly gave Joseph a few minutes ago, he fears she might think *he's* the older guy Drew's been seeing – and now he's contradicted himself over his movements. What his wife is thinking, he can't begin to imagine.

'OK,' Erin says, pushing back from the table. 'There's no point sitting around talking. Let's box up all this food and take it over to Enoch's. Odds-on he hasn't eaten. Right now, the best way we can help Drew is by helping her dad. So let's go over there and do that.'

Joseph drives, despite everyone's protestations about his knee. Erin takes the passenger seat, a cooler bag filled with Chinese food on her lap.

Head-down in her phone, Tilly provides a running commentary of what she's learned. It's always bad news. Or possibly good news. Joseph is so dizzy with stress, and so exhausted from lack of sleep, that it's increasingly difficult to differentiate. What might be good news for him and Max is necessarily terrible for everyone else. He finds himself hoping, beyond rationality, that Tilly's next update will reveal that Drew's been found safe and well, that the girl has called Enoch to explain she smoked too much weed and fell asleep, that she got drunk and passed out somewhere, that her blood is pumping, warm, around her body and she's alive, alive, alive.

He feels Erin's eyes on him as he negotiates Crompton's streets. It's obvious she wants to say something. Perhaps she's waiting until there's no chance of anyone else overhearing. Rarely has he met anyone with intuition as keen as hers. Better that he tell her the truth than she figure it out for herself, but he can't even begin to work out how to have that conversation – nor where it would likely lead. Joseph has made his choice – he intends to protect Max no matter what – but he doesn't expect that from Erin. Certainly not once she learns of her stepson's deeds. And her husband's.

'Joe, red light,' Erin says. Gripping her seat, she shouts, 'Joe, red *light*!'

By the time her words penetrate, it's too late to react. Joseph shoots across the junction without slowing. He senses a vehicle speeding towards his driver's door, hears a shriek of brakes, a horn, and by the time he's unlocked his arms he's rocketed through the lights. In his rear-view mirror he sees a car slewed round in the road.

'Jesus!' Erin yells, unsticking her hands from the door rest. 'Joe, wake up! I told you I should drive. What's got into you?'

'Sorry,' Joseph mutters. In the rear-view mirror, he catches Max's eyes, mouths another apology.

Enoch Cullen lives in a two-bedroom terraced house on the Larchwood council estate, ten minutes from the Carvers'. A rotting and bird-shit-caked caravan sits on the front drive; inside, what looks like worthless junk is piled to half the height of the windows.

Joseph parks on the road and switches off the engine. 'Look,' he says. 'I'm not saying we should keep it a secret indefinitely, but I'm not sure how much it helps the situation by telling Enoch about Max and Drew.'

'What are you suggesting?' Erin asks. 'That we lie?'

'No, I'm not saying that.' He takes a breath. 'I just don't think it'll come up, so I don't see the point in offering it.'

'Good with me,' Tilly says. She glances at her stepbrother for confirmation.

'I guess,' he adds.

When they throw open the rear doors and climb out,

Erin remains in the passenger seat. She stares at Joseph long and hard. Then, shaking her head, she climbs out too.

They have to knock twice before Enoch answers. His eyes are red with booze and small with animosity. He doesn't look scared, not yet. Rather, he seems like he's seething with a cold-burning rage that could explode into violence at any moment.

'Erin,' Enoch hisses, as if he's unsure whether to greet her or bury his fist in her face. His shoulders drop a little when she hugs him, and when her lips graze his cheek he closes his eyes like a man receiving a rubdown after a day spent breaking rocks.

'We brought food,' she says.

'You brought the whole clan,' he replies, squinting past her. He looks Joseph up and down before offering his hand. Joseph really doesn't want to touch it. Coming here was bad enough, but feigning solidarity with the father of Max's victim feels like his worst atrocity yet. He shakes hands because he has to, because decisions of conscience are a luxury for the innocent.

Enoch's grip is hot and slimy, as if he's in the throes of a fever. 'Swear to God,' he whispers in Joseph's ear. 'If someone's hurt her, I will bury him in the ground while he's still breathing. I will fucking *bury* him.'

Inside, the house is a mess. Towers of unwashed crockery stand on the kitchen's food-spattered worktop, among toolboxes and engine parts resting on oil-spotted rags. In the living room, DVD cases are piled around the TV. Against one wall lean the door panels of what looks like an old kitchen. In the corner, an artificial Christmas tree has burst from its cardboard box.

'Have you contacted Drew's mum?' Erin asks.

'I've left messages, but Paula's in Ibiza,' Enoch says. 'She'll be coked up to the eyeballs for the next week, spreading her legs for any dickhead that'll have her.'

190

Erin glances at her daughter, straightens. 'And you've been over to her place? Made sure Drew isn't there?'

'I have and she isn't. Neighbours ain't seen her, either.' From his pocket Enoch pulls out an iPhone in a fake leather case decorated with turquoise rhinestones. 'I did find this, though, up in her room. It's never usually more than a few inches from her right hand.'

The room fades to monochrome, Drew's phone the only point of colour. Joseph sees every detail in bright, laser-focused clarity – the scuffed and hairy edges of the fake leather, the rhinestones catching and bejewelling the light.

The evidence on it – photos, web searches, location history – might be enough to send him and Max to jail. He could seize it from Enoch's fingers, smash it to bits, but then what? He might as well unravel an enormous banner stencilled with GUILTY and wave it in everyone's faces.

'I recharged it,' Enoch says. 'But I can't unlock it – I don't know the code.'

*That's one bit of good news*, Joseph thinks.

'I do,' Tilly says, a moment later. 'Pass it to me.'

# THIRTY-ONE

Enoch nods, but he doesn't relinquish the phone. 'Tell me,' he says. 'I'll type it in.'

Bristling at his lack of trust, Tilly says, 'One-six-three, zero-one-one.'

Joseph glances at Max. Only after the boy's shoulders have risen and fallen in a tiny don't-worry-we're-not-screwed shrug does Joseph notice that Erin is watching, forehead creased and mouth pinched.

'*What?*' she mouths, and Joseph repeats his son's shrug. When her eyes narrow, his stomach feels like it's being fed through an old-fashioned mangle.

Tilly presses her head against Enoch's shoulder, peering at the phone screen. 'Check WhatsApp,' she says. 'OK, scroll down a bit. Let's see who's contacted her.'

The pair spend the next few minutes in silence, opening and reading Drew's messages. Joseph stands by the window, conscious of his wife's gaze, trying to figure out how he'd be behaving were he innocent. 'Shall I sort the food?' he asks.

'You might need to wash up first,' Erin mutters.

Joseph nods, but he can't bring himself to leave while Enoch and Tilly are still investigating.

'It's all just people telling her to get in touch,' Tilly says eventually. 'Mostly from after I put the word out. We should check her texts and call history. We can look at Snapchat, I guess – see if there's anything she hasn't opened.'

For the next minute, Joseph watches his stepdaughter navigate the device for the evidence that might put him away. Finally, his nerves defeat him. He retreats to the kitchen, fills the sink and begins to wash the dirty crockery.

On the windowsill stands an old school photo of Drew. The image is curled and sun-faded, but the girl's stare is no less intense than in Joseph's kitchen yesterday: *I know what you did for Max, and I think it's really brave.*

Doubtless, she wouldn't think that now.

Joseph's about to angle Drew's photo away from him when his wife appears in the doorway. She grabs a tea towel and begins to dry the dishes. Fortunately, Enoch's proximity seems to still her tongue.

Once everything's been put away, they reheat the Chinese food. Then all five of them squeeze around Enoch's tiny Formica table, Tilly perched on a stool because there aren't enough chairs.

Enoch sinks three beers as he eats. Joseph drinks two more. That means he won't be driving home, but he doubts Erin would let him after his near-miss on the way here. Nor will he be visiting the bungalow later, or heading out to Black Down. Considering how long the last grave took to dig, he simply doesn't have enough time.

Right now, Joseph's not even sure if he'll make that trip at all. Burying the dead man was bad enough. He can't imagine burying Drew. Certainly not as he sits at her father's table, drinking her father's beer. And yet he can't leave her in the car much longer.

'You want me to call the police again?' Erin asks Enoch.

'No point. They won't do anything till tomorrow. Best

thing I can do, they said, is stay here in case she walks in through the front door.'

'What about other places she might go? Bars, clubs, gyms?'

'I've contacted them all,' Tilly says. 'And I've posted photos to their social media, too.'

'You called the salon?'

'She never showed up this morning. Never even told them beforehand.'

'Which ain't like her,' Enoch adds. 'She loves that job. It's like her second home. Third home,' he adds, cracking open another beer.

'You checked the hospitals?'

'Course.'

'OK, listen,' Erin says. 'We'll clear away this food, make some space. And then we'll write an action plan, allocate tasks. Drew will most likely show up any moment, but better that we plan now for the alternative than start from scratch should we get there. We need to compile a contact list of everyone she knows: names, numbers, something we can hand to the police the moment they get involved. We need photos of Drew, too – good ones, that show her in the best light. I brought my laptop. We can mock up some flyers. Also, and I don't want to frighten you, Enoch, but they'll probably ask for a DNA sample, from Drew's toothbrush or something similar.'

Enoch stares at her, his eyes even smaller than before. Just like earlier, he looks like he's trying to decide whether she's an ally to be welcomed or a threat whose lights he needs to punch out.

Eventually, lifting his chin, he reaches out and rubs Erin's side, his fingers close to the swell of her breast. His touch is more sensual than fraternal, grimly opportunistic. Erin doesn't flinch, but she does throw Tilly another look.

Whatever her true feelings, she masks them with an empathetic smile.

Five minutes later, they clear the table and Erin sets up her laptop. Joseph finds a jar of coffee in Enoch's cupboard and boils a kettle. Tilly paces between the kitchen and the living room, checking her phone for updates.

Only while Joseph is stirring water into the cups does he notice Max's absence. His son isn't in the living room or the downstairs hall. There's no ground-floor cloakroom to check. On a hunch, he excuses himself and climbs the stairs. Reaching the upper landing, he pokes his head into the bathroom. Max isn't inside. Nor is he in Enoch's cluttered bedroom. At the back of the house Joseph discovers a box room that must be Drew's.

It's a sad little space. Even sadder, now. Drew had done her best to improve it, covering the peeling walls with poster prints of exotic landscapes in cheap plastic frames; destinations that perhaps she'd one day hoped to visit.

On the bed is a collection of cuddly toys; on the windowsill, a single dusty athletics trophy. A mannequin head stands on Drew's dresser; over it hangs a blonde wig so startlingly convincing that the hair must surely be real.

Max, his back to the door, is standing opposite a bureau, the middle drawer gaping open. In one hand he holds a pink bra embroidered with tiny flowers. With the other he's raking through the rest of Drew's underwear.

Joseph tries to ignore what it looks like – because it looks like his son is hunting for the bra's companion piece, intending to complete a trophy. And it's not that. It's not.

'What're you doing?' he asks softly.

Max twists around, his eyes showing white. 'Dad,' he begins. 'I was just . . . I thought I'd check her room. See if . . .' He looks at the bra, blinks. 'If . . .'

'Put it back,' Joseph whispers. 'Close the drawer. Go downstairs.'

Max rolls his tongue around his teeth. Then, his face flushed, he does as his father asks.

Outside, it grows dark. Enoch's house phone doesn't ring and Drew doesn't walk through the front door. Joseph brews more coffee. Enoch drinks another beer.

By eleven p.m., work on the action plan has slowed. Conversation dries up, too. The tick of the wall clock grows louder, as sinister as an old-fashioned movie bomb timer.

By midnight, even Tilly looks like she's flagging. Joseph starts wondering how much longer Erin intends to stay. He's due in the office tomorrow, not that he can afford to go; not with Drew's body still inside the Honda; and not with the bungalow still available for viewings because he's too worried about how it might look should he suddenly take it off the market.

At one a.m., Enoch belches and announces he's going to bed. It's the trigger for a general exodus. Tilly and Erin take turns to embrace him. Enoch clutches Erin far longer than is comfortable for her or anyone watching. Joseph, next in line, shakes hands as briefly as etiquette will allow. Max slides past without touching Enoch at all.

Erin drives them home. As soon as they're through the front door, Max and Tilly go up to bed. Joseph limps into the kitchen. 'You want a drink?' he asks Erin. He knows that a confrontation is coming. Maybe, if he blunts her intuition with alcohol, he'll struggle through.

'It's late,' she says.

'I know.'

Erin massages her neck. Then she sighs. 'Bar tender, pour me a cognac.'

From somewhere he finds a laugh. 'You want to drink cognac in this heat?'

'I know what I want in this heat, but cognac first, with ice. And yes, I know a puppy dies somewhere whenever I mention cognac and ice in the same breath. I hope it wasn't a cute one.'

She throws her bag on to the sofa near the bifold doors and slumps down next to it. 'God, that was hard. Not just hard, actually. Kind of weird. Enoch's a strange guy.'

Joseph grunts. 'Even a missing daughter didn't stop him from copping a feel.'

'Jealous?'

'What?'

'I saw the way you were looking at him.'

'How did you expect me to look?'

She shrugs. 'I like it when you get all protective.'

Joseph drops ice cubes into Erin's cognac. This isn't the interrogation he was expecting. Something's going on here; he just can't figure out what. Opening the fridge, he grabs another beer.

'Careful,' his wife says, sipping her drink. 'Once I finish this, I want you fully functional.'

He flinches at that, hadn't expected it at all. Is Erin switching tack? Is this an alternative ploy to get him talking? Or has Drew's disappearance highlighted her own mortality, and sex is how she intends to fight back? Maybe the drama of current events has energized her. She always seems most alive when she's at the heart of a crisis, directing the response. Her actions at Enoch's, developing a plan for the rest of them to implement, were classic Erin.

Joseph feels her gaze as he pours beer into a glass. When he meets it, he's surprised by its raw hunger. How long has it been since they were intimate? More than a few months, he thinks. Probably not even this year.

It had taken her words at the party to see how bad he'd let things get: *Sometimes it feels like we're two strangers living in the same house . . . Being married to you – it's been lonely at times, particularly these last six months . . . Are you happy, Joe? With me and with Tilly? Do you still want this?*

Strange, really, that while the last seventy-two hours have plunged him into a nightmare, in some ways he feels like he's waking from a dream.

The guilt that's eaten at him like a cancer these last five years – guilt at Claire's death, guilt at embarking on a new relationship, guilt that he'd neglected Max – has achieved nothing but further pain. It shouldn't have taken the tragedy unfolding around him to realize that.

In hindsight, he'd had so much to be thankful for, chief among them Erin, who'd seen something in him to cherish despite his manifest failures. And he never could have anticipated, as their two broken families became one, just how close Max would grow to his stepmother, or how close Max and Tilly would grow to each other.

For it to have happened like it had, for all four of them to have knitted together so seamlessly, he should have felt joy. Instead, he'd felt a mushrooming fear. The knowledge that he couldn't guarantee his new family's safety – that he'd failed at that task once before – had begun to obsess him, overwhelm him. Somewhere along the way, perhaps he'd lost sight of what he'd found: the extraordinary privilege of new love.

Upstairs, to his surprise, he remains fully functional. With the lights off, Erin pushes him on to the bed and straddles him. What follows isn't quiet; nor is it exactly gentle. He listens to his wife's gasps, endures the pain of her nails as she braces herself against his chest. In their three years together it might be the best sex they've had – and the first time Joseph's felt no shame.

Soon, they're so slippery with sweat that Erin's hands can hardly find purchase. For a while, she seems too lost in sensation to realize something's wrong, but Joseph does. From there, it's only a matter of time until his wife notices, too, and how bad it'll be when she does.

At last she rolls off him and lies there, recovering her breath. Then she reaches out and turns on a lamp – and reveals a scene of carnage. Blood covers Joseph, covers the sheets. Erin's palms are crimson with it.

With a cry of dismay, she flips on to her knees. Her eyes move from her bloodied fingers, splayed in front of her, to Joseph. The slash wound across his abdomen gapes red and slick, its reopening caused as much by Erin's gyrations as her nails. 'What the fuck, Joe?' she whispers. '*What the fuck?*'

'I'm sorry,' he says. 'I should have warned you.'

Levering himself on to one elbow, he swings his legs out of bed as carefully as he can. Now that the sex is over, the pain from his wound is hitting harder. It feels like someone's dragged a soldering iron across his flesh, smoking his skin. When he stands, favouring his good knee, the hamstring in that leg feels like it's been Tasered. He hobbles to the ensuite and hears Erin stumble to the family bathroom.

It's quicker to shower than to wash himself at the hand basin. Afterwards, he binds his abdomen with another long strip of Elastoplast. He wraps a towel around his waist, opens the door.

During his absence, Erin has cleaned herself up and changed the sheets. She's sitting on the mattress, hugging her knees. Joseph wonders if his wife's nakedness is deliberate. Perhaps, in showing him she has nothing to hide, she hopes to encourage the same honesty in return.

'You're really starting to scare me,' she whispers.

Joseph limps towards the bed. When she recoils he hesitates.

'How did you get that?' she asks, indicating his abdomen. 'It looks fresh.'

'It isn't.'

Erin shivers, waits for him to speak.

'That stupid, damned axe,' he tells her, after a moment's pause. 'When I went downstairs, Friday night, Max scared the hell out of me, and I must have scared the hell out of him right back. It was dark. We had a . . . a coming together. Just a stupid accident, really. I didn't want you to worry.'

'He *attacked* you?'

'No. Nothing like that. As I said, it was just a clumsy coming together. My fault, really. Not his.'

His wife is quiet for a while. Then she rests her chin on her knee. 'Silly question,' she says. 'And maybe this is on me for not asking sooner. But why do you have an axe in the wardrobe, Joe?'

At last, she's asked him something he can answer honestly, with no fear of the consequences. 'Because I wanted to keep you all safe,' he tells her, 'and didn't feel like I could. The world's a dangerous place. A lot of the time it's a brutal, unforgiving place. And I didn't want to lose anyone else.'

Joseph fills his lungs. Then he starts to tell Erin about the doorstep seller last winter who wouldn't leave, and how powerless he'd felt to protect Max and Tilly. And how that single incident had grown in importance in his mind, a microcosm, perhaps, of more fundamental insecurities.

'So you bought an axe?'

'It's actually a tactical tomahawk, but yeah.' He screws up his face. 'I bought a crossbow, too – some other stuff. The crossbow's in the wardrobe, still in its box, if you want to see. Turns out I'm not much of a home defence guy.'

Erin's gaze moves to the wardrobe as if she's considering his offer, but then something seems to change her mind. Her attention returns to the Elastoplast stretched across his midriff. 'These two disappearances,' she says. 'Angus Roth, and now Drew. Do you know anything about them, Joe?'

'What could I possibly know that you don't?'

'I guess that's what I'm asking. Because in the entire time we've been together, I've never seen you so – I don't know – so *distracted* as you've been these last few days. So skittish and erratic. You drove through a red light on the way to Enoch's, nearly hit another car. When we were sitting around that table with him, you looked terrified. Same with Angus's brother, earlier today.'

Joseph concentrates on his breathing. Slow in, slow out. 'I'm not sure what you think I might know,' he says. 'As for my behaviour, Tilly's best friend is missing. Of course I look scared.'

'Is it something to do with Max?'

'Max?'

'I saw the way you were watching him. Not just at Enoch's but earlier, before we left. I know we talked about this already but something's not right with him, Joe. Don't tell me you haven't noticed.'

'What are you saying?' he asks quietly. 'Because you need to think very carefully about where you're going with this.'

Erin hugs her knees tighter. 'I'm not accusing Max of anything. Obviously, I'm not.'

'Good, because—'

'Do you still love me?'

He blinks, surprised by the swerve, unsettled by how intensely she's watching him. 'Why would you ask that?'

'Because it just came into my head. I practically had to drag you to bed tonight. You never seem interested in that. And we never really talk, not like we once did. We're more like housemates, these days, than husband and wife. Not even good housemates, particularly.'

Joseph doesn't respond. He's worried that anything he does say might lead Erin in directions he hasn't anticipated.

'And yet,' she continues, 'despite your apparent lack of

interest in me, you've started wearing aftershave, started taking an interest in fashion, started being careful about what you eat. I'm not the only one to have noticed. Everyone was commenting at the party, complimenting you. Gemma Robinson seemed a particular fan, based on what I recall.'

Joseph opens and closes his mouth. Can she possibly think he's being *unfaithful*? There's an explanation for every point Erin just listed. But he can't tell her he's started wearing cologne to mask the smell of the dead man; that his clothes purchases were simply the pretext for buying a SIM card to research burial depths; that apart from his gluttonous display at Meghan's, he hasn't been eating and has mainly been puking because his son has taken two lives in the last week.

'What do you think has happened to Drew?' Erin asks.

Joseph shakes his head, as if a wasp just flew into his ear. His wife's question, following so closely behind her observations of his behaviour, is very bad news indeed. 'I think Tilly's theory is the most likely – that she's with this new guy and they just went somewhere, spur of the moment.'

Erin watches him, unblinking. 'What prompted you to go over to the bungalow, yesterday?'

His stomach dives. Because her train of thought is still rattling along the same track, and his attempts to divert it aren't working. 'I told you. I thought I'd go through all the furniture – decide what to sell and what to keep. If we declutter it a bit we might generate more interest. The council tax isn't huge but it's starting to add up. I just want to get shot of the place.'

Erin considers that, head tilted. 'You know what? You're right. That place *is* taking far too long to sell. And actually, it's a good while since I last saw it. I think I'll make some time tomorrow, go over and take a look around. Maybe I'll spot something you've missed.'

She holds his gaze until he nods. Then she unfolds her

legs and rises from the bed. From her drawer she retrieves pyjama shorts and a vest and slips them on. Flicking off the light, she slides under the covers.

Joseph waits a while, standing there in the darkness. Then he shuffles to his side of the bed and climbs in. Erin turns on to her side, away from him. The silence between them is heavier than it's ever been.

He thinks of Thornecroft, the huge house on Hocombe Hill. He thinks of Enoch's miserable two-bed terrace and Drew's sad little room. He thinks of his mother's bungalow, and the isolated spot on Black Down where he buried the dead man. They're dots on a map, blinking away like beacons, waiting for someone to join them up.

He can't let his wife find out from someone else. Nor can he see a future, any longer, where he manages to keep all this quiet.

'Erin?' he whispers, in the darkness.

She deserves the truth. If he can't protect her from it he must, at least, prepare her.

'Erin,' he whispers again.

His wife doesn't answer – and Joseph realizes that while he's been thinking her breathing has slowed in slumber. Perhaps that's just as well. Because if she'd answered just then, he might have told her everything.

It's a moment of weakness he can't afford. Because Max is his North Star. There's no one he won't sacrifice for his boy. Putting his back to his wife, just like she did to him, he reaches out for sleep.

Tomorrow will be difficult. Likely the worst day yet. For a few hours, the sleep into which Joseph sinks is so black and luxurious it's almost indistinguishable from death.

# THIRTY-TWO

Miah Desjardins is prettier in person than she sounded on the phone. She arrives in a purple Fiat 500 emblazoned with the logo of her employer.

As Gabriel Roth climbs out of his hire car, he wonders if Miah's plaid miniskirt, silk blouse and heavy make-up are a lure for prospective buyers. If so, he hopes she'll find him immune. He just spent a cleansing twenty minutes listening to 'Eighteen Songs of a Nomad Flute' and 'High Mountains and Flowing Water'.

Unfortunately, meditation and classical Chinese music aren't offering the safe harbours they once did. These last few days, as the world has darkened around him, brief bursts of violence have become the only release valve for his pain. Hard to know why, after so many years of celibacy, his sexual urges have similarly begun to overwhelm him. He cannot let that continue.

In his readings of Confucius, he's learned to consider the consequences of rage. Now, more than ever, he needs to hold those teachings close. Because when he finds those responsible for Angus's disappearance, he intends to apply another tenet of Confucianist thought: repaying evil not with mindless wrath but cold justice.

'Mr Anderson,' she says. Her lips don't lose their plumpness when she smiles. Her teeth are as white as coconut meat.

Gabriel turns his attention to the bungalow. 'Two bedrooms, you said.'

Miah nods, leading him up the drive. 'It's a lot more spacious inside than it looks. So many people are choosing single-storey properties these days. It's a lifestyle choice, don't you think?' She unlocks the door and swings it open. 'Shall we?'

He indicates that she should go first and follows her inside.

'It's a nice, bright hall,' Miah says. 'The décor might need a refresh but it's only cosmetic stuff. Through there's the living room, which I think is a *lovely* space. Kitchen leads off it to the rear, with a gorgeous view of the back garden.'

Gabriel looks around. Although the bungalow is fully furnished, he sees discoloured patches on the wall where pictures and photographs once hung. No knickknacks are on display, no keepsakes. Everything personal has disappeared. 'Tell me about the vendor.'

'Well, there's no chain, for starters. Which is a real benefit.'

'Is this a probate sale?'

Miah's smile is strained, revealing once again those coconut-white teeth. 'Kind of. I mean, OK, yes, but it shouldn't put you off. I know some people are funny about that but it's not like anyone died in here.'

She laughs awkwardly, as if embarrassed by her own sales pitch.

'That kind of thing doesn't bother me. So who's the vendor?'

'The son of the lady who lived here.'

'What can you tell me about him?'

She shrugs. 'Seems a nice guy. I've only met him a few times.'

'Does he live here? Use the place as an office?'

'I don't think so.'

'How long's it been on the market?'

'A while.'

'Which means what, exactly?'

'Maybe . . . March? I'd have to check the file. If we'd listed it the previous March we'd have sold it in a day, but right now – well, I'm sure you know how the market's been.'

In the living room, an armchair and a side table have been pushed against the wall, revealing the indentations on the carpet where they once stood. All the other furniture – the bookcase, the sideboard, the TV cabinet, the sofa – looks like it hasn't moved.

'You want to see the bedrooms?' Miah asks.

As Gabriel follows her for the tour, he tunes out her sales patter and thinks about that pushed-back space in the living room. He looks inside the built-in wardrobes, checks the bath for stains. He examines the walls and skirting boards for blood splashes, the linoleum and the carpets. He opens the kitchen cabinets to see which cleaning products they contain and in what quantities.

'That leads to the garage,' Miah explains, when Gabriel puts his hand to an interior door. 'Feel free to have a look.'

He opens it and steps through. Inside, the garage is dark. He touches the wall, feels for a switch, flips it. Overhead, a fluorescent strip stutters before casting its light. In the centre of the garage stands a blue Honda hatchback.

The air in here feels like it's being cooked. There's a smell of dust and engine oil and hot metal – and the hint of something more unpleasant, like game meat hung for flavour that has somehow managed to get damp.

Against the near wall is a workbench scattered with equipment. Various garden tools have been stacked in one corner. A rake lies on the concrete floor beside a glass demijohn on its side.

Gabriel crouches down and checks beneath the car. Then he goes to the driver's side window and cups his hands to the glass. He sees nothing of interest on the front seats, none of the usual junk that tends to accumulate inside a vehicle regularly used. Behind the rear seats, a tonneau cover has been drawn over the boot space. Gabriel goes the rear, finds the boot release, squeezes it.

Miah appears in the doorway. When she spots him behind the Honda her eyebrows lift, but she can't see his hand from where she's standing. 'Everything OK?' she asks. 'Anything else you want to know?'

'I'm just trying to figure out if I could park my car in here. It's a lot bigger than this one.'

'I'm sure we have the measurements on the plans.'

'Great.'

She smiles at him again.

Gabriel drops his hand, smiles back.

The boot is locked, as he thought it would be – but he thinks he saw a Honda-branded key fob hanging from a hook in the kitchen. As he walks out from behind the car he notices, trapped between the bottom edge of the boot lid and the lip of the surround, a flap of clear heavy-duty plastic.

It stops him dead, that sight. It empties his ears of sound. He stands there motionless for what might be ten seconds or longer before the gears of his brain re-engage. The pulse of blood in his arteries has become a torrent, a raging flood. He clenches his fists, unclenches them. Wordlessly, he follows Miah to the living room, where he observes once again the chair and table pushed back to the wall.

When he tries to breathe, his diaphragm spasms like a bowstring releasing its arrow. His lips feel numb, his cheeks.

'You ever get scared?' he hears himself ask, his gaze still on that inexplicable tableau.

Miah cants her head. 'I'm sorry?'

'I mean, you don't know anything about me. And yet here we are, together, in an empty house. If something happened, it might be an hour or more before one of your colleagues raised the alarm. In that time . . .' He shrugs. 'I could attack you, rape you. And what could you do to stop me? What *would* you do?'

Beneath the silk fabric of her blouse, Miah's chest swells. She, too, throws a glance at that patch of cleared carpet. Her hand slips inside her shoulder bag. 'I have to say you're scaring me a bit.'

'I should be scaring you,' Gabriel says. 'You should be scared because you don't have a plan. You're young, you're pretty. You're physically weak. That makes you an easy target for those with appetites they can't suppress.'

His own breath is coming a little easier now. 'I'm not going to attack you, Miah, but I want you to think about how you'd react if I did, because I guarantee you one thing – I could close the distance between us before you managed to dial even a single number on that phone you're clutching inside your bag. So the questions remains: what would you do?'

Miah blinks at him, licks those plump lips. Then, softly, she says, 'I'd give you everything you wanted. If you tried to touch me, I wouldn't resist. If you tried to kiss me, I'd kiss you straight back.'

Steadily, she removes her hand from her bag. Instead of a phone, she's holding a switchblade. When she presses the button release, the blade flicks out. Gabriel knows switchblades, and he knows Miah isn't holding a toy.

'This is from Maniago, Italy,' she tells him. 'Locals call the place the Town of Knives, the birthplace of the modern switchblade. Which means when I stabbed you through the neck with this one, you could take solace in the fact that you weren't killed by a cheap Chinese copy.'

# THIRTY-THREE

When Ralph Erikson answers the door, Tuesday morning, he's wearing a traditional Japanese kimono in black silk featuring gold dragons and tigers in a complicated, interwoven design.

'Joseph,' he says. 'What a pleasure. Would you like to come in?'

'Thanks, I will.'

Ralph's kitchen, although well kept, looks like it hasn't been decorated since the eighties: peach walls, wooden cabinetry, terracotta tile floor. Trinkets and collectibles crowd every surface: Disney snow globes, Murano glass paperweights, a menagerie of bone china creatures. Plants share their pots with plastic gnomes and fairies. Mounted on the walls are decorative plates daubed with the names of various holiday destinations, alongside embroidered hoops and display cases filled with thimbles.

Many of the phrases stitched on the hoops reference heaven and the afterlife. Other oddments in Ralph's collection share the same focus. Joseph sees porcelain angels, bronze crucifixes, hand-painted images of tunnels and light.

Among all this clutter are scores of photographs of Carole Erikson, Ralph's late wife. There are snaps of Carole as a young girl; as a woman in her twenties, her forties, her sixties; even a few of her smiling in a hospital bed. Lots of the images sit inside frames stencilled or inscribed with messages:

*Goodbyes are not for ever, and also not the end.*

*Because someone we love is in heaven, a little bit of heaven is at home.*

Some of the messages are more direct, and strike Joseph as more disturbing:

*I am watching you, every day.*

*Tonight, in your dreams, we will dance.*

*Watch for my signs – I'll send them every hour.*

'Would you like some shogayu?' Ralph asks. 'It's a ginger tea, brewed with honey and lemon. The Japanese mainly drink it in winter but I enjoy it in summer, too. Carole loves it. Don't you, darling?'

Joseph frowns, glances around the room – until, finally, he understands. 'I'll try some, thanks.'

Ralph pours him a cup from a saucepan on the stove. 'Please,' he says, indicating the breakfast table. 'We don't get many visitors these days.' He cocks his head as if listening, then smiles. 'Well, you *would* say that.'

Joseph carries his brew to the table. 'You talk to her. Carole, I mean.'

'Unless she's being difficult.' Ralph flinches, then chuckles – as if reacting to a mild admonishment.

'It's nice that you do that.'

'You don't talk to . . . Claire? Is that your first wife's name?'

As usual, when hearing it, Joseph feels like he's plummeting into an abyss. 'It was,' he says. 'And yeah, sometimes I do. But not often. And not in the same way.'

The older man nods. 'You petition her, perhaps. Plead for help. When things aren't going how they should.'

'Something like that.'

Ralph joins him at the table. 'Some might say that isn't really a conversation. They might say it's an appeal to a deity you've disguised as a loved one. They might tell you that a conversation has to flow in two directions, and for that you mustn't simply talk, you must listen. Really listen.'

Joseph thinks of yesterday's cemetery visit. How he'd managed to touch Claire's headstone but not look.

Ralph smiles. 'If it's really Claire you seek, then it's time you opened your ears to her, Joseph. It's time you opened your eyes, too.'

Joseph clears his throat, tries to shake off the dreamlike mood that's stolen over him. 'Saturday night, at the party. We were talking about Erin's intruder. I know it was a false alarm but it got me thinking about security, and then I remembered you offered to show me the ropes on your doorbell cam.'

'I did,' Ralph says. From the depths of his robe he retrieves his phone. Unlocking it, he opens the Nest app and angles the screen. 'The camera's idling right now. But if I press here, it'll wake and show me the live view. See?'

Suddenly, Joseph's looking at an astonishingly high-resolution image of his own house, from the perspective of Ralph's front porch. 'Wow,' he says. 'What's the view like after dark?'

'Great – it switches over to night vision. You can change the sensitivity trigger for what it records, but I like to keep it high – you'd be surprised at how much wildlife you get to see. When you want to check recent events, you just press here. Or, for a full history, here.'

'Would you mind if I had a play around?'

'Be my guest. Would you like some more shogayu?'

'I'd love some.'

Ralph hands over his phone and gets up from the table. Joseph, recalling the instructions he researched on Claire's iPhone, opens the app's settings menu.

He taps **Delete video history**. Then he taps **Delete** to confirm. It's ridiculously easy, ridiculously quick. If what he read online is correct, Google don't keep backups, which means the evidence on Ralph's device has disappeared for good.

'How strange,' the widower says, from where he's standing by the stove, 'that we were only just talking about the importance of opening your eyes. And it turns out you came here seeking better ways of seeing.'

Actually, Joseph came here to prevent others from seeing, but he's not going to argue the point. He jumps out of the app's settings and back into the live view of his house. Thanks to the clock at the top of the screen, he's able to note the exact moment that a police car pulls into his driveway.

# THIRTY-FOUR

Paralysed with shock, Joseph remains at Ralph Erikson's kitchen table. In the space of a breath his world has shrunk to the dimensions of a smartphone screen. He watches the police car's front doors open and two officers step out. They stare at his house for a moment. Then they walk to the front door and ring the bell.

Joseph's heart is a hummingbird in his chest. Vaguely, he hears his feet scrape against the terracotta tiles. Across the street, Erin opens the door. She stands there listening as the officers talk. Stepping back, she lets them into the house.

'Your tea,' Ralph Erikson says.

Joseph kills the live view and puts down the phone. Maybe, if Ralph doesn't see the police car, the police car won't exist. With shaking hands he picks up his mug and drinks. The shogayu is hot enough to burn his tongue. He winces, swallowing a scalding mouthful.

He could call Max, perhaps. They could jump into the car, drive to Crompton, empty the savings account of cash. From there they could go . . . *some*where.

Except Joseph's car is boxed in. Even if they could release it, they wouldn't evade capture for long.

'I'm sorry,' he tells Ralph, pushing up from the table. 'I

just remembered something important.' When he tries to stand, his knee nearly gives out. The pain is instant and electric.

'Well, I'm glad you chose to visit us,' the older man says. 'Perhaps we could do it again. Remember, Joseph: open your ears if you want to listen; open your eyes if you want to see.'

Smiling, wanting to puke, Joseph hobbles across the kitchen. He feels drunk, sick – as if the widower's tea contained a toxin. He knows he has to get home, but he doesn't know what to do when he gets there. Nor what to say.

Outside, he limps down Ralph's drive and across the turning circle towards his house. Overhead, the sun is a white disc in a plate-blue sky. A glorious day and a terrible one. At his front door, he slides his key into the lock.

There's no one in the hall. He hears voices in the living room, the squawk of a police radio.

He's never felt so scared. He's never felt so ill. The living-room door opens and Erin leans out her head. When she sees him standing there, sweat running from his forehead, she opens her mouth in surprise, and perhaps in dismay, and Joseph thinks that she must know everything – that her stepson is a killer, that her husband buried Max's first victim in the Sussex Downs and hid Max's second victim in his mother's car.

Except . . . except . . . his son isn't a killer. He's not.

He's just lost.

*Remember, Joseph. Open your ears if you want to listen. Open your eyes if you want to see.*

'The police are here,' Erin says.

Joseph nods, mute.

'Are you OK? You look terrible.'

'I was just over the road, talking to Ralph.'

'Well, that'd do it.'

'We need to talk,' he says. 'It's important.'

Erin nods, smiles, touches his arm. And Joseph can't help marvelling, yet again, at his wife's refusal to carry bad feeling from one day into another.

'That sounds good,' she says. 'But first I think you might want to come into the living room.'

'Is Max here?'

'He's talking to the police.'

She takes his hand, leads him along the hall. Joseph follows without resistance. The pain in his knee has faded. His entire body is numb. When he enters the room, the two officers he saw on Ralph's live feed – one male, one female – are sitting on the sofa. Max and Tilly are sitting opposite.

Everyone looks up. Erin's voice, introducing him, comes as if through a tunnel. Joseph goes to an armchair and lowers himself into it.

Beneath the female officer's seat cushion is the screwdriver he grabbed yesterday, during Gabriel Roth's visit. There are other weapons here, too, in this room and beyond, but they're useless against the police. He'd planned his security response against intruders. He hadn't foreseen this.

'PC Hopkins,' the female officer says. 'This is PC Kenner. We've just been speaking to your daughter about Drew Cullen. As you must know, she hasn't been seen since Sunday.'

Joseph needs to swallow, but if he does he fears his throat will bulge to the size of a balloon, announcing his guilt. 'There's still no sign?'

'I'm afraid not. It's been a couple of days now, so we're looking at it a little more actively. By far the most likely scenario is that Drew arrives home any minute with an embarrassing story to tell. We're just getting on the front foot in case she doesn't.'

Joseph nods. Finally, he swallows. His throat makes a sound like a sink being unblocked.

The officer tilts her head. 'Casting your mind back, Mr

Carver, did Drew say anything to you on Sunday that might be relevant? I gather you were here with her and your daughter while your wife was up in London.'

*I know what you did for Max, and I think it's really brave.*

Joseph clenches his fists in his lap. 'Like what?'

'Like her plans for the rest of that day? Any mention of someone she was intending to meet? Your daughter suggested an older man.'

Joseph can't decide if maintaining eye contact will make him look more guilty than if he looks away. He shakes his head. His eyes are beginning to water from the effort of not glancing at Max.

PC Hopkins holds his gaze. Just like in the hallway with Erin, Joseph tells himself that she must read the truth in his eyes – and that any moment now she'll ask him to hold out his hands for the cuffs.

When she doesn't, he starts to wonder if something else is happening here, if this conversation is nothing but pantomime, a distraction designed to keep him busy until a search warrant is granted for the house. He recalls, suddenly, the Sainsbury's bag he hid inside one of the kitchen cupboards on Friday night, containing his T-shirt stained with the dead man's blood. Irrationally he wonders if, just by thinking about it, he has somehow communicated that knowledge to the police officer sitting in front of him.

Finally, PC Hopkins switches her attention to Tilly. 'Thanks for that list of contacts,' she says. 'I know you've already put the word out, but we'll follow up, just to be sure.'

'What happens now?' the girl asks.

'We're checking the area where Drew was last seen, seeing if there's CCTV. We'll put out alerts on social media, ask for dashcam footage, doorbell footage, that kind of thing.'

'What about newspapers, TV?'

'Not at this stage, but there's nothing to stop you from

approaching them. Just be prepared that they might not be that interested quite yet. There's no indication anything untoward has happened – and it's not like Drew's a child.' PC Hopkins returns her gaze to Joseph. 'Finally, can I ask where you were Sunday night?'

'Me?'

'It's nothing to worry about. But you're one of the last to see her.'

Erin perches on the arm of his chair. She rests her hand on his shoulder. 'Didn't you go over to your mother's?'

Joseph glances at his wife, appalled. His hope had been that the police, once they started investigating, would remain ignorant of his mother's bungalow, and the car parked in its garage. 'Uh-huh,' he says. 'Just a bit of maintenance work that needed doing.'

'Does she live locally?'

'Saddle Bank.'

Erin rubs his back. 'Joseph's mother passed away last Christmas,' she explains. 'We've been trying to sell her place since probate, but the market's just . . .' She shrugs. 'Dead.'

The word hangs in the air. PC Hopkins glances from Erin to Joseph, then scribbles something in her notebook. 'Well,' she says. 'You've all been very helpful.'

Tilly shows the officers out. Erin follows them into the hall. Joseph looks at Max, gasps for breath. He feels like he just ran a marathon in a clown suit. Somehow, he summons the energy to lever himself up. His body screams in protest; his knee, his hamstring, the line of fire stitched across his abdomen.

Did Erin tell the police about his visit to the bungalow deliberately? Or was she simply trying to be helpful? She'd also told them that his mother was dead and that her place was up for sale.

Moving to the living-room window, he watches PC

Hopkins survey the street. Her gaze lingers on Ralph Erikson's doorbell cam.

*Too late*, he thinks. *I beat you to it.*

Except now the officer is studying Gemma Robinson's house, and Joseph wonders if she has a doorbell cam, too. Gemma hadn't mentioned one at the party. Then again, she'd been more interested in badmouthing her husband.

He watches the police car reverse off the drive and disappear up the street. Beside him, Max says, 'We've got to move her, Dad.'

'I know.'

'We've got to do it now.'

'Listen,' Joseph tells him. 'This has blown up. People are watching us. We can't afford a single mistake.'

'We can't afford to wait, either. Erin—'

'Leave Erin to me.'

'That's not what I meant. I think she—'

With a raised hand Joseph cuts him off, worried their voices will carry. He goes to the door, checks the hall. When he finds it deserted, he checks the kitchen.

Erin is standing by the espresso machine, searching through her bag. In the minute or so since the police officers left, she's pulled on trainers and has tied back her hair. She retrieves her car keys, recoils when she sees him in the doorway.

'Where are you going?' he asks.

'Out.'

'Out where?'

'I thought I'd pick up some things for Enoch. You saw how bare his cupboards were.'

Her tone, now that the police have left, is different. Her manner seems different, too. What if she's lying about shopping for Enoch? Last night, after their bloody and disastrous sex, she'd told him she intended to visit the bungalow.

'I'll come with you,' he says.

'You don't have to do that.'

'I want to.'

'Don't you have work to do?'

'It can wait.'

'Joe . . .' Erin begins. She blinks a handful of times in quick succession. Then she rummages in her bag for her sunglasses and puts them on. 'Fine, but we leave now. I have a meeting later – and I need some time to prepare.'

Joseph nods. When he turns, he sees Max standing in the hall.

*I should come*, the boy mouths.

*No*, he mouths back. *Leave her to me.*

Max shakes his head.

*I've got this. Trust me.*

Teeth clenched, Max stands his ground. Then Erin reappears. 'Are you ready?'

Max backs into the living room. He doesn't look angry, exactly. If anything, he looks scared – like a kid who already lost one parent and fears he's about to lose another. Joseph wants to reassure him, but with Erin watching, there's nothing he can say.

# THIRTY-FIVE

Joseph sits in the passenger seat, peering through the side window as his wife reverses off the drive. It looks like Gemma Robinson doesn't have a smart doorbell, but the Taylors might, his neighbours on the other side. He wonders if any of the houses further down the street have cameras. He can't pull the same trick he pulled on Ralph Erikson with everyone.

In Crompton, rather than driving into the Sainsbury's multistorey, Erin turns left at the train station roundabout and stops the car. Joseph sees that they're almost exactly where he parked yesterday. From here, he has a perfect view of Crompton's police station.

His ears pop and roar. Just like yesterday, he feels, suddenly, like he's trapped inside a tiny ocean submersible, deep below the surface. 'I thought we were picking up supplies for Enoch.'

'Change of plan. There's something I wanted to say first.'

'Here?'

'It didn't feel safe at home.'

'Safe from what?'

Ignoring the question, Erin takes off her sunglasses. 'Joe, do you remember the first time I introduced you to Tilly?'

He does. He'd been seeing Erin for three months, after their friendship at the bereavement group developed into something more. Erin had already met Max; by now, she was regularly staying the night at their old house. But despite Joseph's keenness to meet Tilly, Erin had kept them apart.

Then, one Sunday morning in late spring, they'd been drinking coffee in a Hampton Court brasserie overlooking the Thames when a girl around Max's age had dropped into the seat opposite Joseph.

'I thought it was time,' Erin had explained. She'd introduced her daughter, picked up her bag and walked out.

Joseph had looked at Tilly.

'Hi,' she'd said, with wry amusement.

'Hi,' he'd said right back.

Clumsily, he'd ordered more coffee. Even more clumsily, he'd started to ask her questions.

After ten minutes, their conversation had grown less awkward. Twenty minutes after that, it wasn't awkward at all. Tilly clearly shared her mother's ability to form quick and meaningful connections. The effect was like sliding into a warm bath.

Despite the girl's confidence, Joseph had felt he was talking to someone whose road had perhaps been even rockier than Max's; someone in desperate need of a father; someone who needed stability and protection – all the things love could bring. She'd suffered her parents' divorce, her stepfather's suicide, the fallout from his gambling debts, difficult situations at school.

In Tilly he'd perceived what he'd often perceived in his son since Claire's death: that sense of something tragically broken, albeit better concealed. It had triggered in him an overwhelming desire to repair the damage.

The thought of becoming a protector and a role model to

another child had filled him with foreboding. But – and here was the strange thing, sitting opposite this charismatic and keen-eyed teenager – the thought of side-stepping that role, of refusing it, somehow felt unconscionable.

'I was terrified that day,' Erin tells him. 'It felt like I was rolling the dice on a huge gamble. I was so scared you'd let Tilly down. You had to be perfect, Joe. Rock solid. Because the two men who'd been there before you had failed her horribly.'

Erin stares at the police station, chews her lip. 'I haven't told you much about Tilly's father.'

Joseph keeps his breathing shallow, tries to figure out where this is going. 'You've told me virtually nothing.'

'It's not the easiest thing to bring up.'

He waits for her to elaborate. Once a minute has passed, he says, 'I might be way off, here. But from the few things you've said, I got the impression he was abusive.'

'Unfortunately, your impression was right.'

'I'm so sorry, Erin.'

She picks up her sunglasses, puts them down. 'You read all those stories – of women who don't get out, who let it happen time and again. You grow up thinking you never would because you're too intelligent, too strong.

'And then it does happen. And you tell yourself it's not the same. You're career people, high-fliers, with all the stresses that brings. Yours was a one-off – an extreme situation. And it *doesn't* happen again, until one day it does, and this time you end up sticking around because for some bizarre reason you need to fix it, because you can't accept failure, in marriage or anything else.

'That is, until you find out from your daughter that he's abusing her, too. And in the worst possible way.'

'My God,' Joseph says. 'What an animal. I don't know what to say, Erin. I sensed she'd had a rough time, too. But not that.'

'After the divorce, I'd thought the worst part was over. Then Robson fought me for access and won joint custody. You'd think it could never happen, not with those kinds of accusations flying around. Apparently, it happens all the time. When the court found no evidence of abuse, Robson's legal team accused me of parental alienation. I nearly lost Tilly completely.'

Joseph sees how much the recollections are costing her; and yet he can't help wondering why she's telling him this now, with all these other crises unfolding around them, or why she's brought him within shouting distance of Crompton's police station before sharing it.

'Tilly doesn't see him any more,' Erin continues. 'But back then, thanks to the court order, she didn't have much choice. Only after she'd gone through puberty did her dad suddenly lose all interest.'

She rubs her arms, hugs herself. 'After Robson, there was Mark. He seemed a nice enough guy, but he wasn't much of a dad. Wasn't much of anything, it turned out. You know most of the story from our bereavement meetings. One night he chased down a handful of pills with a bottle of whisky and climbed into bed with me. When I woke the next morning he was already cold. You could live a thousand lifetimes and not put that memory out of your head.'

Joseph closes his eyes. He'd known that Mark had killed himself but not that Erin had woken up beside him. 'I cannot even begin to imagine.'

As nightmarish as that moment must have been, he knows the tragedy hadn't ended there. Mark, a compulsive gambler seemingly devoid of luck or talent, had left behind a trail of loans and maxed-out credit cards, along with a hefty secret remortgage. His life insurance had paid out, but Erin had still been forced to sell the house.

'And then I met you.'

Joseph turns that sentence over in his mind. He tries to frame it among her revelations about Robson, which he hadn't heard before, and the details he hadn't known about Mark.

*Bad things come in threes*, says a voice inside his head. *Don't you get it? Bad things and bad men: Robson. Mark. You.*

He stares at the grey misery of Crompton's police station. He wonders if PC Hopkins and PC Kenner are inside, reporting on their conversation with the Carvers. He wonders if his photograph is tacked to a whiteboard, a dotted line connecting him to Drew; worse, if Max's photograph is up there with it.

'I'm telling you all this,' Erin continues, 'because for the last three years, and for the first time in her life, Tilly's had a proper dad. Someone who keeps his promises when he makes them. Someone prepared to go into bat for her when she needs it. I'd wanted that for Tilly and you delivered. Just like I hope you think I delivered for Max.'

'I do,' he says. 'You know I do.'

Erin sighs. 'But being a dad isn't enough, Joe. I need a husband, too.'

A thirty-foot metal pole stands outside the police station. Three CCTV cameras hang from it, pointed in different directions. One of the lenses faces this way.

Joseph's heart starts to thump against his ribs. 'I *am* your husband.'

'It's more than just a word.'

Yesterday, sitting here, he'd barely glanced at that nest of cameras. Might a group of officers inside the station be watching the live footage, deciding exactly when to come outside and arrest him?

'I know that,' he says. 'Obviously, I know that. But things have been good enough, haven't they? I mean, last night we—'

'Oh, last *night*,' Erin laughs. It's a bitter sound, discordant. 'Yes, that certainly was memorable.'

In a blink he recalls his wife naked on their bed, her palms covered in his blood, shock and horror on her face. When he comes back to himself he realizes that she's studying him.

'I know I asked you already,' she says, 'but is it repairable?'

'What?'

'This. Us.'

'Erin, until Saturday night I hadn't even realized what needed fixing. But my eyes are open, now. Well and truly. I'm committed to this. To us. I want it to last for ever.'

'I know you know,' Erin says.

'You know I know what?'

She closes her eyes, leans her head against the rest. 'Joe, please. This is hard enough without you playing dumb. We can be adults about it, can't we? The question I really want to ask is whether Max knows.'

He sees pain lines creasing her face, cords of muscle standing proud in her neck.

'Whether Max knows *what*, Erin? What are you talking about?'

'Are you really going to make me say it?'

'I guess I really am.'

'Whether he knows about Angus.'

Fireflies stutter and dance in front of Joseph's eyes. 'I don't get you.'

'About me and Angus.'

'You and Angus?'

And then, suddenly, he understands.

There's an itch in Joseph's throat he can't scratch. He coughs, hawks, but he can't get any relief. A sudden, appalling chasm opens up inside him. Rapidly, it begins to expand – a cathedral of black nothing, vast in its emptiness.

'It won't help,' Erin whispers, 'but I'm going to say it anyway. I'm so sorry, Joe. I'm so dreadfully, dreadfully sorry.' At last she turns to him, her eyes swimming. 'I was lonely, heartbroken really. You kept pushing me away. I thought you'd given up on us. And none of that is an excuse.'

His phone starts buzzing. He pulls it out, sees that Max is calling. Dazed, not knowing what else to do, he puts the phone to his ear.

'Dad,' the boy says. 'Don't tell her anything. Don't you—'

Joseph ends the call.

'Was that him?' Erin asks. 'Was that Max?'

'Yes.'

'He knows, doesn't he? Did you tell him? Or did he find out all by himself?'

'Erin . . .' Joseph clenches his teeth. 'I don't know *what* he knows.'

'Did you use some kind of tracker? Hack my phone? Follow me to the hotel? *Look* at me, Joe.'

'I *am* looking at you!' he shouts, his voice cracking. 'I didn't know any of this!' He shakes his head in stunned disbelief. 'Still, what a way to tell me, eh? You park outside the *police* station for this conversation? What was the plan? Test me out with the truth, and if you got a bad reaction lean on the horn and wait for the cavalry? What did you think – that I'd hit you? Start slapping you around? Have I ever – *ever* – given you any reason to suspect I might behave like that? In the entire time we've known each other, I think this is the first time I've even raised my voice to you – and based on what I just learned, you might say I had good reason.'

Not once, during his response, has Erin taken her eyes off him. Now, reaching out, she lays her hand on his. Her fingers are hot, almost like she has a fever.

'You really didn't know,' she says; and Joseph sees, from

her expression, that she must have glimpsed the truth of that in his face, or in his reaction, or both.

He snatches away his hand. 'Did it occur to you that maybe, *just maybe*, if I'd suspected an affair I'd have come straight out and asked you?' Again, he shakes his head. 'Do you love him?'

Erin grimaces. 'No. God, no. Absolutely not. It isn't like that at all. Wasn't like that. It was a horrible, devastating mistake. One that I was in the process of correcting – or at least ending. He was just . . .'

She pauses, and Joseph can tell that she's trying to order her thoughts – that she isn't trying to deceive him, or paint her actions in a more positive light. 'He was just present, you know? In a way you haven't been. We used to be so close, me and you. And then . . . I could never figure out why things changed. I know how selfish it sounds, how awful, but I guess it was just a relief to be away from that for a while. To feel . . . *wanted* again.'

Joseph lets that sink in. 'How long has it been going on?'

'Not too long.'

'Weeks? Months?'

'No more than a few months.'

Erin takes a tissue from her bag. She blots away the mascara running down her cheeks. Her chin trembles, her neck blotchy and red. He's never seen her so distraught. Abruptly, she starts the car, checks her mirror and pulls out into traffic. 'And now, suddenly, he's missing,' she says. 'And Drew is missing, too.'

Joseph watches, bewildered, as Crompton's police station slides past on his right. So – test passed? Is that it? Had she thought her admission of infidelity might wring from him an explanation of Angus Roth's disappearance? How ironic that his ignorance of Erin's affair might have affirmed his innocence in her mind of any wrongdoing.

In the pit of his stomach, a flame of anger ignites. The longer he sits beside his wife, the hotter the fire grows.

Is Erin the key? Suddenly, it seems she must be. He thinks of Max's claim that he'd hit the dead man by accident; the lack of visible damage to the car; the boy's subsequent claim that he'd ended the dead man's life out of mercy. (*It was a kindness, what I did.*)

Did Max discover the affair and act to protect his father? Is that what this has been about all along? He recalls his son's words in the kitchen Friday night, when asked why he hadn't woken Joseph and sought help.

*Because you've already been through so much. Because, on top of everything else, you really didn't deserve this.*

In hindsight, perhaps the boy hadn't been referring to the supposed car accident but to Erin's affair.

The fire in Joseph's stomach erupts with fresh fury. It feels like liquid flame is beginning to run through his arteries. His hands make fists. His knuckles crack like gunshots.

He replays once again what Max had said at Claire's graveside.

*I'm not trying to make you feel bad. It's just . . . if things keep going the way they are, you're going to lose her. The only reason I'm telling you is because I don't want you to end up alone . . .*

*I just want you to think about the future and how that looks. Because if Erin is part of it, you need to commit to her, Dad. If she isn't, you really need to decide now while you still can, while there's still time to start afresh.*

Suddenly, it's heartbreakingly obvious what his son, in whatever damaged capacity, had been trying to communicate.

Joseph had sought to rebuild his family, had hoped to heal Max of past wounds. And all he's achieved is this – this monstrous and horrific calamity.

Fire in his arteries, in his head. It feels like he's burning up, the heat threatening to flash over at any moment. His rage isn't directed at Erin. He loves this woman, regardless of what she might have done; and love – in his experience, at least – doesn't come with an off switch. Instead, his fury is directed inwards, because what Erin said just now was true. He *hasn't* been present, for any of them. He's allowed his fear of losing another loved one to hijack him, threatening the very consequences he's so desperately tried to avoid.

They're heading east, Joseph realizes. Out of Crompton. To the north, he can see the green curtain of Jack-O'-Lantern Woods.

It's growing increasingly obvious where his wife is taking him. Erin slows the car, takes a left. And then they're gliding around the gentle curve of his mother's street.

Just like yesterday, Joseph prepares to see a line of police cars, perhaps a white geometric tent pitched on his mother's front lawn.

'You know what I think?' Erin asks. 'You won't like it, but I'm worried it might be true.'

If Joseph's fists clench any harder, he'll see the white bone of his knuckles burst through the stretched skin. 'Try me.'

The bungalow reveals itself. Joseph sees no police cars. No forensics tent. Erin pulls on to the empty driveway and kills the engine.

Across the street, an old man in a Hard Rock Cafe base-ball cap is shaving a box hedge with electric clippers. Joseph recognizes him – Dell Stephano. His mother used to take coffee with Dell every Wednesday and complain bitterly about his nosiness for the rest of the week. She'd stuck to that routine for as long as she lived in Saddle Bank, so Joseph supposes she must have found something about Dell that she liked.

He watches the man through the wing mirror, imagin-ing how glorious it must feel to have no task more pressing than the trimming of a hedge. Then he looks at his mother's garage and thinks about what lies inside.

Two houses to his left, a sprinkler is flinging jewels of rainbow water into the air. Overhead, an aeroplane is scribing twin white lines across blue sky. The day is idyllic, dreamlike.

Erin slips her sunglasses back on. From her bag she finds a silk headscarf, folds it into a triangle and ties it under her chin. She looks like she's channelling Audrey Hepburn, or perhaps Susan Sarandon from *Thelma and Louise*.

'Well?' Joseph asks. 'Are you going to tell me?'

'Yes, but not out here. Let's go inside.'

Climbing out of the car, she strides across the driveway to the bungalow's front entrance.

# THIRTY-SIX

In the half-second before Joseph throws open his door and follows, a hundred thoughts rush through his head; a thousand.

Last night, lying awake, he'd been ready to tell Erin everything. Not just what Max had done, first to the dead man and then to Drew, but how Joseph had concealed the truth. He'd intended to tell her because he hadn't thought it conscionable to let her find out any other way. Now, just like previous decisions since this nightmare began four days ago, the calculus has fundamentally changed. Because as much as he might still love his wife, as much as he might understand the reasons for her infidelity, he's just glimpsed a side to her he hadn't known existed.

Outside the police station, Erin had begun their conversation by spinning him back to his first meeting with Tilly, a memory she'd known would invoke all the emotions that had filled him that day, all his protective instincts. She'd gone on to share intimate details of her life with Robson, and then Mark, that he'd never heard before. Only once she'd pacified him with the opiate memory of first encounters and neutered him with the horrors of past relationships had she admitted the truth about Angus Roth.

He can't fault her. She has, at least, been honest. But Erin's manipulation of him, however trivial, does highlight something important – his ability to predict her behaviour isn't as accurate as he'd once thought. Right now, right here, that could be his undoing.

Joseph gets out of the car, ignoring his body's various shrieks of protest, unable to ignore the chill of fear his mother's bungalow instils in him. The building seems different, in ways he can't explain. It exudes a tangible menace. Breathing hard, he hobbles after his wife, his fingers hooked like talons, like claws.

Erin slides her key into the lock and opens the door. She sniffs the air, steps through. Joseph pauses on the step, casting a look back at Dell Stephano and the sprinkler flinging its jewels into the morning sky. He wonders if the stench of death rolling out of the bungalow is real or entirely illusory.

Sweat bursts from his pores. It rolls wet from his armpits. Flexing his fingers, he limps across the threshold behind Erin. He elbows the door shut, hears the snick of its latch. Immediately, he finds himself in an entirely different world to the one populated by Dell. It's silent in here, but there's an *awareness* to the silence. The bungalow feels sentient; as if it's poised, alert.

The stench Joseph thought he'd breathed into his lungs is already fading. His imagination must have been playing tricks. The air feels ancient, even so, hot and dead: like the inside of a crypt unsealed after a couple of millennia lying beneath desert sands. Again, he's struck by how alien everything looks. He feels less like he's standing in his late mother's hallway and more like he's entered a—

—*lair*, some part of his mind volunteers.

Erin glances over her shoulder at him, her eyes hidden by her sunglasses. Then she turns away and lifts her chin. 'Hello?'

Joseph baulks at that, stares at his wife in confusion. She knows the place is unoccupied. Who does she think might answer?

'Drew?' she calls. 'Are you here?'

Joseph watches Erin move along the hall, his stomach twisting like an Archimedes screw. She stops at the door leading to his mother's bedroom, ducks in her head.

'What're you doing?' he hisses. 'You really think she might be here?'

Erin ignores his question, disappearing inside. Joseph, his heart kicking like a newborn foal, is forced to follow. What he sensed as he crossed the drive he senses even more strongly inside the bungalow. Something is badly amiss with the heavy, bookish quiet. Even the peculiar fall of the light through the slatted blinds feels wrong.

His mother's room is a desolate space, familiar yet fundamentally changed. The fitted wardrobes – white with decorative gold inlays – look just as they did when she was alive. Her bed, now stripped to the mattress, is crowned by the same rose-velvet headboard.

But just like the rest of the bungalow, the vital touches that made this her sanctuary have disappeared. Her empty dressing table is layered with dust. Joseph remembers it cluttered with make-up and perfume bottles, along with keepsakes and gifts made by Max: the boy's first finger painting; his first handwritten letter; Christmas cards he'd drawn; crude clay figures he'd pushed together; a bookmark cut from felt and badly sewn; a trinket box covered with carefully stuck-on shells; photos of him feeding ducks, or wearing a doctor's dressing-up kit, or standing on a box and turning sausages on a barbecue.

Where did it all go? Joseph remembers clearing the bungalow with Erin, a few months after his mother's death. But now, standing here, he doesn't recall what happened to her most sentimental belongings. He knows he didn't throw them away.

Erin glances at the bed, leans over it. Whatever she's looking for, she doesn't find it. Going to the fitted wardrobes, she opens the doors two at a time, revealing the empty spaces beneath the rails.

Erin closes the last set. Then she returns to the hall. Joseph follows, watching as she performs the same routine in the guest bedroom.

In the living room, he spots the first change since his last visit. Someone has returned his mother's chair and side table to their original positions. Their legs have been slotted, like eight keys into eight locks, back into the same depressions in the carpet.

Did Miah do this yesterday, following the viewing? Perhaps it was the older woman with the Japanese knotweed fixation.

Erin looks around the room. There's nowhere in here to hide a body – not unless you chopped it into pieces and put separate chunks in the sideboard and dresser; likewise, in the kitchen beyond the arch. Perhaps Erin's not looking for a body at all but signs of occupation. Perhaps she suspects Max and Drew have been using the bungalow as a hideaway, that Drew has been camped out here for reasons unknown.

With a lurch, Joseph recalls the way Enoch had rubbed Erin's side last night, his fingers not-so-subtly seeking her breast. He recalls Erin's story about her first husband and how Robson had abused her, and had abused Tilly even worse.

Perhaps *that's* why Erin thinks Drew might be here. If so, she won't be looking for bloodstains or pieces of hacked scalp but crumbs of food, toiletries, a sleeping bag crushed inside a drawer.

In the kitchen, she opens each cupboard individually. She

checks the fridge, the washing machine, the dishwasher. When she turns to him, he still can't see her expression. The sunglasses have given her ant eyes: black, shiny, enormous.

Joseph forces himself not to look at the connecting door to the garage. Erin hasn't checked it. Can it possibly have escaped her notice?

'Well?' he asks, wiping sweat from his forehead. 'Are you going to talk to me?'

'I think Max found out about Angus. I think that's why he's been acting so strangely. And I think that maybe he decided to do something about it. Scare Angus off, or teach him a lesson. Maybe snatch him off the street and hold him prisoner for a while.

'Angus hasn't been seen since Thursday, and it'd take a lot of work to keep him here so long. Max has been seeing Drew. You told me that yourself. I'd wondered if she might be helping him – if that might explain where she'd gone. But she's not here, Joe. No one is. So maybe that's not what happened at all.'

Erin pauses. Then she says. 'Maybe it's worse than that. Maybe Drew found out that Max had done something and threatened to go to the police.'

Joseph laughs, shakes his head – because mockery of her argument feels like his only possible strategy. 'Jesus, Erin. Do you know how you sound? Your evidence for any of this is what, exactly?'

Her chest rises and falls. She folds her arms, then unfolds them. 'All the connections I just laid out. Angus hasn't been seen since Thursday. Friday night Max decides, seemingly randomly, and for the first time ever, to take a drive in an untaxed and uninsured car. When he gets home, he doesn't park outside. Instead, he sneaks into the house, keeping all the lights off. In the morning, the washing-up bowl and the dish scrubber have disappeared. Also – and I didn't mention this before, thought I'd hold it back – someone decided to mop the kitchen floor in the early hours of Saturday, because when I went downstairs first thing it looked spotless and smelled strongly of bleach. And when I asked you, that morning, about what happened when you confronted Max, you told me you—'

Erin stiffens, raises her head. She turns away from him, stares at the connecting door to the garage. 'You told me you drove the car over here with him, in the middle of the night, to stop him from using it again.'

Erin takes off her sunglasses and slides them in her hip pocket. She's breathing even faster, now. For the first time, Joseph thinks he sees something new in her expression – the smallest flicker of apprehension. Perhaps even fear.

She moves towards the connecting door. And Joseph, out of desperation, blocks her path.

'Move,' she says.

'Erin—'

'What've you got to hide?'

'Erin, listen.'

'I said *move*.'

They're inches away from each other. Joseph can smell her perfume, the lingering traces of coffee on her breath. He can see the striations of caramel in her blue eyes, the inky pools at their centres. The tick of her pulse in her neck.

She is, he thinks, quite beautiful. Even now. *Especially* now.

All he wants is to protect his son. To keep Max out of jail, to give him another chance of life. He wonders if Erin can read any of that in his face. He wonders if she understands the lengths he'll go to achieve it. Because he's in this for the finish, now, has resigned himself fully to the task. He loves his wife but he can't lose his boy.

Joseph thinks of what's waiting on the other side of that door: the car, Drew, the garden implements piled in one corner, the workbench against the near wall and the work tools stacked upon it – the screwdrivers, the hammers, the mallets; the saws, the wrenches, the planting spikes; the hand axes, the lengths of hose and rope.

With a huge gulp of air, Joseph stands aside. Erin reaches for the door handle and opens it, revealing a wedge of perfect dark. She hesitates on the threshold, throws him a distrustful look.

It feels like someone has forced a paddle down Joseph's throat and is violently stirring his guts. A muscle twitches in his bicep. His knee sends out a warning shriek.

Forty-eight hours after Drew's passing, twenty-four hours after he wrapped her in plastic and dumped her inside the Honda, Joseph fears the stench inside the garage will be thick enough to coat his tongue. But the air rolling out of it smells toasted, not rotten – an inoffensive combination of warm engine oil and baked dust.

Erin steps forward. Joseph follows. He feels like a cow being led into an abattoir. And then, as if a slaughterman just pressed a bolt gun to his forehead and pulled the trigger, white light flares.

In front of him, his mother's garage resolves, shadows flitting like bats to the furthest corners of the space. Overhead, the fluorescent strip stutters twice and stabilizes.

Joseph staggers past his wife, somehow keeps his balance. He blinks, stares, reels. But there's no denying reality. His mother's car has gone.

# THIRTY-SEVEN

Teri Platini meets the solicitor recommended by Brittany Moore at eleven a.m. in the lobby of the Tamarind Hotel and Spa, a few miles from Crompton.

Saul Faulkner is short, middle-aged and balding. His suit is expensive and well cut, but the impression is spoiled by leather-soled shoes that are scuffed and falling apart. He's sweating when he arrives. He looks like a man trying to flush out last night's alcohol or cocaine.

Teri orders a skinny latte. Saul orders a Bloody Mary with extra Tabasco.

'Talk,' he says. 'I'm all ears. Like an African elephant without the trunk.'

'Is this conversation protected?'

'Protected?'

'Sorry. I mean confidential.'

Saul gulps down half his Bloody Mary and wipes his mouth. 'My elephant lips are sealed.'

'I need you to prepare a will.'

'Easy-peasy-Japaneasy.'

'It's not for me. For my partner.'

'Is he joining this powwow?'

Teri shakes her head. 'He's gone AWOL. And I don't think he's coming back.'

Saul necks the rest of his Bloody Mary and signals the waiter for another. 'Out of interest, how do you know this partner of yours doesn't have a will already, drawn up by another firm?'

'Because he's a narcissistic shithead who thinks he'll live for ever. And because he doesn't have any kids, with me or anyone else.'

Saul nods, blots his forehead with a napkin. 'If you took off my socks right now, you'd see that my toes have turned blue. Because what you're asking for is ih-lee-gal. For the record, I couldn't possibly involve myself with something so inherently unethical. For the record.'

The waiter arrives with a second Bloody Mary. Saul sips it, exhaling with evident satisfaction. When he puts down the glass, his lips are red with tomato juice. 'But it's a nice morning,' he continues. 'And this is a nice enough spot to cure a hangover. And you seem like nice enough company in which to do it, save for your obvious depravity. So I see no harm in indulging a fantasy.'

'Sorry?'

'I mean that while Saul Faulkner, of unimpeachable integrity, would never contemplate something like this – even if you insisted on paying cash, and fat bundles of it – I'm happy enough to help you conduct a thought experiment, explaining all the risks of such a venture, how they might be minimized, and all the potential outcomes. I presume that this document, should it come into being, would make you the sole beneficiary of our narcissistic friend's estate? House, cars, cuddly toys, that sort of thing?'

'It's a possibility.'

Teri watches a bead of sweat roll down Saul's temple. Then she flags the waiter. This time, instead of a skinny latte, she orders a gin and tonic. Saul smiles at that, using a napkin to wipe his face.

They talk for an hour. Saul excuses himself twice. Both times he returns to the table sweatier and more talkative than before, his pupils noticeably dilated. After his third Bloody Mary he switches to whisky. Teri orders a second G&T. By midday, she has a much clearer understanding of her options.

None are without risk. Long-term, they all depend on Angus being dead. Short-term, the outlook is even more uncertain.

Saul tosses back the dregs of his drink. 'The brother is going to be your problem. You realize that, yes?'

Teri's cheeks and forehead throb, still raw from her tumble across Thornecroft's gravel drive. 'Let him try his worst.'

'Did he do that?' he asks, indicating her swollen face, her split lip.

'It's the last time he ever will.'

Saul's grin widens. 'I like you, Teri Platini. You're like a mouse with the balls of a wild horse.' He blinks, frowns. 'Confusing image, I'll admit.'

'So you'll help me?'

'I couldn't possibly. Let's keep in touch.'

Teri stands. Saul's hand, when she shakes it, is wet and gross.

'I have a condition,' he says. 'It makes me sweat.'

'Do you mean a habit?'

'Like a nun's habit?'

'Not exactly.'

He winks. 'OK, Horse Balls. Let's tango again when the moon is full and witches are abroad.' With that, he bows out.

Upstairs in her room, Teri puts on to hangers the clothes she rescued from Thornecroft and arranges her scant toiletries. Then, sitting on the bed, she takes out her notebook and opens it to the most recent entry. There, in her own handwriting, are two words: Barbie Girl. Beneath them, the mobile number she memorized from Angus's WhatsApp.

Teri stares at it for a while, fingernails tapping her teeth. She keys the number into her phone, hesitates. Then she goes to the window and stares at the car park four storeys below. 'Well, Horse Balls?' she mutters. 'Are you going to use them or not?'

Holding her breath, Teri hits the call button.

# THIRTY-EIGHT

Staring at the empty patch of concrete in his mother's garage, Joseph can't quite process what he's seeing. He shuffles forward another step, almost expecting to feel resistance, as if his mother's car might still be there, albeit somehow rendered invisible.

Erin is speaking, but he doesn't really hear her. There's a buzzing in his ears like a faulty dimmer switch.

The car can't be gone. It can't be gone.

The car is gone.

Pressure on his right arm. Erin, gently shaking him. Joseph screws up his face, turns his head left and right. He sees the glass demijohn he kicked over during his last visit. The knocked-over rake.

There's a small, dark stain near the main swing door. He thinks it's probably his blood, from where he crashed down yesterday and ripped open his knee. Or perhaps it's the blood from Max's hands, Sunday night.

'Where's the car?' Erin asks. 'You said you parked it here.'

'I did.'

'Joe—'

'I did!'

She turns towards him. 'So where's it gone?'

He has no answer. Did Max come over and move it after the viewing? Did their paths somehow not cross? He can think of no other explanation. And yet without one their conversation following the police visit makes no sense:

*We've got to move her, Dad.*

*I know.*

*We've got to do it now.*

*Listen. This has blown up. People are watching us. We can't afford a single mistake.*

*We can't afford to wait, either. Erin—*

*Leave Erin to me.*

*That's not what I meant. I think she—*

He snaps out of his stupor. What might the boy have said, had Joseph not cut him off? He stares at the empty patch of concrete. Then he looks up at his wife.

Erin's face is sickly beneath the fluorescent strip. 'The truth, Joe. You really don't know where it's gone?'

'I really don't.'

'Friday night, when you drove over here, did you look inside the boot?'

He shakes his head, not trusting himself to speak.

'Then we have to talk to the police. We do. Because this . . . It looks more and more like Max did something. And I know that's hard to hear because he's your son, and I know how fiercely you love him, but we have to—'

'He not a killer, Erin. He's not. He's just . . .'

'Just what?'

*Lost? Are you really going to say it?*

Joseph flounders. He gazes around the garage: at the sharp and lethal tools lying on the workbench; at the sharp and lethal garden implements stacked against the wall. He can still hear Dell Stephano's hedge trimmer, but only faintly. 'Just a teenage boy.'

'Teenage boys can do bad things. They do them all the time. I want to be wrong about this, obviously I do. And if I am, I'll hold up my hands to both of you. But if I'm right, Joe – if I'm right, and Max did something to Angus because he found out about the affair – then who do you think might be next?'

Joseph opens and closes his mouth. He stares at his wife, incredulous, because he can see that Erin's fear is genuine. Knowing what he does about the events of the last week, he can't even dismiss it as paranoia. Five nights ago, he wouldn't have believed his son capable of killing a stranger in cold blood. Three nights ago, he wouldn't have believed him capable of killing Drew. Only an hour ago, he wouldn't have believed his wife capable of an affair.

Those fireflies are back, dancing in front of his eyes. His gaze returns to the workbench. 'We're not going to the police.'

'Joe, we have to.'

'He's my son, Erin. He's all I've got.'

When Erin's face crumples, Joseph grimaces.

He hadn't thought before speaking, hadn't meant to hurt her with that comment, but there it is, the truth. Eight billion people on this planet – and only one to whom he's connected by blood; only one to whom he owes a debt too enormous to be paid: a son who lost his mother because of his father's naïve belief that the world was a better place than it's proved to be, and that home was a safe harbour where bad things could never happen.

How many of those eight billion souls would he feed into the fire to save Max? More than two, he suspects. Would he ever stop?

'Joe, think about what you're saying.'

'I know what I'm saying.'

'You can't simply—'

'I can rescue this. I just need—'

'Joe, seriously, this is—'

'You're not going to take him *away* from me!'

Erin recoils. Glancing around the garage, she suddenly seems to grasp how alone they are in here. Dell Stephano might be working across the street, but the guy's hearing isn't great. With the hedge cutter buzzing in his ears, he'll be deaf to everything else.

Joseph lowers his voice, speaks slowly through clenched teeth. 'Listen to me carefully,' he tells her. 'Because I'm not going to debate this any longer. You don't get to stand here and unilaterally decide my son's future. You certainly don't get to do that minutes after confessing your infidelity. We're going to get back in the car and we're going to drive home. We're going to speak to Max, see what he has to say – and then, collectively, we'll figure this out.'

Something shifts in Erin's expression, as if her own calculus just changed, too. 'OK, Joe,' she says quietly. 'OK.'

Joseph nods, knows he's storing up trouble. But right now this is about survival, tackling each crisis as it hits, transitioning from one calamitous moment to the next – as if leaping stepping stones across a raging river.

If he can get Erin outside, if he can get her into the car and get the car on the road, he can win himself a reprieve. She's not going to throw herself from a moving vehicle. The tension between them is escalating, but it's not that high, not yet.

'Give me your phone,' he says, holding out his hand. When Erin takes a backward step, he matches her with a forward one. 'Just for the journey home.'

'Joe, what is this? Listen to yourself. Surely you don't—'

'The *phone*, Erin.'

Her jaw muscles bulge. She opens her bag, digs out her mobile and hands it over. Joseph slides it into his pocket.

'Car keys.' She hands those over, too. 'OK, we're leaving. And please – don't make this any harder than it already is.'

Erin seems reluctant to put her back to him. Finally, squaring her shoulders, she turns and steps through the connecting door. As Joseph follows her out, he picks up a claw hammer from the workbench and slides it up his shirtsleeve.

# THIRTY-NINE

Enoch Cullen wakes in his chair, to a ringing so cruelly insistent he wants to yell at it to stop.

It feels like someone drilled a borehole through his skull while he was sleeping and poured in sulphuric acid. He cracks open one eye, just a slit, and pulls himself upright. The sudden movement rocks his stomach and he's nearly sick.

One thought – to stop the ringing and crawl upstairs to bed. On the coffee table, among the crushed beer cans and congealed Chinese food, stand an empty tequila bottle, an empty port bottle and a bottle that might once have contained ouzo.

Enoch stands, belches acid. His moan is long and heartfelt. As it ends, the ringing ceases. He sways on his feet, wonders if the sound was in his head all along. Then it starts up again – a clamorous electronic trilling. On the arm of his chair lies Drew's phone, still in its rhinestone case. Its screen is dark. The ringing sounds like it's coming from behind him.

Enoch pivots, his leg colliding with the coffee table. Beer cans, bottles and Chinese food go tumbling across the carpet. He's frantic, now. He's got to stop that ringing before it splits his head in two. Stumbling into his kitchen, he tries to identify its source.

The light streaming through the window is nuclear bright. Panting, Enoch goes from cupboard to cupboard, yanking the doors wide. When he checks the one above the toaster, the ringing intensifies. He thrusts his hand inside. Tins of soup and corned beef crash on to the worktop like mountain boulders. Finally, he hauls out a phone, the screen lit up with a mobile number he doesn't recognize.

Accepting the call, Enoch presses the phone to his ear. 'Drew?' he rasps. He hears no reply – not even the hiss of an open line – and when he checks the screen he sees that the battery must have died.

He stares at the device, tries to think, wishes he'd memorized the number.

A wave of dizziness hits.

He staggers back into the living room, this time knocking over a stack of DVD cases. When he collapses into his chair, he loses his grip on the phone and hears it bounce across the carpet.

Enoch lays back his head, screws up his eyes. He feels like he's on the deck of a yacht being tossed by an angry ocean. If he can ride out his nausea, navigate his way to calmer waters, he can find a lead for the phone, charge it up.

Enoch's chin touches his chest. He only needs a minute. Just one. Within seconds, he's asleep.

# FORTY

Outside, the day is as idyllic as it was. The flotilla of white clouds overhead looks like it's sailed straight off a Constable canvas. Dell Stephano has put away his hedge cutter and is sweeping up the trimmings. When he sees Joseph and Erin emerge from the bungalow, he waves in greeting.

Joseph waves back. Then he takes Erin's hand. Holding it firmly, he warns her not to engage Dell in conversation. She does as he asks, which is a relief, because he has no plan should she try to shake herself free. He's hardly going to club his wife around the head with the hammer hidden inside his shirtsleeve.

*Certainly not in front of witnesses, eh, Joe?*

Joseph snarls at that voice, tries to smother it.

He unlocks the car and opens the passenger door for Erin. As he walks around to the driver's side, he slides out the hammer from his sleeve, dropping it into the door well as climbs behind the wheel. Then he tries to settle his nerves and catch his breath.

He's still sweating. His shirt clings against his skin. Mopping his brow again, he reverses off the drive. Erin watches him, silent.

Joseph follows the curve of his mother's road, turns right

at the junction and accelerates. Erin can't open the door, escape. Nor can she call the police. For a while he can concentrate on an even more significant problem – the likely whereabouts of his mother's Honda, and the resultant whereabouts of Drew.

Could a burglar, finding nothing of value inside the bungalow, have decided to steal the car? Might someone be driving it away from Saddle Bank at this very moment, ignorant of its cargo? If that's true, Joseph is powerless to control what happens next, but he doesn't believe that's the explanation.

Did Max move the car first thing? He hadn't said anything, and it wouldn't have slipped his mind. Which means if he *is* responsible, he's clearly lost all trust in his father.

'I'm scared, Joe.'

'Me too.'

'I'm so sorry for what I did. I didn't want to lose you, I still don't. I thought I already had.'

'I don't want to lose you, either,' Joseph mutters, keeping his eyes on the road. As he changes up a gear, he hears a tapping sound and worries for a moment that the car is playing up – or, even worse, that someone is locked in the boot. When he glances down, he realizes that his wedding ring is rattling against the gearstick, his left hand violently shaking. The more he tries to control it, the worse the shaking becomes.

If Max did take the car, where might he have driven it? Even without Drew's body, the vehicle is a forensic examiner's wet dream.

Turning on to their street, Joseph drives along it to the cul-de-sac. Their driveway is clear: no Honda, no police cars. He pulls up and kills the engine.

Erin stares through the windscreen at the house. 'I don't want to go in there,' she whispers.

'It's your home,' he tells her. 'Our home.'

'It doesn't feel like it. Not right now.' She glances at him. 'What if I'm right, Joe? Just tell me, before we go inside.'

He looks at her, tries to think. Back at the bungalow he'd told himself that of the eight billion people on the planet, there was only one he'd do anything to save. But is that what he really believes?

'Remember what you told Max last night?' he asks. 'That our house was his sanctuary? That what happens out here doesn't affect what happens in there? That there are no recriminations, only love?'

'You're taking it out of context.'

'Am I? If Max has broken a law, hurt someone, we'll do the responsible thing. Obviously, we will. But the moment you go to the police you'll paint a giant target on his back – and right now you don't even have good reason. That's why we speak to him first, give him every opportunity to explain.' He pauses, tries to work out what she's thinking. 'Will you promise me?'

Erin's chest swells. Then she opens the door and swings her legs out of the car. Joseph climbs out, too. Positioning his torso to avoid Ralph Erikson's camera, he retrieves the hammer from the door well and slides it inside his trousers. Hooking the head over his belt and covering it with his shirt, he accompanies his wife up the drive. His heart is beating like a bird flapping broken wings. Eight billion souls. A thought with which to damn himself. Eight billion souls in exchange for one.

So many times, on TV, he's seen someone incapacitated by blunt force trauma suffer no lasting damage. But he knows from the YouTube guy that such outcomes can't be predicted – and certainly aren't guaranteed.

If Erin tries to call the police, will he physically attempt to stop her? That he's even asking the question demonstrates just how far he's fallen. He loves this woman. And yet he's lied to her repeatedly, has buried her dead lover, has concealed from her the truth about Drew.

All to protect his son. Because without Max, there's nothing left for him in this life.

Erin unlocks the front door. Joseph – his vision stuttering, his left hand twitching as if in horror of what it might soon have to do – follows her inside.

# FORTY-ONE

The second time Enoch Cullen jerks back into consciousness, he can't figure out how long he's been out, whether it's late afternoon or late morning, whether a few minutes have passed or several hours. He can't decide if he was having a nightmare or has just re-entered one.

Struggling up from his chair, he goes to the kitchen, opens the fridge and grabs a beer. He chugs half the can, gasps and wipes his mouth.

The kitchen clock isn't working, the microwave isn't set to the right time and his phone isn't in his pocket. Returning to the living room, he turns on the TV and checks the guide.

It's eight minutes past five, Tuesday afternoon. Last night, the Carvers had left around one a.m. Afterwards, he'd sat up drinking until five. Which means he's slept, give or take, for twelve hours.

He finds his phone wedged between the arm of his chair and the seat cushion, the screen dead and unresponsive. When he goes to the front door, he finds a police contact card on the mat, handwritten with an officer's details, a reference number and a message to call in. Beside it lies a sheet of A4. The word MISSING is printed above his daughter's image, along with a few lines of text. Scrawled in biro along the bottom:

*Made these earlier and putting them on lampposts today. Gave you a knock but no answer.*
*Tilz xx*

Finding his charger, Enoch plugs in his phone. As soon as he switches it on, it begins to chime and buzz with updates: texts, missed calls, voicemail alerts, social media notifications.

The first voicemail is from a wet-as-shit-sounding detective sergeant based in Crompton. The second is from Erin Carver, calling to see how he is. Enoch calls the station first, chugging the rest of his beer while he waits for what feels like a couple of weeks until somebody fetches the right guy. The detective is as useless as Enoch had expected, and he has no real news to share: they're continuing to look for Drew, just want to keep him informed, blah-fucking-blah-blah-blah. Only when Enoch ends the call does he remember something important: a dream fragment, perhaps – but he doesn't think so.

Back in the living room, he rips the seat cushion off his chair and daggers his hand along the cavity around its sprung base. He checks beneath the coffee table, beneath the TV cabinet and around the partially collapsed stacks of DVDs.

Enoch finally discovers the phone beside his boxed-up Christmas tree. Not a dream fragment, then. Nor a false memory created by booze.

The phone is a Samsung, just like his. Taking it to the kitchen, he unplugs his phone and connects the new one. A few seconds later, a lightning icon appears. Enoch holds down the power button until the device buzzes in his hand. While he waits for the screen to load, he grabs himself another beer. While he drinks, he thinks.

The phone can't be Paula's; his bitch ex-wife hasn't visited in weeks, and there's no way the battery could have lasted that long. It had died only when he tried to answer it. That means it couldn't have been in the kitchen cupboard where he first found it more than a few days.

Finally, the phone wakes. Unlike his own, it doesn't immediately freak out with updates. The wallpaper is a half-length portrait of Drew pouting for the camera. It looks like the image was snapped early evening, on the Carvers' back lawn.

Enoch sways on his feet when he sees it. His daughter is wearing pink lipstick, a ruched pink dress and pink opera gloves. Surrounded by globe lights, she's as pretty as a pearl.

'Where are you?' he whispers, and is dismayed at the catch in his voice. It's the kind of tragic drama-queen shit he'd expect from Paula. Not from a capable, hairy-arsed brute like himself.

When he touches the screen, a padlock icon appears. When he swipes right, he's offered the option of a fingerprint unlock or PIN. He tries 1-2-3-4. When that doesn't work, he tries 0-0-0-0 and fails again. Last night, Tilly Carver had told him the code for Drew's iPhone, but however hard he tries he can't remember it. Nor does he know Tilly's number to call and ask.

Enoch presses his index finger to the scanner, baring his teeth in frustration. Then he slams his fist into the cupboard opposite, splintering the panel. Rage is a more useful emotion than despair, even if it leaves his knuckles skinless and bloody. Finishing his second beer, he pulls a third from the fridge. 'What you need right now, boy,' he growls, 'is a moment of fucking clarity.'

Enoch cracks his knuckles, belches. He pops the tab on his beer, takes another long swallow. Then, returning to the hall, he retrieves the MISSING poster from where he dropped it. Beneath the printed text he sees Tilly Carver's contact details.

'Sherlock fucking Holmes,' he mutters. Draining the rest of the beer, he tosses the can into the sink. From the living room he fetches the landline handset. Back in the kitchen, sitting at his kitchen table, Enoch dials his daughter's best friend.

# FORTY-TWO

The house is as quiet as Joseph's mother's. When Erin calls
out, no one answers. Joseph knows that Tilly stayed home
this morning to make another round of calls to Drew's colleagues and friends, and to flood social media with appeals.
By now she'll be putting up her MISSING posters around
town. Where Max is, he has no idea.

'I'm going to make coffee,' Erin says. 'I suggest you call
him, ask him to come home.'

Joseph nods, his left hand violently jumping. Standing in
the hallway, he understands what his wife had meant outside. This doesn't feel like his home at all, more like a stage
set carefully constructed to resemble it. That feeling he'd
had at his mother's – of something not right – steals over
him once again, but he can't attribute it to anything tangible.

Were all the doors down here closed before they left?
They're all closed now. When Erin enters the kitchen, Joseph
almost shouts a warning – and he then waits, breath held,
right hand reaching behind him to the hammer hooked
over his belt.

But his fear, or his paranoia, is unwarranted. No one
seizes Erin as she walks inside. No one swings a bat into her
face or forces a blade between her ribs. Ironically – and this

is tough to admit – perhaps the greatest threat to her well-being is standing directly behind her.

Joseph doesn't want to leave his wife alone – he remains fearful of what she might do – but nor can he let her hear his conversation with Max. From the doorway, he watches her empty the portafilter into the knock box and position it under the grinder. 'You want one?' she asks.

'Thanks,' Joseph says, because the longer Erin is occupied with the machine the better.

She offers him a small smile – and just for a moment he feels himself weakening, his immediate instinct to comfort her, to assuage her fears.

But Erin isn't *the one*, which makes her one of the eight billion, so he resists the temptation and turns away. In the living room, he calls Max's number. The boy answers on the seventh ring.

'Where are you?' Joseph hisses. 'Where'd you go? Where's the car?'

'Slow down. What's wrong? I'm in town, helping Tilly put up posters.'

Joseph grimaces, clutches the phone harder. Because there are so many things wrong with what he just heard. 'Did you move the car?'

'What?'

Joseph goes to the living-room window and looks across the street at Ralph Erikson's house. Through gritted teeth, he mutters, *'Did you move the car?'*

'That's what I thought you said. Why would I take it? What're you talking about?'

Joseph closes his eyes, asks himself if the boy's tone sounds off, if something in Max's words doesn't ring true. His exhaustion, and the steady dump of adrenalin into his system, is starting to affect his thinking. He counts to ten, prepares to drop a nuke. Because if his son isn't lying, their situation is now critical. 'It's gone, Max. The car. It's not there.'

Silence, from the other end of the phone.

Joseph can almost hear the boy's mind racing, its gears sparking. And then the unexpected happens. The line goes dead.

He rips the phone from his ear, stares at it in dumb confusion. Running his tongue around his teeth, he redials, waits for the call to connect, listens as it rings and rings and, finally, switches to voicemail.

Joseph kills the connection. Moving from the window, he returns to the hall. In the kitchen, Erin is still working the espresso machine. She hasn't asked for her phone, which he confiscated for the journey here. The landline handset is on the console table. Joseph puts it in a separate pocket. Then he slides his hand down the wall and disconnects the router. Now she's completely cut off – no mobile, no landline, no internet through her laptop, nor any of their tablets.

Where does he go from here? He can't risk leaving Erin. He can't get hold of Max. He doesn't have the first clue about the Honda's location and the police are actively searching for Drew. Doubtless they'll soon be searching for Angus Roth.

Abruptly, he recalls something that had occurred to him at the bungalow. It won't help his immediate situation, but it'll give his mind a moment's respite. Opening the cupboard under the stairs, he pulls the light cord.

It's a cluttered space. Not just a home for their vacuum cleaner, ironing board and Max's various gym bags but a halfway house for all the stuff earmarked for charity. Joseph doesn't find what he's looking for so next he checks the garage. When he has no luck there, he ducks outside to the garden and investigates the shed, but it looks just like it had the night of the party.

When he returns to the house, Erin is waiting with his coffee. 'What were you looking for?'

'Nothing.'

'That's not true. Were you hunting for Drew?'

'No.'

'Did you get hold of Max?'

'Not yet.'

Joseph leaves the kitchen and goes upstairs. When he gets to the first-floor landing, he finds the blood.

# FORTY-THREE

It's a fist-sized puddle, dry at the edges, still wet and glistening at the centre. Two smaller stains the size of fifty pence pieces mark the floorboards a few inches away.

Joseph stares at the blood in silence. He's still shaking from the abrupt end to his phone call with Max, from his godawful discovery at the bungalow.

And now this.

He checks the hallway runner, the skirting board. He sees no other blood splashes, but a chunk of plaster is missing from the wall to his left, level with his nose. A few fragments lie on the floor directly beneath it.

It's not his blood. It can't be Erin's. And he just talked to Max.

*Oh Jesus*, he thinks. *Oh Jesus, oh Jesus.*

Tilly.

When he stands close to his stepdaughter, he can just about see over her head. If Max had clubbed her as she came out of her room and turned towards the stairs, her skull would have hit the plaster at that exact spot. If she'd tumbled to the floor, the puddle of blood is right where she might have landed.

Joseph's lungs have seized. He puts out a hand to the

bannisters. Tries to stop himself from falling. What does he do? *What?*

First the dead man. Then Drew.

Now Tilly.

Just like the ground floor, all the doors up here are closed, too. He definitely doesn't remember that from before he left the house. Is Tilly lying lifeless inside one of the bedrooms? Is Erin, drinking coffee downstairs, the oblivious mother of a dead daughter? Just like Enoch is an oblivious father?

There's a sickening pressure inside Joseph's head, as if a major artery is about to burst. Max might be his primary reason for living, but Tilly has been a reason for living, too. Since their first meeting in that Hampton Court bistro, they've become like father and daughter. Could he possibly stand by his son if he's done this?

*Of course not*, a part of his mind shrieks. *Of course not!*

He grips the bannisters, forces his eyes to return to that stain. Then he steps over it, opens his bedroom door. Tilly isn't there. Crossing the hall, careful to avoid the blood, Joseph opens all the remaining doors. He doesn't find his stepdaughter behind any of them.

He has to tell Erin what he's discovered up here, he has to, even though he knows that in her terror she'll call the police. He won't have the right to stop her. To even consider it would be monstrous.

Joseph takes a breath, breathes it out. Then, recalling his conversation with Ralph Erikson, he closes his eyes, gets down on his good knee and presses his hands together. 'Claire,' he whispers. 'Claire, please. I'm listening. For the first time, I'm really listening, but you've got to talk to me. Right now, right this very moment, you've got to talk to me, because I really don't know what to do.'

He empties his mind of thought, concentrates on nothing

but his breathing. It hitches, smooths. Hitches, smooths. Hitches, smooths, smooths.

Darkness, a rushing of sound. Silence, then that rushing sound again. As if he's caught inside a giant lung. Or a tunnel through which air is racing in steady pulses.

A memory forms. And then it's more than a memory. Suddenly, Joseph isn't kneeling in his upstairs hallway but bending over an incomprehensible network of pipes and tubes: white ones and clear ones, straight ones and articulated ones. Around him machines suck and whir and beep. Somewhere inside all that equipment lies Claire Carver. And now, at last, he sees her; a part of her, at least. A triangle of smooth cheek. A closed eye.

The machines are doing his wife's breathing and keeping her body alive. Claire's brain, the doctors have told him, is already dead. They haven't yet asked his permission to turn off life support, but he knows that conversation is coming. For now, he just needs to stand here and process the unutterable cruelty of what he's seeing.

Joseph feels strangely calm. Almost a disinterested observer. He finds himself studying the various items of medical equipment. He's never been that interested in how things work, but now he tries to guess the purpose of each machine and the components he might find inside them. He examines the bags of liquid, the beeping displays, all this high-tech wizardry brought here for the purpose of ensuring that Claire Carver's body – for a while longer, at least – remains a living tomb.

She looks like she's just sleeping.

Somewhere beyond the hospital grounds, police are hunting the burglar who attacked her before fleeing; but they'll never find him. Claire's killer won't serve a single day in prison.

If Joseph had listened to her in the bedroom, if he'd gone

downstairs instead of back to sleep, if his antennae for danger hadn't been so poorly developed, her body wouldn't be lying in this bed, the rest of her gone to a place he cannot follow.

Except . . . *except* . . . the vital signs monitor now registers a change in his wife's state. He hears a beeping different to that which has so marked his vigil. Onscreen, the numbers change, showing a spike in heart-rate, blood pressure, oxygen saturation and respiration.

Claire's eye opens. Her pupil contracts, then dilates. Her mouth, forced open by a tracheal tube, begins to move. And Joseph hears her voice, not in his ears but inside his head: *Protect our son, Joe. Whatever it takes.*

He staggers, feels his balance going, and then he's not in the hospital at all. He's on one knee in the upstairs hall of this house he bought with Erin, trying to work out what just happened.

In the hospital that day, Claire hadn't spoken, hadn't opened her eyes and looked at him, because despite the steady rise and fall of her chest, and the regular ping of the machines, she'd already departed.

*Protect our son, Joe. Whatever it takes.*

His eyes are burning. His throat, too. He stares at the puddle of what can only be Tilly's blood and pulls himself up. What he's about to do is inexcusable, indefensible. And he's going to do it all the same.

Limping to the bathroom, he tears two fistfuls of toilet paper from the roll. Back in the hall, ignoring the pain of his injuries, he mops up Tilly's blood as best he can. It's a messy job; most of it has congealed, leaving grim, jellylike trails on the wooden boards. Once it's done, he collects the tiny pieces of broken plaster.

Downstairs, he hears Erin open the fridge and close it. A kitchen cupboard bangs. Joseph flushes away the blood-soaked toilet paper, returns to the hall. Then, lifting the runner rug, he drags it towards him until it covers what's left of the stain.

In the ensuite, he scrubs his hands with soap and water. He tries not to think about what he's just done. Better to focus on each new task exclusively and prevent his mind from wandering.

Joseph retrieves the landline handset, removes the batteries and hides it under his pillow. Then he leaves his bedroom for Tilly's. On her desk he sees a stack of MISSING flyers, freshly printed.

There's no evidence of violence in here, no clues to aid Joseph's understanding of what might have happened. Did his stepdaughter hear an intruder and decide to investigate? Did Max, waiting in the hall, call out to her?

*Protect our son, Joe. Whatever it takes.*

Joseph leaves Tilly's room and pauses on the landing. He needs to find Max, but he can't leave Erin. He needs to locate Tilly, and tell Erin what has happened, but he can't let Erin call the police. He needs to find the Honda, find Drew.

If Tilly has a head injury, she could be bleeding out. Erin might be about to lose her daughter without even knowing it. The thought of that turns his insides into daggers, makes him soul-sick. And yet if says anything he'll lose his son.

Joseph calls his stepdaughter's number, hears it divert to voicemail. Putting away his phone, he grips the handrail and begins to descend the stairs.

Hard to understand any of this. Impossible, really. How did his wife's affair lead to the deaths of two people, maybe even three? In less than a month, Max is due to start medical school, the culmination of what feels like a lifetime of preparation. He'd wanted to be a doctor from an early age; the lost photo on his grandmother's dresser is testament to that. The boy's room is a trove of medical texts and equipment, from stethoscopes and blood pressure sleeves to the foam hearts and brains bought for him by Claire to encourage his interest.

But it was the burglary, and Claire's death, that turned Max's passion into an obsession. Rather than grieve, he took solace in his studies. It's what makes the events of this past week so difficult to process, the boy who dedicated himself to saving lives taking them instead – and all to protect a father who didn't deserve protection, who should have opened his eyes and seen what was happening around him.

All of this, Joseph's fault. All of it.

At the bottom of the stairs he turns towards the kitchen. Erin is sitting at the breakfast bar, elbows on the worktop. She stares at him, cat-like, over the lip of her coffee cup.

He has to tell her.

Now.

He has to tell her.

As he limps into the kitchen their eyes meet. And then a bass thumping starts behind him. The floor shivers beneath his feet.

Erin slides off the stool and comes around the island. Joseph's breath is in his throat. He twists his head towards the door, sees it reverberating in its frame, sees shadows moving beyond the dimpled glass.

And suddenly he can't breathe at all.

Did Erin manage to call the police despite his precautions? Maybe she has a phone he doesn't know about – one she'd bought solely for contacting Angus.

The banging escalates. Joseph's head pounds in tandem. Erin slips past him, pads down the hall to the door. 'Wait,' he croaks. 'Don't answer.'

She hesitates, just for a moment. Her expression seems almost one of pity. 'Joe, I don't think they're going away.'

'Please, you can't—' he begins, but Erin's hand is already

on the latch. The moment she twists it the door bursts open, nearly knocking her off her feet.

Into the hall staggers Enoch. His eyes are small, networked with red capillaries. The knuckles of his right hand are bloody, the skin scraped and raw. 'Tilly,' he growls through clenched teeth. 'Get her now.'

Erin takes a backward step. 'Enoch, has something happened? What are you—'

'I found this,' he says, lifting up a phone. 'Hidden in a cupboard. Only came across it when it rang. Got to be Drew's. Not the one I found yesterday Something's got to be on it – otherwise why would she hide it? Tilly might know the code. Where is she?'

Erin takes a breath. 'OK, Enoch, let's figure this out together.' Hands raised, palms outwards, she skirts around him and closes the door.

Enoch watches, sweat running into his eyes from his forehead. Joseph can smell him: a fug of body odour and sour beer breath. Abruptly, he recalls how he'd caught Max raking through Drew's underwear drawer. Last night, he'd closed his mind to it, because the very worst explanation was simply too troubling to consider – that his son was hunting for a trophy.

Now, a conviction seizes him that the target of Max's search was the phone in Enoch's hand – which means whatever's on it will implicate the boy if discovered, sending him to prison for life.

Joseph's hand twitches. He has to get that phone off Enoch, but any move to take it will implicate him. If Enoch raises the alarm, the house will be searched, the bungalow, too.

Joseph's bagged and balled-up T-shirt, soiled with the dead man's blood, is still hidden at the back of a kitchen cabinet. Hidden in his ensuite is the dead man's wallet. At this point, taking the fall for everything that's happened would almost be a relief – except Max has already indicated he wouldn't allow that; that he'd insist on revealing the truth.

His vision begins to stutter again. These next few moments might dictate how this all ends.

'Tilly isn't here,' Erin says, 'but I can call her.'

Enoch shakes his head. 'I just tried. She wasn't picking up.'

'She might pick up for me. Why don't you come through?'

His eyes narrow further. Finally, he grunts his agreement.

They assemble in the kitchen. Erin opens her bag, searches through it. 'Oh,' she says. 'I forgot. Joe, I think you might have my phone.' She smiles tightly. 'I gave it to you in the car on the way home. Remember? It's in your front pocket.'

Joseph stares, trying to read her intentions. Can he trust her? An hour ago he wouldn't have asked the question, but in the last sixty minutes so much has changed. He certainly has no right to that trust. Not after what he just did upstairs.

Returning her fake smile with one of his own, he passes her the phone, holding it a fraction longer than necessary when she takes it.

If Erin understands the message, she gives no outward sign. Dialling her daughter, she lifts the phone to her ear.

Joseph retreats to the archway leading to the utility, within reach of the baseball bat he keeps hidden there. Enoch watches like a man primed for violence, veins standing proud on his neck.

Erin lowers the phone, shakes her head. 'No answer. But we might not need her, Enoch. What codes have you tried?'

'Just the usual. One-two-three-four. Four zeros.'

'What about the number Tilly gave you last night?'

He grimaces. 'I don't remember it.'

'I do. Sixteen-thirty-eleven.'

'This phone only wants four numbers.'

'Let's try the first four, then. Sixteen-thirty.'

'Wait,' Joseph says. And instantly realizes it was a mistake.

He'd spoken without thinking, and now both Erin and Enoch are looking at him strangely.

'Wait for wait?' Enoch demands. His grip around Drew's phone tightens.

Joseph's mouth has turned so dry he can barely speak. 'I just think . . .' he begins, but the rest of the sentence fails him, because there's no credible reason in existence to delay or second-guess any initiative that might locate Drew.

'Joe?' Erin asks. 'What is it? What's going on?'

His guilt must be written large on his face, because Enoch slides the phone back into his pocket and draws himself up to full height. He raises his bloodied hand and points his index finger at Joseph. 'You,' he whispers, 'fucking know something. Don't you?'

# FORTY-FOUR

Joseph steps forward, out of the arch, hoping to convey that he has nothing to hide. Except, looking at Enoch's face, the opportunity has already passed. 'Of course not,' he says. 'I'm—'

'I can see it, clear as day.'

'Joe,' Erin says carefully. 'I think you need to explain why you wouldn't want us to unlock that phone.'

Since Friday, Joseph has known that to survive this with Max he'll have to become a competent liar. Now, when it counts most, it feels like there's a tightening iron band around his chest, steadily crushing his ribs.

'Joe?' Erin asks.

The longer he's silent, the worse this gets. He has to say something, anything, but his tongue has glued itself to the roof of his mouth. He glances at Erin in mute appeal, sees nothing encouraging in her expression.

'Even your wife doesn't believe you, you piece of shit. What do you know? What don't you want to tell us?'

'I don't know anything,' Joseph says, finally managing to speak. But he hears the lie in his voice and knows they've heard it, too.

Enoch's eyes shrink into slits. 'Tilly said there was an older man. Fucking hell, it's you. Isn't it?'

'Enoch, please,' Erin says. Her gaze flicks between the two men. 'Just hold on a moment. Joe hasn't—'

'Where is she?' Enoch hisses. 'You tell me right fucking now.'

And Joseph, looking at him, realizes that this really is the inflection point, the moment at which his efforts to save Max will need to become something else entirely – because he simply cannot let Enoch see whatever evidence is on that phone; and because this conversation has already reached the point of no return.

He thinks of Claire, lying brain-dead in her hospital bed. He thinks of the man who killed her walking free. He thinks of the doorstep seller, last winter. The depthless chasms of guilt into which his heart plummets each morning. The powerlessness he feels every day.

He thinks of Max.

His North Star.

His everything.

*Protect our son, Joe. Whatever it takes.*

Joseph has never been in a fight, has never climbed into a boxing ring or stepped on to a martial arts mat. Enoch is younger, stronger, far more fierce. A physical confrontation would likely have only one outcome. Attacking him unprovoked, while Erin looks on, is simply unthinkable.

Joseph believes that right up until the moment he doesn't.

He strikes Enoch square in the face with his leading left fist, following it with a swinging right which snaps the taller man's head around.

Enoch crashes into the kitchen worktop behind him, his skull cracking off a wall unit. Erin cries out in shock.

Blood running from two split lips, Enoch roars. He lunges forward, grabs Joseph's shirt, shoves him back. Joseph staggers. His knee gives out and his feet slip from under him. The world upends. The floor punches him in the back, emptying his lungs and driving the hammer head tucked behind him into his spine.

He doesn't even have time to breathe before Enoch is straddling his chest, blood and saliva spilling from his mouth in glossy strings.

'You want to take me on?' the man spits. 'I'll fucking take you on.'

He grabs two fistfuls of Joseph's hair, yanks his head off the floor and slams it against the tiles. The impact knocks loose a shower of silver sparks across Joseph's retinas. Before he can recover, Enoch's hands encircle his throat.

'Stop this!' Erin screams. 'I'm calling the police! Right now!'

Joseph tries to warn her off, can't find his voice through the stranglehold. He tries to prise Enoch's fingers from his throat but the grip is impossible to break. It feels like his brain is swelling in his skull, his eyeballs bulging in their sockets. He flails with his fists, hoping to strike Enoch's face, but his reach is too short.

Shocking how quickly this has turned around. He's spasming from lack of air, knows he has mere seconds before he passes out. He can't get to the hammer wedged beneath him. Sweeping his hands back and forth, he searches for a weapon, something he can use as one, anything.

His fingers scrape the kickboard beneath the cabinets. They hook a door, yank it open. He touches cereal boxes, a bag of rice, bottles of olive oil and balsamic vinegar.

Around him the kitchen darkens, as if a shroud has fallen over the day. Joseph uses the last of his strength to snag an oil bottle. He shatters its base against the floor tiles and stabs the jagged edges into Enoch's arm.

Enoch shrieks, pitching on to his side. Joseph crabs backwards. He gets one leg under him, takes a whistling lungful of air, drags himself up.

Erin is hunched over her phone, fingers busy on the screen.

'No!' Joseph shouts, slapping it out of her hands. It ricochets off a cabinet and clatters towards the bi-fold doors.

Spider-like, Enoch flips into a crouch. He dives forward, all his weight behind one shoulder. This time Joseph is punched into a wall, demolishing a framed print behind him. Glass shards and wood splinters rain down.

Leaning over, grabbing the back of Enoch's belt, he uses it as a pivot to swing the man into the wall. It wins him hardly any respite – Enoch straightens and lurches forward again, fists swinging. He connects with a left, then a right. They're devastating blows, rattling Joseph's brain inside his skull.

Erin screams again, yells at them to stop.

Joseph stumbles backwards, slips on oil, nearly goes down a second time. He snatches at the knife block beside him, tips it off the worktop instead. When it hits the floor five blades flash out, spinning like silver fish across the tiles.

Joseph gasps, his balance all wrong, his head still not clear. He tries to blink away his dizziness, feels the colours in the room smear around him.

'No!' Erin cries. 'Don't you dare!'

And through his confusion Joseph realizes that Enoch has snatched up one of the knives. He backs towards the sink, passes the espresso machine, sees the coffee Erin just made him on the drip tray. Grabbing it, he tosses the contents in Enoch's face, then throws the cup, which misses by a yard and shatters against the wall.

Enoch bellows in agony. Scalding coffee runs down his cheeks. Joseph backs into the kitchen island, feels the sharp angles of the hammer head press into his spine. He reaches behind him, tries to get his fingers around it. Enoch walks him down, slashes with the knife, misses, thrusts with it instead. Joseph sidesteps, the hammer still trapped in his belt. Finally he wrenches it free, but his grip is awkward, the head inside his fist, the shaft emerging from his fingers. It's not even a stout piece of wood. Certainly no good as a weapon. It blocks Enoch's second knife slash but not the third, which opens Joseph's shirt at the bicep. He feels the cut even though there's no pain, senses it's deep.

And now Enoch is pressing against him, his forearm wedged under Joseph's chin, his face so close that the pores in his skin look like craters, his beard stubble like thick black spears. Pearls of blood cling to his yellow teeth. He smells ripe: vinegar sweat and rank breath. 'Tell me,' he hisses, spittle flying from his lips. 'Tell me where she is. What you've done with her. *Tell me.*'

And Joseph sees, in that moment, not an assailant but a fellow father, a man plainly terrified for his child. Enoch's eyes, poached in booze though they may be, are filled not with rage but an awful, desperate need.

'She's gone,' Joseph whispers.

And with that admission everything stops.

The pressure of Enoch's forearm against his chin ceases, as does the pressure of Enoch's chest against his own.

There's no more movement, only sound: the steady drip of blood and coffee; Joseph's laboured breathing; the tick of the kitchen clock, counting off the seconds.

Enoch's pupils dilate. The muscles in his face slacken.

Joseph places a hand on the man's chest and gently pushes him back. And then, because he's known how this must end since the very moment he saw that phone in Enoch's hand, even if he hadn't wanted to believe it, he reverses his grip on the hammer and swings it with all his strength into the side of Enoch's head.

There's a crunch like breaking glass. A sound of kinetic energy transferring from metal to bone – and the bone not surviving intact. A spray of something wet hits Joseph's face.

Time freezes once more, as if the entire universe has ground to a halt. And then Enoch drops, instantly lifeless, his head sucking free of the hammer. He crumples into an awkward sprawl at Joseph's feet.

# FORTY-FIVE

Sitting behind the wheel of his late grandmother's Honda, Max Carver pulls into a rest spot on one of the quieter roads through Jack-O'-Lantern Woods. His phone is ringing, and he knows who's calling. When he answers, he activates the speaker.

'Where are you?' his father asks. 'Where'd you go? Where's the car?'

'Slow down. What's wrong? I'm in town, helping Tilly put up posters,' Max says, staring through the windscreen at the trees.

Behind him, he hears muted rustling. It sounds like the thick plastic wrapped around Drew is settling after its bumpy ride here. That is, unless some dark forest magic has reanimated her. Checking the rear-view mirror, he sees that the tonneau cover is still pulled taut across the boot space. There's no bulge from a plastic-encased head.

'Did you move the car?' his father asks.

Max blinks, angles the mirror down. Across the Honda's rear seats lies Tilly. Plastic ties secure her wrists and ankles. Her head wound has leaked a lot of blood – the seat fabric looks stained beyond repair.

Not that Max or his father could ever have contemplated keeping the car, once this was over. Not that he would have wanted to.

It's so strange seeing her like this. These last few years, Tilly has become far more than a sister. She's been his counsellor, his guide; in many ways she's reinvented him.

She might not have shared his passion for medicine. For Tilly, the innumerable ways a body can fail, and the more numerable ways, with knowledge and with skill, that it can be put back together, hold little interest. Despite her disregard of academia, he'd thought her wise in ways he will never be, sagacious beyond her years. Tilly's knowledge comes not from books or formal learning but seems entirely empirical, gained through close attention to those around her. In that, she's similar to her mother.

For three years Tilly has enthralled him, bewitched him. How bizarre, then, that seeing her like this, bound and bleeding, seems to have dissolved the last threads of that enchantment. For the first time in weeks, he almost feels like he can think straight. Tragic that it might have come too late.

She's not his sister. He mustn't think of her like that. Tilly's something else, something *other*. A cuckoo chick that hatched in what was left of his family's nest. A threat to him and his father – although not the only threat, it seems.

Shaking his head, he tunes back in to his father's voice. 'What?'

'*Did you move the car?*'

'That's what I thought you said. Why would I take it? What're you talking about?'

'It's gone, Max. The car. It's not there.'

More rustling, then a moan. Checking the rear-view mirror again, he sees that Tilly's eyes are open. She blinks, lifts her head from the seat, winces. It takes her a moment to realize she's bound, and a moment longer to realize where she is. When her gaze shifts to the mirror and meets his own, he sees a panoply of emotions: shock, fury, disbelief – and, unmistakeably, fear. He looks at her for as long as he dares. Then he turns to his passenger beside him.

# FORTY-SIX

In the aftermath there is only Joseph, and Erin, and the fact of what he has just done. For a while neither of them speak, nor even make eye contact. Blood is inching across the floor, forming a growing pool.

Joseph cannot deal with what he thinks he just witnessed: the light of consciousness disappearing from Enoch's eyes. It's simply too immense. 'I'm . . .' he begins, pausing when his head grows light. He puts the hammer on the worktop, tries not to look at it.

The pool of blood is still spreading. Limping to a drawer, he takes out a couple of tablecloths. Then, easing himself down, he slides them under Enoch's head. When he catches sight of the wound his stomach flops.

'It's so red,' Erin mutters, staring at the blood. 'There's so much. What have you done, Joe? Why did you do that?'

Gingerly, Joseph gets to his feet and fetches a first-aid kit from the utility. When he returns to the kitchen, Erin hasn't moved. He takes out bandages and dressings. Lowering himself once again to Enoch's side, he presses a dressing to the man's head wound, binding it tightly.

Erin crouches down, putting her fingers to Enoch's neck.

'Joe,' she says, as he's tying off the bandage. 'There's no point. Where you hit him – you only had to look. He's—'

'I'm not trying to save him,' he tells her. 'I just want to stop the blood.'

Erin grunts, coughs. 'I don't understand. Is this real? You just . . . you literally just ended his life in front of me.'

Joseph's head feels hollow; a legacy, perhaps, of the two stinging blows Enoch delivered before he died. Maybe he's simply in shock. One arm of his shirt is soaked with blood. On the floor by his feet lies the knife that did the damage.

'Take it off,' Erin says, indicating his shirt. 'Let me see how bad. And Joe, please – if there's a reason, tell me why you did this.'

He doesn't know if she's being genuine, is trying to deceive him, or, like him, simply cannot process the enormity of what he's just done. He unbuttons his shirt regardless, his gaze moving around the kitchen. Blood is splattered across the nearest wall units. Shards of ceramic and glass litter the floor, along with splinters of picture frame and olive oil from the broken bottle.

When Erin peels off his shirt, he sees the deep incision in his arm, its red lips.

'This needs stitches,' she says. 'At the hospital.'

'No.'

'Joe, you—'

'I said no.'

Erin leads him to the table. 'I think we have some wound closure strips. Maybe they'll . . . I . . . maybe they'll do for now.'

For the next minute, Joseph submits to Erin's attention as she works on his arm. He watches with awe and grief: awe that she would try to help him, even now; grief at what he must tell her, and the ruination it will bring.

Eventually, he says, 'Angus Roth is dead. Max killed him Friday night in Jack-O'-Lantern Woods. He told me he knocked him down on his way to Drew's. Just some random guy who stepped into the road.'

Erin stops what she's doing, glances up at him. Her eyes are blue planets, vast in range, each with a hollowed-out core. Her breath comes in shallow sips.

Joseph licks his lips. 'At the time, I didn't know about . . . about what was going on. And I had no reason to think he was lying. I didn't want Max to lose his whole future over what seemed like a tragic accident. So I decided to cover it up.'

Erin's eyelids stutter. Her breathing is more audible now. 'Angus is dead?'

'Yes.'

She looks around the room. Her gaze falls on Enoch, quickly moves away. Removing the last bandage from the kit, she winds it around Joseph's arm. Her hands are shaking almost as badly as he is. 'You're saying Max knew about Angus? And that's . . . that's why . . .'

'I don't think it was a coincidence that they were in those woods, together, Friday night. I think he must have known, yes.'

Erin shudders. She digs into the first-aid kit and removes a safety pin. Perhaps the task of bandaging his arm is helping to order her thoughts. Once the task is complete, she laces her fingers over her stomach, like an expectant mother unconsciously protecting her child.

'So where's Angus now?'

'I buried him Sunday night. Drove him out to Black Down, dug a grave, filled it in. I tried to do it Saturday, after the party, but I didn't leave myself enough time.'

Gently, still cradling her stomach, Erin begins to rock. 'And Drew?'

'Max says she knew about Angus. That she was scared, wanted to tell someone. That it was only a matter of time before she went to the police.'

'She's gone, too?'

He can't bring himself to answer that, because he still can't reconcile himself to the reality.

Erin coughs again, makes a small sound of distress. 'When did she . . .'

'Some time on Sunday night. I went back to the bungalow after burying Angus. Max was already there. Drew was in the living room, laid out on a plastic sheet.'

'My God, Joe.' Those blue planets swirl. 'Where is she now?'

'Yesterday, she was still in the living room, which is why I tore over there when you told me about the viewing. I . . . I got her into the Honda just in time.'

Silence, for a while. Then Erin says, 'So where's the car?'

'That's just it. I don't know.'

'How can you not?'

He shrugs, opens his hands.

'Did Max take it?'

'He said no. But maybe.'

Erin casts another look at Enoch. 'None of what you've just told me explains this – what you just did.'

'Last night, when we were over there, I caught Max searching Drew's room. He was looking for that phone. There's something's on it that'll implicate him. Something that'll send him to prison for life, if anyone sees.' He passes his fingers through his hair, feels blood where Enoch's rings must have cut open his scalp. 'If I can save Max, I will. I don't care, any more, about the right or wrong of it. Or what I have to do. I'm not sure I even care what he did. I just want him to survive this, Erin. I just want to keep him close.'

'Three people are dead.'

Joseph examines his knuckles. The skin is scuffed, rucked back in white layers.

Erin says, 'Three people are dead because of me.'

When he realizes where her mind has gone, he shakes his head. 'Not because of you. It's more complicated than that.'

He stands on shaking legs, asks himself if he believes his own words. He's believed a lot of things these last four days. Most of them have turned out to be false.

He limps over to Enoch and slides the phone from the man's back pocket. 'I need to see what's on here. But before I do, I need to tell you something else. And it's going to be difficult.' Joseph pauses. Then he says, 'I think Max has Tilly.'

# FORTY-SEVEN

Erin groans as if she's taken a kick to the stomach. She staggers up, her chair scooting away, and braces herself against the kitchen worktop.

Watching her, Joseph recalls once again the deer he hit last summer: not the fawn, observing from the undergrowth, but the mother; the panic in her eyes as he'd approached with the torque wrench; the knowledge of her impending fate.

'Tilly didn't answer when you called,' he says. 'Nor when I tried her earlier. If you go upstairs and pull back the hallway runner, you might see what's left of the blood I just mopped up. If you check the wall outside her bedroom, you'll see a fresh dink in the plaster. That blood wasn't there when we left the house. Something happened, here, while we were out.'

Erin stares at him a moment longer. Then her face collapses. She pulls herself along the worktop, as if she's in the deep end of a swimming pool and has forgotten how to swim. When she reaches the corner unit, she lunges into the hall. He hears her thump up the stairs.

Forcing back the darkness still pressing at his vision, wondering how much of his humanity is left to shred, Joseph turns his attention to the phone. When he presses the side buttons, it wakes. Staring at him from the screen is Drew.

The photo is a recent one, shot in his back garden. It might be the last ever image of the girl alive. He holds her gaze for as long as he can bear. Then he swipes with his thumb and brings up the PIN screen.

Floorboards creak above him. A sound of anguish follows, like nothing he's ever heard.

Joseph keys 1-6-3-0 into the phone, sees the screen change.

He checks the call history first. The most recent inbound one was received half an hour ago, from a mobile number with no contact name. Scrolling back through the log, Joseph sees that all the other calls are to or from a contact labelled *SCORPION*. Checking the contacts folder, he sees that *SCORPION* is the sole listing.

Joseph opens WhatsApp next and finds a single chat log, again with the *SCORPION* contact. He scrolls back to the first message, so fast that the images and text blur. Then he begins to read. The conversation, initiated a few weeks ago, is chatty at first. Progressively it turns more flirty.

To some of Drew's later messages, she'd attached selfies. None are intimate but all are revealing. Joseph finds only one photo sent in response, a shot taken on a boat somewhere exotic. Centre frame on deck, beside what might be a 500lb blue marlin, crouches Angus Roth.

The colours in the room smear again. Joseph screws up his eyes, tries to draw meaning from what he's seeing. Scrolling to the end of the log, he reads the last few exchanges. They detail the pair's plans to meet.

Joseph thinks of that photo in the living room, of Erin and Tilly and Drew at the Huntingdon Manor fundraiser. Angus Roth had been there that night, too.

Returning to the home screen, he taps a thumbnail called **Gallery** and finds a video file created last Thursday night.

Footsteps crash down the stairs. Erin appears in the doorway, her face so ravaged it looks like she's suffering from anaphylactic shock.

'Police,' she gasps. 'We're calling them right now. If you try to stop me, Joe, I'll run.'

'Listen to me before you do. Because how we choose to deal with this probably dictates how it ends. I know you're scared for Tilly. And I know what's happening here is as bad as it gets. The choices I've made – I'm not going to defend them. But I think we have a better chance of resolving this if we work together, instead of handing control to the police.'

'That's insane. We can't—'

'Think about it: did the police manage to stop Tilly's dad from abusing her – or abusing you? Have they worked out what happened to Drew? Five years ago, some guy broke into our house and killed Claire. The police never even found him. Do you really want to put Tilly's life in their hands?'

Erin sways on her feet, her eyes glassy. 'I just want her back.'

'I want them both back. I think I know where Max is taking her. And I think we still might have options. But only if we deal with this ourselves.' He lifts the phone, displays the screen. 'While you were upstairs, I learned something else. Seems like you weren't the only one seeing Angus Roth. Because Drew was seeing him too.'

Erin lurches as if kicked.

'There's video,' Joseph says. 'I think we should watch it.'

# FORTY-EIGHT

Sitting in the passenger seat as they bump along the track through Jack-O'-Lantern Woods, peering through the windscreen at the night, she still can't quite believe this is happening. Can't quite believe what she's about to do.

What *they're* about to do.

Beside her, Angus Roth looks like a man contemplating a fine dining experience several months in the planning. In reality, of course, it hasn't been that long. Only a few weeks have passed since their first exchange of messages. Everything about this has been fast.

On their left they pass a wood pile, beyond which lies a clearing.

'Here's a good spot,' he murmurs, wiping the sweat from his forehead. 'No chance of being disturbed.'

She's perspiring, too. Her body heat has intensified the perfume she borrowed from Erin Carver's dresser. The scent fills her nose.

Stones pop and crunch as Angus turns the wheel. Fronds of giant bracken fold beneath the bonnet.

Drew looks down at herself: at her watermelon-pink dress showing just the right amount of cleavage; at the fake blonde curls falling off her shoulders; at her freshly manicured nails, her tanned legs. She's shaking a little from adrenalin, but not too badly.

The burner phone she's used for all her communications with Angus is in her lap. Taking a last peek, she opens the app that can shoot video while the screen is turned off and hits **Record**.

Angus kills the engine, then the headlights. Moments later the cabin lights fade up, turning the windows into black mirrors. With the phone now dark, Drew places it on the central armrest, lens aimed at the ceiling, and releases her seatbelt. The leather upholstery squeals against her bare legs as she turns to face him. 'It's so *hot*. Can you put the windows down?'

He thumbs two buttons on his door rest. Warm night air feathers in, carrying sounds of the forest. Close by, something shrieks in the darkness.

Drew glances through Angus's open side window. Then she turns her attention back to him, catching her lower lip in her teeth for a moment before she grins. It's a move as old as these woods, but it produces the result she was anticipating. He leans over, kisses her.

Drew closes her eyes, submits. When he touches her breasts, her back arches.

She tries to imagine he's someone else. When her brain conjures an image of Max Carver, she latches on to it. She's admired Tilly's stepbrother for as long as she's known him, but she's been careful not to reveal her feelings.

Max is one of the good guys: compassionate, dependable, generous with his time. He's always treated her as someone to be valued, perhaps even to be treasured; but however well they get on, the hard facts are that Max is heading to medical school and a bright future after that; and even though Drew has big dreams, too, she knows she'll never leave Crompton. The most she'll ever be is his friend.

While the fantasy that she's kissing Max sustains her for a while, it's impossible to ignore whose tongue is in her mouth. And when Angus's mouth presses harder against her own she puts her hand against his chest and pushes him away.

'Easy, Romeo,' she laughs, wiping her mouth. 'I don't know what you're used to. But with me you don't get everything all at once.'

He smiles, lunges forward, snatches another kiss. 'Is that right?'

'Play nice,' she tells him. 'Be a good boy. And eventually you'll get rewarded.' Again, she glances past his shoulder at the night.

'How nice?' Angus asks.

She frowns. 'You hear that?'

He cocks his head, turns to the open window and scans the darkness. 'Nope.' Rearranging himself in his seat, he slides his hand up her thigh.

Drew squirms away. She's kissed him, let him touch her through her clothes. Despite what she just told him, she doesn't have the stomach for anything further. 'Seriously, I think I heard something.'

'We're in the woods, at night,' he says. 'Of course you're going to hear something.'

'Still, maybe we should find a different spot. Somewhere closer to town.'

'Are you fucking kidding me?'

Drew cringes – knows, instantly, that she's screwed up. His gaze travels down her legs to her footwear: strappy pink heels, not exactly tuned for running. Still, if it comes to it, she can kick them off, escape in bare feet. She may have left school with few qualifications, but she did win that athletics trophy.

Angus reaches out, touches her face. 'What if I don't want that?' he asks.

She blinks. 'Don't want what?'

'To be a good boy.'

His earlier flash of anger has vanished, replaced by a look she knows well: the charmless confidence of a man who fully expects to get his way, regardless of any objections.

Angus flicks on the headlights, illuminating the clearing. 'Come on. It's a clear night. I've got a picnic blanket in the boot. Let's get out and watch the stars for a while.'

'I just want to go back to town.'

'Well, it's a long walk. I don't envy you. Or – you can join me for ten minutes of stargazing and then I'll drive you. Your choice.'

Drew holds his gaze, sees he isn't kidding. Throwing open the passenger door, she grabs her phone from the central rest and swings her legs out of the car. When she stands, her heels sink into soft mulch. Cursing, because the shoes are brand new, she bends down, unfastens the straps and steps out of them.

Angus's door opens. He emerges, looking smug. Going to the boot, he raises it.

Drew scoops up her shoes and walks barefoot around the front of the car so she doesn't have to pass him. She gets a few yards up the track before she hears Angus rush up behind her. He grabs her arm and spins her around. 'Where do you think you're going?'

'Home,' she tells him. 'You told me I had to walk.'

'Don't play games.'

'I'm not.'

'You're the one who chose these woods. We could have gone to a hotel.'

'And now I'm choosing home.'

'Just come and sit.'

'No thanks.'

'I brought vodka,' he says. 'There's a bottle in the glovebox.'

'Oh, Jesus.' Drew rolls her eyes. 'What am I, fourteen? Get off my arm.'

'So you're a tease. Is that it?'

'Yeah, I guess that's it.'

'Fuck you, then.'

'Fuck you back, Comrade.'

His eyes blaze. Releasing her arm, he slams her shoulders with his open palms.

Drew stumbles backwards, but she can't compensate fast enough. She sprawls on to her back, grunting with the impact. Her shoes go flying but not her phone, which she brandishes before her like a crucifix.

Angus swears, seems to realize he's gone too far. And then Tilly Carver emerges from the darkness. She's holding one of the logs from the wood pile, and as he turns towards her she swings it with all her strength into his face.

# FORTY-NINE

It's a devastating blow, bone-cracking and tooth-shattering. Angus staggers, trips, falls. Drew, still lying prone, can't quite believe what she's seeing. His mouth is a mush of pulverized flesh and broken teeth. It looks like his jaw has detached. He splutters, coughs, launches a fountain of blood drops that glitter like rubies in the glare of the Lexus's headlights.

As he elbows himself backwards across the leaf litter, Tilly walks him down.

'Tilz, stop, what the fuck!' Drew yells, because she doesn't understand what's happening, here. She'd agreed to lure Angus to this part of Jack-O'-Lantern Woods, had agreed to kiss him so that Tilly could film their liaison, had even agreed to a little harmless action in the front seats. She hadn't agreed to this.

Tilly lifts the log above her head. Angus raises an arm to block it. There's a crack of breaking bone.

Drew screams, sits up straight.

Tilly's third swing goes undefended. The damage it inflicts is cataclysmic, driving Angus's nose and cheekbone inside his skull. He twitches once, his heels kicking. Then he lies still.

Tilly drops the log and kneels at Angus's side. She looks grimly satisfied.

Drew tries to catch her breath, angling the burner phone away from Tilly's eyeline. Despite the fog of her horror, instinct tells her to keep recording – because her friend has clearly gone nuts. 'What did you do?' she moans, climbing to her feet. Then she shrieks the same words.

'He was attacking you,' Tilly says. 'I stopped him.'

Drew chokes, sobs. The awful reality of what she's just witnessed – and her own unwitting role in it – is starting to sink in. Perhaps even more shocking than Angus's brutalization is her friend's calm demeanour.

Never, before tonight, has she seen Tilly display any capacity for violence. She'd heard the story of what had happened at school, but she'd believed her friend's version of those events, had thought Tilly's actions justified. 'Is he breathing?' she asks. 'He might still be alive.'

Tilly leans over Angus. 'Hey, dickhead. Are you breathing?' She prods his chest. Then she places her ear close to his ruined mouth. 'I'd say he's officially checked out.'

'No,' Drew groans. 'No, no, no, I don't . . . Why, Tilz? You'd already put him down. You didn't have to—'

'He got what he deserved. This piece of shit would've wrecked my mum's marriage, torn my family apart.'

Drew puts one hand on the bonnet, steadies herself. 'But that was the whole *point* of this. You'd film us in the car, show him the footage, scare him off.'

'And I did film you. But this is better.'

Drew sags, can't believe what she's hearing. She slides the burner phone behind her back, tucking it inside the belt of her minidress. She doesn't know if the mic will still capture their exchange – or if she'll need that. She does know Tilly mustn't find out she'd decided to make her own recording of tonight's liaison – protection in case things went south. 'What're we going to do?'

Tilly searches Angus's pockets, removing a wallet, a

294

phone and a set of keys. 'First thing *you're* going to do is get his car out of here. Move it to another part of these woods.'

'Me?'

'I can't drive, Drewster, so it has to be you. Besides, you've already draped yourself across the seats. No point adding my DNA to the mix.' She stands, walks over. Drew stiffens, resisting the urge to back away.

'Listen to me carefully,' Tilly says, 'because this is important. If you do as I say, no one will ever connect this back to you. Other than move the car, all you have to do is keep quiet. The last thing I want is to see you thrown in jail. Honestly, it would break my heart.'

Drew's mouth falls open. She glances at Angus, gags when she sees his cratered face. 'Why would I be jailed?'

'Think about it: you're the one who contacted him, who flirted with him these last few weeks, who lured him to the woods under false pretences. Whereas there's not even any proof I was here.'

'But that's . . . I didn't even . . .'

'I know. And it sucks, believe me. But that's how these things work.'

Drew shakes her head, her panic rising. This simply doesn't feel real. 'We should call the police, explain what happened. Tell them the truth – that he attacked me.'

'You lured him out here, Drewster – and then I killed him. However we try to frame it, it's going to look premeditated.'

'What are you saying? You want us to walk away? Pretend it never happened? Just leave him lying here?'

'Of course not. Better that he disappear than he's found like this. We'll drag him somewhere more discrete. Then I'll persuade Max to help us get rid of him.'

'My God. *Max?* You can't be serious.'

'Trust me. Max is a puppy. He'll do anything I ask. When I tell him what's happened, and he sees all the ways this might end, there's no chance in the world he won't help. If Joseph finds out about my mum's affair with this shithead it'll break him. Even more so if we get locked up for trying to stop it. Max won't want that, I guarantee it.'

Drew closes her eyes, because she knows Max probably *would* help, that Tilly would manipulate him as easily as she manipulated her into contacting Angus. 'You can't drag him into this. It's not fair.'

'Of course it's fair. He gets to protect his dad.'

'But he's starting medical school next month.'

'So? He's not Jesus. He's no better than you or me. Besides, by the time I've worked my magic he'll think it was his idea anyway. Right now, all we need to do is make sure none of this traces back to us.'

Tilly takes out her phone. As her fingers move across the screen, her face is bathed in ghoulish blue light. 'There,' she says. 'I've deleted my footage. And tomorrow I'll get a new phone and destroy this one, just to be doubly sure. I've already got Angus's. Where's yours?'

'I left it at home, like you asked.'

'What about the one I bought you to WhatsApp him?'

'That's at home, too,' Drew says, feeling it press against her spine.

'Why would you leave it?'

She opens her arms. 'Look at me, Tilz. This dress doesn't exactly have pockets.'

'You didn't bring a bag?'

'Do you see one?'

Tilly studies her closely. She waits a beat, then tosses Drew the car keys. 'When you get home, you smash that phone to bits and get rid of it. Understand?'

'Sure.'

'You'd better get moving.'

# FIFTY

The clip ends. Joseph rocks back in his seat. For a while he sits motionless, unable to order his thoughts.

Since the early hours of Saturday, a nightmare has enveloped him of Kafkaesque proportions. He's reacted with a ruthlessness and a single-mindedness he hadn't realized he possessed. All to protect his son. And now it turns out he wasn't protecting Max at all.

From the start, everything about this catastrophe has felt off. He'd never really accepted that Max could be responsible for the violence he's just witnessed on that phone. Now, faced with the truth, he can't process the implications fast enough.

Once he takes away the possibility that Max killed Angus, it leaves no possibility in his mind that Max killed Drew. How Tilly managed to get into the boy's head so effectively that he not only agreed to bury Angus Roth, but concocted a story to fool his father, is difficult to fathom. Part of the answer, no doubt, lies in Tilly's extraordinary gift for manipulation. But another part, Joseph thinks, might lie in something his son said at this table, Friday night: *Because you've already been through so much. Because, on top of everything else, you really didn't deserve this.* Max, quite clearly, has been trying to protect his father all along.

It's a discovery all the more devastating for its timing. Joseph just took Enoch's life in a desperate attempt to prevent the phone evidence incriminating Max of murder. And now it turns out it exonerates him.

Lifting his head, he forces himself to confront Enoch's slumped form. A father, just like him, intent on protecting his child. Except Enoch, albeit it unwittingly, had lost that battle even before it started.

Erin, sitting opposite, looks as bloodless as a corpse. Joseph can't imagine the carnage wreaked inside her head. She's just plunged into the very nightmare he's been living these past four days. For him, at least, it had built in stages: a car accident; a body hidden in a boot, an act of misplaced mercy; and then, two days later, Drew.

For Erin it's arrived all at once. Compounding the shock, she's just witnessed something Joseph had been spared: the horrifying visual brutality of her daughter's actions. Finally, and possibly worst of all: as Erin's affair seems to have been the catalyst, she'll believe herself directly responsible.

If he could take some of his wife's pain on to himself he would. One thing he's learned, these last four days, is his seemingly endless capacity for it.

'What do we do, Joe?' Erin whispers. 'I can't think straight.' She looks up at him. 'You said you knew where Max was going.'

'I said it so you wouldn't call the police. After what we just saw, I've no idea. The blood upstairs might not even be Tilly's. More chance, now, that it's his.'

A multitude of emotions twist across Erin's face when she hears that. It's like watching wind change direction over a lake, the surface flayed first one way and then another.

Joseph hauls himself to his feet. 'I need you to stay here,' he says. 'I won't be long.'

'Where're you going?'

'Ralph's. There might be something on his doorbell cam that'll help us.'

'I'll come.'

'No. If we both go, it might ring alarm bells. We want to keep this low-key. I'll be five minutes, no longer.'

'Joe?'

'What?'

'You better put on a shirt first. Clean yourself up.'

He blinks, looks down at himself, dismayed at what he sees. Is he really so punch-drunk that he'd have walked over to Ralph's stripped to the waist and spattered with blood? It's on his hands, his trousers; he feels it clotting in his hair, drying stiff on his ears and cheeks.

Upstairs, he strips off his trousers and cleans his face and neck as best he can. His knee has split open again. He binds it with the last of the Elastoplast. Then he pulls on fresh clothes, hiding his damaged scalp under one of Max's base-ball caps.

Outside, he passes Enoch's van and crosses the turning circle to Ralph's front door. A minute later, he's sitting in the widower's kitchen, waving away the offer of an aloe yoghurt drink and explaining what he needs.

Ralph listens in silence. Then he unlocks his phone and relinquishes it. Retreating to the sink, he fills a small water-ing can and starts attending to his house plants. 'If you're in trouble, Joseph, if you need help, we're here for you in every capacity.'

Joseph glances up. Less than ten minutes ago he ended Enoch Cullen's life. Now, he's with Ralph Erikson in this weirdly Zen-like space.

He knows the widower's offer was genuine. Perhaps that's what surprises him. His currency, this past week, has been death and dishonesty, barbarism and betrayal. He's inured himself to the worst of human behaviour, has done things almost too awful to comprehend. And now Ralph Erikson – a man he hardly knows and has spent little effort befriending – has just shown him something important: that there's good in the world, even now. Sometimes in the most unexpected places.

It's a truth Joseph realizes he'd forgotten. Or had simply stopped believing.

He thanks Ralph and opens the Nest app. The most recently captured video shows him crossing the street to the widower's front door. The prior clip shows Enoch arriving in his van. The third clip back along the timeline shows Joseph and Erin arriving home after their visit to the bungalow. The fourth clip was recorded fifteen minutes before that. In it, the driveway is clear. The garage door rises on its winch, revealing a dark interior. And then, impossibly, the Honda rolls out, sunlight glinting off its windscreen.

Joseph stops breathing. Because what he's seeing makes no sense. Was the car already here when he left with Erin for the bungalow? Or did it arrive while they were out? With a grunt, he remembers that he's watching these clips in reverse, which means the vehicle's entry into the garage should have been captured in footage he's yet to view.

The car stops on the driveway. Then the driver's door opens and Max gets out. He stands there for a moment, staring across the street at Ralph's house, almost as if he knows his father is watching.

What Joseph sees next convinces him of that – because Max, looking as solemn as he's ever been, raises a hand and waves. Immediately afterwards he returns to the garage and hits the electric release. As he re-emerges, the door begins to close. With a final glance towards Ralph's camera, Max climbs behind the wheel. The car rolls off the drive and disappears out of shot.

Fingers shaking, Joseph scrolls to the previous video. In

this one, the Honda is parked on the driveway. The garage door rolls up and Max emerges. He gets into car and backs it into the garage. The door rolls closed.

The next clip, shot five minutes before the one Joseph just watched, is even stranger. The Honda is on the driveway again. Max enters shot on foot, from further up the street. He stands motionless for perhaps thirty seconds. He approaches the car, peers inside. Then he moves to the front of the house. He hesitates at the door as if listening, looks behind him and surveys the street. Finally he unlocks the door and slips inside.

The next clip was recorded twenty minutes earlier than the last. It shows the Honda pulling on to the drive. The driver's door opens and Gabriel Roth climbs out.

Joseph rears back, nearly drops Ralph's phone. Onscreen, Gabriel opens the side gate beside the garage and disappears around the back. The video rolls for a few seconds longer. Then the image freezes.

Across the kitchen, Ralph is still busy with his houseplants – or at least he's pretending to be. Joseph blinks, tries to think, but his mind is a vortex of awful possibilities. Sweat rolls down his sides from his armpits. His bowels feel horribly loose.

The fog inside his head is making it difficult to concentrate. Watching the captured footage in reverse order has added to his confusion, so he tries to reorder it. While he'd been at the bungalow with Erin, Gabriel had arrived in the Honda, entering the house around the back; Max had arrived home shortly afterwards. Something must have happened inside, evidenced by the blood Joseph found upstairs. But Max hadn't looked injured when he'd shut the garage door and driven off.

The reflections on the windscreen had obscured the car's interior as it disappeared up the street. Had Tilly been inside with Gabriel before Max got home? If so, Joseph's intuition that it was her blood in the upstairs hall was likely correct, albeit for the wrong reasons.

He pinches the bridge of his nose, presses his lips together. Should he delete this footage? Keep it? The implications either way could be huge – and he has little time to decide. None of it implicates Max; if anything, it shows him acting under duress.

Still, the more evidence that exists, the fewer his options to fit a story around it. Quickly, he deletes all the files and switches off recording completely. Then he closes the app and rises from the table.

Of everything he's just seen, what scares him most was the expression on Max's face as he waved at Ralph Erikson's camera.

It looked like he was saying goodbye.

# FIFTY-ONE

Standing in the kitchen of his brother's place on Hocombe Hill, Gabriel Roth stares through the window at the Honda parked on the drive.

Earlier, returning to the bungalow in Saddle Bank after the estate agent had left, he'd forced the back door and found one of the vehicle's key fobs, still hanging on its hook in the kitchen. Standing behind the car, he'd prepared himself for the unimaginable. But when he'd unlocked the boot and raised the lid, he'd discovered, wrapped in plastic, the body of a young woman.

Barbie Girl.

Real name Drew Cullen.

Angus's latest plaything.

And Tilly Carver's best friend.

Any remaining hope Gabriel might have had for Angus's survival had died in that moment.

All men, pushed beyond the limit of what their ego can endure, are capable of murder. But Joseph Carver has demonstrated a depravity beyond anything Gabriel had anticipated. Instead of reserving his wrath for those who crossed him directly, he's rampaged far beyond the natural boundaries of vengeance, his killing indiscriminate.

In truth, Drew Cullen's fate has moved Gabriel only in relation to his brother's. What he fears most is that Carver killed her first, intending to terrorize Angus in his last moments. Gabriel will have to respond in kind. He'll take no pleasure from it – this is a dead world, now, in which anger and hatred are redundant – but perhaps he can find a measure of satisfaction in retaliatory justice. Gabriel has suffered the loss of everything he held dear. He'll ensure Joseph Carver suffers the same.

Now, taking out his phone, he dials a number committed to memory. When the call connects, he says, 'She looks even more like you in the flesh.'

For a while he hears nothing but ravaged breathing.

'Have you hurt her?' Erin Carver whispers.

'Not yet.'

'We found blood.'

'She's a little banged up. Nothing a few painkillers won't fix.'

'What do you want?'

'What I want is my brother. But I think we both know I can't have that. So by way of recompense I want your husband. And I want you to deliver him to Thornecroft within the next hour.'

'Gabriel,' Erin says. 'I know how badly you must be hurting, but—'

'You have no *idea*!' he screams. For a moment, his grief and his rage meld into something so hot he nearly surrenders to it.

Closing his eyes, he visualizes plum blossom falling over a slow-moving river. He imagines floating downstream among the petals, the water cool and cleansing. Gradually, his pounding heart slows.

'Don't talk,' he says. 'Just listen. You need to listen because you have a very serious decision to make, and not much time to make it. I'm afraid you don't get to walk out of this with your whole family intact. None of us do. But if you're brave enough you can at least bring your daughter home.

'Deliver Joseph to Thornecroft. I don't care how you do it. Call me when you're here and I'll trade Tilly for your husband. You're an intelligent woman, so you don't need me to explain the consequences if you deviate even one degree from what I've asked.'

More tortured breathing. Then: 'What about Max?'

'What about him?'

'He's family.'

'Not by blood, he isn't. Why do you care?'

'I just told you. Because he's family.'

Even in the silence that follows, Gabriel can hear Erin Carver's fear. He listens to it for a while. Then he ends the call.

Crossing Thornecroft's grand entrance hall, he opens the door to the formal dining room. At the head of the table, secured by zip ties to a chair, sits Joseph Carver's only son.

Their eyes meet.

'If you—' Max begins.

Gabriel closes the door and goes to Angus's office. Tilly Carver is lying on a couch beside the window, her bandaged head supported by a cushion. He'd applied the dressing himself. No need to treat her discourteously until it's time. She can't go anywhere – not with her wrists and ankles bound.

'How're you feeling?' he asks. 'How's your head?'

'It hurts,' she says, her voice small enough to thaw any heart that remained whole. 'But not quite as much as it did.'

'I'm sorry I had to do that. There was no malice in it.'

Tears gather in Tilly's eyes. When she blinks, one of them breaks loose, taking a stuttering path down her cheek; Gabriel, to his surprise, finds himself supressing an urge to go to her, reassure her, blot the tear away.

'I think I know what you want with us,' she whispers.

'You do?'

'Uh-huh.'

Before he's quite realized what he's doing, Gabriel has moved closer to the couch. 'What do I want?'

'Your brother is missing,' she says. 'And you want to find him because you love him. But you think my stepdad was cross with him and did something bad.'

She reminds him, in that moment, of Teri Platini.

Sunday morning, as he'd questioned Teri, she'd acted increasingly childishly. He'd treated her more harshly as a result, because he'd known she was putting on an act to illicit sympathy.

Tilly Carver, by contrast, seems utterly genuine.

He perches on the edge of the couch. One of Tilly's sandals has fallen off, revealing a delicately arched foot. There is, he thinks, something quite compelling about its shape. 'How do you know that?' he asks.

'Because Max told me.'

'Max?'

Tilly blinks, spills another tear, takes a shuddering breath. 'My stepdad wouldn't hurt anyone. I know he wouldn't.'

She winces, rotating her bare foot at the ankle.

Gabriel watches, transfixed.

'It's cramped up,' she says. 'Is there any chance you could loosen the ties? Just a little? My wrists hurt, too.'

'Maybe later,' he murmurs. He can't take his eyes off that foot, its lazy revolutions and the way the light winks off her nail polish. He feels his pulse rate climbing, his breathing beginning to quicken. 'I could massage it for you.'

'Would you?'

She has her mother's eyes, he thinks. Her mother's lips. But unlike Erin Carver, Tilly is unspoilt by age or motherhood. When he touches her foot, he feels a spark of electricity pass between them.

'There's something you don't know,' she says. 'And I really think it would help you.'

'I'm listening.'

'It's about Max, but I'm scared of saying. Because . . .'

'Because what?'

'Because he scares me.'

'Your stepbrother scares you?'

She nods, her eyes huge.

'Listen,' he tells her. 'You don't need to be scared. But you do need to be honest.'

Her foot is warm in his hands. When she breathes, his gaze is drawn to her chest.

'Once you know who hurt your brother,' she says, 'what's going to happen to me?'

'Do you think I'd hurt you?'

'I don't know.'

'I wouldn't.'

'You hurt me already.'

'Am I hurting you now? I bandaged your head, gave you something for the pain. I'm even massaging your foot.'

'You're doing a good job. It's feeling a lot better.'

'What do you want to tell me? Because now really is the time.'

Tilly takes a deep breath. 'Max was seeing Drew. They were boyfriend and girlfriend. He really loved her. Then your brother came along.'

She looks through the window at Thornecroft's landscaped garden before returning her gaze to Gabriel. 'Who do you think she wanted more? It wasn't even close. But then Max found out, and he . . .' She puffs out her cheeks. 'He went mad.'

Gabriel falls still. He'd known about his brother and Drew Cullen from Teri Platini, but he'd never guessed that Drew was Max Carver's girlfriend. If that's true, he might have been looking at this all wrong. He might already have Angus's killer bound to a chair in Thornecroft's dining room.

Releasing Tilly's foot, he stands. He needs a moment, space to think. Leaving the office for the kitchen, he braces his palms against the worktop and lowers his head. He has to bleed off a little adrenalin, compose his thoughts. Now, more than ever, he cannot allow emotion to dictate his actions.

The killing of a twin isn't one death; it's two. But it's far worse than that – an irreversible severing of souls.

Stepping into the boot room, Gabriel takes a set of keys from his pocket. Secured to the far wall are two gun cabinets. He opens the first, revealing Angus's three shotguns and two hunting rifles. He won't use any of these; Thornecroft's grounds might be extensive, but the sound of a discharge will carry far beyond them, and he doesn't intend to be rushed.

Locking the first cabinet, he opens the second. Inside, among boxes of cartridges and rifle rounds, he finds what he's looking for: a collapsible police-issue baton.

Returning to the dining room, he stands in front of Max Carver. 'Your stepsister says Drew Cullen was your girl-friend. Is that true?'

The teenager blinks. He looks dazed, as if he can't quite believe what's happening. Or if he's trying to figure out what Gabriel wants to hear.

'Is she telling the truth?'

Max blinks faster. 'I . . . no.'

'So she's lying?'

'Not . . . maybe not lying. Just mistaken.'

'You know what I think?' Gabriel asks. 'I think *you're* the liar. But we'll get to that, don't worry.'

He leaves the dining room, returns to the office. In his

absence, Tilly has dislodged her other sandal. When he pulls out a Stanley knife, she shrinks against the couch.

'Lie still,' he says, slicing through the zip tie securing her ankles.

Tilly draws up her knees, watches him.

'You know Drew Cullen is dead?' he asks.

She's silent for a while. Then, gasping for air, she says, 'Drew was my b-best friend. And Max . . . He . . . He . . .'

'It's OK. Can you stand?'

Tilly heaves another breath. 'I'll try.'

Gently, he helps her up. 'Did he kill my brother, too? I need you to tell me the truth.'

'He did,' she whispers. 'I'm so sorry to be the one to tell you.'

Gabriel nods. There it is, then. But Tilly is only confirming what his heart had already surmised. The world doesn't change, because the world was already dark.

'When you have a twin,' he says, 'you sense when something is wrong. I already knew Angus had passed. Not only because he'd never have stayed out of contact this long, but because when I reach out I don't *feel* him. I realize how strange that must sound – almost a kind of witchcraft – but that's what our bond was like.'

'It doesn't sound strange. It sounds . . . magical, beautiful. Which makes it even more tragic, more heartbreaking. I can't imagine what you must be feeling, Gabriel.'

'How long have you known?'

'Since . . . a few days, maybe. I've been so scared.'

Plum blossom on slow-moving water. The art of Dong Yuan and Juran.

'I want to thank you,' he says. 'Telling the truth was the right thing to do. Hold out your wrists.'

She complies. He severs the plastic tie and puts away his knife. 'What kind of man do you think I am, Tilly?'

'I'm . . . I don't know you.'

'Do you think I'm the kind to hurt a young woman with bound hands and feet?'

Tilly blinks. Her gaze moves from her freed wrists to the collapsible baton Gabriel just extended at his side.

She steps backwards, which helps, because it gives him more room to swing.

The blow lands hard into her side. She doubles up, collapses on to all fours.

Gabriel leans over her. 'You stayed silent about my brother's death for two days,' he says. 'I can't excuse that. Because it's inexcusable.'

Lifting the baton, he goes to work.

# FIFTY-TWO

Seconds after leaving Ralph Erikson's house, Joseph is back at home. The air inside the kitchen churns his stomach; Enoch's blood smells like old pennies and something vaguely sweet. Erin is still sitting at the table, clasping her phone like it's a religious icon. She looks stricken, desolate.

Joseph goes to the bifold doors. Finding no damage, he steps into the utility. The back door looks intact, too, but when he opens it, he sees pieces of handle and lock mechanism on the step.

'Gabriel Roth,' he says, returning to the kitchen. 'I think he has them. I just saw him on Ralph's camera. He drove the car over here while we were out, broke in.'

Erin's hand moves to her chest. She looks even worse than before. 'Did you see Tilly?'

'Just Max, but he didn't look injured. Scared shitless but not hurt. Gabriel turned up before he did. I think Tilly must have been here alone when he arrived.'

Thinking of the blood he found upstairs, Joseph lets that sink in. He knows Erin's love for her daughter won't have been extinguished because of what she watched on that phone, however diabolical it had been.

'This is bad, Joe. Really bad.'

She stares at him, her eyes lost, and Joseph tries to ignore his growing belief that no good endings to this nightmare remain possible. He's endured four days and four nights of horror – all in the service, perhaps, of delaying the inevitable, of refusing to accept that life has thrown him another tragedy. And now, at the last, the battle he thought he'd been fighting has morphed into something unrecognizable.

It feels like there's so little of him left – but he can't stop until he's exhausted every possible means to save his boy. He may have damned himself by taking Enoch's life, but he's going to see this through.

'Listen,' he says. 'Right now, we've got one thing in our favour: we know what's going on, and he doesn't know we know. Tell me everything you can about Gabriel Roth.'

Erin doesn't have much insight. Angus, she says, hadn't talked about Gabriel often. Not because he was dismissive of his twin – the brothers' relationship had seemed so incredibly tight that Angus refused to grant outsiders access.

She does know they were brought up in care, that they have no blood family other than each other – and that while Angus, in adulthood, pursued property and wealth, his twin chose a life of travel. Gabriel has no permanent address, moving from place to place and living largely off-the-grid.

The more Joseph hears, the more disquieted he grows. Because it sounds like they're dealing with a man who could slip out of sight as quickly as he appeared. A man who doesn't fear any consequences for his actions.

'Angus's house on Hocombe Hill,' he says. 'Did you ever visit?'

'Just once,' Erin says. 'A few weeks ago.'

The thought of her at Thornecroft is a knife in his gut. She must see his pain because she grasps his hand, squeezes it.

'Doesn't matter,' he tells her. 'That's for later, if we ever get there. Look, I think Gabriel is mostly likely at his brother's. It's a big place, private, and he probably knows it well. I don't know about Angus's girlfriend – I think I saw her there yesterday, but if Gabriel's moved in, I doubt she'd have stuck around.'

'I think you're probably right.'

'So that's where we go. Once we're there, we do whatever's necessary to bring Max and Tilly home.'

Erin glances at Enoch. Then she looks at Joseph, ashen-faced. 'Not that. I can't do that, Joe.'

'If it comes to it, I think you can. Because I'll be honest with you, Erin. That's where I think this is going. He believes I killed his brother. And instead of calling the police, he walked into our house and snatched our kids.'

'So what are you thinking? We can't just turn up and ring the bell.'

'As I said, right now he doesn't know we know. That's to our advantage, but it might not last long. We need to surprise him there – and soon.'

Erin looks at him in silence. Eventually, she says, 'How did we get here, Joe? How did all this creep up on us, unawares? How could Tilly . . .'

Her words falter. He opens his arms and pulls her close.

'What kind of mother am I to let this happen?' she sobs. 'What kind of wife?'

'This didn't happen because of some mistake you made. It didn't happen because of Angus Roth. You saw the way Tilly was on that clip. That was something else.'

'I should have seen it coming. I should have seen the signs, picked up on them.'

'Then I should have picked up on them as well. I've lived with her long enough.'

'It's not the same, Joe. You know it isn't.'

He releases her, steps back. 'As I said, there'll be a time to talk about all this, but first we've got to get them back.'

He looks around the kitchen – at Enoch, at the debris from their fight, at the blood streaked across the cabinets and the floor. 'We have to move him, too. Clean up in here. If a forensics team goes over the place we're screwed, but that's another thing for later. For now we just need to make this look like it never happened.'

'How's your knee? Tell me the truth. Could you run?'

'It'll hold up,' he says, knowing he can promise no such thing.

Erin nods. 'I'll get started down here.'

Joseph limps upstairs. In his bedroom he retrieves his crossbow box from the wardrobe. Removing the user guide, he flicks through it to the English-language section. A few minutes later he's attached the fibreglass cross-piece to the barrel. Next, he attaches a stringing aid and uses the cocking system to pull it into the latch. With the limb under tension he strings the bow. Finally, he loads five carbon-fibre arrows, each with a razored-steel broadhead point, into a speedloader and drops it into the magazine.

The weapon feels cold in his hands. Brutally capable. Catching his reflection in the mirror, he hardly recognizes the person he sees. His skin appears bloodless. His eyes look like they've already glimpsed his own death.

He returns the empty box to the wardrobe and retrieves his tomahawk, his torch and his police-issue cuffs. From its hiding place in the ensuite, he grabs Angus Roth's wallet.

He carries everything downstairs and puts it on the kitchen table. In his absence, Erin has swept up the broken glass and the shards of broken ceramic. Now she's scrubbing the cabinets with stain remover.

Joseph fetches his baseball bat from the utility. Then he helps with the rest of the clean-up.

'What do we do with Enoch?' Erin asks. 'I can't lift him on my own. I doubt you could either, with that knee. If something happens to one of us . . .'

'You want to take him along?'

'I don't think it's wise to leave him in the house.'

'I guess if we can get him into the van, we can drive that to Thornecroft. At least Gabriel won't recognize it. Afterwards . . .' He shrugs, casts about. 'Honestly, right now I've no idea about afterwards.'

After locating Enoch's keys, Joseph opens the garage door and reverses the van right up to it. Even with Erin's help, the task of lifting the man inside proves far more difficult than he'd anticipated. By the time they've completed the job, they're both sweating.

In the kitchen, Erin points at the crossbow. 'You want to show me how to use that thing?'

Picking it up, he gives her a quick tutorial, demonstrating how to cock it after each shot and how to replace the speedloader.

'Is it traceable back to you?' she asks.

'I paid cash. Some prepper's shop on the south coast that was closing down. So no. I don't think so.'

While Erin goes upstairs to change, Joseph digs out a large sports holdall from the cupboard under the stairs. He fills it with everything he may need – not just the crossbow and tomahawk but the baseball bat and some of the other weapons secreted around the house. He throws in an old birdwatching scope of Claire's, a daysack. Then he finds the Sainsbury's bag containing his blood-stained top and throws that in, too.

Erin comes downstairs, wearing black cargo trousers,

desert boots, a black vest. She looks grimly determined, like she's about to go to war.

'Ready?' he asks.

She pulls her hair into a knot. 'Not in the slightest.'

'Me neither. Let's go.'

# FIFTY-THREE

Joseph drives, despite his injured knee. Erin, beside him, looks deep in thought, as if she's wrestling with something existential.

'There were signs,' she says, eventually. 'I didn't miss them. I ignored them.'

Joseph pulls up at a junction, waits for the lights to change.

'You've heard a lot of the school stuff,' Erin continues, 'but not all of it. When Tilly was twelve, a group of girls started bullying her. Name-calling, mockery, the usual nonsense. One day something happened between Tilly and the ringleader, a physical clash in the toilets. The other girl was hurt – very badly hurt. She needed corrective surgery, the works. Another pupil came forward as a witness, but only after Tilly went to see her. She said Tilly had defended herself against an unprovoked attack. If it hadn't been for that, there might well have been charges. We still had to find her a new school.

'Then there was what happened with Robson. Six months after he won joint custody, his solicitors said he wanted the agreement terminated, along with all his parental rights. They said he'd woken a few times in the night to find Tilly at his bedside, staring down at him – that she'd scared him shitless. That on the last occasion she'd had a knife.

'Tilly denied it and I believed her. Or at least, I guess I decided not to think too much about it. The main thing was it was over. He was out of our lives for good.'

'And then you married Mark,' Joseph says, recalling that relationship's tragic end. 'Do you think—'

'No,' Erin replies, her tone vehement. 'Mark had his problems – his gambling debts were crippling us – but he was getting help, and I'd found a job with a higher salary. Tilly knew that I loved him. She's not a monster, Joe. She's just . . .'

*Lost?*

Joseph studies his wife as he waits for the lights to change, because he's experienced the same cognitive dissonance and knows the tricks it can pull. 'Did Tilly and Mark get on?'

Quietly, Erin says, 'She hated him.'

By the time they've skirted Jack-O'-Lantern Woods, the sun is bleeding its last red light through the trees. At this time of day there's little traffic. As they roll past the big houses on Hocombe Hill, they're the only vehicle on the road.

'I'll slow down as we pass,' Joseph says, 'but I won't stop. Get the best look you can.'

A minute later they reach Thornecroft. Despite their reduced speed, the surrounding trees allow only a brief glimpse down the drive before the house is swallowed up again.

As Joseph accelerates away, Erin turns in her seat. 'I saw the Honda,' she says. 'Plus two cars I know belong to Angus. But not the Mercedes Gabriel was driving yesterday.'

'I think that was a hire car,' he replies. 'Maybe he already returned it. We'll find somewhere to pull in. Then we'll double-back on foot. Do you know if the house has a security system?'

'I'm pretty sure it doesn't. And if we go through those trees to the back we can avoid the drive.'

Joseph finds a suitable parking spot a few hundred yards from Thornecroft, a grass verge between two huge private residences and their grounds. Grabbing the holdall, he locks the van.

On this side of the road there are no houses, just open woodland. Joseph leads Erin into cover before they flank the road towards Thornecroft.

A minute later he spots the entrance. Dropping the hold-all, he transfers the birdwatching scope into the daysack and slips his arms through the straps. Then he takes out the crossbow, the tomahawk and two sheathed knives.

'Joe?'

The setting sun has turned Erin's skin golden, in stark contrast to her dark clothes. In this light she looks like an avenging angel, her beauty somehow terrible.

The look she gives him is full of sorrow. 'I just wanted to say I love you, Joe. I know how empty that might sound, but it really is the truth. We've never said it enough, and this may be our last chance.'

Joseph holds her gaze, asks himself how he feels about her words. And then he goes over and kisses her, holding her in the fading light.

'I can't lose Tilly,' she tells him. 'Whatever she's done, however damaged she may be, she's still my daughter. If this goes as planned and I get her back, I swear I'll fix her.'

'We both will,' he replies, but he doesn't really believe it. He doesn't think Tilly can be fixed. Strapping a knife to his belt, he hands the other one to Erin. Then he offers her the crossbow.

Erin stares at it a while before accepting. Joseph picks up the tomahawk and feels instantly light-headed. Because the weapon, in truth, is anything but ridiculous.

They emerge a short distance from Thornecroft's drive-way, hurrying across the road and ducking back into cover.

There's no border fence, just more of the same deciduous woodland. Keeping the driveway on their left, they move through the undergrowth towards the house.

Above the trees, the red hues of sunset have turned crimson. Joseph skirts a patch of bracken, staying as low as he can, and finds a hollow where the shadows are already deepening. He lowers himself to his good knee, takes out Claire's birdwatching scope and focuses the lens on Thornecroft.

The building is huge: triple-fronted with three enormous chimney stacks rising high above its gables. Light glows from the windows of all the ground-floor rooms. Inside the covered porch, the two half-arch entrance doors stand open in mocking invitation.

Joseph sees his mother's car on the drive, parked between a Lexus and a vehicle hidden by a tarp. Erin was right about the tree cover. It should be possible to circle the main residence without being spotted.

'Joe,' Erin says, behind him. 'I'm sorrier than you'll ever know – but I have to do this. I've no choice.'

Joseph lowers the scope. When he turns his head, he sees that she's lifted the crossbow to her shoulder, placing him at the centre of its sights.

# FIFTY-FOUR

By the time Gabriel's rage has run its course, his breathing is ragged and his clothes are soaked through with blood and sweat.

It's the first time he's lost control in years, the first time he's allowed the cage door to swing open fully and release what he usually keeps chained.

Sunday morning, he'd opened that door a crack, giving Teri Platini a glimpse of the beast that lurked within. Yesterday, he'd returned to Thornecroft and showed her a little more of it. But he hadn't let it escape.

Near the window lies the bloodied heap that was Tilly Carver. The only part he still recognizes is her bare foot, the nails a cheery yellow. Blood is dripping from her ankle in a steady rhythm.

In the kitchen, he leans his head under the cold tap and drinks until he's sated. Then he holds his hands in the flow and watches Tilly's blood swirl into the drain. He scrubs his forearms, washes his face. Afterwards, he opens the duffel bag he brought along and takes out a knife, more zip ties and a seventy-metre length of climbing rope.

The beast is back in its cage; he won't let it out again. His task isn't vengeance but the cold application of justice.

In one of Thornecroft's outbuildings he finds a two-wheeled sack truck and tows it into the house. As he enters the dining room, Max Carver arches his back and asks, 'What did you do to her?'

Ignoring him, Gabriel drags the back legs of Max's chair on to the sack truck's toe plate. He braces his foot against the axle, tilting the wheels and lifting the boy off the floor. Then he tows him out of the dining room and along the entrance hall.

They pass the office. Max groans when he sees what lies inside. 'Is she . . .' he begins. 'Did you . . .'

Gabriel wheels him into the orangery and tilts him upright. Then he throws open the exterior doors. Outside, the setting sun has lit a fire in the heavens. As he drags the sack truck across the grass, the colours of lava and flame surround him, bleed over him.

When he reaches the ancient oak that crowns Angus's garden, he parks his load beside the three dining chairs he positioned here earlier, facing the tree. He slides the rope off his shoulder, pays out a good length and cuts it with his knife.

Max Carver's eyes are enormous, reflecting the apocalyptic sky.

'You'll burn for what you've done,' Gabriel tells him, winding one end of the rope around itself. 'But first you'll hang.'

Once he's made the noose, he slips it over the boy's head. He throws the remaining coils over a bough twelve feet above the ground.

'Please,' Max says. 'Don't do this. I didn't—'

'Speak again,' Gabriel tells him, 'and I'll cut your throat

first.' He severs all the zip ties except the one around the boy's wrists. 'Up. On to the chair.'

When Gabriel receives no response, he heaves on the rope looped over the bough. The noose tightens around Max's throat. He struggles up, his eyes bulging. And then he climbs on to the chair as instructed.

# FIFTY-FIVE

It takes Joseph a moment to fully appreciate what's happening. The light beneath these trees is failing fast. Erin, standing fifteen feet away, is more shadow than light. The arrow's razored steel tip is the brightest thing he can see.

'Erin,' he says slowly. 'What is this?'

Tears are coursing down her cheeks. 'Everything I told you just now was true. Which makes this the hardest thing I've ever done. The hardest thing I'll ever do.

'I've never stopped loving you, Joe. But Tilly's my daughter. I have to put her first. If anyone understands that it's you. Look at everything you've done, these last four days, to protect Max. Even when you thought he'd hurt her, your instinct was to cover it up. Crazy as it sounds, I don't even blame you. No one really knows how far they'll go until they're in this situation, do they? And now it's me being asked the question.'

Cautiously, Joseph rises to his feet. He takes a careful step towards her.

Erin braces the crossbow's stock against her shoulder. 'Don't, Joe. Please. I don't want to shoot you with this thing but I will if I have to. It'll kill me but I won't hesitate. Unclip that knife and throw it over. Don't unsheathe it.'

Joseph sees from her expression that she isn't bluffing – that she's approaching the edge of what she can bear. Keeping his movements slow, he follows her instructions. 'Erin, I'm not going to fight you,' he tells her. 'But whatever you're planning, just think. I know we can't be certain, but Tilly and Max are probably inside that house. If Gabriel's in there with them, he doesn't know we're coming. If we work together, stick to the plan, we—'

'He does know.'

Her comment stops him dead. He stares at her, his thoughts stalling.

Erin takes one hand off the crossbow. She digs in her pocket and pulls out the cuffs he'd put on the kitchen table earlier. 'I'll do everything in my power to stop him hurting you, Joe, but first I have to prioritize Tilly – just like you've been prioritizing Max. Here,' she says, 'put these on.'

Joseph catches the cuffs, tries to focus.

If he complies with Erin's demand it's a death sentence, but if she shoots from that distance she can't miss. He knows how much damage that steel broadhead will do. He's watched YouTube clips of them ripping through sides of beef. 'He got to you, didn't he? When? How?'

'He called while you were at Ralph's, gave me an ultimatum. If I don't do this, if I don't bring you to him . . .'

'And if you do? What do you think will happen then? That he'll hand Tilly over and let you both go?'

The crossbow trembles in Erin's grip. Her finger is millimetres from the trigger. If she isn't careful, she'll shoot him entirely by accident.

'That's what he promised.'

'And you trust him?'

She blinks away tears. 'Of course not. But what choice do I have?'

'The choice for us to go in there together and get our kids.'

'That's suicide.'

'*This* is suicide.'

'He knows we're coming, Joe. That advantage you were talking about – we don't have it.'

Joseph stares at her in disbelief. A brutal truth is beginning to reveal itself: that his determination to save Max might be countered by Erin's determination to save Tilly; that his success might depend on her failure; and that his failure might be a prerequisite for her success.

In one phone call Gabriel Roth has managed to make them rivals – and right now Erin is winning.

'You're just going to hand me over?'

'I'm sorry, Joe. As I said, the moment Tilly's safe . . .' She indicates the handcuffs. 'Put them on.'

Joseph closes his eyes, just briefly. He has one last card to play, but this isn't the moment to reveal it. Slowly, carefully, he slips on the cuffs.

Erin takes out her phone, dials. 'It's me, we're here. Yeah. I'm looking right at him.' She pauses, then says, 'No, not yet. Not until I see Tilly.' Erin frowns. 'But you—'

She listens, then flinches, perilously close to putting an arrow through Joseph's sternum. Looking dazed at what she just learned, she returns the phone to her pocket.

'I'm guessing he refused your request,' Joseph tells her. 'Maybe he doesn't want you to see what he's done to Tilly.'

'Actually,' Erin says, sounding broken, 'he wants you to see what he's done to Max.'

# FIFTY-SIX

Suddenly, it feels like every muscle in Joseph's body is singing with tension – as if he's become a giant tuning fork struck hard on its tines. He doesn't want to consider the meaning behind Erin's words. When he tries to breathe, he can't pull air into his lungs fast enough.

That strange resonance transmits through him to the earth. And now it feels like everything around him is vibrating at the same frequency: the trees, their branches, the saplings pushing through the leaf litter, the roots plunging into the soil.

Has he just lost his son? That can't be true.

But he's felt this resonance once before, when Claire died. Perhaps it's the sound of the universe rearranging itself around a proscribed event – and unwittingly revealing its workings.

Erin says, 'He's waiting for us around the back.'

Joseph blinks, tries to cast off the unworldly sensation that's stolen over him – of a change to the natural order so perverse that everything around him is trying to reject it. 'What else did he say? Just tell me. So I know.'

Erin looks bereft, like she's operating on nothing but fumes. 'Honestly, Joe, that's all he said.'

She studies his face, must see the agony in it, just like he sees the agony in hers. Cursing, she digs out the keys for the cuffs. Removing one from the fob, she drops it into his breast pocket. 'I know promises are meaningless at this point, but don't make me regret that. I won't let you put Tilly in danger. Now please – turn around and walk.'

Joseph complies without further comment, stumbling through the undergrowth to what awaits.

Is the blood-red sky a portent? Perhaps he's lucky and a meteor has struck, somewhere on the other side of the planet, and at this very moment a blast wave is racing around the earth towards him, obliterating everything in its path. Because it seems, now, that he's at the end of things. Likely the very end.

He limps forward regardless, his right leg dragging, his left knee popping each time it flexes.

It's impossible to move stealthily. Twigs snap beneath his weight. His feet tangle in roots and rip them from the soil. He passes Thornecroft on his left, hears Erin following close behind.

The garden reveals itself in silhouette.

Joseph steps on to a black lawn that climbs towards a black oak spreading its branches across a red sky. Four dining chairs have been arranged around the trunk, all of them facing a sight Joseph's brain tries its best to reject.

Because Max – his only son, his everything – is hanging by his neck from one of the oak's boughs.

# FIFTY-SEVEN

When he falls to his knees, he barely feels the impact. The world smears, an Expressionist palette of scarlet and black. The air drains of warmth, becomes frozen. *This can't be real,* he thinks. That's not his boy hanging there. Because Max has a future, a whole life to live.

But Drew had a future too. As did Enoch, and Angus Roth.

He hears commotion behind him, sounds of a struggle, and turns to find a swarm of busy shadow. When it resolves, he sees Erin lying prone – and Gabriel, crossbow in hand, standing over her.

Joseph turns away, no longer cares. His gaze returns to the silhouetted oak – and the silhouetted form hanging from it. He gets a foot under him. Tries to stand.

Once he's struggled to his feet, he limps up the sloping lawn. It doesn't matter what's behind him, doesn't matter how much his body is hurting. All he wants is to be with his son. He'll gladly die in the attempt.

He's halfway to the tree when his perspective begins to shift. The flat silhouettes of the objects arrayed at its base take on depth, revealing their relative positions.

Joseph staggers, nearly falls, recovers himself – doesn't

know if he can trust what his eyes are showing him. Because from this angle Max's feet don't look like they're swinging freely. Instead, the tips of his trainers appear to be touching a chair seat.

Gasping, Joseph breaks into a run. When he reaches the oak, he discovers that his hope was justified and that Max, by standing on the balls of his feet, has just enough rope to breathe.

'Dad,' the boy croaks.

'I'm here,' Joseph says. 'I've got you. I'm not going to leave you.'

But even though this feels like a reprieve, he knows it isn't; because Gabriel Roth put that noose around his son's neck and waited for him to arrive.

'Please,' Max whispers. 'Help me. I can't . . . stand much longer.'

'You can. You will. You're strong, Max. Just hold on.'

Joseph glances behind him, sees Gabriel Roth marching Erin across the grass. The knife he stripped off earlier now hangs from Gabriel's belt.

Turning his back, he tries to fish the key from his breast pocket, but the cuffs frustrate him, and by the time he's figured out how to dig for it with his thumbs it's too late. Gabriel grabs his shoulder, wrenches it around.

Joseph stares at him, this man who intends to kill his son. The day's dying light has turned Gabriel's eyes to precious stones.

He feels a rush of blood through his arteries – some primal instinct switching off his pain, readying muscle and sinew for one last burst of violence.

If he acts now, with his hands still cuffed, he's guaranteed to fail, but every second he hesitates is a second closer to losing Max. He thinks about slamming his forehead into

Gabriel's face, but he's unlikely to incapacitate him with a single blow. One kick of that chair is all it'll take to set his son swinging.

He looks at Erin, sees the torment scribed into her face. Their eyes meet for just a moment before she sweeps the rest of garden with her gaze. He knows she's searching for Tilly, that she cannot comprehend why her daughter isn't here, nor what that might mean. He wants to scream at her for what she's done, even though he understands the desperation that made her do it.

Worst of all is the knowledge that Joseph now has no choice but to respond, actively working against the woman he loves and who he knows loves him too.

Gabriel wraps his fist around the cuffs, gives them a shake. Satisfied, he turns to Erin. 'Key.'

She blinks, looks at him in bewilderment. Finally, his words seem to penetrate. 'Where's Tilly?' she asks. 'You said—'

'I know what I said. Key.'

'Gabriel,' she begs. 'Please. I just want to see that she's OK.'

In response, he drives his fist into Joseph's stomach. 'Key. Now.'

Joseph collapses, gaping, on to the grass.

'My back pocket,' Erin moans.

Gabriel finds the key and lobs it across the garden. Then, his attention still on Erin, he points to one of the chairs. 'Sit.'

She glances left and right, a cornered prey animal contemplating its last move.

Watching her, trying to sit upright despite his body's shrieks of protest, Joseph fears his wife is about to do something stupid, that in her desperation to find Tilly she'll try to run; and that Gabriel will either put an arrow in her back or, worse, kick away Max's chair as punishment.

'Erin,' he hisses. 'Just do it.'

She casts him a panicked look, and perhaps something in his expression pacifies her, just a little, because she sinks down as instructed, her bound hands clutched between her knees.

Gabriel places the crossbow on the grass. He pulls more zip ties from his pocket and begins to secure her to the chair.

Joseph looks at the weapon. He stands little chance of reaching it before Gabriel, an even smaller chance of firing it while cuffed. Instead, moving slowly, he brings his hands towards his chest and inverts his thumbs. He's sliding them into his breast pocket when Max, above him, starts to gasp.

The boy's heels touch the seat and the noose tightens. Max chokes, barks out a cough. His face darkens. From somewhere he finds the strength to raise himself up again, but the noose doesn't loosen completely. His lungs whistle as he tries to suck in air.

'Jesus Christ, he's an eighteen-year-old fucking boy!' Joseph shouts. 'He had nothing to do with this! Cut him down!'

From the base of the tree Gabriel retrieves a second rope, a noose already tied at one end. He throws its loose coils over the bough and strides towards Joseph, who snatches his thumbs from his pocket just in time.

Gabriel fits the noose, grabbing Joseph by the hair and forcing back his head until it's done. 'I'm not interested in creating a spectacle,' he says. 'Or drawing this out to cause more pain. This isn't about vengeance. It's about righting a wrong. I just want to get it done.' He goes to the loose end of rope hanging from the tree and pulls until it's taut.

Joseph scrabbles up because he has to. 'Max didn't kill your brother,' he says, through clenched teeth. 'And nor did I. Drew Cullen lured him into the woods, Thursday night. Tilly killed him, and Sunday night she killed Drew.'

Erin stiffens in her chair. 'Joe, what are you saying? That's not *true*.'

'No,' Gabriel says. 'It isn't. And he knows it.' He drags over a chair. 'Climb up.'

'Listen to me,' Joseph hisses, his words coming faster. 'Because if this really is about justice, about righting a wrong, then you need to hear what I've got to say. Your brother was sleeping with my wife – I'm guessing you already know that. Somehow Tilly found out about it and used Drew to set him up. Her plan was to film Angus and scare him off. But when it backfired, Tilly killed him.

'She's a damaged kid. I had no idea how damaged. But Max isn't responsible. She is.'

Erin's back arches. 'Joe, that's ridiculous. She's not capable and you know it.'

As Joseph meets his wife's gaze, his heart crashes away from him. He wonders how it's possible to feel such overwhelming hate and also such overwhelming love.

'Tell the truth,' he begs her. 'Erin, for fuck's sake. You can see what's going to happen if you don't.'

'I am, Joe,' she sobs. 'I don't know what you mean.'

Gabriel points at the chair. 'Up. Now.'

Erin's sobs grow louder. 'Can we please slow this down? You don't have to do this, Gabriel. There must be another way.'

'Tilly killed your brother,' Joseph says. 'And then she killed Drew to stop her talking.'

'Joe,' Erin moans, 'you fucking *buried* him!'

He flinches at that, thinks that his wife, albeit unwittingly, might just have buried him, too. He feels the rope chafe at his neck. Sees Gabriel's eyes burning even more brightly than they were. With Erin deploying all her guile to make him a liar, perhaps his only defence is the truth.

'Yes, I did,' he says. And with his admission it feels like the whole world has frozen on its axis, waiting in anticipation of what comes next. 'Because at the time I thought your brother's death was a tragic accident. I was scared for my son, what that might mean for him, and I didn't want one tragedy to become two.'

'Dad,' Max croaks. 'Don't do this.'

Joseph's mouth is so dry it's difficult to speak. 'I put Angus in my car and drove him to Black Down. If you don't know, it's a beauty spot fifty or so miles south of here. I can take you there if you want. He's buried in rough ground a hundred yards from a road I found near the summit.

'Max isn't the reason this happened. If he's guilty of anything it's naïvety, but that's not a crime that deserves his life as punishment. Tilly killed your brother, Gabriel. She killed Drew, too. And then I covered it up.'

Gabriel waits a beat, as if satisfying himself that he's heard everything. Then he whispers, 'Up.'

And with that, Joseph realizes he's failed. He doubts he even has the strength to climb on to the chair, but when Gabriel pulls on the rope, he finds it from somewhere. Even once he's up there, the pressure around his neck doesn't slacken. He feels his head beginning to swell.

Beside him, Max's heels drop a second time. The boy makes a sound like tearing tape. This time he looks too exhausted to lift himself back up.

'Erin,' Joseph pleads. 'You can't just sit there and let this happen. Please. For God's sake – do the right thing before it's too late.'

Gabriel turns to her. 'You want me to cut down his son? Put your daughter up there instead?'

Joseph stares at his wife. Never has he seen such an agony of conflicting emotions in a human face. She glances at him, tears rolling down her cheeks. And then, teeth clenched, she shakes her head.

Gabriel begins to secure the rope's loose coils around the tree trunk.

So much adrenalin is rushing through Joseph's system that his teeth start clattering inside his mouth. He looks at his son, at his wife. He looks at the first stars beginning to glimmer in a red sky.

And then, addressing Gabriel, he says, 'If you don't believe my words, at least believe your eyes. Drew captured your brother's death on her phone. She filmed it from start to finish. It's a hard watch, but you need to see it, because it'll show you that everything I just told you was the truth.'

# FIFTY-EIGHT

It was his last card. And now he's played it.

Gabriel turns, studies him with those end-of-days eyes. He drops the rope and approaches, slow as a stalking tiger. The cadence of his breathing has changed.

'The phone's in my back pocket. Code is sixteen-thirty.'

Gabriel halts in front of his chair.

That strange resonance Joseph felt earlier is back, humming in his chest, buzzing in his fingertips, vibrating through his bones to the chair, and through its wooden legs to the turf.

Gabriel slides his fingers into Joseph's pocket and removes the phone. When its screen wakes, he keys in the code.

Erin's head collapses on to her chest. She begins to weep, quiet sounds of exhaustion and defeat.

Gabriel brings up the video file. Moments after it begins to play, Drew's voice issues from the phone's speakers. '*It's so hot. Can you put the windows down?*'

Gabriel's chest fills. He goes to an unoccupied dining chair and lowers himself on to it. There's a solemnity to him, now. A terrible, expectant silence.

'*Easy, Romeo,*' Drew laughs. '*I don't know what you're used to. But with me you don't get everything all at once.*'

Then Angus Roth says, *'Is that right?'*

Gabriel inhales sharply. His muscles move beneath his shirt.

*'Play nice,'* Drew says. *'Be a good boy. And eventually you'll get rewarded.'*

Joseph opens his right fist. In his palm, stained red by the dying light, is the key he lifted from his breast pocket just before Gabriel put the noose around his neck.

Keeping his movements to a minimum, he manoeuvres the key until he's gripping it between thumb and forefinger. Then he tilts his hands and examines the cuffs. Earlier, to improve his ability to free himself should he get the chance, he'd attached them with the lock mechanisms palm-side. Fortunately, Erin hadn't known to double lock them, which would have increased the key turns required to disengage the arms.

*'How nice?'* Angus Roth asks.

Joseph guides the key towards the lock. His hands are shaking so badly that metal clinks against metal. The key rattles as it goes in.

*'You hear that?'* Drew asks. *'Seriously, I think I heard something.'*

Joseph glances at Gabriel, but the man still seems engrossed in what he's viewing. He switches his attention to Erin, sees that she's watching him through her tears. Her gaze slides down to the cuffs, travels back up.

There's no reason for her to draw attention to what he's doing. Their escalatory back-and-forth has reached its conclusion. Any moment, Gabriel will learn the truth of his brother's fate. Afterwards, Erin will need all the help she can get.

That is, unless she's so terrified for Tilly – and so sceptical of Joseph's ability to intervene – that she'll do whatever it takes to delay that moment as long as possible.

His blood runs cold inside his veins. Goosebumps break out across his skin.

'*I've got a picnic blanket in the boot,*' Angus says.

Joseph turns the key, hears a click as the pawl retracts, releasing the rachet teeth. One arm of the cuff glints red as it falls loose. Holding his breath, he extricates his wrist.

Beside him, the toes of Max's trainers squeal against the dining chair. Erin shifts in her seat, her muscles tensing despite her bonds.

It's time, irrefutably, to act.

# FIFTY-NINE

Tilly Carver staggers into Thornecroft's orangery and collapses against a wicker sofa. Around her the room spins as if in mockery. Blood and saliva spill from her mouth, sliding to the floor in thick gobs.

*Fucking gross, Tilz.*

There's no escaping how badly Gabriel Roth has broken her. She can't move her jaw without pain so acid-bright her heart threatens to burst free of her ribs. When she probes her mouth with her tongue, she finds jagged points instead of teeth. Her lips have ballooned, mushy and sticky. Underneath her surface pain is a deeper ache of pulverized flesh, bruised bone.

Beyond the orangery's windows the red sky is everywhere – as if an erupting volcano has filled the heavens with magma. Behind her she sees the blood slick marking her progress through the house.

Tilly coughs, sprays more blood. When she blinks, the light fractures into glass shards that slowly melt back together.

The orangery's external doors gape open. A night breeze wafts through. The gravity in here feels wrong, as if Angus Roth's house is orbiting the earth rather than anchored to it.

Tilly forces herself upright. She staggers to the external doors, her hands making red prints when they clutch the frame. Difficult to believe how weak she is. How each burst of movement requires a rest twice as long.

Outside, around a silhouetted oak at the top of the lawn, she sees silhouette figures, a scene that makes no sense. She steps on to cold flagstones. A few steps more and the flagstones surrender to grass. As she weaves across the lawn, those silhouette figures grow sharper. More surreal.

There's her stepbrother, standing on a chair, a noose around his neck. Her stepfather is on another chair beside him. Gabriel Roth, the sick bastard who broke her, is holding a coil of rope from which dangles a second noose.

But it's the fourth member of the group who captures Tilly's attention and holds it, who triggers a euphoria so potent it's a temporary anaesthesia for her pain. On a third chair, head bowed, sits her mother: the woman who raised her and protected her, and whom she has striven to protect in return – from bad relationships and bad men.

Tilly's euphoria, although potent, vanishes as quickly as it appeared. Because if she's to save her mother again, she has hardly any time to do it. And she needs to save Joseph, too.

For three years Joseph Carver has been the father she'd long hoped to find. He's cooked her meals, washed her clothes, ferried her places she's needed to go. Even more importantly, he's been the husband her mother has always deserved.

Robson, Tilly's birth father, had abused Erin verbally and physically. Mark, who'd come next, had treated her almost as badly. Fortunately, Tilly had been old enough by then to intervene directly, without needing to invent more claims of child abuse.

Joseph, by contrast, has given her not a single reason for

doubt. He's treated Erin well, has shown her love, warmth, endless kindnesses. Crucially, unlike those before him, he's never attempted to turn Erin against her daughter. For three years he's been a safe and stable presence in their lives. To reward him, Tilly had even taken his name.

And then, six weeks ago, she'd overheard Erin on the phone, arranging to meet Angus Roth at a hotel.

She still doesn't understand why her mother fell into bed with a man so manifestly unsuitable. She *had* understood that she needed to save Erin once more – this time from herself.

The fallout from Jack-O'-Lantern Woods has been challenging to manage, but Tilly doesn't regret what she did – nor any of her actions since. There's nothing she won't do to protect her mother.

Drew would have done well to realize that. Her loyalty hadn't lasted, evidenced in a growing number of betrayals. Given long enough, doubtless she'd have gone to the police.

Max's betrayal has in some ways been even worse. Tilly had learned of it Sunday morning, overhearing Drew's comment to Joseph: *I know what you did for Max, and I think it's really brave.* Later, she'd dragged the full story from her friend.

The revelation that Joseph had done what his son hadn't managed – and had been discreet enough to keep it from Erin – had vindicated yet again Tilly's belief in him.

Now, she hears him speak, and even though the fear in his voice is palpable, so too is the resilience.

'*Jesus Christ, he's an eighteen-year-old fucking boy! He had nothing to do with this! Cut him down!*'

New strength fills Tilly's muscles. Gabriel Roth may have brutalized her, but he must have believed her lies about Max. It's not the ending for her stepbrother she'd foreseen, but she hadn't foreseen Angus's twin.

From the outset of this mission to save her mother's

marriage, the most logical danger to guard against has been a police investigation into Angus's disappearance. She'd sought to prevent any evidence pointing towards her family, because Joseph would have been the natural suspect. She'd needed a contingency plan, even so, and her stepbrother had been the answer; acceptable collateral damage.

If police search his room, they'll find Angus's wallet hidden inside his footstool. At the bottom of one of his gym bags they'll find Angus's phone. Then there's all the DNA evidence in his car.

Her solution had never been perfect – Joseph would have been devastated at his son's incarceration, and Erin would have blamed herself – but Tilly had only ever intended it as a last resort. Now, if she's smart enough, she might not even need that.

Across the garden, Gabriel Roth has started talking, but he isn't shouting, and she's too far away to hear his words. Tilly continues her unsteady advance. She glances again at her stepbrother. When he turns his head, their eyes meet.

For three years, Max Carver has been as malleable in her fingers as wet clay. But in the aftermath of Drew's death, that malleability had stretched to breaking. Tilly had been forced to change tack.

She's not sure, any more, if her threats had worked as well as she'd assumed. Perhaps Max, albeit belatedly, had been working on a plan to save himself.

She still doesn't know why he'd claimed he was seeing Drew. She does know it'll backfire spectacularly if the police ever become involved, because it'll offer further motive for a conviction: Max killed Angus to avenge his father; and he killed Drew because she betrayed him with the same man.

Inching closer, she sees Gabriel force the noose over Joseph's head. He throws the rope over the bough, which he uses as a pivot to haul Joseph to his feet.

Erin cries out in dismay. Tilly's swollen lips curl back over her splintered teeth.

Important to move silently, now, as she crosses this last stretch of lawn. Important to show the same resilience as Joseph.

He's speaking again, and although she doesn't catch his words in full, she's close enough to catch most of them.

They nearly stop her heart.

'. . . didn't kill your brother, and nor did I. Drew Cullen lured Angus into the woods, Thursday night. Tilly killed him, and Sunday night she killed Drew.'

Tilly sways on her feet. Because what she just heard makes no sense. How could he think her responsible?

Through the fog of her confusion, Tilly hears him again.

'She's a damaged kid. I had no idea how damaged. But Max isn't responsible for any of this. She is.'

Her outrage at his duplicity – and his denouncements within earshot of her mother – is barbed wire in her veins, far worse than a broken jaw, splintered teeth or a body leaking blood. Joseph Carver has just eviscerated her for his own gain, cutting her open from breastbone to navel and letting her bowels spill on to the grass.

Tilly crumples slowly, silently, as if her bones have turned to paste. The air she pulls into her lungs is a poison, reducing her further.

Every man she's ever known has let her down. And Joseph Carver has just shown himself to be the worst of them.

On the ground, close to her mother's chair, she sees the crossbow he keeps in his wardrobe. Clearly, he'd arrived here hoping to save Max, while throwing his stepdaughter to the wolves.

Tilly's fingers, as they contract, scratch crumbs of soil from the lawn.

*Fucking get up.*

*Fucking end this.*
*Fucking now.*
She rises.
Not a Carver.
Something else.

# SIXTY

Holding Drew's phone before him, Gabriel Roth watches his brother die.

And Joseph, standing above him, tells himself that it's now, it has to be now, beneath these freshly minted stars piercing a red sky.

Because here, at the end of things, this task falls to him alone.

From the phone he hears the bone-splintering impact of Tilly's first swing with the log. Moments later, Drew's cry: '*Tilz, stop, what the fuck!*'

As smoothly as he can, Joseph reaches up. He loosens the noose around his neck and lifts it over his head.

Another impact sound. Drew's scream.

Gabriel contorts as if skewered.

Then comes the blow that ends Angus Roth's life – the act that destroys first one family, then two, then three.

Joseph allows himself to fall. As gravity takes hold, he pushes off from the chair and launches himself at Gabriel Roth, who looks up in time to see him but not in time to react.

Their coming together is as violent as it is destructive. Joseph is almost horizontal as his shoulder slams into

Gabriel's sternum. The chair bursts apart and Gabriel is driven through the wreckage, his back thumping into hard turf. Joseph's momentum carries his legs over his head. The ground swings up and punches him, as unyielding as a granite slab. He lies prone, his neck and spine vibrating, the shock dissipating through his bones. His diaphragm spasms, unable to pull in air. Above him, all around him, he sees red fire and distant suns.

He has to move but he can't. Has to find the crossbow, can't see it. He's a broken thing, a beached carcass. A ship impaled on rocks.

Above him, Max rattles out a breath, the last of his energy spent. The noose tightens around his neck.

Somehow, Joseph manages to roll on to his front and lift himself on all fours.

Gabriel Roth has already found his feet. From his belt he draws the knife Erin confiscated earlier. It's a savage-looking piece, ruthlessly capable, the blade coated with black ceramic.

Joseph stares at it, his horror rooting him to the grass. Then he crawls forward and seizes the largest piece of wreckage from the chair they both destroyed – the slatted backrest still connected to the rear legs. It's a defensive tool at best, and then it's not even that, because Gabriel snatches it from his hands and pitches it across the lawn. In doing so he reveals, behind him, a sight initially too complex for Joseph's brain to process.

A silhouette has detached itself from the falling dark. Shadows gather to it, or flow from it; he can't be sure. It approaches with marionette-jerkiness – like a reanimated corpse shuffling on grave-rotten limbs.

For a moment Joseph thinks the dead man must have clawed his way out of the Black Down soil and journeyed here to join his brother. But the truth is perhaps even worse – because this isn't Angus Roth, returned from death. It's Joseph's stepdaughter.

How Tilly is managing to stand he doesn't know. Nor how she's managing to see. Her face has taken such a beating it looks like it's been inflated by a high-pressure pump, the skin so taut it's in danger of splitting or bursting.

Tilly's mouth is a shattered cavity from which blood has sheeted in torrents. Her nose is a pulped ruin, her cheekbones smashed and sunken. Her eyes are like the slivers of wet flesh glimpsed inside a wound.

In Tilly's hands Joseph sees the crossbow. She's pointing it not at Gabriel Roth, but at him. In her eyes is a fury murderous in its intensity.

And then he can look at her no longer because Gabriel Roth blocks his view, closing on him with the knife.

Joseph worms backwards on his elbows. He opens his mouth, tries to speak, realizes his voice has abandoned him. Gabriel walks him down.

Under the tree, Max starts to strangle.

Joseph moans, elbows faster. When his shoulder knocks against Erin's chair, he gets a foot under him, two.

Gabriel continues to stalk him.

Joseph pushes out of his crouch, feels something godawful happen inside his knee, as if bone and cartilage and flesh have twisted together to form something diabolical before immediately tearing apart.

Even with adrenalin flooding his system, the pain is crippling, nauseating, but he hardly cares about that, because as he rises he draws Erin's knife from the sheath still attached to her belt – and now he has the means to cut down his boy from that tree, even though it's likely the last thing he'll do. He circles Erin's chair, using it to put a little distance between him and Gabriel, hears his son continue to choke.

As Gabriel steps around the chair towards him, Tilly slides back into view. And then Joseph hears it: the *snap-thud!* of the crossbow as it releases.

Except the *thud!* isn't the sound of the string as it transfers its energy to the arrow, but the arrow transferring its energy into living meat.

Joseph doesn't feel the impact straight away. He stagger-hops across the grass, Gabriel following close behind

He sees his son, so close. Sees Tilly crank the crossbow's stock. Hears another arrow drop into position.

The air collapses from his lungs.

*Snap-thud!*

Joseph cringes, clenches his teeth, stumbles. His legs nearly buckle beneath him. The pain is overwhelming, everywhere all at one, his knee its white-hot source.

'Oh my God, no,' Erin sobs, and Joseph cannot work out if her words are for him, for Max, or the human wreckage that's her daughter.

Tilly reloads, looses off another arrow.

Joseph grunts, takes another faltering step towards his son, but he knows he'll never manage to climb up on that chair. Changing direction, he inches towards the tree trunk, where the other end of Max's rope is tied.

Gabriel Roth changes direction, too, twisting towards Tilly as she pumps the stock and reloads. As he does, Joseph sees the black fletchings of two arrows protruding from Gabriel's back – and a bloodied hole in his shirt where a third arrow has passed clean through him.

Joseph swings with his knife. He severs the rope binding Max to the tree, hears his son crash to the grass from his chair, sees him scrabble at the noose around his neck and take a gasping lungful of air.

Their eyes meet, just briefly. A thousand things pass between them in that moment.

Gabriel looks down at himself, at the blood coursing from his abdomen, at the broadhead tips of two arrows glistening with lumps of shredded meat.

He frowns, switches his gaze to Tilly. His eyes flare in recognition of what she's done. 'You'll never—' he begins.

Her fourth arrow takes him in the neck. He drops his knife, goes down on his knees.

Tilly cranks the stock. Her fifth arrow disappears inside Gabriel's chest. He remains on his knees a while longer. Then he keels over on to the grass.

Joseph drops his knife. He sees his stepdaughter reload and swing the barrel of the crossbow towards him. Tears streak her face, mixing with the blood. 'I thought you were dead,' he whispers.

Tilly shakes her head.

'You did the right thing.'

She stares at him.

Joseph glances at the crossbow. He can't remember, now, how many arrows were in the magazine. 'I need to check on Max.'

Tilly blinks. Her trigger finger twitches. Then she lowers the crossbow and turns towards her mother.

# SIXTY-ONE

It's a family meeting like no other. They hold it outside, as the red sky fades to black, as more stars appear above them. Joseph knows they don't have long to create a story. The challenge is that it needs to be watertight.

Tilly refuses to let anyone come near her. Despite her difficulty forming words, she does manage to make herself understood. The first person she wants to hear from is Joseph – exactly what he knows, and how he came to be at Thornecroft with Erin.

In his response, Joseph holds little back. Whatever he might think of his stepdaughter, however deep his horror, he realizes he needs her onside to stand any chance of surviving this.

He explains how he buried Angus at Black Down and is surprised to learn that she already knows. She obviously hadn't known about Enoch, but she displays very little emotion when he tells her – unlike Max, who seems broken by the news.

He describes how he'd found blood in the upstairs hall, how he'd gone across the road and watched Ralph Erikson's footage before deleting it. He doesn't tell Tilly he'd thought the blood was hers and had cleaned it up so that Erin wouldn't see.

Fortunately, Erin doesn't volunteer that either. Initially, she says very little, unable to tear her eyes off the nightmare of her daughter's face, but she takes over once Joseph's finished speaking.

She focuses on their digital footprints first, making each of them narrate in detail where they've taken their phones, these last five days, and what the geolocation data might show. Afterwards, she progresses to email, social media, texts. Any story they concoct will have to fit the evidence perfectly.

Tilly had switched off GPS and activated airplane mode before taking her phone into the woods, Thursday night – a revelation that makes Joseph wonder if the possibility of violence had been in her head all along. That night, she'd instructed Drew to leave her contract mobile at home. She's incensed to learn that Drew had taken the burner phone to the woods instead, covertly filming what happened. She does confirm that Drew hadn't taken either phone to the bungalow the night she died. Tilly also admits that she has Angus's phone, which has been switched off since she killed him – although she won't say where it's hidden.

Joseph had taken Claire's iPhone on his two trips to Black Down, fitted with the SIM he bought in Crompton. Enoch had arrived at the Carvers' with the burner phone Drew used to contact Angus, but not his own.

There are multiple calls between Angus and Erin, but their work relationship can explain those. Hopefully, Erin's phone records won't be checked anyway, meaning her call to Gabriel at Thornecroft will remain undiscovered.

They carry the dining chairs from the garden into the house, along with the sack truck Gabriel used to transport Max. Afterwards, they collect up the lengths of rope and put those inside too. They leave the crossbow on the grass where Tilly abandoned it. Joseph is as confident as he can be that it won't be traced back to him. He takes out Angus Roth's wallet, cleans it thoroughly, and switches it for the one in Gabriel's pocket.

Erin moves Enoch's van on to Thornecroft's drive. Then comes the task that Joseph and Max perform alone. Opening the Honda's boot, they lift out Drew's body as carefully as they can. They carry her into Thornecroft's dining room and lay her on the table. Only once Max has left the room does Joseph free Drew from the plastic.

Facing her again – twenty-four hours after he last saw her – is even more difficult than he'd imagined. It forces him to confront, once more, the appalling travesty of her death, this time with the knowledge that he killed her father.

Outside, Erin has retrieved the tomahawk that Joseph abandoned in the woods, along with the birdwatching scope, the sports holdall and his baseball bat. She stows everything in the car and closes the boot.

Finally, they lift Enoch out of the van and carry him into Angus's office. Standing on Thornecroft's front steps, Joseph turns to his stepdaughter. 'You're clear on everything?'

She nods, grunting something unintelligible.

He climbs into the Honda with his wife and son. Glancing in his rear-view mirror as he pulls on to the road, he watches Tilly go back inside the house.

# SIXTY-TWO

Tuesday night, at the Tamarind Hotel and Spa, Teri Plat-ini eats a late room service dinner alone. Afterwards, she channel-surfs for a while, glancing periodically at her phone.

At ten p.m., she turns off the TV and climbs into bed. She thinks about texting Brittany, decides it's too late. She thinks about calling Barbie Girl's number again. Decides against that, too.

Dousing the bedside light, she lies there in darkness, her mind on Thornecroft. And on Gabriel Roth. Her face throbs, the skin raw. Her lips sting when she licks them.

An hour later, she's still no closer to sleep. Throwing on jeans and a hoody, she grabs her keys and rides the lift down to the lobby. It's a ten-minute drive home from the hotel. On Hocombe Hill, the only vehicle she meets is a small hatch-back that blasts past in the opposite direction.

Teri parks on a grass verge a few hundred metres from Thornecroft and heads back along the lane on foot. When she reaches the driveway she pauses and studies the house.

Its two entrance doors are gaping open, the lights in the ground-floor rooms all burning. Outside, she doesn't see Gabriel's Mercedes, but Angus's Lexus and his tarp-covered Morgan are there – plus a dirty panel van she doesn't recognize.

Teri checks her watch, waits. Two minutes later, she's spied no movement. She edges down the drive towards the house, using the panel van to screen her final approach. Pausing at the passenger-side window, she peers inside. All sorts of junk has been stuffed between the dashboard and windscreen; fast food bags, crushed coffee cups, crumpled flyers. She wonders who drove it here, and where they are now.

Climbing the porch steps, she peeks inside the entrance hall.

Since her last visit, someone has removed the wrecked console table and fragments of broken vase. Gabriel, most likely; Angus hadn't employed a cleaner, insisting that was her job.

The house is silent, no sounds of conversation or TV. Then Teri notices the blood.

It's smeared along the far wall connecting the east and west wings. Beneath it she sees a trail of bloody footprints.

Adrenalin stitches threads of sensation up and down her spine. She thinks about getting out of here, running back to her car, but that's how old Teri would have reacted. Those prints were made by small feet. Someone inside the house might need help. Besides, if she's serious about her plan to retain Thornecroft, she needs to understand what happened here.

Silent, Teri crosses the hall to the junction of the two wings. To her left, the blood is heaviest outside Angus's office, where she thinks the trail must have originated. Teri turns right, following it to the orangery, careful not to disturb the prints.

Inside, the glass exterior doors have been thrown open to the night. There's blood on a wicker sofa back, red handprints on the doorframe. At the top of the garden, near the oak tree, she sees a human-shaped black mound.

Teri's skin contracts on her flesh. Again, she thinks about getting as far away from Thornecroft as she can, but the prone figure near the tree exerts a pull impossible to resist.

Outside, she feels like she's gliding above the grass rather than walking upon it. Moments later, she's standing over Gabriel Roth, trying to make sense of what she's seeing.

He looks more like a butchered carcass than a man. In the moonlight, the blood that's soaked his shirt shines like black paint. Two glistening arrowheads have burst through his chest. A third arrow, shot from a different angle, has penetrated up to its fletching. A fourth shaft is lodged in his neck.

Gabriel's eyes are glossy pools. She thinks he must be dead – until the reflections in those pools ripple, and his gaze slides over her.

Teri stiffens. She glances away from Gabriel, checks the rest of the lawn. A few metres away lies the weapon that must have done the damage: a squat but powerful-looking crossbow.

Gathering her courage, she lowers herself to a crouch. The person who did this might still be here, but fear hasn't crippled her. She thinks again of the small feet that made those prints.

The arrow lodged in Gabriel's neck must have nicked an artery rather than severing one; otherwise he'd already be dead. Still, there's no coming back from his other injuries. Even if she calls an ambulance, he likely won't survive until it arrives.

'I want you to know something,' Teri whispers, holding his gaze. 'You and Angus don't have any power over me.'

A blood bubble forms on Gabriel's lips, slowly inflates.

'You only had what I gave away freely, and now I'm taking it back. I've been frightened too long. I won't let anyone frighten me again.'

His eyes roll away from her. The bubble on his lips bursts.

Teri grimaces, but she doesn't recoil. And then she follows his gaze – and sees that they're not as alone as she'd thought.

The teenager standing a few metres away is a broken thing; a pulverized ruin. Her face looks like a fruit that ripened until it burst and spilled its pulp. In one hand she's holding a jerry can. In the other she grips a knife. Behind her, across the lawn, the door to the outhouse where Angus keeps his petrol mower is hanging open.

The newcomer isn't Barbie Girl – that's obvious despite her injuries – but she's very similar in age.

For a while, the pair don't speak, the silence between them finely balanced. Finally, Teri says, 'You need a hospital. I can drive you.'

The teenager shakes her head. Her fingers tighten around the knife.

Raising her hands, hoping to communicate that she's not a threat, Teri asks, 'Did he do that?'

The girl nods. With the knife, she gestures at Teri's swollen eye, split lip and grazed cheeks. Her voice, when she speaks, is a wet rasp. 'That?'

Teri nods in return, then indicates Gabriel. 'You did this?'

Another nod. A glimmer of broken teeth that's almost a smirk.

'He's still alive.'

The girl rocks on her feet, limps closer. Carefully she lowers herself to the grass on the other side of Gabriel; and Teri sees, in his eyes, something she'd never expected: more than just fear; a blossoming terror. It doesn't make her feel good, but it doesn't make her feel awful, either.

The girl watches him for a while, impassive. Then she lifts her gaze to Teri, waiting as if for a signal.

Air rushes into Teri's lungs. Because suddenly the question she's being asked is very clear. She closes her eyes, opens them, sees the girl still watching her. She thinks of the past year with Angus; the past week with Gabriel; the life she wants to lead. And then she nods.

The girl leans forward. Wrapping her fingers around the arrow shaft, she twists it like a screw. Blood wells, a sudden flood. Gabriel sighs, his chest sinking. And then it's done.

Teri shudders. She can hardly believe what she just witnessed; the seismic consequences of her consent. 'Angus,' she says. 'Is he gone, too?'

The girl nods. Then she points at Gabriel. 'Angus,' she croaks. 'Angus.'

Thinking she understands, Teri says, 'What now? What do I—'

'Go. Never here.'

She rubs her arms, glances at the jerry can. 'What will you do?'

'Go.'

Teri looks across the lawn at Thornecroft, the house Angus built to hoard his treasures. She thinks of its bloodied walls and floors; of the violence and the humiliations it's hosted, not just tonight but all those days and nights previously.

This isn't the ending she'd planned, but maybe it's more fitting. Twenty minutes later she's back in her room at the Tamarind Hotel and Spa. Switching off her phone, she climbs into bed.

When Teri Platini falls asleep, she dreams not of Angus or Gabriel Roth, but of flying like a bird above the earth.

# SIXTY-THREE

Joseph drops Erin and Max at the house, then drives to his mother's bungalow in Saddle Bank. He parks in the garage, locks the car and cycles home through sleeping streets. During his absence, his wife and son have showered, and filled a binbag with the clothes they'd worn at Thornecroft.

'You'd better do the same,' Erin tells him.

He stands under the hot water for as long as he can bear, blasting the blood and grime from his skin. Afterwards, Erin puts fresh dressings on his injuries and helps him into a loose-fitting shirt. Max shoves the binbag of soiled clothes into a rucksack. He's gone twenty minutes and returns empty-handed.

They do a final check around the house. Erin collects the pieces of broken door handle from the back step. Joseph stuffs the crossbow box into their wood burner and tosses in a match.

At midnight, they report Tilly missing. Because of the link to Drew's disappearance, two police officers arrive straight away.

Erin does most of the talking. She tells them her daughter had spent the morning publicizing Drew's disappearance on social media, and that afterwards she'd left the house to put up posters around town. Her phone, when called, diverts straight to voicemail.

The officers ask to see Tilly's room and Erin shows them. They don't seem to notice the dink to the plaster in the upstairs hall. They do spot the stack of MISSING flyers on Tilly's desk, and take one with them when they leave.

Joseph drinks a beer, opens another. Despite his exhaustion, he can't slow his brain, can't stop hunting for things he might have missed. He thinks of the woman he saw at Thornecroft on Monday. Wonders where she is now.

At three a.m. the police return, this time in far greater numbers. Before he answers the door, Joseph embraces Max and sends him upstairs. A while later he finds himself in the back of a patrol car with Erin, on the way to the hospital where, an officer tells him, his stepdaughter is recovering from an abduction almost too savage to contemplate.

# SIXTY-FOUR

.

Wednesday morning, at the hotel, Teri Platini waits until she's finished her second coffee before switching on her phone. It immediately goes crazy with updates.

There are twenty-six messages from Brittany Moore alone. Teri hasn't scrolled through more than a handful before the phone trills in her hands.

'Babe?' Brittany shrieks. 'Are you freakin' *kidding* me? Where are you?'

'A hotel outside Crompton.'

'I've been going out of my *mind*, hon. Why haven't you been picking up?'

'I've had my phone off.'

'Your phone off? What are you, insane?'

'No, I—'

'Did the police make you do that?'

'The police?

The line goes silent. A few seconds later, Brittany says, 'Hon, check your freakin' DMs. Have you even seen the news?'

Thirty seconds later, Teri is watching shaky amateur footage of Thornecroft, shot at night. The house is ablaze, fire erupting from every window. When part of the roof collapses, bright snakes of flame curl heavenward. The three vehicles Teri saw last night are burning, too.

Emergency workers are everywhere: paramedics hurrying in and out of ambulances; firefighters reeling out hoses; police officers talking on radios. Overhead, a helicopter circles, its searchlight arcing down. The scene is almost too apocalyptic to process.

Teri pushes away from the table, pulling her car keys from her bag. When she reaches Hocombe Hill, she finds its entire length has been sealed off. Thin smoke is still rising above the trees. Emergency vehicles are parked nose to tail. A second helicopter is now hovering above the trees.

Teri gets out of her car and walks to the barrier. The two police officers stationed there wave her off at first, until she explains who she is and where she lives. Soon after, she finds herself in a command vehicle, repeating her story to a harassed-looking senior investigating officer. From there she's driven to Crompton's police station, where she gives a full statement. She's back at the hotel by late afternoon.

A uniformed officer collects her from the lobby the next morning and drives her to the hospital in neighbouring Shipley. There, she's met by two pathologists. They explain that she can't touch the body she's about to view: that the post mortem can't begin until formal identification has been made, that there's still forensic evidence to be collected. They warn her the experience will be difficult.

Gabriel Roth is lying beneath a white sheet. Teri's tears are genuine, borne not of heartbreak but overwhelming relief.

'That's him,' she says. 'That's my boyfriend. Angus Roth.'

An hour later, in the hotel bar, she sinks three gin and tonics and calls Saul Faulkner, the solicitor she met two days ago. 'Angus is dead,' she says. 'I just identified him.'

'You poor, sweet child.'

'I want to talk about probate.'

'OK, maybe not so sweet.'

'Oh, and the house burned down.'

Saul barks out a laugh. 'That was naughty.'

'It wasn't me.'

'Silly question, but are you insured?'

'We are, but will they pay out on arson?'

'Not to the arsonist.'

'I told you it wasn't me.'

'In that case, congratulations. You're about to become a very wealthy girl.'

'Woman,' Teri says. 'Not girl.'

# SIXTY-FIVE

*Two months later*

Joseph meets Max in the St Andrews Botanic Garden, a mile or so west of the seafront. When he sees his son, his heart lifts. Wordlessly, the pair embrace. 'How's the course?' he asks.

'First dissection was a little dicey. Couple of fainters and a walk-out. But it's everything I hoped and more.'

Joseph smiles to hear the enthusiasm in his son's voice. 'I thought we could stroll down to the harbour,' he says. 'Have a look around.'

'Sounds good, Dad.'

Joseph enjoys the walk. The air here is fresher than down south. The ancient buildings, the rugged land and wild sea imbue in him a peace he hasn't felt in months.

After sunset they find a pub and head to a quiet corner.

'So,' Max says. 'How're things at home?'

Joseph sips his beer, wonders how to answer that. Because the truth is worse than he's prepared to admit.

The whole world, it seems, is going crazy for Tilly Carver's story. Everything she says or does seems to intensify the media furore further. Joseph can see no signs of it letting up.

The police investigation into what happened has been as

poorly managed as the hunt, five years ago, for Claire's killer. The working hypothesis is that Angus Roth developed an obsession with Tilly and Drew after meeting them at the Huntingdon Manor fundraiser. After abducting and killing Drew, he'd snatched Tilly two days later. Somehow, Enoch Cullen had deduced that his daughter was at Thornecroft. On his arrival Angus Roth had killed him. Afterwards, Angus had torched the house, intending to burn Tilly with the other bodies. Miraculously, she'd managed to free herself, killing him with his own weapon.

When all the national newspapers offered interviews, Tilly negotiated an exclusive with just one. A US network paid for a TV exclusive and syndicated it around the world. They led with the heart-breaking yet strangely life-affirming 999 call she'd made from Thornecroft – worthy of an Oscar should anyone have known she was acting. In it, despite grievous injuries, Tilly's only concern was for her dead friend.

Media organizations publish countless photographs of the pair before their abduction, each one deliberately selected by Tilly to highlight their closeness, their youth, their obvious beauty. Images of the friends in bikinis do particularly well.

The photos Tilly releases of her slow recovery, unflinching in their honesty, win her further praise. She's lauded by victim groups for her resilience. On social media she's celebrated for her strength.

The GoFundMe page, set up by supporters to pay for dental work and facial reconstruction, ticks higher with every media appearance, every radio phone-in, every photograph documenting her recovery.

'You know she has an agent, now?' Joseph asks his son. 'And a book deal?'

'Don't.'

'She's meeting this ghost writer twice a week. There's

talk of something happening with Netflix. Every time she opens her mouth I worry she's going to trip herself up, contradict herself, bring us all down with her.'

He drinks his beer, looks around the pub. 'There's something I wanted to ask. Because we never really got to talk about it before you left. I think I know the answer but I'd still like to hear it first-hand.'

'Shoot.'

'Why did you protect her for so long? Even after Drew? Why did you protect her at all? You let me think you'd killed someone. First by accident, then deliberately.'

Max picks up a beermat, fiddles with it. 'She gets her claws into you, Dad. Messes with your head. When she came to me that Thursday night, she told me she'd discovered Erin's affair and had tried to sabotage it to save your marriage. She said she'd known how devastated you'd have been if you'd found out. That she'd been trying to hold our family together. And that Angus had attacked Drew, and Tilly had no choice but to intervene.'

Max pauses, drinks. 'You've seen the tape, I haven't. She told me she only ever hit him once.'

'It was more than once,' Joseph says. 'She could've stopped and she didn't.'

'I know that now, but at the time I had no reason to doubt her – and at first Drew backed up her story. They would have gone to jail, Tilly said, because it would have looked pre-meditated.

'I couldn't do anything Thursday night so I took the car over there on Friday, when everyone was asleep. It was too late to bury him so I put him in the boot, parked around the corner and came home.'

No wonder that Angus's decomposition had seemed so advanced: he'd been killed a day earlier than Joseph had realized.

'And then you found me in the kitchen,' Max says. 'I pan-icked, I guess. Came up with that bullshit about an accident. When you insisted on seeing the body, I had to invent more bullshit to explain his injuries.'

'You could have told me the truth.'

Max nods. 'And then you'd have found out about the affair. We thought you'd have ended the marriage. I didn't want you to go through that. If I'm honest, I didn't want it to break up our family. And Tilly convinced me that she could get you guys back to a better place.'

'Tell me more about Drew.'

'She came to me after the party, told me the truth about how Tilly had gone nuts. She was terrified, said she had a recording of Angus's death that she wanted to give to the police. Trouble was, by that point you'd already buried him – at least, you said you had. When I told her, she agreed to keep quiet.

'Somehow, Tilly caught wind that Drew was having second thoughts. Sunday night, she told me to meet her at the bungalow. When I got there, Drew was already dead.

'Tilly was . . . Jesus, Dad. You wouldn't believe it if I tried to explain. She said she wasn't going to mess around any more, that she'd done her best to save our family but wouldn't go to jail for it. She told me she knew you'd buried Angus, that she'd got the truth out of Drew before killing her.

'She was furious. Said if I didn't take responsibility for Drew's death, she'd find a way to implicate me. She'd tell the police about you, too. When you showed me Angus's wallet and said you'd found it in my footstool, it was pretty clear she was serious.

'I knew she still had his phone, his car keys. I was scared shitless she'd plant them somewhere and throw us both under a bus. The one thing that might have saved us was that footage, but Drew hadn't told me where she'd hidden it.'

'So that's what you were looking for at Enoch's.'

The boy puffs out his cheeks, nods. Then he says, 'I don't know how you can bring yourself to stay inside that house with her, Dad.'

'Because the whole world is watching, for a start,' Joseph replies. 'But mainly because Erin's my wife and I love her – and because I can't let her deal with this alone. I know that must sound crazy to you. Half the time it sounds crazy to me. But everything she said and did at Thornecroft I did back to her and worse. When you have a son, or a daughter, there's not much you won't do to keep them safe.'

Max drains his glass, shakes his head. Then he goes to the bar and orders two more beers.

# SIXTY-SIX

The next morning Joseph takes a cab to Leuchars, where he catches a train to Edinburgh. From there he boards a second train for the long journey home. The peace he'd felt in St Andrews evaporates as he approaches Crompton.

Last night, in the pub, he'd purposely kept some things back. He hadn't told Max that these days he does most of the cooking. That he avoids eating anything Tilly's made unless he can randomly choose a plate. Most of the coffee he now drinks he buys from Costa.

He no longer believes that his wife's second husband died by suicide. He's convinced that Tilly poisoned Mark to protect Erin and safeguard their mother–daughter relationship. Now, through his words to Gabriel at Thornecroft, Joseph has likewise proved himself a threat: *She's a damaged kid. I had no idea how damaged. But Max isn't responsible. She is.*

Their house is no longer stocked with weapons he could call on in an emergency. Instead, he's filled it with CCTV. Two cameras cover the front of the house; another two cover the rear. Inside, three more keep a constant watch, including one hidden inside a smoke alarm. Each night before he gets into bed, he locks the bedroom door.

In the last few weeks, he's discovered something else

disturbing, the answer to something he'd noticed during those four hellish days in August: the fate of the personal items from his old life with Claire.

Tilly hadn't touched his bereavement box, nor Max's, but in the attic he'd discovered a few storage crates stuffed with keepsakes he still cherished. There hadn't been many. The rest he guesses she'd destroyed. Perhaps she'd decided that reminders of his late wife posed yet another threat to Erin's wellbeing.

Since her release from hospital, Tilly has treated him much the same as before. The friendliness is still there – and the banter. But sometimes he's caught her looking at him with an expression that's anything but friendly. Her smile has always come quickly. And then the moment is over until the next one.

She'd be crazy to try anything, especially with all the media attention she's attracting. He wishes he could draw more comfort from that than he does.

Erin meets him at Crompton's station, kissing him when he climbs into the car. 'You smell good,' she tells him. 'Is that a new one?'

'Something I picked up in Edinburgh.'

'Well, I like it. How was Max?'

'Worried about me and you. How've things been here?'

'She's accepted that mentor role. Apparently there's now a magazine column on offer.' Erin shakes her head. 'What the hell are we going to do, Joe?'

'Right now, I really don't know.'

She kisses him again. 'I've missed you. Thank God you're back.'

Inside the house, he finds Tilly curled on the sofa with a glass of wine.

Hard to believe it's the same girl he saw at Thornecroft,

her face a smashed ruin. Tilly's right cheekbone is still a little sunken, but an upcoming surgery should fix that. Her new teeth look even better than the old ones. Recently, she's had dermal fillers injected into her lips to improve her smile.

'Hey, Axe Man,' she says. 'How was Bonnie Scotland and Bonnie Max?'

Joseph smiles tightly. He hates it when she calls him that. 'He seems to be enjoying the course.'

Tilly sips her wine, studying him over the rim of her glass. 'You want a brew?'

'Thanks, but I had one on the train.'

'You must be hungry,' Erin says, rubbing his back. 'How about some food?'

Joseph looks around the room. He sees that in his absence the photograph from the Huntingdon Manor fundraiser has disappeared, as he'd thought it might. 'Maybe we could order from Mr Wu's.'

# SIXTY-SEVEN

Joseph wakes to darkness, with no idea how long he's been sleeping.

As always, the first moments of consciousness belong to the *before* and not the *now*. When his heart rebounds, he reaches instinctively for Erin. Beside him she's warm in slumber.

He hears something, then, or thinks he does, even if he can't describe it. Maybe he just senses it. A wrongness about the house. A feeling that something chaotic has crept close while he's been sleeping. Something ruinous and wicked.

His chest tightens.

And then a floorboard creaks, further along the hall.

On his bedside table his phone buzzes, lights up.

Joseph grabs it, sees the notification – a video shot by the camera no one knows about, hidden inside the smoke alarm mounted on the hallway ceiling.

He hits play, sees Tilly's door swing open. His stepdaughter emerges, wearing her favourite Pokémon nightdress. The image is monochrome. Her eyes are sharp white dots.

She glides along the hall, navigating the darkness with one hand extended in front of her. When she reaches Joseph's bedroom door, she stops.

For the next ten seconds she stands motionless. Then her fingers find the door handle. She turns it gently, but the door itself doesn't move. Tilly remains there a moment longer. Lifting her head, her white eyes slide towards the hidden camera. It looks like she's staring right at him. Her lips retract, forming a smile. Finally, she creeps back down the hall to her room.

Joseph returns the phone to his side table. He can't understand how Tilly can have learned of the camera. He recalls what Erin had told him about Robson: that after winning joint custody, Tilly's birth father had woken in the night to find her leaning over his bed; that on the last occasion she'd had a knife.

Joseph wonders what his stepdaughter is planning.

Silently, he begins to plan too.

# ACKNOWLEDGEMENTS

Huge thanks to my fantastic editor, Thorne Ryan, who supported this book at every stage of its creation – from the initial idea, pitched during a breakfast meeting where the scrambled eggs made more sense than I did, and through multiple drafts to the final story. Thanks also to my agent, Sam Copeland, at RCW, and to everyone at Transworld. Finally, a gigantic shout-out to Noah Jones, who offered valuable advice along the way.

# ABOUT THE AUTHOR

**Sam Lloyd** grew up in Hampshire, where he learned his love of storytelling. These days he lives in Surrey with his wife, three young sons and a dog that likes to howl. His first three thrillers, *The Memory Wood*, *The Rising Tide* and *The People Watcher* were published to great critical acclaim.